12 SHORT STORIES

AND THEIR MAKING

Edited with an Introduction by

PAUL MANDELBAUM

A Karen and Michael Braziller Book
PERSEA BOOKS / NEW YORK

For permission to reprint or for any other information,
write to the publisher:

Persea Books, Inc.
853 Broadway
New York, New York 10003

Library of Congress Cataloging-in-Publication Data
12 short stories and their making / edited, with an introduction by Paul Mandelbaum.—1st ed.
p. cm.
"A Karen and Michael Braziller book."
ISBN 0-89255-312-X (original trade pbk. : alk. paper)
1. Short stories, American. 2. Short story—Authorship.
3. Authors, American—20th century—Interviews. I. Title: Twelve short stories and their making. II. Mandelbaum, Paul, 1959-
PS648.S5A143 2005
813'.0108—dc22
2005002694

Designed by Rita Lascaro

Manufactured in the United States of America

First Edition

12 SHORT STORIES AND THEIR MAKING

Other Persea Anthologies

THE RESILIENT WRITER
Tales of Rejection and Triumph from 23 Top Authors
Interviews, with an introduction by Catherine Wald

THE ELOQUENT ESSAY
An Anthology of Classic and Creative Nonfiction
Edited, with an introduction by John Loughery

THE ELOQUENT SHORT STORY
Varieties of Narration
An anthology edited, with an introduction by Lucy Rosenthal

IMAGINING AMERICA
Short Stories from the Promised Land
Edited, with an introduction by Wesley Brown and Amy Ling

OLD GLORY
American War Poems from the
Revolutionary War to the War on Terrorism
Edited, with a introduction by Robert Hedin
Foreword by Walter Cronkite

CONTENTS

IV. SETTING

V. STRUCTURE

VI. THEME

INTRODUCTION

For lovers of contemporary short fiction, the idea of being able to engage a favorite author in detailed conversation about a much-admired story ranks among the most pleasant of fantasies. What might you want to know? Something about the story's inspiration, probably, and the process of its development. How does its powerful ending manage to feel so inevitable only in hindsight? Maybe you'd pay tribute to that particularly thoughtful turn of phrase on the second page, third paragraph—or a passage you'd found personally gratifying.

From such musings, this anthology.

I'd been acclaiming the twelve short stories collected here for some time—years, in many cases—to friends, family, and students. The stories are remarkable not just for their overall fineness and the reading pleasures they offer, but also for the exemplary uses to which they each put one of the following elements of fiction writing: character, plot, point of view and voice, setting, structure, and theme.

So I had questions. Many of them about technical issues of craft, as well as broader questions about the story behind each story and also about the art of fiction in general. To my delight, each of the approached authors graciously agreed to participate. The interviews were all undertaken exclusively for this anthology, sometimes conducted over the phone, other times via e-mail. They're printed here directly following the story that inspired them. And the stories have been arranged according to those fiction elements mentioned above, starting with character.

Walter Kirn's story "The Hoaxer" and Elizabeth Tallent's "Prowler" provide a master class in delineation of character, each exercising a broad use of descriptive, sensory, pensive, and behavioral modes as well as highly inventive devices. For instance, the lonely father in "The Hoaxer" invents an alter ego named Howling Johnny, whose woeful history further illuminates the father's own special brand of desperation. In "Prowler," Tallent has matched her protagonist's most severe transgression to resonate meaningfully with his vocation as architect. "Intrusion is for him an entirely conscious act," she explains in our correspondence. "He's not someone who can trespass innocently. It's as if a heart surgeon damaged someone's heart."

In his interview, Kirn describes how he imagines character as a Method actor might, by reaching into his store of memories for people he's met who hold some glancing or head-on similarity to the person he's building, then transplanting a feature here, a penchant there. He also describes a useful process for creating character motivation: inferring backward from a behavior that intrigues him. Why, for instance, would a grown man *want* to fake UFO sightings?

Plot presents special challenges to the writer of literary fiction. Should plot overpower character, a story can end up in the realms of high-concept or so-called genre fiction. But the two stories included here effectively harness large, vigorous plots and put them to higher purpose.

Kim Edwards, in "The Story of My Life," makes use of an actual, well, *plot*—a conspiratorial intrigue—that illuminates the characters involved. In her e-mail correspondence about its creation, she describes a dedicated, sometimes perilous process of revision in which she struggled to find the story's true path.

George Garrett keeps the rollicking spree of "A Record as Long as Your Arm" on track through a careering, farcical humor. To some of the more outlandish plot twists the narrator deliberately calls attention, which readers will likely find part of the joke but also reassuring, because it signals that the hijinks are under control and are being employed within a serious piece of work—gravely serious, as it turns out.

Choosing the right point of view from which to narrate is perhaps the most fundamental decision a short-story writer has to make. Charles Johnson's "China," about a middle-aged, out-of-shape postal worker named Rudolph who revitalizes himself through kung-fu, becomes an even larger story—about the challenge to a marriage and to an entire way of life—by virtue of its being told through his wife Evelyn's eyes. In our interview, Johnson explains some of the factors he tries to consider when assigning point of view, including his readers' likely ability to empathize with that character.

Allan Gurganus, in "Condolences to Every One of Us," relates the details of a violent uprising in Africa through the viewpoint of a widow from Toledo, Ohio. "The most logical witness might seem some expert on international terrorism. But for me," he says, "one ordinary woman's attempt to comprehend these ghastly crimes outstripped in validity any professional pundit's opinion." The efficacy with which the story delivers its moral arguments derives in part from its narrator's humble voice and the power of her gentleness.

Ursula K. Le Guin's "Sur" and Jhumpa Lahiri's "The Third and Final Continent" offer compelling reminders of how setting not only provides a story's sense of place, time, language, and custom but also can form the very backbone of its conflict. Especially when its characters arrive from somewhere *else*, and the new place is strange to them, challenging, and, in the case of "Sur," sub-zero. Le Guin says she'd avidly read about Antarctic expeditions since early adulthood, so when her story's inspiration eventually came to her, she already knew the terrain quite well.

Lahiri, who, like Le Guin, is often celebrated for her evocation of place, demonstrates throughout "The Third and Final Continent" how the ordinary can seem fresh when experienced by a newcomer—in this case a man newly arrived in Massachusetts from India via Great Britain. "I am a very visual person," she says of her own painterly eye. "It's how I relate to the physical world." Both stories use their vividly observed details of setting to simultaneously convey mood, or inform us about the observer, or emphasize an idea.

Tobias Wolff discusses his story "Smorgasbord" and in particular its affecting structure. Focused on a night of adolescent selfishness, the story is in fact told years later, after the haunting consequences of the narrator's ill-considered choice have fully manifested. "The simultaneity of these two different periods in this narrator's life is part of what makes the story," says Wolff. "It *does* make the story. I don't think you really have a story without that older narrator. You have an anecdote." This dimension of hindsight is so delicately layered overtop the dramatized remembrance—like a borderless glass frame—that its execution seems worthy of careful, detailed consideration.

Embodying a very different structure, Gail Godwin's "Dream Children" resembles a collage, which seems well suited to a story about the mutability of time and space, and about a woman who, in the aftermath of a trauma, has become either delusional or perhaps enlightened. In her interview, Godwin relates how she came to develop her method for creating structure from nonlinear "episodes" and how and when she decided to reveal details about her protagonist's ordeal.

Ellen Gilchrist in "Rich" and Sandra Cisneros in "Never Marry a Mexican" both tackle bold, large themes that make their presence felt throughout all levels of the work. In "Never Marry a Mexican," the idea of betrayal's echo finds expression in the story's unusual two-part structure, in the ingenious device of addressing two separate characters directly as the story's listener, and in the image of a set of Russian nesting dolls, as well as in the title itself, which the narrator initially hears as a caution but later feels as a devastating personal indictment.

"Rich" addresses the tremendous damage inflicted by social snobbery and the painful problem of needing to belong. It does so through its main storyline as well as through its details and embellishments, like the vignette about a hapless fraternity pledge who falls victim to inimical forces similar to those that will later undermine the main character.

Ellen Gilchrist, to my surprise, claimed to be unaware of some of the thematic connections I'd long credited "Rich" with making and at one point in our conversation even went so far as to aver playfully that she didn't know "what a theme is." She's not alone in stressing the role of instinct and the subconscious in her creative process. In many of the interviews, authors describe how they move through a story by feel or might be drawn to specific moments or by the compelling voice of a first-person narrator. "I write in a very instinctive and organic sort of way," says Kim Edwards. "I trust my intuition. I don't mean, by saying this, to imply a lack of respect for the intellectual and analytical. Indeed, what I called intuition has been informed by years of study, practice, and reading, reading, reading."

While focusing on each story's most conspicuous element provides a basis or starting point for the interviews, it's important to remain aware, as Charles Johnson reminded me, "that we have abstracted that single dimension from the Whole in order to examine it. . . . All parts of the fiction refer to all *other* parts, so we must think about art in a holographic way: character is the engine of plot, viewpoint is anchored in character."

In fact, readers may notice that several stories could easily have been chosen for more than one category. And so the interviews address some of these other issues, too, as well a number of topics about the writing life. Retreating to the countryside, for example. And the mixed experience of working with mentors in an MFA program. Racing to meet a contractual deadline. And the time spent on a single short story (Charles Johnson works virtually nonstop, usually completing one within five days; Tobias Wolff can take up to five months).

Through these vibrant interviews, we gain a stronger understanding not just of the represented stories and their making, and of the authors who wrote them, but also of our own notions and values concerning the art and craft of fiction.

—Paul Mandelbaum

CHARACTER

THE HOAXER

Walter Kirn

PROWLER

Elizabeth Tallent

THE HOAXER

Walter Kirn

My father was a hoaxer. In his spare time and with no thought of profit, the way other men fish or build radios from kits, he perpetrated frauds against the public. He did his share for the popular phantoms—Bigfoot, extraterrestrials, ghosts—while promoting a number of minor phenomena that were, I like to think, closer to his heart. Some of these lesser-known entities, such as the Minnesota Lionbird and a strange atmospheric condition known as Burning Snow, had a basis in folklore and merely required a plaster-cast footprint or a blurry snapshot to refresh their legends. They were the easy ones. More difficult to foist upon the public were the myths and marvels dreamed up by my father himself, monsters such as Howling Johnny, the mummified wolfboy of Glacier National Park, whose shrunken, rodent-gnawed body was my father's crowning achievement. In the world of scientific fakery, a world more extensive than outsiders know, the man was an original. He was not impressed with ordinary oddities. Indeed, I like to believe that my father had high hopes for his deceptions and thought of himself as a teacher—though of what set of truths or values, I don't know. I do know what it was like to live with him, and what it is like now without him.

It's early, a couple of hours before dawn—time to drive out to a nearby cornfield and make it look like something landed there. I am thirteen years old, an eighth grader, and this is my first time. My father sits up high behind the wheel of his four-wheel-drive Ford pickup truck, steering with one finger, and I can tell by his locked-ahead gaze and unaccustomed silence that

I am on probation. We pass dark farmhouses flanked by looming silos. Bats dive and bank in our high beams. The cross breeze through the rolled-down windows smells of rain-soaked earth, of night crawlers drowned by the thousands. I feel anxious, tired, and honored. My father woke me up this morning when he easily could have snuck out alone.

"Under the seat there. The thermos," he says, and I am quick to reach down and grab the bottle. Its cap, which I unscrew, is a cup. I fill it only halfway to prevent a spill and place it in my father's outstretched hand. The steam from the Postum fogs his eyeglasses and he sets the cup on the dash to let it cool. The glasses are dummies (I tried them on once, the lenses were plain glass), and my father's refusal to leave the house without them is just another trick. He has even developed certain tics, such as blinking when he puts the glasses on or suddenly acting blind while wearing them and whipping them off to be polished on his shirtsleeve.

My father is not a normal man. I've learned this.

"Here's how you're going to help me," he says, holding out the cup for more Postum. Because of his blood pressure, he can't drink real coffee. "I'll walk to the field and make the circle while you sit tight in the truck and stand guard. You can turn the radio on, but keep it low. Sound carries miles on a night like this."

He raises the cup to his lips and blows. He knows I'm disappointed. He had promised when he woke me up that he would show me how to make the circles, how to fabricate a landing site. Guard duty is an insult, a gyp. I've been waiting for this day for months, ever since the Sunday night he led me into his workshop after dinner, shut the door so my mother couldn't hear, and took me into his confidence.

He chose that night to reveal himself, I think, because he'd been fighting all weekend with my mother and he wanted the companionship. The fight was the same one they were always having, about my mother's demands for affection and for material things. So far as I knew, the argument had started well before I was born, which may have been why my parents' yelling didn't bother me: I'd heard the racket so often it had become elemental, expected. In fact, the quarrels often made me sleepy, and I would wake up when the screaming stopped.

My father was calming himself with a cigarette when he sat me down at the drafting desk in his tidy, fluorescent-lit workshop. He showed me an album of newspaper clippings dating back to the year I was born. The articles dealt with mysterious events that I, a straight-A science student, immediately knew to be made-up. My father read some of the headlines aloud in an anchorman's phony baritone: " 'Ogden Boy Scouts Report Strange Lights'; 'Grizzly on the Vegas Strip?' " He shut the album and asked me what I thought.

"Somebody was playing pranks," I said. "There aren't any grizzly bears in Nevada."

"Correct," my father said, and he gave me a deep, long squinting stare.

"Was it you who did those things?" I said.

He put a heavy, warm hand on my shoulder.

"It's a hobby, Travis. It started back in engineering school, me and some buddies goofing around. Believe me, I'm not the only one who does this."

I nodded as if I already knew that.

"There are lots of us," my father said, "spread out all over the country. We're professionals, mostly. Intelligent men. Does that make sense to you?"

I waited for him to make it make sense, but suddenly he seemed distant and anxious, caught up in his thoughts. He shut his eyes and reached under his glasses and pinched the bridge of his nose. I wondered if he was regretting his decision to let me in on his secret life. I hoped not. I hadn't wanted to know about this stuff, but now that I did, I needed to know it all.

"Do you ever meet up?" I said. "Is this a club?"

"We are a club," he said, opening his eyes, "but not one that meets. Not meeting is the point. We'd rather pick up a newspaper, read about a Bigfoot track discovered in Wyoming, say, and realize another one of us is out there. It's our way of saying hello to one another. Of sending smoke signals."

I said I understood and for the rest of the evening I asked no more questions, just sat there with the album on my knee as my father disclosed true stories behind various clippings. The Ogden UFO scare, for example, was the result of panicky phone calls to several late-night disc jockeys. By changing his voice for each call and varying his descriptions of the spacecraft, my father had stimulated other sightings throughout a four-state area and over the course of the following three nights. He said I was sick with the croup at the time and neither he nor my mother could sleep; whenever she got up to quiet me, he would sneak down to the basement and monitor the reports of fresh sightings on a police-band radio. By the second night, he said, the hoax had developed a life of its own.

"That happens sometimes. You forget you started it. But then you remember and that's what makes it fun."

We turned a few more album pages, and afterward, my father made me swear to keep our conversation to myself. Not a word about the altered Polaroids that proved the existence of the Vegas grizzly. Not a breath about the St. Paul taxidermist who fashioned the Lionbird remains my father had sold to an Iron Range museum. As I made my vow, I could hear my mother through the door noisily clearing the dinner plates. I sensed that whomever else my father's jokes were on, they were mostly on her.

Still, I made a promise. My father's odd pastime became our secret, despite the wall it immediately placed between me and everyone else in the world. And that's why on this morning six months later, the morning of the crop circles, I will settle for nothing less than full and equal participation.

"But we don't need a guard," I say. "Nobody's going to come by here. It's not even four o'clock yet."

"You don't know farmers' hours," my father says, pumping the brakes and stopping the truck. "Ever wonder why it's country people who see all the UFOs? They're up so early. Still half dreaming when they do their chores."

He backs the truck off the paved country road and onto a grassy two-track, proceeding for twenty or thirty yards, until we are safe behind a clump of sumac. Wordlessly, we climb out of the cab and walk around to the back to unload our tools: a coil of rope and a long metal stake with a swivel eyelet. I consider what we are about to do together. In just a couple of hours we will be back in our normal lives—me at school and my father at his office—but the circle will be out here, waiting, ready to drive people crazy. . . .

By the glowing green dial of my father's watch, the work takes almost two hours. We plant the iron stake in the ground and tie one end of the rope to the swivel ring. I hold the stake with both hands and steady it while my father stretches taut the rope and walks in a series of widening circles, sweeping down the cornstalks as he goes. The noise of the bending and snapping stalks seems bound to give us away, yet no one comes. I hear a dog bark and a new fear hits me: no one will ever see what we're creating here and the only people the circle will drive crazy will be my father and me, waiting for it to be discovered.

The thought of this makes me feel lonesome, foolish, and as I watch my father sweep the corn down, I wonder what satisfaction there can be in duping people you will never meet and piling up secrets for the sake of it.

Our family moved a lot in those days because my father was always quitting. It wasn't that he couldn't hold a job, but that he had no reason to; the moment he felt bored or unappreciated, he left and found another one. His field was computer programming back when that was new, and though he had trouble obtaining promotions because he hadn't finished engineering school, he never lacked for entry-level offers. For him, obtaining a new position was merely a matter of driving to a city, looking in the local yellow pages, and making a few calls from a pay phone. My mother and I would watch him from the truck, wiping circles in the steamed-up windows, since it always seemed to be winter when we moved.

The winter I was fourteen, four months after a startled crop duster discovered the St. Cloud saucer site and all the TV stations went out to film it, my father announced over his morning bran flakes that we would be moving to Rockford, Illinois, as soon as we could pack up the truck. My mother rose from the table when he said this and walked as if in a trance to her bedroom. I heard the screech of wire clothes hangers being ripped from the bar in her closet, followed by snapping suitcase latches. My father sipped from his third mug of Postum and browsed through the latest issue of *Popular Mechanics.*

"She's sad," he said. "That's natural in a woman. It's biological. They get attached to places. Through the smells." His gaze remained fixed on the magazine, whose cover showed plans for a do-it-yourself infrared burglar alarm. "What about you?" he said, turning a page. "You up for Illinois?"

To show solidarity with my angry mother, I frowned and said, "Don't know," though the truth was I couldn't wait to leave St. Cloud. Ever since the uproar surrounding the "Circles of Mystery," the place had become ridiculous to me, a city of hicks and fools. What's worse, my school year so far had been disastrous. My classmates had changed during summer vacation, growing sideburns, adopting baffling slang, forming new and strange alliances based on shared tastes in sneakers and haircuts. Being polite to teachers was out and defiant public nose picking was in. These new ways had caught me by surprise and I knew I wouldn't be able to catch up. My only hope was a fresh start somewhere else where no one remembered my hair in a crew cut and I could claim that math had *always* bored me.

"Before you go pack your stuff," my father said, "I want to tell you something." He closed his magazine. "Travis, a man is just a human being."

"I know," I said.

"I know you know. It's your mother who thinks differently. She thinks I control the universe."

I listened.

"And I made her think that. I built myself up big. I made her believe I had powers."

I stood there.

"Women demand it," my father said. "Then they punish you when they learn the truth."

"I'm sorry," I said.

"You ought to be. You're next."

I was never quite comfortable with him after that.

The one-story house we rented in Rockford had a partially finished basement. My father spent most of his evenings down there, assembling gizmos from *Popular Mechanics* and imagining schemes that I wanted no part of but had to hear about anyway. I began to dread eating dinner at home, knowing I might be invited downstairs the moment my mother stood up from the table. My father said she knew nothing of his hobby, that she thought of him as an ordinary tinkerer, and her willingness to leave me alone with him told me he was right. Once or twice a week, he would lead me down into his dungeon, promising to show me "something fascinating." He was focused then on fake ancient artifacts. I remember handling a set of chisels, a dictionary of Aztec pictographs, some chunks of marble salvaged from old buildings. I remember a long and manic riff concerning the fallibility of the carbon-dating process.

"This notion that things have determinable ages," I remember my father saying, "is baloney. It's science's big lie. The only way to date a thing is to date a more familiar thing that's near it, and the only way to date *that* thing, of course—"

"May I go upstairs now, Dad, and watch TV?"

"There's nothing on."

"There is, though. There's a lot on."

I stopped going home after school. I hung out. My plan to revamp my image had succeeded and I had joined a ninth-grade clique that centered on two cute girls who liked to smoke pot in the park by the river and discuss such things as telepathy and witchcraft and life on other planets. Both Karla and Jan were only-daughters of single mothers who worked, meaning they could do anything they wanted, anytime. I pretended I was equally free, and sometimes I stayed out with them until seven or eight o'clock at night. Their interest in the supernatural made me feel protective toward them, as though my inside knowledge of the subject required me to ease them toward the truth.

"Flying saucers," I told them once, "are usually just that: plates thrown in the air."

"So you think humans are the only life-form in all the universe?" Karla said.

"That's an arrogant view," Jan said. She was the pretty one, the one I liked.

"I'm saying there aren't UFOs," I said. "There might be other life-forms. Moss or something."

"What about Bigfoot?" Karla said. "I mean, do you think everyone just *lies?"*

"People make things up," I said. "I can't believe you don't know that, Karla."

"Lay off my friend," said Jan.

"I'm sorry."

Jan said, "You're such a cynic, Travis. God."

The girls got sick of me soon enough, so I spent my after-school hours by myself, yelling at older kids driving by in Firebirds, lobbing snowballs at dogs chained up in yards, spitting off freeway overpasses. When I got home, there would be food wrapped in tinfoil in the kitchen and my mother would either be off at Red Cross or in her bedroom reading a Harlequin. My father would be in the basement, too busy with his latest creation to notice my arrival. I would eat in front of the TV and fall asleep on the sofa with a show on.

In March, our family moved again, first to Lincoln, Nebraska, for a month, where my father did not even bother to find work because of his dangerously elevated blood pressure. Then he decided on Denver. When he announced this move, my mother phoned her parents in Florida and asked them to send her two plane tickets, one for her and one for me. The tickets arrived a few days later and my father made my mother cash them in and then spent the money on truck repairs. We drove to Colorado in a blizzard, using four-wheel drive the whole way and playing car games like license-plate Scrabble. I sat squeezed in tight between my parents, forming the link and keeping us a family. A thin line down the middle of my body was all that I felt was left of me.

We arrived in downtown Denver at lunchtime. My father ushered us into a diner crowded with businessmen smoking cigarettes and told us to sit at the counter while he made a phone call. He motioned the waitress over and ordered two BLTs and two split pea soups and nothing for himself. On the napkin beside my mother he laid two one-hundred-dollar bills. I remember thinking the money was counterfeit, something my father had printed himself, and that we would go to prison if we used it.

As my father strode off toward the pay phone mounted on the back wall of the restaurant, the collar of his jacket was turned up and his hands were thrust deep in his pockets. That seemed odd to me. I ate some soup. I watched our waitress swirl mayonnaise on toast and lay down parallel strips of wrinkled bacon.

I felt my mother's hand touch my hand.

"We're leaving," she said. "Your father's gone. Come on. We planned this so there wouldn't be a scene."

She picked up the bills and rose from her stool. I turned and looked down the aisle. A man in a suit was talking on the pay phone, covering one ear with his free hand. Next to the phone I saw a door with a lit-up red EXIT sign over it. The door was open slightly and I could see trapped cigarette smoke rushing out through the crack.

"Travis, please," my mother said. I saw she had the truck keys in her hand. They were on a new ring: a rabbit's foot.

"We're giving each other some time to think," she said. "We'll probably get back together in a month, with all these little problems ironed out and everyone just as happy as before."

"He's coming back?" I said.

"He's coming back."

"Do you still love him?" I said.

"I love him dearly."

My mother could be a hoaxer sometimes, too.

About a year later I went to see my father in Helena, Montana. My parents' divorce had gone through a few months earlier, the week I'd turned sixteen, and the judge had ruled that the summer was to be time with my father. After my grandparents' crowded condo in buggy, polluted Florida, his trailer in the mountains was just what I needed. I felt like I could breathe again and my acne began to clear up. My father, though, had deteriorated. He had grown a black beard, which made his skin look paler. When he spoke, his words were run together or sleepily strung out. I noticed he was drinking real coffee now and forgetting to watch his salt.

"You're looking good," I told him my second day there. We were sitting in plaid nylon lawn chairs on his sloping, home-built deck. Between us, on a little metal table, was a family-size bag of barbecue potato chips that we sometimes reached into.

"Baloney," my father said. "I'm eating worse, sleeping less, drinking more, and feeling shittier every day."

"I didn't know. I'm sorry."

"I threw away my life," my father said. "I hated computers. They bored me stiff. Everyone thinks of computers as clever, but in fact they're the definition of dumb. They aren't electronic minds at all. Imagine a person who all he can do is repeat what you tell him, not even twist things. Imagine spending twenty years with him."

As we ate our snack and watched the sun go down, I wondered if my father had kept up with his strange pastime. All winter in Florida I had scanned the newspapers, particularly the supermarket tabloids, looking for stories with Montana datelines, but no luck. All the tall tales seemed to come from other regions. There was a haunting in a Long Island mansion, sea monsters in the Finger Lakes, crucifix-shaped hailstones in Missouri. A pair of elderly lobstermen in Maine claimed to have watched a group of gray whales spout in unison between a hovering mothership. America was seeing things, but my father appeared to have no part in it.

Then he told me about Howling Johnny and I realized my father had not retired—he had raised his sights.

It was August, hot. We placed the bones and relics in a flour sack, closed the sack with baling twine, then stowed it in the trunk of my father's rusted Cutlass. The metal fried my fingertips as I slammed the trunk lid. My father stood off to the side with pen and notepad, giving instructions and checking off our steps. He had on a wrinkled pink polo shirt, dark glasses, and a baseball cap from *Popular Mechanics.* I sensed that he thought he looked inconspicuous, but to me he looked absurd. Also, profoundly, utterly fulfilled.

"Gasoline," he said.

"I filled the tank."

"Once we're inside Glacier Park," he said, repeating this point for the third or fourth time, "we're on our own. They don't have service stations."

"That's why I filled the tank," I said.

His lack of faith annoyed me. I had been working hard to keep his confidence ever since the night in late July when he had spread a white bedsheet on the deck and carefully set out the Johnny remains and the other gravesite relics. He showed me the bones out of jealousy, I think. He had been drinking bourbon during dinner and grilling me about my mother's boyfriend, a Coast Guard officer named Percy Finn. After ridiculing his name and the concept of the Coast Guard, my father asked me if Percy Finn had ever let me visit his cutter. I said yes and my father's face changed color. He said, "I'll bet that was interesting," and pressed me until I admitted that it had been. Then he rose on wobbly legs and disappeared into his trailer. A few minutes later he came back out carrying the bundle.

The remains themselves—an adolescent male skeleton purchased from a defunct museum and some hair my father had saved from his own head—were the least part of the Howling Johnny hoax, which was based, my father said, on an actual unsolved missing-persons case. In 1939, the story went, a six-year-old boy named Johnny Hale, budding musical prodigy and only child of Thomas Earle Hale, a leading San Francisco banker, disappeared from his parents' lakeside campsite in Glacier National Park. A massive manhunt was launched immediately, but after weeks of intensive search, the teams of divers, bloodhound handlers, and Native American trackers had failed to turn up the slightest clue to the child's fate. Park officials presumed the boy dead—killed and eaten by bears or wolves—but Thomas Hale rejected this conclusion. Until his death in 1975, Hale senior had offered a standing reward of half a million dollars for information about the lost boy's whereabouts. The reward created a small but steady stream of Johnny sightings, Johnny lore, and even one or two Johnny imposters, but no satisfying explanation was ever found.

My father intended to close the case. As we headed north on I-15, rolling cool Coke cans across our baking foreheads and listening to a Merle Haggard tape, we carried with us the makings of an American roadside legend. Far from being eaten by wild beasts, Johnny Hale, the world would soon discover, had himself become a beast: a hairy wildboy, maker of crude stone tools and weapons, and yet, because of his musical upbringing, an artist as well—a kind of Stone Age Mozart. Stashed in the rotting, handstitched deer hide rucksack that would be unearthed beside the bones were rustic antler harmonicas, crude flutes, even a tiny lute-like instrument strung with braided elk gut. When my father first showed me this primitive orchestra, he bragged that he'd outdone himself, and I had to agree: Johnny's instruments were works of genius, implausibly plausible. It was the closest my father had come to his ideal—to create something fantastic which actually might have happened.

We stayed that night in a campground just inside the park's east entrance. Neither of us slept. Howling Johnny was too much with us and I kept seeing the moon-outlined image of his thrown-back head as he piped strange tunes across high mountain valleys. His motives for choosing this savage, lonesome life would never be fully known, of course, but perhaps a partial explanation lay in the faded newspaper clipping my father had planted in Johnny's rucksack. The clipping, obtained from an actual old copy of the *San Francisco Chronicle,* was a review of little Johnny Hale's first public recital, noting his "somewhat skittish fingering" and "oddly romantic choice of material." So apparently the six-year-old wonder could not take criticism, and had fled to the rocky moraines of Glacier Park to work out his musical gifts in solitude.

"And you know why it's perfect?" said my father, turning over in his sleeping bag and going up on one elbow to face me. "The moment this thing gets discovered and reported on, people will know there's a master out there. It's better than Piltdown Man."

"You're right," I said.

"People won't *want* to explain this thing. It's magical."

We folded the tent around 2 A.M. and climbed in the Cutlass and drove for an hour on the moonlit Going to the Sun Road. We parked at a trailhead posted with a sign warning hikers of grizzly bears. We divided the Johnny remains between two knapsacks and walked for an hour straight uphill. I noticed my father getting short of breath and I offered to take his pack for him. I was surprised when he accepted. We climbed another hundred yards or so and he sat down on a rock and put his head down. I shined my flashlight on him. He looked awful, with damp, matted hair.

"Let's stop," I said. "We'll do it here."

My father shook his head. "It has to be near the snow line. Off the trail more. Also, we need a cliff he could have fallen from. It has to make a story."

By this time, my father was shivering hard and his color had turned a sickly pink. He wrapped his arms around his chest and eyed me pathetically. His breathing was quick and fluttery, as if his lungs had turned to crinkly paper.

"I'll do it myself," I said. "I won't be long. You sit tight and keep warm, okay? Don't move."

I shrugged off my fleece-lined denim jacket and draped it over my father's shaking shoulders. I asked him if he was all right and he nodded. Then I strapped on both knapsacks, took a breath, and went up the mountain to bury the bones.

Five months later, my father died. The news of his stroke came as no surprise to me. During my last few weeks in Montana, in the lull that followed our trip to Glacier, my father had gone on a binge of strong black coffee, alcohol, and salt. When I'd begged him to take his blood pressure medicine, he'd cursed me like he didn't even know me and said the pills had made him impotent, which had ruined his marriage and ruined his life. His bitterness and fury, long pushed down, flew out in terrible rants and screaming fits, often directed at Percy Finn, who had become an obsession by then. I left for Florida five days earlier than planned, vowing not to return the following summer and sensing that perhaps I wouldn't have to.

My mother and I did not attend the funeral, which was paid for by my father's company, a Helena data-collection firm. He had gone back to computers, after all—to the machines that had faithfully supported him. His boss sent us a snapshot of the urn containing my father's ashes and he offered to send along the urn itself, but I told my mother I didn't want the thing.

I had a better way to remember my father, a memory that was mine alone, hidden where the world couldn't touch it.

When my father died, Howling Johnny had still not been uncovered, as I'd taken pains to make sure he never would be. I had simply buried him too deep.

WALTER KIRN DISCUSSES
"The Hoaxer," character, and the truth about Santa Claus

PM: In this story and other work of yours, you focus on the father-son relationship; what especially appeals to you about it as a vein for fiction?
WK: Aside from the fact that I think subjects choose us as often as we choose them, it appeals to me because it's a mysterious relationship. Love and romance and friendship—all of those are chosen relations that have to do with affinity, but it's one of the abiding mysteries of life that the most important relationships we have aren't chosen, they're thrown at us by fate, and we have to work out their significance on the job, so to speak.

I think that's why I find the parent-child relationship perennially fascinating—it's one that's thrust at people; it's not chosen; it's one where one of the parties has an inordinate amount of power and the other party is extraordinarily vulnerable and alert and impressionable. There isn't much that can happen between a father and son actually that isn't dramatic, or isn't worthy of recording or exploring.
PM: What led you to this particular father in "The Hoaxer"?
WK: In a way, it's a metaphor for something that I think is true of the father-son relationship in general: there comes a time when your father is exposed as a fraud. Whether he's a Supreme Court justice or works in a sawmill, it is universally true that the time will come when his son sees through him or understands his importance in the world to be less than he formerly thought. As an extension of that basic truth, I made this father a conscious liar, a conscious faker. I really think kids journey through the forest of their parents' mistakes, exaggerations, and misrepresentations to find the truth. That's what

growing up is. And this was a way of making that process outsized and conspicuous.

Part of the character of the father in this story came out of my fascination with the personalities of these hoaxer types themselves. It's a small group of people that enjoy putting one over on their fellows. We all do to some extent, but there are some who become consumed by it, you know?

It's a curious profile: I've seen it in people who always have to be the one playing the practical joke, always have to be in control of information somehow, the people who make a big deal out of April Fool's Day or spend too long trying to keep their kids in the dark about the true nature of Santa Claus. All parents—I'm a parent—to some extent for the first few years at least of their children's lives are engaged in a masquerade with them. But that part of all of us is hypertrophied and overgrown in this fellow.

PM: What helps keep such an outsized, quirky character tethered to the orbit of universal human experience and to your reader?

WK: Personally, I do a few things. I don't take an idea and then sheathe it in flesh and then put clothes on it and give it an accent and consider it a character. That to me is a failed character, when all you've done is dress up or costume an idea. The way it comes about for me is a little bit more complex. I use memory a lot to bring back to me the pictures, habits, dress, and behavior of people who remind me of the character who's sprung into my mind. In this case, because the character started with a proclivity for lying and for fooling others, I think about the people I know who share it. And it's as though parts of those people, parts of real people, parts of people in memory and just the sort of general association with people I've seen, draw to themselves clothing, speech, etc. To me that's the fun of it.

And whether you've done it well is always a question of: do you believe them line by line, paragraph by paragraph yourself? I can't always say when I'm doing it right—I can't always say when somebody's living, real, or convincing—but I *know* when they're not. I know when I've lost it. It's often the case of drawing someone until something looks out of place and pulling back, trying to regain the original impulse, the original truth of the thing and proceeding *again* until you hit a wall of unreality or unbelievability. And so it's fumbling in the dark to some extent. But you always know when it doesn't ring true. And keeping that b.s. detector about character tuned is the most important job.

PM: Is it more pleasurable going through this process with a character who, like the father, is closer to the fringes?

WK: It's my personal belief that the marginal, the rejected, the ignored, the obscure, the flawed are almost always more interesting subjects for art than the successful, the conventional, and the approved, unless you have something new to say about them.

PM: Tolstoy's "unhappy family" principle—

WK: Well, it's partly that "all happy families are alike," true, but it's also that there's more to discover in the unexplored and the underappreciated than there is in the familiar and successful. When people go with the exploratory impulse, they don't head for downtown New York City; they head for the moon, or the bottom of the ocean, or the edges of the continent. That's a pretty pervasive impulse, to try to find something important or new in the underappreciated or unknown. And so I do find that characters who've not shown up on the radar of literature quite as often are more interesting than the ones who have, or certainly than the ones who show up every day in the newspaper.

PM: When portraying a character as quirky and large as the father, how did you keep him from upstaging Travis?

WK: The father in the story is acting, and the child is reacting. That's the nature of being a child. You react and react to characters larger than yourself. The key is making those reactions real and making Travis's voice vivid, convincing, and persuasive.

In *The Great Gatsby*, Gatsby should by all rights upstage everybody else, but he doesn't because the story's being told to us by someone whose curiosity and impressions are actually more vivid. Larger-than-life characters are strangely a dime a dozen; people who can see through them and somehow make something meaningful out of them are actually rarer. And Travis's predicament in this story is just more appealing and widespread than the father's. I mean the father's wrestling with some peculiar problems, but Travis is dealing with *the* problem, which all of us in some sense share, which is: How do we relate? And how do we love and continue to honor people, authority figures, who so often let us down?

PM: The narrator says in the introductory section that he'd like to think of his father as a teacher—"though of what set of truths or values, I don't know." What set of truths or values do *you* attribute to the father?

WK: "Don't be anyone else's fool." He's trying to teach his son by letting the son in on his masquerade, the theater he makes out of life. Not to trust in appearances, not to be a chump. And at the same time he's trying to teach him what we're all trying to teach our kids when we ask them to believe in Santa Claus, which is there's a place in the world for willed and willful fantasy. If you want this world to be magical or mysterious, you have to create that mystery and honor that side of life.

And it's the tension between the desire to have faith and the desire to live in reality; in some ways this father is a teacher of that. Or a guide to that process.

PM: The father's inventions certainly have a spiritual flavor to them and a sense of magic. But at the same time that he's opening that door for his son, he's spoiling any genuine belief the boy might have been inclined to have.

WK: Right. The father in this story is a kind of embittered rationalist. He sees through a lot. He's skeptical, he's logical, and I think that whatever magic or penumbra of mysticism that he experienced as a child, he's very bitter about the loss of. And he's not teaching any direct lesson in some linear, pedantic way. He's struggling with his own ambivalence about the lack of mystery in life.

I think about these people who make crop circles; somebody had to fake all those UFO photographs. (Pardon me if I sound like I don't believe in UFOs.) Faked the Bigfoot footprints. And somebody had to spin the legends of Loch Ness. And I wonder: Why? And I think that those types have a dual motivation: it's a projection of power to see others all worked up about some phenomenon which you secretly know to be a fraud, and it also represents a longing in those types for there to *be* another dimension.

PM: So it's a very ambivalent relationship with materialism.

WK: Yes, exactly. Exactly. The father is a pretty disappointed character in this story. Pretty limited. Like people who set out to build the world's largest ball of string or to collect every issue of *National Geographic* ever published, or something like that, there are people who are disappointed in ordinariness, who will go to great compulsive lengths to make themselves extraordinary or protest . . . I think the father is protesting daily life. He's protesting against rationality. There's a romantic there. And yet there's a rationalist who can't feel it.

PM: Can't feel the romance?

WK: Yes. I think what he's really teaching his son about, what he's really displaying for his son, is his own ambivalence about mystery. When Wordsworth says, I was a child, and everything had a gleam about it and an aura, and then it all passed away, and life is gray now, and I can't get back to that, he's expressing some of the emotions that operate in this father.

And it's interesting, when you read for example about shamans and medicine men; they tend to know that they're playing tricks. And that they are seeking to elicit belief though fraud. And I think the father is, in this strange way, a kind of a shaman who is trying to create for others the magic or the sense of wonder or the sense of mystery that he is unable to feel himself.

PM: So in that first scene where he takes Travis out to make crop circles, he's initiating his son into a priesthood.

WK: Yes, he is, exactly. It is a story about being initiated against your will into a very quirky priesthood. And yet that is a rite of passage that I see go on in all kinds of father-child relationships. The first time the big brother is let in on the mysteries of Christmas night, so as to enchant the little brother—that represents the initiation. I think more than anything this is his father's only way of being close to this child. Or to anyone.

By taking his son into his confidence in this con game that is his hobby, he is trying desperately to form a bond with him. We often think about the intimacy of thieves in a gang, or between conspirators. He's making his son a co-conspirator. It's the only way he knows how to have a relationship.

PM: Let's talk about Howling Johnny, this pet project of the father's, which also seems to be a helpful device for *you*; it gives you an extra dimension through which to delineate the father's character.

WK: Howling Johnny externalizes the father's loneliness. This is overwhelmingly a story about loneliness, about a very, very lonely man. His pièce de résistance is a materialization of his own soul. Inventing that device or that character, if we're going to call Howling Johnny a character, came out of my contemplation of who these mysterious beings like Bigfoot and the Alien often are: they share a family resemblance; they're always lonely, misshapen, misunderstood, feared. I guess in Jungian terms, they represent the—I don't know, the anima, or the repressed side of people. That part of us that we fear is ugly, unacceptable, alone, disfigured. And these monsters are often, and it seems typically, pathetic. Outcast characters. So Howling Johnny comes in that sort of line. It's a child, too.

PM: Who's regressing into a more and more primitive state, not unlike Travis's father.

WK: It's his Frankenstein monster made up of parts of himself, the parts of himself that didn't work or were marginalized or cast off. I think that Howling Johnny represents his fears for himself and a fantasy of extreme isolation and loneliness brought to life.

PM: He's creative, though, too. It seems important that

Howling Johnny isn't just surviving, he's creating all these musical instruments.
WK: Right, right. As I say, this figure of Howling Johnny came out of my contemplation of monsters in general, and they often tend to be possessed of strange talents or powers. Certainly aliens have attributed to them all kinds of gifts and extraordinary faculties. It seems to me revealing that we didn't create aliens as average, low-intelligence creatures who just bumble through the universe. No, they do things that we wish we could do. And Howling Johnny kind of makes a successful creative existence out of the barest of materials and in that sense is a fantasy for those like the father who feel unappreciated, obscure, alone.
PM: Skipping to the opposite end of the spectrum, we've got Percy Finn. He's in the Coast Guard and his name is ridiculously suited to his work, and just those couple of details seem to convey that he's part of the establishment and probably content about it.
WK: He represents a lot of options that the father didn't take. A lot of characteristics that the father can't inhabit. He represents the conventional and the satisfied and the confident. And the socially successful. Because if there's one thing the father's not, it's socially successful. The father literally has to create this fantasy figure for company.
PM: The story also seems to suggest that there's something less than ideal about being so conventional.
WK: Yes, the Percy Finns of the world are, for the father, less than alive, less than fully human in some way. The father seems to identify most closely with the values of creativity—the father's an artist, he's an artist without an art. And there is something very appealing, very kind of noble in his ability to do a lot with very little material. Life has handed him very little to work with—very few paintbrushes—but with what little he has, he's done all he can.

I think if we're talking again about the values that he's promoting, one is the respect for oddness and individuality. The son will certainly never be able to voyage innocently among the unimaginative after having been his father's co-conspirator. He might have longed to be normal, but he won't be. He's had a taste of this cultic secret reality.

PM: Not that it will likely give him pleasure. He's stranded in this narrow middle ground.

WK: Our family experiences narrow our options in life, it's my feeling. The kinds of behavior and outlooks that we learn and have modeled for us tend to set us on a fairly narrow path, I think. Travis didn't *ask* to know any of these secrets, he didn't ask to be let in on any of these stories; he was given them for some reason. And his character will be formed accordingly, just as I think the children of alcoholics and of people with mental illness are consigned to a certain extent to wrestle with those same things, and the set of problems that Travis has been handed and attitudes that he's been handed to wrestle with are no one else's, and they're not particularly common. And yet here they are, you know?

Our parents dump a set of preoccupations and predicaments and aptitudes and inaptitudes on our doorsteps, which are ours, and I guess this story's fairly fatalistic about that process. Success in dealing with them seems to be defined by how honestly you can do it, or how fully you can do it, not by how far away you can run.

PM: Were you ever tempted when drafting this story to articulate Travis's trajectory a beat or two further?

WK: Beyond this point?

PM: Yes, since the story is being told in hindsight.

WK: Yes, the story is told in hindsight, without many explicit clues as to what has happened in the gap between its ending and its telling. That's a gap I like to leave open, because that's where the reader gets to think and feel and speculate.

It was a habit of early storytelling to take every story right to the end. If the story ended when someone was eighteen, there was an addendum about how they got married and lived to an old age. But I think that that was a kind of ritual reassurance that storytellers felt obligated to provide. And it was never really the best part of the story or the most sincere; it was just the bow you always tied the package with.

I didn't tie this story with that bow because I think I left Travis at the point at which all the major ingredients for his life were now in place. And to some, that's the definition of an unsatisfying ending, an ending which is really a beginning, but to me that's the definition of a good ending. Because unless you're telling a story on through to the death of the character, there's some point at which you have to say, *And then* (laughs) *all was dark, or was a mystery*, or whatever.

I write a lot about adolescents for the same reason it's probably over-represented in literature generally, which is that it seems to be in some ways the most dramatic time of life. Because we go from partial knowledge to a fuller knowledge of who we are, and who the people around us are, and what the society is that we find ourselves in, and then we're handed our backpack and told to march with what's in our bag. And I feel that the reader's imagination about future paths for Travis is most stimulated at the point where I leave things. All the questions have been asked most vividly. All of the potential problems have been stated most clearly.

PM: In a way, it would be problematic to nudge this story even the slightest bit further, because you've left him right at the brink of a very ancient dilemma.

WK: He's poised between two equally powerful forces and instincts. One is rationality and one is a sense of mystery, of the unknown, fate, and so on. But that alternating current will be the energy that powers his life. That, we know. And this issue—bouncing between these poles, trying to square this circle—will be the stuff of his future. And so for me it is a conclusive ending, because it shows me—and the reader, I hope—exactly what the issue's going to be with this young man; it will be this issue and not another.

And that is a way of defining character. Every character is, in a way, a problem. And if you want to know someone or some character, you have to know what the problem that drives them is. What is the dissatisfaction or the difficulty that keeps them moving? And by the end of this story, I think we know what it is for Travis.

PM: Travis tells us he "buried the bones too deep" for Howling Johnny ever to be unearthed. With that final gesture you manage to dramatize some of the paradoxical nature of his "problem." Because the gesture seems to suggest both respect as well as rebellion.

WK: I remember writing that, and I remember that I was trying to express the irredeemably private nature of our family relationships. That which we know best and most fully is often beyond communication, and I think that gesture in some way and that statement are Travis's way of saying that this story is part of me now. It's not going to be scavenged by others, it's not going to be turned up by passers-by; it's in my very substance now.

And I think it's exactly what you said—it's two things. It's a rebellion: he's made a failure of his father's project, in that it was intended for an audience that it will never have; it's going to remain forever secret. But that is a form of honoring him, too, in that he's made himself his father's sole audience. I think one of the things Travis is saying is: "Unless you knew the guy, you wouldn't understand. You wouldn't understand this artifact the way I can."

PM: One of the things "The Hoaxer" also seems to capture is the relationship between the artist and his long-suffering family. Do you ever think of fiction writing as a form of hoaxing?

WK: I definitely think of fiction as hoaxing. Fiction is an attempt to cast a spell by people who know exactly how that spell is cast. It's a peculiar profession in that we're sort of disillusioned types trying to create illusions for others a lot of the time. And the father in this story is definitely for me a version of the fiction writer. Maybe the unpublished fiction writer *(laughs)*. He has this very complicated relationship with truth, and so do fiction writers. We're trying to teach or impart truth through fabrication, which may be one of the reasons why things like the memoir and nonfiction seem to be winning out in the publishing world, because it's hard for the audience, and even the writers, to remember exactly how this process is supposed to work.

Fiction writers have not made a very good argument, and professors haven't either, for why made-up stories can actually be relevant to real life. And I think we've kind of lost that thread as a culture. It's an increasingly quixotic enterprise to try to enlighten through falsehood. And that's why people want true stories that they can take away a clear moral from, rather than ambiguous, made-up stories that will somehow—how can I put it?—increase their wisdom.

So I think that the father in this story represents some of my own conflicting feelings about writing fiction. I mean, it's never been an entirely reputable occupation. Plato pretty much said flat out that artists were deceivers and creators of useless, untrue objects, and I don't think we've ever gotten over that as a society.

WALTER KIRN is the regular book reviewer for the *New York Times Book Review* and a contributing editor to *Time*. He is the author of a story collection, *My Hard Bargain* (1992), and the novels *She Needed Me* (1992), *Thumbsucker* (1999), and *Up in the Air* (2001). A graduate of Princeton University and Oxford University, he lives in Livingston, Montana.

PROWLER

Elizabeth Tallent

A new development, and more than he can bear: his ex-wife is suddenly back from Europe, her boyfriend of the last two years nowhere in sight. The tortoiseshell glasses she has never worn before alert him that Christie, confronting him across the living room, has reinvented herself yet again. That the glasses still excite her as a novelty, a kind of prop, is plain to Dennis only because he knows her so well. She has a new gesture, index finger laid against the bridge of her nose to give the specs a tiny upward shove, brown eyes widening, that manages to get across the impression she is taking life more seriously, yet her account of the last year smells of evasiveness. Déjà vu, because his own sense, with Christie, was often that she was skipping details that might not reflect well on her, editing and enlarging as she went, and that he was essentially helpless to pin her to the truth. Christie is all in baggy black, her legs crossed, one black, doltish boot swinging. She wants their son for the summer.

"George has stayed behind," she says with a faint, enigmatic tone of apology. Not even that is clear. Not "I've left him" or "It was all a mistake," but "George has stayed behind." In Paris, where she lived with him for the last year.

By a coincidence, he and Christie both began second families last year, she with George, Dennis with his young wife Francesca. Christie's baby girl has been left in Santa Fe with a sitter. His twins are asleep upstairs with their mother, all of them exhausted by the cold they have been sharing back and forth. Andy, his and Christie's thirteen-year-old, is away overnight with his best friend; when Dennis heard a car grind to a halt in the rocky drive, he had a scared flash that Andy and Leo had got into trouble and somebody had been sent to tell him so. For next to no reason, Dennis distrusts Leo, a smart, good-looking kid, self-assured around adults in a way Andy never will be, not until he's one himself—maybe not even then. Leo's girlfriend works in a record store where Andy and Leo are always hanging out. Andy can't drive yet, of course, and neither can Leo. It's real proof of Leo's fast-talking charm that he has a sixteen-year-old girlfriend. Leo's mother, who doesn't approve of the girlfriend, drives the boys to the mall, because otherwise, she says, they'd hitchhike. Maybe it's Leo's mother Dennis dislikes. She gives in to the boys too easily. She was Christie's lawyer, trim and venomous, during the divorce.

What kind of trouble does he imagine his son getting into? Dennis has no very persistent or obsessive idea, just occasional glints in which Andy pockets a Baggie of white powder or, with faked knowingness, hoovers a furled five-dollar bill over a mirror, talked into these idiot risks by Leo. None of those fears come true; instead an altogether different problem materializes. The car that startled him belongs to Andy's mother.

Christie's never been in this house before, and one of his reactions to letting her in strikes Dennis as inappropriate, even disturbingly so, and he hides it: he'd like to know what she thinks. An architect, he is constantly exposed in his work to the wanton quest for the famous New Mexico light, which is especially sought after by new arrivals from the grayed-over, greenhoused cities of the East Coast. It's as if light is another aspect of the West they can seize and display, the way their walls are now hung with pristine longhorn and bison skulls whose flesh—the new arrivals don't trouble to learn this—has been boiled from the bone in oil drums, not worried away by coyotes. Dead Tech, Dennis's partner calls it. When Dennis first came across this house, it was a warren of low-ceilinged rooms whose windows were unfashionably small and few. Huge cottonwoods grew right up to the walls. Such a shaded, wood-fragrant, down-at-heels little place; he wanted it. In renovating, he changed it only minimally.

"Nice," Christie says of the room, sitting, crossing her black legs, beginning to pick at the cuticle of her thumb, and he asks himself why he wanted more of her. Glancing up, she reads his disappointment, and makes a face. *What do you expect?* the face says. This is where you live your new life. The face implies that she knew such a muted reaction would hurt. More than anything, he wants her to stop picking away at her cuticle. If she can get at him so fast, so nonchalantly, he'd better watch it.

"Can we turn on another light?" she asks.

When he does, he has to admire the kinked mass of her dark hair, backlit. Even with the stupid glasses, she looks good. She's already lost whatever weight she gained with the baby.

"Coffee?" he says, for a chance to leave the room. He pokes through a drawer for filters, then stares around the kitchen, catching his emotional breath, reorienting himself. "Tea," Christie calls. Her tone's not rude, and he's no longer annoyed with her, but it troubles him that, this long divorced, it's taken them all of five minutes to fall back into marital shorthand. O. K. Tea. By the time he carries their two cups back with him, he's both more guarded and surer about where to begin.

"Christie, weeks went by when you didn't call him. Once you let it go a month. February, right?"

She has too much at stake to lose her temper. That would have been her familiar next move, but she holds it fast, though her black thug's boot kicks air. "It costs a fortune."

"Do you think he understood being abandoned for a year? Then you show up here and you'd like to pick up right"—Dennis snaps his fingers—"where you left off."

"Did he tell you he felt abandoned by me? Are those his words?"

"The agreement that you get him summers depended on your trustworthiness."

"You're saying I have to be as predictable as you are, Dennis. You're saying I should never have had George in my life. I don't think that was the agreement."

A sort of ongoing record of their exchange—the conversation as he will replay it for Francesca—runs through his mind. Francesca, as she will sit up in their bed, listening, taking everything in, sometimes shaking her head or marveling aloud, is his sanity. Francesca illustrates children's books. Christie's mercurial excess, which prevents her carrying anything through to the end, and Francesca's serene attention to detail—to root, trunk, twig, and every small, slanting leaf in the forest—could not be further apart.

What fairy tale is it, where someone comes back at last for the beloved child? Because she's never seen well in the dark, he walks Christie out to her car. When a rock trips her, he catches her arm, and in the darkness she twists to face him before shaking off his hand. She would rather have fallen. They could be any bitter couple walking in the woods, tired of each other, tired of the way nothing is ever resolved between them. He had thought he was protected from such vivid involuntary remembrance of her past lives: her zazen phase, with its hours of formidable silence; the year during which she was convinced she was an actress; the macrobiotic diet she starved herself on; the novel she'd finished half of. Leaving her had been so plainly necessary that he should not find himself surprised to be here, where everything, the house behind them, the wife sleeping soundly in that house, even the trees closing in around them, speaks of the care with which he has constructed an existence of his own. There is an infant's car seat in the back of her Volvo, and she has wedged a bag of groceries into it, upright. So this visit really was on the spur of the moment.

Leaning into her window as she starts the Volvo, wanting to end on a friendlier note, he asks whether she's found a place to live. She did. A week ago. In one of those apartment complexes where there's always something empty; he knows it.

But then she can't resist circling back to their quarrel. "So you're saying no for the summer?"

"Too much has changed for that agreement to hold."

"What's changed is that you're even more judgmental than before."

"You hurt him," he says.

"Dennis, we need to talk about this again." She takes a hand from the wheel, raking her hair from her face, the dark-rimmed glasses picking up spots of light from somewhere. "I'll call," she says, and he can't tell her not to.

Tonk, plunk: something goes in upstream, where half-submerged boulders catch direct moonlight. All around Dennis, cottonwoods yield to the wind with saddling-up creaks. By the moonlight he observes them, the only trees he will ever think of as his own. A head black and broad as a Labrador's, and as purposefully at home, shaves across the glassy, swelling smoothness that is the deepest part of the river. A beaver, a big one, and upwind, or it would have known Dennis was there. *Castrados,* the beavers are called in Spanish, because after a fight the victorious male scythes off the scrotum of the loser, or so it's said. Dennis finds it hard to believe, but since hearing it he likes beavers less than he did before, when he thought they mutilated only his ancient cottonwoods. Another bit of folklore: the piss of a man connotes a proprietary interest that the beavers tend to respect. Each night Dennis liberates a different tree from possible destruction. Barefoot, brooding, he smells the odor his urine gives to dry, grateful old bark, and taps the last drops onto a golden leaf. The spring wind, balmy and humid, blows across the river, and as it stirs Dennis's hair there is that slight, single instant in which he feels himself blameless.

His divorce seems a tight black tunnel he once forced himself and Andy through, fearing each forward move, fearing still more getting stuck to suffocate. A blindly crawling exit from pain, his shy kid shoved along before him. So Andy loves motorcycles, which do not creep, which proclaim in every line speed and certainty. Christie didn't ask, or didn't think she could ask, to see Andy's room. Dennis believes it tells everything about Andy. Photo-realist motorcycles, chrome and highly evolved threat, grace the walls, along with a passport photo of Kafka razor-bladed from a library biography, a sin so small and inexplicable, and finally so appealing, that Dennis uncharacteristically forgot to mention it to Andy. If Andy's motorcycle paintings, done in this hyper-attentive style of glisten and mass, are depressing, surely jug-eared Kafka promises complexity, contradiction, hope? When he was a little boy, Andy painted houses with peaked roofs, surreal cats and dogs and birds, petroglyph parents—Dennis and Christie—with their hands linked over the head of a smaller, round-eyed creature, Andy himself. Orange sun, blue house, green grass, all's well. The garish houses dwindled; cats and dogs were supplanted by snakes and wolves; Dennis and Christie were replaced by superbly muscled superheroes, and Andy was seven. Ten was the year of the divorce. Thirteen is this plague of motorcycles, Leo's flawless smile, and hanging out at the mall. Oddly—at least Dennis wouldn't have predicted it—Andy wrote regularly to his mother in France. Because Andy didn't seem to consider them particularly private, Dennis sometimes read the letters over Andy's shoulder. The light of the computer screen glowed on his son's clear forehead. He wanted her to know that he liked having a little sister. He wanted her to know that he thought about her. He really worked on the letters. None of the obvious things (When was she coming home? Ever?) were in the letters. His son knew by thirteen not to ask Christie certain questions.

At the kitchen table Dennis eats slices of bologna folded into cold tortillas and drinks a beer, then scrapes and washes the day's dishes while the twins' bottles come bobblingly to a boil on the back of the stove. When Gavin wails, Dennis climbs the cantilevered stairs. Tim howls, coming to consciousness alongside his brother. Dennis lights a candle, his habit so that the overhead light won't blind Francesca, blinking awake. Dennis lays Gavin and Tim side by side on the bed, and Francesca sits up. Theirs is a four-handed assembly line, the twins' bottoms bared, wiped, and rediapered, neither boy crying, both staring from their giant calm father to their giant calm mother, who are talking softly together. Francesca takes Gavin. He can't lunge at the breast fast enough, and she laughs down at him. Though they're almost over the cold, the twins' breathing remains raspy. The wings of Francesca's nose are coarsely red, and her chest has the tonic stink of Vicks Vapo-Rub, which neither boy seems to mind. Dennis cradles Tim, leaning back in an old chair whose upholstery is a kind of friendly maroon moss worn away, on the arms, in matching bald spots his elbows fit in as he angles the bottle up. Tim's warm head rests in a hand large enough to cup it completely. What weight was ever this good? A baseball fresh from the sporting-goods store, or his high-school girlfriend's breasts released from lacy bra cups in a dark Chevrolet. Maybe. Francesca is uneasy, Dennis can tell. She's not sure she understands exactly what is wrong, though he's told her everything that was said.

He says, "She can't have him this summer."

"Andy has a father *and* a mother."

That lightly stressed *"and"* is criticism, and subtle as it is, it pricks him to argue, "You wouldn't know that by the last year."

"She was far away."

"That's no excuse," he says, knowing she knows it's not, having advanced it only so that they could both examine its weakness—could study, through the excuse's transparency, Christie's habitual irresponsibility. For a time they sit quietly, each with an urgently sucking baby, until, in Dennis's arm, Tim yawns, a thumb gliding into his mouth, his body's weight going sated and more vague, so that it's only a matter of settling him into the crib. Then Dennis leans to take Gavin. This is tense: Gavin's crying, if it starts, will rouse his brother, but Gavin sleeps. Ah, silence. "We're good," Dennis says, and the answer is an amused "Good? Great." He sits on the bed, not ready yet to climb under the covers, some chord in him still vibrating at a tense, post-Christie pitch. Francesca stretches, then narrows her attention until it includes only him. To do this, she very deliberately excludes sleep. The intense, the velvety deep desirability of unbroken sleep is what Dennis senses most strongly whenever he enters this room. In any competition he wages for her against sleep, sleep's going to win. It has only to lap inward from the dim corners of the room to close over her head, and she has only to let herself slide luxuriously under, while what he wants, in wanting to make love, would ask effort of her, and an energy she doesn't have.

"Showing up here with no warning," Francesca says.

"It was weird."

"No wonder you resent it, but what convinced you she can't have Andy?"

"She's lost the boyfriend."

Francesca says, "What has that got to do with it, really?"

"How many guys does Andy get to see come and go?"

"In three years there's been George. Not exactly promiscuous."

"Now Andy has a sister he knows only from pictures."

"The sister was born in Paris," she says reasonably. "Andy can get to know her here."

He wants Francesca on his side, not mediating between him and Christie. "She kept talking in non sequiturs." He places his hands, palms facing, in the air before her, implying the gaps between what Christie said and what she said next, but Francesca leans forward until his hands slide into a caress of her face, until, with two fingers, he tucks hair behind an ear, and then idly revolves the pearl resting against that ear's lobe, as if he were turning a tiny screw, tightening some connection that had, minutely, loosened.

"What's her baby's name?"

"Emma." He feels strange, saying it.

"I'd hate to see you be so unforgiving toward me," she says.

After a time he tells her thoughtfully, "I couldn't be," but she's asleep, her mouth open, an arm flung out before her, her fingers touching the wall, her entire body relaxed, loose, her fingertips' pressure against the wall too negligible, too accidental, to suggest she is meeting any resistance, even in a dream.

The next afternoon Andy comes in, home from somewhere, on his way somewhere else, and is struck enough by his father's expression to say, "You look weird." Dennis, lying back on his son's unmade bed under the portrait of a glitteringly malign Harley-Davidson, squeezing a racquetball in his left hand, answers, "Your mom's back."

Two squeezes of the ball before Andy risks "Yeah?" He is careful not to let slip how pleased he is, but in a lilting involuntary movement, younger than he is, he goes up on his toes, his long legs braced, and bounces, one arm holding the other arm at the elbow.

Dennis says, "Uh-huh. Just last week. She came over last night."

"She did? Is that what's wrong with you?"

"What's wrong with me is no sleep and I didn't shave and that makes me feel old." He dents the blue racquetball with his thumb, and it oozes back into its sphere as he remembers that when his own father used to say he felt old it was a threat that Dennis suffered with an obscure and embarrassed guilt.

He reads in his son the same stiffening, the same resentment, as Andy, at his dresser, fidgets a drawer open and shut, and Dennis says to his back, appealing to the cocky set of the shoulders and the vulnerability of the nape exposed by the cruel Leo-like haircut, "Look, I wanted you to know, but I was really thinking you could spend the summer here. With us."

"You hate her," Andy says intensely, talking down into the drawer, and Dennis starts to say "No, Andy, that's not it" when Andy strips off his sweatshirt, tearing it over his head, its shapely unknowable stubbornness so much like his mother's, and Dennis sees the violent bruise marbling his son's arm. The bruise resolves into a tattoo of a skeleton on a motorcycle, leaning forward as if into wind, black eye sockets, spiked helmet, the whole evil deal, grinning on the freckled, pale, still baby-fattish curve of adolescent biceps. Dennis slams the racquetball at the wall. It caroms past Andy's shoulder. "Dad!" Andy cries, and Dennis is up, taking two fast steps, grabbing the arm. Andy twists away to stand against the wall, cornered.

"My God, it's ugly." Dennis hears the hoarseness of his own voice, the sound of a father's barely controlled anger. "I didn't want to believe it was real. Was this Leo's idea?"

"No. Mine. Dad, it didn't hurt. The needles were really clean. I watched the guy sterilize them. That's the first thing you see when you walk into his place, this big sterilizer. Dad, it's my body. You would have said no. You know you would have said no."

It's my body. Dennis can't believe that. He can't conceive of having no say in what happens to this body, in no longer being needed to protect it. Andy is five, shuddering in his arms; he has fallen into a doorjamb, slitting open his lower lip, and for some reason Dennis is catching the blood in his hand. Andy is two, shrieking down at his own bare leg as the needle eases in. The nurse has told Dennis, who wanted to hold Andy in his lap, facing his chest, that it's better if Andy sees that it's the nurse who's hurting him. That way Andy won't come to distrust his own father.

"What does it mean?" Dennis asks.

"It doesn't mean anything. It's just cool."

"You're thirteen years old," Dennis says, "and you'll be living with this the rest of your life."

"I want to live with it." Andy pulls on a clean sweatshirt from his drawer, and the tattoo disappears under a sleeve. What Andy's defensive about, it hits Dennis, is that he does not regret the grinning little leather-jacketed Death on its motorcycle. Part of him would like to drum up regret if that's the clue to his father's forgiveness, but the truth is he's too old to summon emotion on demand, and too honest to fake it, without being insulated enough to fight his father without a fair amount of pain. Dennis catches himself making an abrupt accommodating shift, with this insight, in the direction of understanding his son as someone strictly separate from him. Perhaps the tattoo has accomplished what it was meant to. Perhaps it was meant to be something that couldn't be undone and something he couldn't possibly like about his child. That's it. His adoration has been unconditional. He's made Andy have to wrestle it off. Something has changed between them, and here Andy is, watching him covertly for signs that this is over. Over, so that he can go.

"You were so perfect when you were born," Dennis says, and is blindsided by the idea that the only other person who will truly mourn that perfection as he does is Christie. "You're grounded," Dennis says. "You're not leaving this house."

When the phone rings that night, Francesca answers and mouths, "It's her." Dennis shakes his head. Holding Gavin against her shoulder, Francesca mouths, "Come on." He holds his left hand flat in the air, his right vertically below it, a T. Time out. Francesca, exasperated, has just enough grace to smile at him. She says, "Christie, he must have gone out. I didn't hear him leave. Andy?" Dennis is shaking his head furiously. "Andy's out with Leo. Sorry. I'll tell them both you called."

Two nights later, and this time Francesca's side of the conversation is "He never called you? I gave him your message. I am sorry. His partner's away, so, you know. I'm sure he'll get back to you as soon as he can." Francesca listens a moment before adding, "I *agree* with you this can't go on much longer." When she hangs up, Francesca says, "Did you hear that last part?"

"I need time," he says.

She shakes her head at his hard anger, at how far he's willing to take this. "She's not helpless," Francesca says. "She can always call her lawyer. I think you're in the wrong."

Without her on it, his side begins to strike him as stale, small-minded, and increasingly indefensible, and a day later it comes to him that it's time he talked to Christie. Francesca seems relieved, looking up from a drawing of a wolf, forepaws resting together on a green satin coverlet, one incisor exposed, caught outside the lip in accidental malice, the whiskers long, flexed back against the muzzle in a grimace of grandmotherly welcome.

"Nice," Dennis says, and amends this to "Great. That wolf has eaten people."

"Did you know your eyes are red?"

"It's insomnia, not your cold. Don't worry."

"How can anyone not sleep?" she says. "I love sleep."

They're both startled by a sneeze, followed by syrupy coughs, from the bedroom overhead where the twins nap, and Francesca says, "If they get sick again, I'm going to kill myself."

He leaves his office early to go to Christie's apartment. It's in a stucco complex of separate four-story buildings spaced around culs-de-sac and traffic islands spiked with dying yucca. He should have called her first, but somehow, for all his keyed-up restlessness, he never got around to it. "You look terrible," people kept telling him all day, and he got tired of his own small joke, "I feel much worse than I look." Well, she surprised him, showing up without warning. Surely she can't be too put off if he does the same. When his knocks go unanswered, he scratches in the dirt under a flourishing white geranium. Christie's houseplants always thrived. She always left a key under one of her plants by the front door, though he'd asked her not to a thousand times. He lets himself in, telling himself he's going to call out to see if she's there after all, but once inside he makes no sound. Stealth, it strikes him, is no small thing, but very physical. He's breathing faster than he likes, as if he'd run two miles on the river road, his heart banging. Her baby's toys lie all around. The bright clutter, for some reason, panics him. In his own house, he would begin picking things up; he'd know how to go about setting things straight. Here, he can't. He's stymied by the very fact that he's an intruder. An intruder is an unreasonable thing to be. *You are in the wrong,* maybe more deeply than ever before. Leo's mother could make a capital case out of this. As if with foresight, he dressed for the part. His Levi's are torn, and his shabby sneakers, gray with age, let him move neatly, brimming with guilt and yet slightly high on it, through the mess, which seems to him evidence of happiness, her happiness, which he long ago divorced himself from, which he has no right to know anything about. All this, everything he sees, is contraband. A jack-in-the-box has been left as it was, sprung open, the vacantly grinning head hanging upside down from the long caterpillarlike sleeve of the body, and here is a naked doll seated in a chair, and on the couch *Vanity Fair* open to a picture of Kevin Costner, leaning back, his shirt loose, glass in hand. Dennis feels scathingly appraised by Kevin Costner.

On the far side of a narrow counter is the kitchen, whose paint-splattered furniture she must have got at the Salvation Army. Four straight-backed chairs are dashed with brilliant blue, while the small table is a scarred palette of yellow, turquoise, hot pink, and silver. It looks as if an Abstract Expressionist went insane here. There are crumbs of burned toast in the high chair's tray. The floor is fifties linoleum, tan tiles, with faint white cirrus clouds drifting across them, and on one tile, Christie—or someone—has painted a tiny airplane. She has been using *The Frugal Gourmet,* which is propped open by her mother's (he remembers) tin recipe box. In the refrigerator, nothing much—milk, bread, juice, the usual, and a half-empty bottle of Beaujolais with the cork floating in the wine. She never handled corkscrews well. Peanut butter. Garlic, fat cloves in mauve-white paper. He takes the garlic out—garlic doesn't belong in the refrigerator—but, holding the crisp little weight, he doesn't know what to do with it. If he leaves it out, she's going to know somebody was there. He has to put it back. He does.

Emma's room, sunny and disheveled, the crib against a wall on which hangs a small Amish quilt, its corners frayed, a powdery-pleasant baby smell and folded clothes in wire drawers under a changing table. A basket of teething rings. A kazoo. A child's rocker. Balled up in the crib, a pair of baby tights and a striped sock. A second small bedroom, darker, shades down, must be meant for Andy. There's something wonderful in being in this room, and he's still high on his amazed apprehension of his own wrongdoing, floating on it, willing to stay with it a little longer now that he's come this far. His hearing is sharp, but there's nothing, no sound, and his sense of what he's seeing seems magnificently, magically clear. He wouldn't have known any of this. She would never have told him. Even if she'd wanted to tell him, he wouldn't have listened. Here are things she thinks Andy will like: a cowboy bedspread, a glaring African mask, an aquarium filled with water, oxygen percolating through it, no fish yet but some kind of seaweed hypnotically weaving, and, clinging to the glass, snails small as capers. A desk fashioned from a sheet of melamite laid over sawhorses. A bright-blue dresser. The drawers, when he opens them, are empty, except that the last drawer contains a Hershey's Kiss.

As he sits heavily on the bed, his exhilaration dies. It doesn't so much desert him in a rush as evaporate, and a befuddling gray fatigue fogs over the vacuum it leaves in him. This stupid midafternoon sleepiness feels entirely ordinary. He lies back on the bed and puts an arm over his face, breathing in the smell of himself—slightly sweaty, salty guilt. Still no sound. It feels good. He even feels he's in the right place.

He dreams a dream he thinks of later as intended for Andy. Andy should have dreamed it; by accidentally falling asleep in this bed, Dennis got it. In it, Christie is younger, Andy barely old enough to work a scissors, the two of them sitting on the floor with their dark heads together, cutting animals from construction paper, the air between them charged with great, disinterested tenderness, and they're not talking. The animals they cut out come alive. A monkey jumps to his knee, and Andy giggles. Christie sets a blue giraffe down on the floor and it canters stiffly away. Waking, Dennis's first thought is that he's dreamed a dream he wasn't in. He can't remember ever having had such a dream before. In some subtle shift in the room's shadows he reads a new degree of lateness, of sheer wrongness in being here, and his body responds with a rising thrill of adrenaline, but he still doesn't move. He wonders if what he really wants is to get caught. In another minute he's able to tell himself *That would really be the height of stupidity,* and he sits up. His body hates his refusal to get moving. He shakes his head to clear the last of the sleep from it, but the mysterious peacefulness of the dream still has a hold on him. What he's seen won't let go so easily.

Back through the apartment, each object in its place, everything exactly as he found it, it begins to appear to him that he's getting away with this. He lets himself out and finds that it's later than he thought, probably six-thirty or so. When he checks the parking lot two stories down, she's not there: her dark-rimmed glasses aren't aimed upward in accusation, and though he fumbles, locking the door, her Volvo does not materialize. He twitches geranium leaves out of the way, sliding the key back where she likes it.

This is not happiness, just a gaudy physiological response to not getting caught—light head, hands shaking, legs he has to will steady to get himself down the stairs, world that looks entirely strange.

"I thought I couldn't leave the house until I was thirty-two," Andy says, his feet on the dash, looking around the maze of stucco buildings he's never seen before.

"You can't," Dennis says. "The one place you can come is here. I want you to call me for your ride home. No taking off. No improvising."

"But I can stay the weekend."

"You can say the weekend if you want."

"Why?"

"I was wrong before," Dennis says. "I was just wrong."

"But how did you see you were wrong?"

"You don't get to know all the details."

"Does Mom?"

"I haven't talked to her."

"You mean she doesn't know I'm coming?"

"She's home. There's her car, right?"

"I don't like surprising her," Andy says.

"O.K. You really don't like it, we turn around, we drive home, we get on the phone, we arrange this for some other time. Is that how you want to do this?"

He hesitates, and then says, "I guess so." Dennis starts the car; maybe this was a bad idea, but he'd liked the feel of it. He'd wanted to change things all at once. He'd wanted the suddenness of his reversal on his side in convincing Christie that things were going to be different from now on, and he hadn't guessed that it might be Andy who didn't like the idea, who seemed unprepared for it.

"Stop," Andy says, removing his feet from the dash, sitting up. "I'm going, O.K.?"

"Whatever you want to do."

"I'll call you."

"Call."

He's gone. He's on the stairs, bag on his shoulder, lighter-footed than his father can remember ever being, taking the two flights of stairs as if they are nothing. Then Christie is at the door in black jeans, a man's T-shirt huge on her, her son taller than she is. That she's amazed is clear in every line of her body. She and Andy don't step nearer or embrace. They just stand talking, and then Dennis sees Christie move to her porch rail, looking down at him bewildered, and he waves at her, a wave that means *I can't explain it.*

ELIZABETH TALLENT DISCUSSES

"Prowler," character, and a fork in the road

PM: You took a somewhat different path to fiction writing, having majored in anthropology as an undergraduate and very nearly attending grad school in archaeology.

ET: You know, I'd recommend anthropology to young writers rather than English, which they so often consider the only field of study for a writer. Cultural anthropology exposes you to a gorgeous, tormented spectrum of human resourcefulness, from the ways people counter desperation to how they address death and what they know about love and what they deem beautiful.

Ethnography's aim then was a very lucid, complex kind of prose, and the author was supposed to strip away her own cultural bias and discover an ideal suppleness of perception. You were supposed to think from inside another culture, to see with eyes not your own, and because everyone understood the seductions of convention and the anxiety of seeing a thing fresh, honesty was revered. This was the greatest tutorial I could have had in thinking about fiction.

PM: How did you decide you wanted to be a fiction writer?

ET: At the Lubbock Lake Site in Texas we were required to keep daily journals that included detailed accounts of what we found, and in trying to describe the skull of a Pleistocene antelope, I fell in love with writing. I loved the written skull more than the real one surfacing centimeter by centimeter from the caliche-ridden earth. I couldn't get used to the strangeness of the real skull—lying on your side in the dirt, you gazed into its eye socket, polishing the arch with a child's toothbrush, then at night you lay in an army cot and scribbled away in a dirty notebook, trying to get at how strange it was that you'd gazed into the space that had, ten thousand years ago, been an eye.

Writing took over: I'm not saying this was good, or that it was smart, but in reality I didn't seem to invest anything else with the kind of energy I put into writing, so I didn't pursue grad school. To me writing and archaeology were very close. In both, there was a kind of unearthing, in both tremendous care was required, and exactness, and patience. In both, details could be revelatory. In neither was there any kind of guarantee, and I liked that. You were never sure what you would find, only that the material you were handling so carefully *could* surprise you.

PM: About that decision not to pursue grad school—didn't this involve a rather dramatic turning point?

ET: My then-husband and I were on the way to Albuquerque, where I was to attend the University of New Mexico's grad school in archaeology. We'd gotten married, then driven day and night from the Midwest in our old car, and when the highway forked, south to Albuquerque, north to Santa Fe, I said wistfully, "We've never seen Santa Fe," and he took out a quarter and said, "Heads it's the weekend in Santa Fe, tails we drive right to Albuquerque." When it came up heads I must have looked doubtful because he said, "Two out of three." Once we got to Santa Fe, we didn't leave for ten years.

PM: What led you to write "Prowler"?

ET: I had an inkling, like a recurrent but vague daydream, of someone breaking into another person's space, and of this trespass being somehow illuminating. It was a light kind of pressure, the premonition of a story, no more than that. But it didn't matter that it was vague: I was *very* interested in it, and it was a question of quietly waiting for the unknown breaker-and-enterer to become a character, or the beginning of a character. Once he was present even in shadowy form, relationships sketched themselves in around him, and I began to understand whose space he was going to break into.

Then *she* got interesting to me—the person whose space would be violated.

PM: You give us just a few brushstrokes of Christie physically—her glasses, her hair, her black clothes—and leave the rest to our imaginations. How do you know which are the right few brushstrokes for a given character? Do you have certain favorite areas?

ET: Dennis wants to keep his perceptions of Christie minimal—clear, distinct, but not too evocative, so there's this objectivity in the tone that's probably right for his perceptions but is almost too limiting. I know I kind of chafed at that description, that there wasn't *more* of her.

Yes, I think I have favorite details I lean on in characterization. I like eyes. I like hands. It's an impediment to really generous description, this kind of favoritism, because it's not as fluent as perception is. It's a narrowing-down. It's stylized, and you have to work against that.

PM: Each character detail or mannerism that you mention vibrates with significance. For instance, Christie's new glasses suggest she "has reinvented herself yet again," and this interpretation sheds light not only on Christie but also on Dennis the observer, as well as the relationship between them. How do you arrive at such three-dimensionality? Are you able to imagine the moment whole, or is it built through layers of perception?

ET: The kind of detail that I love best comes of a character's perceptions, but is original, surprising in itself and to the character. By this I mean that we rely so much on our preconceptions of each other that it's hard for us to seem *vivid.* I like that moment when one person comes into vividness for another. Often some kind of stress figures in such a moment, or a degree of disorientation, and that's good for what you're calling "three-dimensionality," because it makes the observing character present in a more complex way than he would be if he were seeing what he usually sees and thus feeling what he usually feels. The answer to the either/or of your last question—whether the moment's seen whole or whether it's gradually built up—is both, I think, because it can happen either way, and there are those lucky times when you envision a complex moment or scene "whole" and you're just kind of transcribing, but there are more times when you feel some *part* is right, but the rest isn't good enough. So you write *up* to that level of rightness, because you can't bear to default on it.

PM: Just before Dennis grounds his son—a typical, knee-jerk parent thing to do—he has a series of beautifully insightful thoughts about the boy. Contrasting the rich inner life with the cliché of Dennis's behavior is poignant; it gives his character greater depth and suggests stores of potential. When did you begin to experiment with this technique, and what's your favorite classic example from your reading?

ET: But isn't it a great puzzle, how to live by what we know? Perception is so *shy*. It's de-realized by the suasions of habit. That's why the way epiphany works in short stories is so unreal and at the same time so attractive, because we wish insight meant transformation. It's as if built into the form of the short story there's this lovely fable of the way insight transfigures existence. In the primacy it grants perception, it's a very optimistic form, probably more vulnerable than the novel to pretending that consciousness is coherent; it can neglect the paradox that lots of people can articulate complexities they have no chance of honoring in their behavior, because this paradox makes for messiness. You find a fearlessness about mess and incongruity in Alice Munro, though. It's as if she were held by the heel as a babe and dipped in the river of verisimilitude.

PM: What beyond mere contrast do you strive to impart between a character's inner and outer life?

ET: You want to get at what the cost of this failure to reconcile inner and outer will be, because in that gap lives terrific narrative tension. For me the most irresistible instance of this gap between insight and act is Marcel in [Proust's] *The Captive,* when he's been browbeating Albertine, spying on and lying to her even as he's aware she's beginning to suffocate. When he hears her window thrown open in the night in defiance of his abhorrence of drafts, he can imagine she's thinking, "This life is stifling me! I don't care, I must have air!" There's discernment, there's empathy, and there's a terrific failure to treat her any better, though he knows losing her will cause him anguish. He talks about how almost impossible it is for real understanding to find its way down "the highway along which passes what we learn to know only from the day when it has made us suffer: the life of other people."

PM: When Dennis calls Francesca's wolf picture "nice," using the same understated and possibly hurtful word Christie used to describe his new home, he quickly corrects himself and amps up his praise. At what point in your process were you receptive to creating that small bit of "rhyming action," as Charles Baxter might call it?

ET: In that essay of Charles Baxter's, "Rhyming Action," you can find the smartest advice about handling time in fiction, and one advantage of rhyming action that he points out is that we're "watching an intriguing pattern unfold before we know exactly what the pattern is." So if in drafting a story you feel a pattern nudging its way up through the sliding surface of events, you try, I think, to realize it, to encourage it to unfold, before you know what it means. Then in revision you think the repetition through, to see if it's valuable, and in this case, I thought that Dennis was enacting that dynamic of trying to evaluate the hurtfulness of a new wound by identically wounding someone else—to see how they react; often the person you wound is someone you think is a little more whole than you—and that this was true to his character, but that he was also smart enough to recognize what he'd just done and try to make amends.

PM: I've had students question Dennis's reliability. I think they raised the issue because he's judgmental but ultimately mistaken, and maybe, too, because of that gap between his inner and outer life we spoke of above. Do you have any thoughts about the boundary between ordinary self-delusion and a full-blown unreliable narrator?

ET: Only that to me "ordinary self-delusion" is fascinating. It can mean there's a double searchingness built into the narration, because the character's trying to get at truth, and the reader's trying to get at truth, though the truths they see might not be the same and they may not even be looking in the same places. Still, in a sense the reader's and character's desires are intertwined. We're *eager* for these desires to fuse completely, for difference to be erased, and that's another kind of plot, isn't it? When a narrator's what James Wood calls "reliably unreliable," meaning reliably wrong in his understanding of other people, you lose the tension of this highly charged gap between the reader's and the narrator's perceptions.

PM: Dennis's line on page 30 ("'The agreement that you get him summers depended on your trustworthiness'") really opens some interesting doors. Like who is in charge of assessing her trustworthiness? And what on earth had she done to evoke such a bendable injunction against her? What do you want readers to think about this?

ET: Custody's weird because it's an arena where deep emotion comes up against not only fixed legal language but also what you're calling "bendable" injunctions, because whatever a court dictates, in practice custody can involve a lot of negotiation and improvisation. I do feel an attraction to situations in which the culture tries to inscribe some solution, and people resist it and try to come up with something else. I don't have in mind what I want readers to think, really. If I had that in mind, it would doom the story for me. But I do want the feelings to get across—a convoluted kind of frustration, impatience, several kinds of love.

PM: It seems all fictional characters are inspired by some mix of the writer herself, or people she knows, has seen, or read about. Can you recall a couple of examples of how such amalgams have been created in your own work? For instance, Christie likes to rake her hair from her face, which I've seen you do many times.

ET: That gesture turns up in the work of my students, too, unfortunately. I'd rather be in charge of attributing that little vanity to my own characters, but spend time with writers and you get *seen.* I've got a scar under my lower lip, and though I haven't yet used this myself for a character, my students have.

What's really funny is to observe three or four writers simultaneously hearing the same terrific line, especially when this is spoken by someone innocent of its charm. It's as if a nest of magpies spot a gold ring in the grass. It's whoever gets there first.

To me that gesture signals a self-consciousness and anxiety that worked for Christie. My relation to my characters is pretty visual. Often I see them before I hear them, and their voices come a little harder to me.

PM: When you do interject yourself, or a person you know, into a character, how conscious are you of that? How often do readers or friends notice?

ET: A character's consciousness, when I'm writing well, feels real to me, "other," as if I've encountered someone in the world of the book who may or may not have ghost-counterparts in the real world. From these ghost-counterparts, including myself, I get my bearings. Even when I think I got something right, I'm not sure how often readers or friends who might in some way have figured in the life of the character really notice. People don't necessarily identify with those traits or details that might seem most revealing to a writer, which might be a way of saying that the interior life is less easily intuited through gesture and behavior than, as a writer—a certain kind of realist writer—I like to believe. My ex-husband used to find something of himself in a character called Sam who figured in some linked stories, but because he found him relentlessly *good* he called the character "Saint Sam."

PM: Some authors like to imagine copious background information about their characters that's never intended to make it into the actual work—do you?

ET: A friend of mine keeps notebooks for characters, but they're not just written, they're also visual, like scrapbooks, and to me that sounds wonderful, like making a kind of Cornell box for the character. And I've tried that, imagining things not meant to go into the actual work, but what happens to me is that I get so interested in whatever details come up that I end up finding a way to get them into the story. Basically I'm bad at distinguishing background from foreground. In a story called "Love Song, for a Moog Synthesizer," John Updike has a line about falling in love, that you can't fall in love entirely on the basis of what you can fathom about a person, you have to encounter aspects you didn't foresee and couldn't have imagined, "those faults and ledges of the not-quite-expected where affection can silt and accumulate." For me this is true of fictional characters. I have to run into aspects I couldn't have foreseen, or the character won't come alive for me. And once someone's alive for us, what is "background"? We're looking hungrily at the whole person.

PM: Being an architect is not just a job to Dennis; he understands people through their use of space. How do you go about discerning or assigning your characters' careers?

ET: In the fifties American suburban ethos of my childhood, work was fate, work was character, it was the source of safety even as it was the realm of tremendous anxiety, manipulation, rivalry, longing, ego-bruising setbacks. So work had this marvelous contradictoriness, a contradictoriness to rival love's, and I always loved hearing about work, all kinds of work. What I hope is that details of the character's work will unfold different metaphors. Because Dennis has an architect's awareness of the liminal, an eye for thresholds and how these are demarcated, intrusion is for him an entirely conscious act. He's not someone who can trespass innocently, because he so loves the notion of safety. He can't get enough of it, he wants to design it into the world, to make spaces that will read as safe, as home. What he does is complicatedly wrong, wrong not only in itself but because this particular violation answers to his reading of reality. It's as if a heart surgeon damaged someone's heart.

There are kinds of work I've always wanted to write about that I have not yet found the character for. I badly want to write about a botanist, because botany insists on a peculiarly slowed-down, minutely observant relation to the green world, which is now experiencing such damage. So I read and listen to botanists when I can, and hope something will come of this.

PM: Once you've created a character for a story, how likely is he or she to reappear in a different story? What are the potential advantages and drawbacks of that?

ET: When I get to the end of someone's story, I can't know if I'll ever see them again. That extra-narrative sense of parting—the author's sense of loss—I almost think it figures emotionally in the ends of stories. When a character comes back, the problem is that the absence, the not-written, that separates the linked stories must seem right. You're not going to write this gap, you're going to imply it in the way one story doesn't quite touch another, but the beginning of the second story isn't just a beginning, it has this sneaky other thing to accomplish, establishing its fit, in time and in significance, with the first story. It's fun.

PM: Aspiring writers are sometimes cautioned against using dreams to further narrative, but you've employed one in a crucial moment of the story. Talk a bit about your decision to do that.

ET: I think any writer who's cautioned to exclude any aspect of experience should prick up her ears. What is the reason for it? It makes a better story if we habitually exclude something we experience but find difficult to write about? I suspect there's a cultural bias at work in this advice, a sturdy American preference for the forthright, the rational, for the plain light of day, but fiction isn't supposed to honor a culture's construction of reality. It's supposed to seek its own original relation to experience.

I think, early on, I heard this advice and accepted it as an inhibition from which it took a book to free me. When I read *The Interpretation of Dreams* I knew I wanted to try dreams, because the dreams Freud describes possess an uncanny vitality. As revelation of character, they're fantastic. They teem with incongruity, with desire, with the wickedest, most ingenious puns, with this deep playfulness. Who wouldn't want to try to write that?

PM: You once mentioned that your editor at *The New Yorker* convinced you to cut Dennis's urinating on the trees. Why didn't

she like that territorial gesture, and why did you decide to put it back in when the collection was published?
ET: *The New Yorker* then had a sense of decorum that's hard to imagine now, and some things, mostly to do with the body, didn't work for the magazine. When I really rued an omission, I fixed it when I could. I rued that omission because more than one man I knew did this thing of urinating to establish possession of his land, and it fit with the story's interest in boundaries.
PM: What's your ideal relationship with an editor?
ET: Provocative, I think. Strenuous, honest. I say this, but I do love reassurance and am always angling for it.
PM: What lingering questions continue to intrigue you about the story and its characters?
ET: All of them. A story *is* its own questions, I think, and the writers I know tend to stay interested in these questions, and to revisit them. Really, *linger* is a good word for it. I still wonder about the ways love is flawed by irresponsibility, and still want to write about that.

ELIZABETH TALLENT's work has appeared in *The Paris Review, Harper's,* and *The New Yorker*. She has published a novel and three story collections, the most recent of which is *Honey* (1993). "Prowler" was included in the 1990 *Best American Short Stories*. She teaches in Stanford University's Creative Writing Program.

PLOT

THE STORY OF MY LIFE
Kim Edwards

A RECORD AS LONG AS YOUR ARM
George Garrett

THE STORY OF MY LIFE

Kim Edwards

You'd know me if you saw me. Maybe not right away. But you'd stop, lots of people do. I bet you'd look twice at me, and wonder. I'd be an image lingering in your thoughts for days to come, nagging, like a forgotten name on the edge of your mind, like an unwelcome memory twisting up through dreams. Then you'd catch a glimpse of me on television, or gazing at you from a poster as you hurried down the sidewalk, and you'd remember. I'd come into your mind like a vision then, a bright and terrifying light.

Some people see it in an instant. They call out to me and stop me on the street. I have felt their hands, their vivid glances, the demanding pressure of their embraces. They have kissed my fingertips, have fallen to their knees and wept, have clustered around me, drawing the attention of a crowd. Once, a girl even grabbed my arm in the parking lot at school. I still remember the darkness in her eyes, the panic clinging to her skin like mist, the way she begged me to give her a blessing, to relieve her of her great sin, as if I had a direct line right to God.

"Hey no," I told her, shrugging her away. "You've got that wrong. You're thinking of my mother."

You've seen my mother too, guaranteed. See her now, the star of the evening news, standing with several hundred other people in a parking lot in Buffalo. It is hot for May, the first fierce blast of summer, and heat waves rise around these people, making them shimmer on the screen. But that, of course, is pure illusion. The truth is these people never falter, they never miss a step. Theirs is a holy path, a righteous vision, and if they must stand for twelve hours a day in the blinding heat, thirty days in a row, then they will do it like a penance, they will not think twice. This Buffalo clinic is at the edge of the university, and the protesters with their graphic signs draw increasing crowds. For days we have watched the news clips: ceaseless praying, bottles of red paint splattering brick walls, scared young women being led through the hostile crowd by clinic escorts in bright vests. Mounting tension, yes, the sharp edges of impending violence, but still it has been a minor protest, something witnessed by motorists on their way to work, then forgotten until the evening news.

It is nothing compared to what will happen now that my mother has arrived.

See her. She is young still, long-boned and slender, with blond hair that swings at the level of her chin. She favors pastels, crisp cottons, skirts that brush against the calf, shirtwaist dresses and sweater sets. On the evening news the cameras pick her out, her pale yellow dress only a few shades darker than her hair, the white collar setting off her tan face, her sapphire eyes. Unlike the others with their signs, their chanting anger, my mother is serene. It is clear right away that while she is with this crowd, she is not of it. Her five assistants, surrounding her tightly like petals on a stamen, guide her slowly to the steps. The banners rustle in the hot wind, fluttering above the famous posters.

See me, then, my sweet smile, my innocence. It is a black-and-white shot, a close-up, taken three years ago when I was just fourteen. My mother strides before these posters, passing in front of one of me after another, and when she pauses alone at the center of the steps, when she turns her face to the cheering crowd and smiles, you can see it. The resemblance was striking even then, and now it is uncanny. In the past three years my cheekbones have become more pronounced, my eyes seem wider. We could, and sometimes do, pass for sisters. My mother waves her hand and starts to speak.

"Fellow sinners," she says, and the crowd roars.

"Turn it off, why don't you?" Sam says. We are sitting together on the sofa, drinking Coca-Cola and eating animal crackers. We've lined the elephants up, trunk to tail, across the coffee table. Sam's eyes are the same dark blue as my mother's, and the dark curls on his head are repeated, again and again, down his wide chest. When I don't answer he turns and presses his hand against my cheek, then kisses me, hard, until I have to pull away from him.

We look at each other for a long moment. When Sam finally speaks, his voice is deliberately grave and pompous, twisting the Scriptures to his own advantage.

"Nichola," he says, drawing a finger slowly down my arm. "Your body is such a mystery to me." There is longing in his voice, yes, but his eyes are teasing, teasing. He knows I know these verses, the ones my mother always uses to begin. *My body is no mystery to Thee, for Thou didst knit me together in my mother's womb.* He must also know that it seems near sacrilege to me, what he says, the way he says it. And truly I am flushed with his audacity, the breathless danger of his words. I am thrilled with it. Sam watches my face, smiles, runs his hand down my bare arm.

"You know what comes later," I remind him, hearing my mother's voice rising in the background. "*Deliver me from evil men.* Remember?"

He laughs and leans forward to kiss me again, his hand groping for the remote control. I get to it first and sit up straight, keeping a distance between us. I am saving myself, I am trying to, though Sam Rush insists there is no need because one day we will marry.

"Not now," I tell him, inching up the volume. "She's just about to tell the story of my life. It's the best part."

Sam catches my wrist and pulls the remote control from my fingers. The TV snaps off and my mother disappears to where she really is, 257 miles away.

"You're wrong," he says, sliding his hands across my shoulders, pressing his lips against my collarbone.

"What do you mean?"

"That's not the story of your life," he whispers. I feel his breath on my skin, insistent, pressing the words. "This is."

My mother worries, or ought to. After all, I have her looks, her blond beauty, her narrow hips. I have her inclinations. But my mother has a high and shining faith. This is what she tells me every time she leaves the house. She holds my face in her two hands and says, *You'll be good, Nichola. I know that. I have the strongest confidence in you, I know you are not a wild girl like I was.*

Well, it is true in a way, I am not a wild girl like she was. Sam is the only boyfriend I have ever had. And for a long time I was even good like she means. Those were the days when she used to take me with her, traveling around the country from one demonstration to another, standing in the rain or snow or blazing heat. There are snapshots of my mother and me from those days. In many of them I am just a toddler perched on her hip, while she squints into the camera, gripping half a banner in her free hand. She wore pantsuits, all creaseless polyester, with wide cuffs at the wrists and ankles. She had maxiskirts and shiny boots and her hair was long then, falling down her back like the thin silk of corn. For years she was just a part-time protester, like anybody else. But then she got religion, and got famous, all in a single afternoon.

I was five years old that day. I remember it, the heat and the crowd, my mother's pale blue dress, and the way she held me tightly when the preacher started speaking. "Amen," my mother said. "Amen, oh yes, AMEN." I remember the expression on her face, the way her eyes closed shut and her lips parted. I remember how we moved so suddenly toward the steps where the preacher stood with his microphone, leading everyone in prayer. Another moment and we were up there with him. My mother put me down and turned to the crowd. When she took the microphone from the startled preacher and began to speak, something happened. She called my name and touched my hair, and then she said, "I am a sinner. I have come here today to tell you about my sin." People sighed, then they drew in closer. Their faces filled with rapture.

I know my memory on these points is pure, not a story that was told to me, or one that I saw much later on a film. We have a copy of the newsreel now, down in the archives, and it is still a shock each time I watch it and see how many things I missed. My mother held my hand and her words rained softly down. I felt so safe, standing there with her, but I was too young to really understand. I didn't see the anger on the preacher's face as my mother wooed his congregation. I don't remember how the crowd changed beneath her voice and followed her, forming a circle before the clinic doors and lying down. I did not even notice when the police arrived and began hauling them away. But on the film, it happens. My mother and the preacher pray while the circle around them is steadily eroded. I see myself, as the circle shrinks, lifted up and handed blindly into the crowd, to a woman with a patchwork skirt who smelled very clean, like lemons. And then, I see on film the most important thing I missed that day. I see the way my mother rose to power. She stands right by the preacher, praying hard, until just he and she are left. That handsome preacher glances at my mother, this interloper, this surprise. It's clear he's thinking that she will be taken first. He expects her to be humble, to concede the stage to him. My mother sees his look and her voice lifts. She closes her eyes and takes a step back. Just a small step, but it's enough. The police reach the preacher first. He stops praying, startled, when they touch his arm, and suddenly it is just my mother speaking, her eyes open now, sustaining the crowd with the power of her voice alone.

People rise up sometimes, start their lives anew. That day it happened to my mother. She burned true and rose high above the others, like ash borne lightly on a flame. When they came for her she did not cease her prayers. When they touched her she went limp and heavy in their arms. Her dress swept the ground and her sweet voice lifted, and on the news that night she seemed almost angelic. They carried her away still praying, and the crowd parted like a sea to let her pass.

People rise up, but they fall down too. The preacher, for instance, fell so far that he disappeared completely. Others are famous one month, gone the next. They hesitate when boldness is required, they grow vain and self-important and go too far. Sometimes, they sin. In those days before she rose herself, my mother watched them, and she learned. She is smart, careful, and courageous, and her story gives her power when she steps before a crowd. Still, she says, it is a brutal business we are in. There are always those who would like to see her slip. She trusts no one, except for me.

Which is why, when I hear raised voices in her office one afternoon, I pause in the hallway to listen as they talk.

"No, it's too much," Gary Peterson, her chief assistant says. He is a young man with a thin mustache and a great ambition, a man who is a constant worry to my mother. "If we go that far we'll alienate half the country."

I glimpse my mother, standing behind the desk with her arms folded, frowning. "You saw what happened in Florida," she insists. "A clinic closed, and not a soul arrested."

A cleared throat then, a low and unfamiliar voice I can't quite hear. I know what they are talking about, however. I watched it with my mother on TV. In Florida they used butyric acid to shut the clinic down. Everyone spilled out, doctors and nurses, secretaries and patients, vomiting and choking, the building ruined with that putrefying smell. My mother watched this happen, amazed and also envious. "That's bold," she said, turning off the TV and pacing across the office. "That's *innovative.* We're losing ground, I'm afraid, with the same old approach. We have to do something stunning before we fade away entirely."

And so I wonder, standing there, what idea she has asked them to consider now.

"It's too risky," another voice insists.

"Is it?" she asks, "When we consider the unborn babies who would be rescued?"

"Or lost," Gary Peterson interjects. "If we fail."

They go on. I lean against the wall, listening to their voices, and press my hand against my lips. It smells of Sam, a clean salty smell of skin, the old vinyl of his car. In another week or so my mother goes to Kansas City, and Sam has put it to me clearly: He wants to come and stay with me while she's away. He's going crazy, that's what he says, he can't wait any longer. He says it's now or never. I told him I would think about it, let him know.

"Anyway," I hear Gary Peterson say. "Your plan involves Nichola, who isn't exactly reliable these days.

The men laugh and I go still, feeling myself flush bright with anger. They are talking about a year ago in Albany, about the day Gary Peterson made children block the clinic driveway. "Go on," he said to me, though I was sixteen, older than the others. He put his arm around me. Gary Peterson, tall and strong and slender, with his green eyes and steady smile. I felt his hand on my shoulder. "Go on, Nichola, please, these little boys and girls need someone like you to be a leader." The pavement was hot and dusty, scattered with trash, and the cars barely slowed when they swept in from the street. I was scared. But Gary Peterson was so handsome, so good, and he leaned over and whispered in my ear. "Go on, Nichola," he said. "Be a leader." And he kissed me on the cheek.

I was drawn in then. I remember thinking that my mother was a leader, and I would be one too. Plus I could feel his lips on my skin long after he had stepped away. I looked to where my mother was speaking on the steps. The protest was going very badly, just a few stragglers with signs, and I knew she needed help. And so I did it. I spread myself out on the asphalt in a line with all the others. The sun beat down. Some of the little ones started crying, so I led them in a song. We sang "Onward Christian Soldiers." It was the only song I could remember all the words to. Everyone got excited, and someone called in the TV crews. I could see them arriving from the corner of my eye, circling us with their black cameras. That film is in the archives now, thirty of us lying there, singing. All those sweet small voices.

The camera crew was well-established by the time the first doctor got back from lunch. She cruised into the driveway, determined to speed past the growing group of protesters, and almost ran over the smallest child, who was lying at the end of the row. Her car squealed to a stop near that girl's left arm. She got out of her car, livid and trembling, and went right up to my mother, grabbed her arm. I stopped singing so I could listen. That doctor was so angry.

"What in the name of heaven," she said, "do you think you are doing? If you believe in life, as you claim, then you do not put innocent lives at risk. You do not!"

My mother was calm, in a white dress, angelic. "Close your doors," she said. "Repent. The Lord will forgive even you, a murderess."

"And if I had hit that child?" the doctor demanded. She was a small woman, delicate, with smooth gray hair to her shoulders, and yet she shook my mother's arm with a power born of fury. "If my brakes had failed? Who would have been a murderess then?"

Lying there on the hot asphalt, I saw her point. The others were too little to understand, but I was sixteen, and suddenly I saw the danger very clearly. Other cars were pulling up, and there we were, a soft pavement of flesh. Their tires could flatten us in a second. Gary Peterson was hovering near the cameras, talking to the reporters. More crews had come, and the crowd was growing, and I could see that he was pleased. If one of us were hit, I thought, we would make the national, maybe the international news. I was suddenly very frightened. I waited for my mother to recognize this, to understand the danger, but she was intent on making her point in front of the doctor and a dozen TV cameras.

"Repent," my mother yelled. "Repent and save the children!"

As she spoke another car drove up, too fast and unsuspecting, and bumped the back of the first. The doctor's car jerked forward a foot, so that the last little girl was lying with her arm against the doctor's tire, the bumper hanging over her face. She was crying hard, but without making a sound, she was so scared. That was when I stood up. "Hey, Nichola." Gary

Peterson was shouting, and then he was standing next to me, grabbing my arm. "Get back down," he hissed at me, still smiling. "No one's going to get hurt." But already I could feel him fixing bruises on my arm. "No," I said. "I won't." And when he tried to force me, I screamed. That's all it took—the cameras were on us. He let me go, he had to, and stood there while I helped those children up, one by one, brushed them off, and led them out of danger. We made the national news that night after all. My mother was upset for days, but Gary Peterson, who made the front page of several papers, was quite pleased.

It's because I am so angry that I step into the doorway.

"Nichola!" my mother says. She must see from my face that I have overheard the conversation. She nods at me seriously and asks me to come in. "There you are, honey. Come say hello to Mr. Amherst and Mr. Strand and of course to Gary. They are here to discuss the upcoming work in Kansas City." She glances at them then and smiles, suddenly calm, almost flirtatious, all the tension gone from her face. "We're having a little disagreement," she adds.

They smile at this small joke, and look soberly at me. We get all kinds of people here, from the real religious freaks to the bored rich ladies from the suburbs, and I can tell which is which by the way they react whenever I show up. The religious people, they get all emotional. They say, *So that's your little girl, your baby that was saved, oh she is sweet.* Some of the ladies even weep to see me, the living embodiment of all their strivings and beliefs. These men, though, are not moved. In fact, they seem uncomfortable, as if I remind them of something they'd rather not know. My mother calls me her secret weapon when dealing with such people. Against these men, with their college degrees, their congregations, their ways of doing things, I am my mother's strength. Because there is no one who can argue when they see me, the walking, talking evidence of my mother's great sacrifice for life.

"Nichola," my mother says softly, glancing at the men. "I wonder if you could help us out."

"Sure," I say. "What do you need?"

"These gentlemen would like to know—just as a sort of general inquiry—exactly what you are prepared to do, Nichola? What I mean to say is that there's some concern, after the incident in Albany, about your level of commitment."

Our eyes meet. I know that I can help her. And even though I feel a little sick, as if a whiff of butyric acid were puffing through the air vents as we speak, I do.

"I'd do whatever I could to help," I say. This is not exactly a lie, I decide.

"Anything?" Gary Peterson repeats. He looks at me hard. "Think about it, Nichola. It's important. You'd do anything we asked?"

I open my mouth to speak, but the next words won't come. I keep remembering the hot asphalt against my back, the little voices singing. My mother's expression is serious now, a frown streaks her forehead. This is a test, and it will hurt her if I fail. I close my eyes, trying to think what to do.

Nichola. I remember Sam's touch, the way his words sometimes have double meanings. *Your body is a mystery to me.*

And then I open my eyes again and look straight at them, because suddenly I know a way to tell the truth, yet still convince them.

"Look," I say. "You know I am His instrument on earth."

Gary's eyes narrow, but my mother smiles and puts her arm around me, a swift triumphant hug, before anyone can speak.

"You see," she says. She is beaming. "I told you we could count on Nichola."

Something shifts in the room then. Something changes. My mother has won some victory, I don't know what exactly.

"Perhaps you're right," Mr. Amherst says as I am leaving. I hurry, relieved to get away. Whatever they are planning doesn't matter, because I already told my mother I won't go to Kansas City. "Perhaps it would be best to escalate the action, to make an unforgettable impact, as you suggest."

I smile, heading up the stairs. I smile because my mother is winning her argument, thanks to me. And more, I smile because today Sam kissed the inside of my elbows and said that he could not live without me, that the blood is always pounding, pounding in his brain these days. Thanks to me.

"You are asking for trouble with that outfit," my mother says the next day, when Sam drops me off after school.

I flush, wondering if my lips are red, like they feel. Parked in his car, we argued for an hour, and Sam was so angry that I started to get scared. He kissed me at the end of it, so hard I couldn't breathe, and told me to decide tonight, no later. "You love me," he insisted, gripping my arm like Gary did. "You know you do."

"Nichola," my mother insists, "that sweater is too tight, and your skirt is too short. It's provocative."

"Everyone dresses this way," I tell her, which is not entirely true.

My mother shakes her head and sighs. "Sit down, Nichola," she says. We are in the kitchen, and she gets up to make some coffee. She looks so ordinary, so much like any other mother might look. It is hard to connect her with the woman on TV who can hold a crowd of thousands enthralled. It is hard to picture her standing on a platform, offering up the story of my life, and hers, to the tired crusaders. For that is when she tells it, when people are growing weary, when the energy begins to lag, when "Amazing Grace" goes terribly off-key and the day is as hot or as cold as it will get. She stands up on the stage then with her hand on my shoulder and says, "This is my daughter, Nichola. I want to tell you the story of her life, of how the Lord spoke through her, and thus saved me."

She tells them how it started, how she was young and beautiful and wild, so arrogant that she believed herself immune to the consequences of her sins. From the stage she gives them details to gasp about, how beautiful she was, how drop-dead gorgeous. How many men pursued her and how far she let them go, how high she climbed on the ladder of her ignorance, until the world below seemed nothing but a mirage which never would concern her. They envy her a little, despite themselves, and after a while they begin to hate her just a little too—for her beauty, for the power that it gave her. My mother makes them feel this way on purpose, so that when she tells them of her fall they can shake their heads with secret pleasure, they can murmur to each other that she got what she deserved.

My mother knows her audience. In her weakness lies her strength. She tells them how she wound up a few months later, pregnant of course, abandoned by her family and her friends. They sigh then, they feel her pain, her panic. They understand the loneliness she felt. When my mother flees on a Greyhound bus the crowd is with her. They wander by her side through the darkest corners of an unfamiliar city. She grows fearful, yes, and desperate. They, too, grow numb and lose hope, and finally they climb with her to the top of the tallest building she can find. They stand at the edge, feeling the wind in their hair and the rockbottom desperation in their hearts, and they swallow as she looks at the city below and prepares herself to jump.

It is such a long way down. She is so afraid. And she, poor sinner, is so beyond herself that she does on impulse what she would never plan: She prays. She whispers words into that wind. She takes another step, still praying. And that is when the miracle occurs.

An ordinary sort of miracle, my mother says, for she heard no voices, saw no visions, experienced no physical transformation. No, on that day the Lord simply spoke to her through me. She tells how she grew dizzy suddenly. From hunger, she thought then, or maybe from the height, but she has realized since that it was nothing less than the hand of grace, a divine and timely intervention. She stumbled and fell against the guardrail, sliding on the wire mesh, scraping her arm. Brightness swirled before her. She put one hand on the cold concrete and the other on her stomach and she closed her eyes against that sudden, rising light. For a moment the world was still, and that was when it happened. A small thing, really. An ordinary thing. Just this: For the first time, she felt me move. A single kick, a small hand flailing. Once, and then again. It was that simple. She opened her eyes and put both hands against her flesh, waiting. Still, as if listening. Yes, again.

At this point she pauses for a moment on the speaker's platform, her head still bowed. Her voice has gone soft and shaky with this story, but now she lifts her slender arms up to the sky and shouts, *Hallelujah, on that day the Lord was with me, and intervened, and everything was saved.*

"Nichola," my mother says now, sitting down across from me and pouring cream in her coffee. I watch it swirl, brown-gold, in her cup. "Nichola, it's not that I don't trust you, baby. But I know about temptation. I know it is great, at your age. Next week I am going to do that mission work in Kansas City, and I want you to come with me. It will be like the old days, Nichola, you and me. We could stop in Chicago on the way home and go shopping."

She offers this last one because she can read my face, like a mirror face to hers, but with opposite emotions.

"Oh, Nichola," she says wistfully. "Why not? We used to have such fun."

She is right, I guess. I used to think it was fun. I sat on the stage with my mother and watched her speak. I felt the pressure of all those eyes, moving from the posters and back to me, as my mother told our story. That was when I was still a kid, though, and it was before the protests got so strong, so ugly.

"Look, I already told you. I'm too busy to go to Kansas City."

"Nichola," she says, an edge of impatience in her voice. "I promised people that you would."

"Well, unpromise them," I say. "They won't care. It's you they come to see."

"People always ask for you," she argues. "Specifically for you."

"I can't," I say. I'm thinking of the heat, the hours of standing in the group of prayer supporters, of the way there is no telling, anymore, what anyone will do. "I'm so busy. I've got a term paper due. The junior prom is in three weeks. I just don't think I can leave all that right now."

"Leave school, or leave Sam?" my mother asks.

I'm starting to blush, I can feel it moving up my cheeks, and my mother is looking at me with her gentle eyes that seem to know everything, everything about me. I fold my arms, my left hand covering the place where Sam held on to me so hard, and then I say the one thing I know for sure will change the subject.

"You know, I've been wondering about my father again," I tell her.

My mother's face hardens. I watch it happen, imagining my own features growing still and thick like that.

"Nichola," she says. "As far as your father is concerned, you don't exist."

"But he knows about me, doesn't he? And don't you think I have a right to meet him?"

"Oh, he knows," she says. "He knows."

She pauses, looking at me with narrowed eyes, the same expression she wore in the office, negotiating about Kansas City with Gary and the others. Her face clears then, and she leans forward with a sigh.

"What if I told you that you'd get to meet your father, if you come with me to Kansas City?"

"What are you saying?" I ask. Despite myself, my heart is beating faster. This is the first time she has ever admitted that he is alive. "Is that where he lives?"

She shrugs. She knows she has my interest now. "Maybe," she says. "He may live there. Or maybe he lives right here, or in another city altogether." She sits back and looks at me. "I don't think that you should meet him, Nichola. I think once you do, you'll wish you hadn't. I'm keeping it from you for your own good, you know. I just don't want you to get hurt."

She waits for me to say what I have said every other time: that she is right, that I don't want to meet him after all.

"All right," she says at last, when I don't speak. "All right then. Here's the deal. Come with me to Kansas City, Nichola.

Do exactly what I ask there. And then, I promise, I'll tell you all about him."

I sit still for a moment, tempted, but thinking also of the dense crowds, the stink of sweat in air already thick with hate, with tension. I try to imagine a face for the father I've never known. I think of Sam, of the answer he's expecting, and how afraid I am right now to tell him anything but yes. My mother waits, tapping her fingers against her empty cup. I wonder why she wants so much for me to go. I remember what I promised in her office.

"I don't want to do anything . . . anything terrible," I tell her. I say this so stupidly, but my mother understands. Her face softens.

"Oh, Nichola," she says. "Is that what this is about? I know how much you hated that business with Gary. It won't be anything like that, I promise you." She leans forward and puts her hand on my arm, speaking in a confidential voice. I can smell the coffee on her breath, her flowery perfume. "It's true I need you to do something, Nichola. Something special. But it's not a terrible thing, and anyway it's more that I just need your support, hon. It's going to be big, this protest. The very biggest yet. It would mean such a lot to me if you were there."

It is because she asks like this that I can't say no. I hesitate. That is my mistake. She gives me the smile she uses for the cameras, and pushes back the chair, stands up.

"Thank you," she says. "I prayed for this. You won't regret it, honey."

It's true that for a few minutes I feel good. It's only when she's gone that I realize how much I have given, how little I have gained. It's only then that the first slow burn of my anger begins.

My mother's bedroom is done in rose and cream. A few years ago, when she started getting paid a lot to do Christian TV talk shows, she hired a decorator to redesign the whole house with a professional look. The decorator was one of those angular women with severe tastes, and you can see her mark everywhere else—black-and-white motifs, tubular furniture, everything modern and businesslike. It's only my mother's room that is different, soft, with layers of pillows and white carpet so thick it feels as though you are walking on a cloud. Sometimes I close my eyes and imagine I could fall right through. I wonder if this is how my mother thinks of heaven, a room like white chocolate with a strawberry nougat center.

I know where she keeps things. I have sat on her bed, amid a dozen quilted and ruffled pillows, and watched her paste newspaper photos into her private scrapbook. She trusts me, the one person in her life she says she can trust, and I would not have imagined that I'd dig into her secrets.

Still, when my mother leaves the next day, when she phones me from downtown and I know for sure she is safely away, I go into her bedroom. I know just where to look. The box is in the closet, wedged into the corner, and I pull it out from beneath my mother's dresses. It smells of her perfume. I untie the string and lift the things out carefully, the scrapbooks and the yearbooks, the photos and the letters. I note their order. I arrange them precisely on the carpet.

At first I am so excited that I can barely concentrate. I pick up each letter feeling lucky, as if the secrets inside are giving off a kind of heat. In fact, however, I find absolutely nothing, and soon enough my excitement begins to fade. Still, I keep on looking, pausing only once when the phone rings and Sam's voice floats into the room on the answering machine. "Nichola," he says. "I'm sorry. You know you are everything to me." I listen, holding still, feeling shaky. I told him not to call today. I listen but I don't pick up the phone. Once he hangs up I go back to the papers on the floor.

I read. I sort. I skim. Much of it is boring. I sift through a pile of checkbooks, old receipts, a stack of unsorted pictures of people I have never met. I shuffle through the letters from her fans. It's just by chance that I see the one that matters. The handwriting is so like mine, so like my mother's, that I stop. I turn it over twice, feeling the cool linen paper in my hands, the neat slit across the top. I slide the letter out, and money, two hundred dollars in twenty-dollar bills, falls into my lap. I unfold the paper slowly, and then I begin to tremble as I read.

> I don't know if you got my other letters. I can only hope that they have reached you. I don't understand why you would do this, run off without a word. Yes, we were upset at your news but we are your family. We will stand by you. I am sending money and I am begging you, Valerie, to come home. I cannot bear to think about you out there in the world with our little grandbaby, in need of anything.

I put the letter down and finger the bills, old, still crisp. My mother told me that they kicked her out, that they severed ties with her forever. At least, that is what she always says, speaking to the crowd, how she begged them to forgive her and they would not. How she was cast out into the world for her sins, alone to wander. I came up here looking for my father, but I sit instead for a long time with that letter in my lap, wondering about my grandparents, who they are and where, and whether or not they have ever seen me on TV. Sam phones again. I hear the longing in his voice, the little flares of anger too, and I do not answer. Instead, I read that letter again, and yet again. The return address is smeared, difficult to decipher, but the postmark helps: it was sent from Seattle, and dated six months after I was born. Seattle, a place that I have never been. I put the letter aside and go through everything again. I look hard, but there is nothing else from them.

I am still sitting there a long time later, studying that letter, when the fax comes through. There's a business line downstairs, but my mother keeps this one for sensitive communications that she does not want her secretary—or Gary Peterson—to see. It has never occurred to me that she might not want me to see them either, so when it falls from the machine I'm hardly even curious. I'm still thinking about the grandparents I always thought disowned us. I'm trying to figure out how I can find them. I scan the fax, which is from Kansas City. It starts out with the usual stuff, hotel reservations and demonstration times, and I'm about to toss it down when I see this line: "So glad that Nichola has seen the light at last."

What light?

I read. The words seem to shift and change shape beneath my eyes. As with the letter, I have to read it several times before I can get the meaning straight and clear in my mind. I'm sure that in all my life I have never read so slowly, or been so scared. For in my hands I have their plans for Kansas City. The usual plans at first, and then references to their bold plan too, the one that will keep them in the news. I can see at last why my mother needs so much for me to join them. Like pieces of white ice, her lies melt clear in my hands, and suddenly I see her true intentions. What did she promise me? *It's a small thing, not terrible not at all.* But it is terrible. Oh yes. It's the worst thing yet.

Suddenly the room seems so sweet to me, stifling, that I have to get out. I feel I am inhaling sugar, and it hurts. I leave the fax on the carpet with the other papers, and outside I lean against the narrow black banister, breathing deeply. I am so grateful for the clean lines, the clarity, the sudden black and white. Because it is obvious to me now that what I have taken to be the story of my life is not that at all. It is not my life, but my mother's life, her long anger and relentless ambition that have brought us to this moment, to where we are.

Kansas City swelters in the heat, and every day my mother speaks of sin, her voice a flaming arrow. The crowd listens and ignites. The National Guard spills out of trucks and the nation waits to see how this protest, the longest and ugliest in the history of the movement, will end. I wait too, watching from the fringes as she steps from her cluster of bodyguards, smiling shyly at the crowd, which cheers, enraptured, ready to believe. "I am just a sinner," she begins, softly, and I look right at her as the crowd responds. I whisper, "That's right, you are a sinner and a manipulating liar too." She goes on speaking to the nation. I watch her, as if for the first time, I see and even admire her skill at this, her poise. For the very first time I see her clearly. I watch her, and I wait to see if she will make me do this evil thing.

It is on the third day that she leaves the stage and comes to me. It is late afternoon and her face is tanned dark. There is sweat on her forehead and above her upper lip. When she puts her arm around me her skin feels slick. She seems tired, but also exhilarated, for the protest is going very well. *Don't ask,* I think. Maybe she just wants to go for dinner. *Please, don't ask.*

"Come on, Nichola," she says. "It's time for you to do that favor."

We take two cars, the one with me and Gary and my mother, the second with tinted windows and three men I've never met. We drive for a long time it seems, maybe half an hour, and as we reach the suburbs they tell me what they want me to do. It is, as my mother said, a simple task, and if I did not know better, I would do it without flinching, I would not think twice.

"O.K., Nichola," Gary says, stopping on a suburban block where lawn sprinklers are hissing against the sidewalks and the trees are large and quiet. The other car parks in front of us. "It's about a block down, number thirty-four eighty-nine. She comes out every night at eight-thirty to walk the dog. You know what to say?"

"Yes," I tell them, swallowing hard. "I know."

"Good luck," my mother says. "We'll be praying."

"Yes," I say, getting out of the car. "I know."

I walk slowly through the dying sunlight, feeling their eyes on me. Number 3489 is big but ordinary, with fake white pillars and a wide lawn, flower beds. There is no sign of a teenage girl. I keep walking, but slowly, because I am scared and because I do not know yet what I'm going to do. Behind me in the car my mother trusts that I will keep my word, and before me in the house the doctor and his family finish dinner, do the dishes, glad that today, at least, no protesters have gathered on the lawn. You can see where the flowers are all crushed from other times. There are bars on the lower windows too. In a few minutes the daughter will come out of the house with her Scottish terrier on a leash and take him for a walk. My job is simple. I must walk with her, make her pause, and talk to her. About the dog, about videos, about anything that will distract her so she doesn't see them coming. That is all. Such a small thing they have asked of me, a five-minute conversation. They have not told me the rest, but I know.

At the end of the block I pause, turn around, start back. It is 8:35 and I can see the sun glinting off the chrome edges of the two parked cars. This time when I near the house two people are outside, on the lawn. I hesitate by the hedge. A man is squatting by his car, soaping up the sides. A bucket and a hose lie next to him on the ground. The car is old and kind of beat-up too, more like Sam's car than my mother's. On the thick grass a small white dog is running here and there, sniffing at bushes and spots on the lawn, while the young girl whistles and calls to him. The dog's name is Benjy. I do not know the girl's name, though her father is Dr. Sinclair. At the demonstration they emphasize his name. *Sin*clair, *Sin*clair. His daughter has short hair and is wearing a T-shirt, shorts, and sneakers. She is holding a leash in her hand.

Suddenly, her father, who has been rinsing the car with his hose, stands up and sprays a little water at her back. She shouts out in surprise, then turns around, laughing, letting the water rain down around her. The little dog runs over, jumping up, trying to get in on the fun, and suddenly I wonder what it would be like to be that girl, to have grown up in this ordinary house. I know I should walk away, but I can't. I can't get enough of looking at them. In fact, I stare so long and so hard that the father finally sees me. Our eyes meet and he turns his head, suddenly alert. I start walking across the lawn then, trying not to think.

"Hi," I say, when I get close enough.

"Hi," the girl says, looking at me curiously. Her father smiles, thinking I'm a friend of hers. I had this idea that they would know me right away, like I know them. I thought that they would look at me and see my mother, but they don't. They just stare. I'm so surprised by this that for a moment I can't think of what to say. So I just stand there, looking at this doctor. I have only seen him from afar, as he darted from his car into the clinic. Now I notice how small his ears are, how many wrinkles there are around his eyes. His smile fades as the silence grows between us. He takes a small but perceptible step closer to his daughter.

"Can we help you?" he asks. Despite his wariness, he is kind.

"Look," I say. I glance back at the road and then reach up and release my hair, shake it out to my shoulders. They ought to know me now, it should strike their faces like ice water. They should turn and flee without another word from me. But they do not. The doctor gives me an odd look, true, and glances past me then, to the quiet street, the row of bushes that hides his house. There is nothing there. Not yet. They are waiting. He looks back at me, and after a long moment more, he speaks.

"What is it?" he asks. His voice is very gentle.

His daughter picks up the little dog and smiles at me, to help me speak. She is younger than I am. I think about how they want to shove her into the back of the second car and drive away. A few hours in a dark place, and then they'll let her go. They don't want to hurt her, though I'm sure they are prepared for anything to happen. Scare her, yes, they want to do that. They intend to show her the wrath of the heavens, and to this end the men in the car are waiting with their ski masks and their Bibles. Perhaps she will be saved, but that's not the point. What they really want is to terrify her father, to make him repent for the lives that he has taken. They want the world to know that there are no limits in this battle.

I look straight at the doctor then. I don't smile. "Dr. Sinclair," I say. "You should know better than to trust a stranger. It's very dangerous. Especially tonight. I wouldn't walk that dog."

I'm ready to say more, but he understands at last. He reaches for his daughter, and they hurry to the house, leaving the bucket of water, the hose still running. I see the front door close and hear it lock behind them, and I wonder if they watch from their barred windows as I walk through their backyard to the alley, then out of sight. I walk for miles like this, between the quiet yards of strangers, and when it's finally dark I get on the first city bus I see.

It's hard to do this. I know I'm leaving everything behind. My mother and Sam, my whole life until this day. But it was not really my life, I know that now, it was always just the reflections of the lives of other people. I finger the letter my grandmother wrote, the money folded neatly. Seventeen years is a long time. They may not be there anymore. They may not want to see me if they are. But it is the only place I can imagine to begin.

Already, though, I miss my mother. I will always miss her, the force of her persuasion, her strong will. I wonder how long she will wait before she realizes that I've failed her, that I've gone. Outside the window Kansas City rushes past. The air is black and hot, and sprinklers hiss against the sidewalks. The bus travels fast, a lean gray shadow between the streetlights, and elsewhere in the dark Sam gives up on me and turns away. I imagine that my mother waits much longer. It seems to me I know the exact moment when she finally sees the truth. She sighs, and presses her hands against her face. Gary Peterson starts the car without another word. They drive off, and at that moment I suddenly feel the pressure ease. The other people on the bus don't notice, but all this time I have been growing lighter and emptier, until at last I feel myself emerge.

See me then, for the first time.

You do not know me.

I am just a young woman, passing through your life like the wind.

KIM EDWARDS DISCUSSES

"The Story of My Life," plot, and the ripple of events

PM: It seems this story could easily have been sparked by some specific event in the news. Was it?

KE: In the late 1980s and early 1990s, I lived and worked for five years in various parts of Asia—Japan, Malaysia, and Cambodia. During those years I traveled back to the U.S. just a handful of times and, having immersed myself so deeply in other ways of seeing and being, life in my own country often seemed strange to me.

"The Story of My Life" began on one such visit. I was in Newton, Iowa, visiting my in-laws, and one morning the *Des Moines Register* carried a story about a protest against an abortion clinic somewhere in the Midwest. I'd been away for a couple of years by then, and as a consequence I'd missed the incremental but steady escalation of violence against clinics and doctors who provided abortions. I found the story startling and deeply disturbing. This particular group of protesters had made children lie down on a clinic driveway to block traffic. For days I kept thinking of those children, their small limbs and shiny hair, their tender skin pressed against the hot asphalt, the dip and weight of a car turning into the driveway. How had any group of adults come to find this scene acceptable?

In retrospect, I suppose the news story resonated for me in an especially powerful way because I'd been living in a very conservative area of Malaysia, where the bodies of women were quite visibly a landscape for the expression of political ideologies. Malaysia is a multi-ethnic, multi-racial country where it isn't illegal to show your arms or legs or your hair, but at my school on the rural east coast, which comprised only Islamic

Malays, the young women were under a constant and unrelenting pressure to cover, and most eventually did. It troubled me, then, to find this same sort of dynamic running wild in my own culture: groups of conservatives demanding control of women's bodies, using the name of God to enforce their personal ideologies, putting small children at risk. The contradictions were compelling, and I couldn't stop thinking about them. What would it mean to these children to have been complicit in something they couldn't fully understand? What would happen when they grew older and gained a wider perspective?

I made a few notes, but this story didn't really begin to take shape for another two years. I was back in the U.S. for a few weeks, in Buffalo, New York, preparing to go off to Cambodia, and I found myself driving every morning past a clinic where a group of protesters gathered with their signs and their chants. One morning the voice of this story rose up as I drove past them. The voice, and the first line: "You'd know me if you saw me." I went straight to the SUNY Buffalo library and wrote the opening pages in a great exhilarating rush. The story wasn't close to being drafted, but once I had that voice in my head, I knew there was no going back.

PM: What particular challenges did you encounter writing something that contained a factual, topical basis? What guidance would you give an aspiring writer who is drawn to a headline and is contemplating the special task of alchemizing it into a work of invention?

KE: Writing "The Story of My Life" was a tremendous challenge. In fact, for a long time I resisted this story. I wasn't concerned so much about addressing an issue in history, though this wasn't a particularly fashionable stance to take at the time, at least not in this country, where domestic particulars and minimalism were all the rage. We live in history, after all, our individual lives intersecting with particular moments in time and in place, and it has always seemed to me a source of great strength to write from one's own place of knowledge even while seeking what's universal in human experience. Plus, in Asia I'd discovered a wider world and writers who were unabashedly locating their characters in the sweep of history. Nadine Gordimer and Anita Desai and V. S. Naipaul and Yukio Mishima, Paul Scott's *Raj Quartet*—I used to travel down the coast of Malaysia to a great used-book shop in Singapore and pile the whole world into the trunk of the car.

All the same, I was wary of this story. It seemed so full of risks, a gem buried somewhere within a minefield of polemics. Until I had the voice, I couldn't even attempt to write this piece. The voice was the crucial discovery—and I suspect it's always the crucial discovery. In literature we tend to care about the political only to the extent that it touches and shapes the individual lives of characters. Stories aren't about issues, they're about people. More than anything else, "The Story of My Life" is a coming-of-age story, one young woman's painful and exhilarating discovery of her own unique identity. So I'd urge any writer to embrace what's happening in the world—absolutely, don't look away—but also to know quite clearly going into the narrative whose story is needing to be told, and why.

PM: You start this story outside of time, and hence outside of its plot, which is ironic given plot's large role in the story.

KE: I hadn't really thought about it in this way before—the story's first line was powerful and sure and felt completely instinctive—but I suppose this opening serves to set the story up as Nichola's own, to anchor the narrative in a voice and a sensibility strong enough to sustain the coming action. The story also begins in the second person, with this demanding, imperative voice, which creates an immediate bond between narrator and reader. It also invites readers to step into the story and to see the world as Nichola sees it. To become, in a sense, her intimate confidant.

Going back through the story, I'm struck now also by how the voice changes and by how powerful silence becomes in this narrative. The intense, lyrical voice of the opening tells the story of Nichola's shared life with her mother—the life of performance—but that voice changes as Nichola discovers her own. Likewise, midway through the story, in a crucial conversation with her mother Nichola chooses not to answer at all, thus shifting the dynamics of their relationship and gaining more control over her situation. At about that time, Nichola also stops telling the reader everything she knows. This creates suspense, of course, which was why I chose to do it structurally, but it's also thematically fitting; as she claims her own story, Nichola becomes less open about what she reveals, and when and how. The reader, once so close, is pushed back a few steps, just as the mother and Sam and Gary are. That works well to shift the dramatic motion of the story from action to character, doesn't it? I didn't do it on purpose.

PM: Both Sam's and Mom's plans for Nichola are scheduled to culminate during the Kansas City trip. There's something very agreeable about that balance and the fact that it manages to avoid feeling constructed. Could you discuss how the Sam subplot is functioning as a dramatic counterpoint to the main storyline?

KE: Nichola's relationship with Sam grew up very naturally in the narrative and was there from the beginning, though it did evolve during revision. I knew from my earliest notes that Nichola's emerging self, her own desires and dreams, would shatter the world her mother had built so carefully. The first exchange between Nichola and Sam also became a way of showing Nichola's keen awareness of the way he's trying to manipulate her by "twisting the Scriptures to his own advantage." She's not willing yet to acknowledge this dynamic in her other relationships, but the fact that she sees it here sets the stage for her later discoveries. It's interesting, because on the surface Sam seems to be in direct counterpoint to Nichola's mother. He wants exactly what her mother forbids. In reality, however, Sam is pressuring Nichola in exactly the same way her mother is: both want her to meet their needs without regard to her own perceptions and desires. The competing pressures from these two important people in her life finally force Nichola to find her own strength and sense of self and direction—to be her own person, to make her own discoveries, to shake off all agendas but her own. Despite all the action and external conflict, this is a story that turns on internal discovery and change.

PM: You create a parallel linking the moment Gary grips the narrator's arm at the protest to when Sam grabs it in the car. Also the mother flees by bus as a teen, followed at the story's end by the narrator doing the same. What connections did you want the reader to make from those?

KE: I wanted the moment when Sam grabbed her arm to contain and to evoke the previous moment with Gary. Structurally, it worked well to link the two sections together through such a tangible and dangerous moment, but I also wanted Nichola to begin to be aware of other, unspoken parallels between these different parts of her life. The circle of risk is widening, and this repeated gesture was a way of revealing that to the reader as well as to Nichola. Likewise, I wanted there to be an element of narrative movement in this gesture. Nichola was too surprised and distracted to respond to Gary, but she's a different person in the second scene with Sam, and her response—her refusal to see him anymore—shows this. Likewise, when Nichola flees, she repeats her mother's actions, but with different motivations. She's seeking a connection, her own history. Implicit in that, I believe, is the possibility of a greater generosity to her mother at some future point than her mother has been able to show to Nichola's grandparents in the past.

PM: Wasn't there an earlier unpublished draft of this story in which Nichola does track down her father, who turns out to be an abortion doctor?

KE: Right—that did happen in an early draft. Despite all my best intentions and the power of the narrative voice, I lost my way for a while. It would be nice to blame this on the polemics in the story, but that wouldn't be fair. I knew from the very beginning that this was Nichola's quest for self-definition; even in my earliest drafts she is aware that the life she is living is not a life she chose, but one that's been very carefully constructed for her. (The earliest working title was "The Right to Life.") I knew all that, but I made a wrong turn anyway.

This is fundamentally a story about Nichola's break with her mother in the quest for her own sense of identity; though the final ending is exhilarating, it's also full of loss. In the earlier draft I'd found it easier to look in another direction rather than face the hard truths implicit in this story. I introduced the father and had Nichola and her mother in some kind of sympathetic collusion together at the end. However, the mother-daughter dynamic and Nichola's own growth were the essential truths of the story—the narrative strength and motion have their source there. So I went back and stripped away the first ending. I started researching and making notes—doing a lot of unstructured free-writing to explore. The new ending evolved very naturally, though quite gradually, from there. Once I'd broken open the form of the earlier draft, there was room and freedom for the story—and the characters—to grow as they needed.

PM: Making such a large change usually sends ripples throughout the entire story, which often must be re-imagined in light of the new element. What was your experience with this story?

KE: Yes, it wasn't at all a matter of tacking on a new ending; I had to rethink many other parts of the story. With the father gone, present only in Nichola's yearning to know him, I found myself looking more closely at the character of the mother to see why she would be motivated to act as she did. I also, for the first time, did some research, and that's when I discovered that the violence against clinics and doctors was not random but part of a systemic movement with no holds barred. The more I learned about the protest groups, the more I came to understand that they had their own particular dynamics, and that personal power was a large factor in the decisions they made. Often, there was a single charismatic leader driving the actions, but in every case I studied, that leader was a man. Once I realized this, I understood Nichola's mother in a new way. Her position in this group was precarious. She'd been powerless and she'd become powerful, and she was protective of that power. Seeing her in this context made her character seem more complex to me. What she does is awful, yes, but in an odd and convoluted way she's trying to protect the life she's built for herself and Nichola. That she can't see the cost of her actions, for herself and for her daughter, is a kind of tragic flaw. She became more fully human in the revision, and Nichola's relationship with her became much clearer. This was the real discovery I made when I stripped away the first ending. The action of the final version grew out of these important dynamics between the characters.

PM: Is there a particular method you employed in plotting and re-plotting this story? For example, did you backtrack from a destination? Did you decide on certain ideas or feelings you wanted to evoke at various points and figure out how to get to and from them?

KE: No, not really—I don't think of plot in such a deliberate and organized and predestined way. If I start with an idea of anything, it's with what I would imagine is the story's theme—it's beating heart, why it matters. Usually this is contained in some image or voice or bit of dialogue that generates the story. I let the characters take it from there. I write in a very instinctive and organic sort of way; I trust my intuition. I don't mean, by saying this, to imply a lack of respect for the intellectual and analytical. Indeed, what I called intuition has been informed by years of study, practice, and reading, reading, reading.

PM: The short story writer is always prioritizing events for the reader, conveying the essence of her character's story through a small number of scenes. How did you decide which scenes to dramatize and which to summarize?

KE: Perhaps because there is so much narrative action in this story, the scenes I dramatized all have to do with the evolving relationship between Nichola and her mother. Scenes that did not include this—butyric acid piped into a clinic, Sam's anger—were less important to the overall narrative arc and were done in summary. But this was not really a conscious decision; it simply felt right to do this at the time.

PM: In the hands of a less adept writer, Nichola's discovery of the fax could have seemed overly fortuitous, but you disarm that by stressing how focused she was on her grandparents' letter.

KE: In the earlier draft, Nichola discovered her father's identity in that scene, which was much shorter. That is, there was no internal reaction to the discovery. However, after I'd ripped away the first ending and turned my attention to the true heart of the story, things became much more complex and interesting. I remember not knowing, as I wrote that scene, what was going to happen. It was a surprise to me when Nichola found that letter from her grandparents. The scene works because it grows naturally out of the mother-daughter dynamic in the story. The mother's real betrayal—the shocking betrayal of denying Nichola her family—came years ago. That news about her grandparents is far more important to Nichola, far more personal, than the news in the fax, though both moments come together to redefine the mother in Nichola's eyes.

PM: It also helps that the sequence of events leading to the fax is so well-motivated: Nichola invades her mother's privacy because she feels gypped by how little her mother has promised to reveal about the father; the mother promised so little because she's unhappy Nichola brought him up; Nichola brought him up because she's upset that her mom's pressuring her about Kansas City. . . . How do you gauge the authenticity of your characters' motivations?

KE: If you understand who your characters are and what their state of mind is in a given moment, it's not such a leap to imagine the next moment.

Probably in this regard, the hardest character to write was the mother. She was the character toward whom I felt least sympathetic and the one I understood the least, as well. In a very early draft of this story I wrote out a scene where the mother approached a back alley abortionist when she discovered that she was pregnant with Nichola. I was still trying to discover the mother's story then, trying to understand how she'd gotten to this point in her life. The scene didn't work at all; it descended almost immediately into cliché, and though I was trying to mix up and diffuse the polemics, this scene had the opposite effect. Beyond that, it shifted the focus to external circumstances rather than to internal discovery.

Now the mother's moment of desperation and conversion is both more persuasive and more revelatory, and it explains why she behaves the way she does later in the story. Her investment in this protest movement is not superficial; it's deeply personal and speaks to the core of who she believes herself to be. This was another of the great discoveries of revising this piece.

PM: Can we talk about flashbacks? What do you think are the most appropriate times to use them?

KE: I generally think of flashbacks as a way of illuminating a character's state of mind, elucidating the lens through which s/he sees the events of the narrative. In "The Story of My Life" this is so, but it's interesting to me that the flashbacks here are almost entirely the story of the mother, as told to Nichola and as seen through her eyes. In an early one, when describing her mother's first moment on the stage, Nichola contrasts what she remembers with what she can view now on film. This sets up the contrast to come between what Nichola sees and what really exists, so there's a structural parallel here, too.

PM: For a literary writer, what's the proper perspective to consider plot in relation to the other elements of fiction writing? How does one prevent plot from taking over and dragging a work into high-concept or so-called genre fiction?

KE: It's probably a good idea here to pause and clarify what I mean by plot: I see plot as the action of the story, the narrative motion of a piece. Characters both make events happen and respond to events beyond their control. Plot is not static and imposed, but rather generative and creative. Thus, as both a writer and a reader, I'm in favor of plot, by which I mean that I like things to happen in a story. I advocate event and action and the full response of characters. I've been fortunate to live a very exciting life, full of travel and adventure and unexpected twists and confluences. I wouldn't wish to deny my characters those possibilities or to deny myself the pleasure of exploring them in fiction.

Katherine Anne Porter said it well in her *Paris Review* interview: event is the stone dropped in the water; what matters is not the stone, but the ripples it sets off. This is how I see it, too: things happen, to our characters or to ourselves, that we can't control; we make decisions for which we can't foresee all the consequences. What's interesting in fiction is exploring how those events or decisions affect a particular life or set of lives: how they ripple. How a particular moment, even a very ordinary moment, can come to define a life. As long as the characters are distinctive and clearly articulated, they will generate the action of the story, rather than the other way around.

KIM EDWARDS is the author of *The Secrets of a Fire King* (1997), which was a finalist for the PEN/Hemingway Award, and *The Memory Keeper's Daughter* (2005). Her short fiction has appeared in numerous journals, including *The Paris Review, Ploughshares*, and *Zoetrope*, and has received many honors including a National Endowment for the Arts Fellowship, a Nelson Algren Award, a Pushcart Prize, a Whiting Writers' Award, and inclusion in the *Best American Short Stories*. "The Story of My Life," which first appeared in *Story,* was part of that magazine's winning fiction entry in the 1994 National Magazine Awards. She currently teaches at the University of Kentucky.

A RECORD AS LONG AS YOUR ARM

George Garrett

Ray, old buddy, one of the things I'll never be able to forget is the look on your face when you strolled into your bedroom and discovered me there with your wife.

You were supposed to be away for the whole weekend with the Debate Team. Only they called it off, and so you got back home a little after midnight on Friday. Walked into the house happily, already slipping out of your clothes, with a whole unexpected, unplanned weekend ahead of you. You were tiptoeing (you thought maybe she would be asleep). Otherwise we would have heard you, I think. Maybe. Actually we were each and both reaching that state of being where the explosion of a bomb in the driveway or the front yard wouldn't have distracted us. If we'd heard at all. You tippy-toed into your own bedroom, switched on the light, and got about halfway into some familiar, cheery greeting when you saw that smile and cheer being wasted on the large, inadvertent, pale and glowing moon of a bare ass. Mine. . . .

After that things began happening kind of quickly. But I can, by some oversimplifying, impose an order and sequence on events. Geraldine is free of me as if repelled by an electric shock. She has got the sheet all around her—thus even more fully exposing me to chilly light and chill air—and she is trying to curl up under the pillow. You, still, without a full word, have turned toward the bureau and snatched open the top drawer. I have not yet moved. Not purely out of shock and fright, mind you, but also because I can vividly imagine a large, blue-black, shiny, well-oiled, well-kept revolver, probably a .38 Police Special, resting in the bureau drawer just beyond your fingertips. And naturally I am amazed that you would have a gun in there. You know how strongly I feel about the necessity for gun control. My position on the possession of handguns has always been quite clear. Politics and ideology aside, however, I am thinking that I am sure enough about to be shot at, but with luck I may yet come out of this alive. I am betting on the fact that you are (1) completely surprised, (2) naturally a little nervous, (3) basically nonviolent, (4) hopelessly inept with mechanical things, and (5) probably a lousy shot. My first thought is that I must begin by offering you a target, something to shoot at, but which, if hit, will likely do the least permanent damage. Hoping that luck, thick muscle, and adequate fat will save my vital organs, banking on the expectation that one good clean messy hit will bring you to your senses, I therefore exaggerate the somewhat awkward position which Geraldine has left me in, trying with the facility of a contortionist to curl up completely behind that largest of muscles. Hoping that the bland bare sight of it will so enrage you as to cause you to miss me altogether.

Instead of a shot, however, in this timeless instant, I listen to your deep breathing and some considerable rummaging in the bureau drawer. Things start landing on the floor. I decide I'd better sneak a peek, even though it may be my last one. Therefore I shift my strategy and my stance slightly, rising up higher. To view you more or less as, say, the center sees the punter on fourth down.

At which point, precisely, you turn back toward the bed, twist, rather; twist your head to look at the bed. Our glances meet. Upside down, of course. And I am happy to see that you are empty-handed.

What else can I do, then, prior to resuming my original position, what can I possibly do but wink?

"Geraldine!" you shout.

Muffled noise from beneath the pillow.

"Where the hell is my fucking gun? I left it in the top drawer."

Ah, a familiar domestic situation. In a trice and a twinkling Geraldine is back in charge.

"Well," she says clearly and distinctly, "I haven't touched it. Try the bottom drawer."

Clutching her sheet—in fact all of the sheets pulled out from under me in one smooth deft yank—she is now rising with every intention, it seems, of helping you search for the gun.

Wrapped in her cloud of sheets, she is suddenly between us.

And I? Off of that bed in a roll. Scooping up my undershorts like a third baseman handling a hot grounder. Out the window without wondering if it's open or not.

Discovering, a good hundred meters away from the house, that indeed it had been open and all I have wrapped around me is the screen and its frame. A picture entitled "The Wages of Sin" is moving twinkle-toed, screen and all, through a series of almost identical backyards in the Whispering Pines Subdivision. Tangling blindly with rows of hedges while trying to take them like low hurdles. In one case having a memorable encounter with a portable outdoor grill on wheels. Which sails me along merrily as far as a blue plastic swimming pool, through which I thrash and splash, half-drowning, while packs of dogs begin to bark and various lights come on.

I shall pause in my headlong flight through the awakening neighborhood, suspenseful and pathetic as it may be, to say, "Meanwhile, back at your house . . . "

Now, Ray I have to confess that this next part is not purely imagination. I got it from Geraldine the next time we met. I do not give my unqualified credulity to her version, of course. Geraldine, bless her heart, has a tendency to lie grandly when she can or has to. And when she cannot, she will certainly do a little needlepoint upon the plain pattern of truth. So I do not believe that part of her story—how later she managed to con you so that, when the time for apology could no longer be deferred, it was you who apologized. And then were deeply grateful for her forgiveness.

It's possible, I'll grant you. Perhaps also true, but I prefer not to accept it. Nor, for that matter, to think about it very much. However, I am willing to accept other elements as basic facts.

The two of you together searched through the bureau for your pistol. No pistol. In your perfectly understandable anger and dismay, you turned on Geraldine and accused her of having hidden the damn thing, just in case this ever happened.

Very dumb move, Ray.

She denies it. Did not touch, has not ever touched that damn dumb fuckingpistol of yours. Would not either. Being as how she, for one, knows how to respect another person's goddamn privacy. Then she reminds you how you were down in the basement, cleaning the pistol, a couple of days ago.

Maybe, you allow. But you wouldn't have just left it down there.

Yes, you did. You did! Because you got a phone call from the Dean. You had forgotten all about that—the meeting of the Committee on Educational Policy. You had to haul ass over there, fast as you could.

Now you remember it all—the call, a wild, fast drive over to school in the Triumph, tearing up four flights to the Dean's Office, two clumsy steps at a time, bursting into the room a half hour late and suddenly all those astonished, hostile faces looking at the doorway and you standing there in work clothes, panting, both hands all grubby with oil and grease.

Down you go to the basement, Ray, to look and see for yourself. And I go with you, even now. Feeling it all. Stiffness and the slight vague pain in your bad leg. Stooping at your height, under the low ceiling, moving toward the worktable. Where, sure enough and just as you left it, there's the pistol amid rags, an oil can, toothbrush, patches, and a stiff wire brush for the bore. You stand there a moment, testing the cool, pure, clean weight of it. Then a brief flash of inspiration, a flicker of a smile. Yes, she has got you cold, dead to rights and right back in your place. But you smile to yourself, poor deluded Ray. You climb back up the basement stairs. Slow, regular, noisy. Conveying decision and direction. Clump, clump, clump, the ever-so-slight drag of the gimpy leg, through the kitchen, diagonally across a piece of darkened living room, and back into the bedroom.

To find her changed into her best nightie, sitting at her dressing table, back to you, but able to see you enter in her mirror. What happens next I can't claim to know; but either, without missing a stroke with her hairbrush as you approach, she informs you that you'd be a whole lot more scary if that gun were loaded; or equally likely, she reacts with operatic fright, so convincing that you immediately reassure her by showing her the gun is not loaded, whereupon you find yourself having to apologize for frightening her half out of her wits.

In any event, apologize you will, must, and do. And now you are ready to talk about it, to discuss the whole thing.

She is not ready, but a light is in her eyes. She's got an idea. John Towne is lucky to be alive. He needs to be taught a serious lesson. You can agree on that much, if she keeps talking and you don't stop to think about it. If you had shot me when you first came in, you'd have been within your rights; if you proceed to shoot me now, however, even assuming you do find the shells for the pistol, it will technically be first-degree murder. Geraldine says she hates the thought of you in jail. She needs you. She needs you near and available. Maybe you could get off on grounds of temporary insanity, but . . .

You are practically hypnotized by then, Ray. What's more, she has an even better idea. The two of you should get in the car and drive over to my place. I should be there by now. You will wake us up and scare the wee-wee out of me with the big gun and making a horrible face like you did when you came sneaking back into the bedroom trying to be funny. You can take the clothes and shoes I left behind, and hurl them on my living-room floor, enjoy fully the look on Annie's vapid, pretty face as she discovers, at long last, the truth about the two-faced, two-timing, sonofabitching sex fiend and monster she is married to. Then turn with pride and dignity and leave them to each other. She has all the money, such as it is, you know. A taste of poverty will serve Jack right. At that point, Ray, you accept her logic. Partly because it is better than doing nothing, and no question, you do love that Geraldine.

And who wouldn't? She may be a little tacky, but she is a truly first-rate piece of ass.

So you gather up my clothes and get in the station wagon. Solemnly, with even a certain stiff ceremony to the occasion. I bet you even held the door open for Geraldine when she climbed in.

It is, or will be, important you are not driving the Triumph. You are behind the wheel of a John Wesley College wagon, the one you checked out earlier to drive the Debate team.

I'll bet—I can actually see it happening—you haven't driven two blocks before Geraldine, her spirits and confidence now fully restored, has punched on the radio and is humming along with the music of an all-night record show.

Meanwhile, Ray, I had made it safely home. Out of Whispering Pines, though the fringes and edges of town across town, skirting the campus but using the park and the cemetery to good advantage, part way along the railroad tracks, and finally home, over the plowed field behind our (Annie's) literally Colonial house. The real thing, only all furnished in blond Swedish and Danish and probably Finnish modern, with rugless, highly polished, wide-board floors, damn few *objets,* barish light-colored walls. Only a very few choice pictures and prints hanging, and those changed regularly. Fresh cut flowers, artfully arranged. Some old musical instruments that nobody plays, mostly stringed things all out of tune. Pots and ceramics made by Annie herself, together with a few elegant examples of her stitchery. And not to forget the brick and board bookcases; the big stereo setup that can rattle every windowpane in the house. The nursery for Allison, not out of *Winnie the Pooh* at all, but instead as sparse as everything else, with strictly functional toys. One bare cold bathroom upstairs with a high, claw-footed, stained, wheezing turn-of-the-century tub. A toilet with an honest-to-God chain pull. And ancient, scratchy towels (oh long before Margaret Drabble tried to make them popular!). Hardly a mirror in the whole house except for the one in the bathroom—small, old, distorted, badly lit, silvered—over the medicine cabinet. Where, if you peeked, you find it as neat and bare as a G.I.'s footlocker. Only the most basic toilet gear, a bottle of Listerine, and a bottle of aspirin so old that the tablets were crumbled to powder.

Did I mention the bedroom? Most of it occupied by our big, low bed. Which was really only a mattress and an inner spring set up on wood blocks.

Maybe that's what first attracted me to Geraldine. Such a good old simple broad, you know? Everything phony and wonderfully cluttered. Fancy bathroom with all the latest equipment and the soft, colored toilet paper, the covered seat for the john, the cute and vulgar stack of reading material. I think you even had a bidet. I may be wrong. But when I try to picture your bathroom, I always see a bidet gleaming there. And who could forget the full rich medicine cabinet of Geraldine Wadley? I picture everything I can imagine and then I multiply by two. Then add a little forest of pill bottles, every kind of prescription from a couple of dozen different doctors. All about half full. And Geraldine had big soft, expensive, wraparound towels just like in the movies.

Ray, I have to admit I really liked your bathroom.

So anyway, winded, battered, and bruised, toes stubbed and feet full of splinters, eyes teary from twigs, I find myself home at last, sneaking in. Why do I sneak? She's wide awake, reading a book in the living room. Oriental kimono, smoking a Schimmelpenninck cigar, reading a book and listening to Segovia.

When I come in, Annie looks over the top of her book and reacts. Very cool, as ever and always.

"Hi, Jack, is anything wrong?"

"I'm afraid I may be in a little trouble."

"Oh . . . what kind of trouble?"

So I explain how I was in the Library working late as usual. And how I got a phone call from Geraldine Wadley. All frantic about how some kind of an animal is loose in the house. Big bat or a flying squirrel or something like that. Ray is away on the Debate trip and she is scared out of her mind. Would I, as a very big favor, please, please come out there and get rid of it?

I was, naturally, playing on every decent chord I could reach. Annie loves animals. All kinds of animals indiscriminately. Supreme contempt for any woman who is frightened of any animal. Besides which Annie has always had a dim view of Geraldine. Convinced Geraldine is a slut and a hussy and a Jezebel. Cheap and tawdry temptress. Two-dollar whore, etc., etc., etc.

Of course, Annie liked you a lot, Ray, and thought you were patient and long-suffering.

I continue to create my simple fiction. I get out there (never mind how, Annie doesn't ask) to your house and discover a flying squirrel is indeed in the basement. In passing I mention the fact that Geraldine greets me at the door wearing only her panties and bra. Insisting that she was so upset and panic-stricken that she probably forgot all about her personal appearance.

Knowing better, Annie smiles and permits me to continue my tale.

Well, Geraldine has this big pistol and she wants me to shoot the flying squirrel. I will have none of that. Truth is, I couldn't bring myself to kill a flying squirrel. But I explain it to her in more practical terms. I am liable to shoot up her lovely home. A .38 slug could easily carry over to a neighbor's house. Anyway the explosions will wake up the whole subdivision. What I will do, I say, is catch the beast and release him outside.

"Catch a flying squirrel? You?" Annie laughs at that.

"Scoff as you may and must," I answer her. That's exactly what happened. In the limited space of the basement I was able to run the bugger down and trap him in an old badminton net. But not before I ripped my trousers on a nail, dirtied my shirt, and soaked my shoes in water leaking from the ancient hot-water heater.

After I set the squirrel free in the yard and returned, Geraldine seemed very grateful. She insisted that the least she could do was to sew up the rip in my trousers and run the shirt and socks through her washer and dryer. (Annie is sternly against dependence on appliances.)

I remind Geraldine that it is getting pretty late and that the

Library is already closed. I better go on home as is. Nonsense, Geraldine insists, wouldn't dream of sending you home like that. What would Annie think? I am urged to go into the bedroom, hand my stuff through the door, stretch out, relax, watch TV or something. And she'll be through in a jiffy. Should I call Annie? No use worrying Annie about it. She's probably asleep by now anyway.

In trusting innocence I did as she suggested. I did, however, notice that while I had been crawling around down in the basement she had modified her outfit. Changing into a black, powdery, filmy sort of a peignoir. And once I was inside the bedroom I noticed (one each) panties and bra draped across a chair. But I honestly never stopped to think . . .

"You're too naïve," Annie concludes.

"Maybe so," I am willing to concede.

I stretched out on their bed. Since I share my dear and loving wife's supreme contempt for TV and since there are no books in the bedroom, merely some old copies of *Cosmo* and *Mademoiselle* . . .

"She has always dressed too young."

. . . I dozed off briefly. Eyes tired from my long hours of study. An intimate touch, the odor of an unfamiliar perfume waked me. There she was, on the bed beside me, as bare-assed as Eve in Eden, an amorous glint in her eye if I ever saw one . . .

"That bitch!"

But wait. Nothing really happens. Then suddenly everything happens. Who drives up, lights flashing across the bedroom walls, but my good friend Ray? What will I do? If I try and explain everything, will he believe me?

I never had a chance to decide what was the right thing to do. For just as Ray came in whistling and limping into the house, Geraldine made a unilateral decision. She hollered rape at the top of her voice. Ray came into the bedroom just in time to see me bail out of the window.

God knows what will happen next. They might even call the police.

Now, Ray, here is where Annie really surprised me.

"What happens next, sport, is that you get some clothes on, and we will drive over there and straighten the whole thing out."

"Don't you think it might be better to wait until morning? Let things cool off a little?"

"No."

"I'll see Ray at school tomorrow anyway and tell him the complete story. No use your getting involved too."

"Don't be such a coward," Annie says. "Whenever something serious happens in our lives, you always try to avoid it. Usually by comedy. You will go right to the center of a scene and then cop out with a gag line."

"Show me a gag line and I'll go after it like a dog chasing a stick," I say.

But there is no getting out of it. I get dressed to go. I am thinking, what the hell, Ray will never shoot me down in front of Annie. And she will attribute your fantastic story to your sense of misguided nobility—the desire to protect Geraldine's (ho-ho-ho) reputation.

I will give it one last try, though.

"We shouldn't go off and leave the children all alone."

"Nonsense," Annie says. "I woke up Andrew. He is perfectly capable."

And away we go. Laughing and scratching.

Here comes the next problem of that evening. Happens that our car is in the garage. Guy was supposed to have it ready, but he didn't. We have a loaner. Good enough. Not long at all, a few blocks maybe, as we drive toward Whispering Pines, our heap drives right past a John Wesley station wagon. But we think nothing of it. We are looking for a sporty red Triumph. You are on the lookout for a new Pinto, not an old Plymouth.

Ships that pass in the night . . .

We get to your place, hang around awhile. Then decide maybe you went to our house. We go back, passing without noticing, almost certainly, a John Wesley station wagon. You arrive home and find Annie's crisp, curt, cool, condescending, and correct note. We get home to find Andrew highly amused by something.

"Mr. and Mrs. Wadley were just here. Mr. Wadley had a gun with him. He said Daddy is a very bad man and he's going to shoot Daddy."

I get myself a big drink. Annie lights up a cigar and considers the situation. Since they haven't called, it behooves us to go back and try again. As we drive away, I hear, faintly, our phone begin to ring. Annie doesn't hear that well, especially when she is thinking. Andrew won't answer it, you can count on that. He hates the phone.

I think I could save us all a lot of trouble if I drove into a telephone pole or something. Except the local cops know me too well already. They will nail me for drunk and reckless driving. Engine trouble? Annie knows more about cars than I do. The whole thing is, Annie likes Ray and Ray likes Annie. And I . . . ? Well, I like Geraldine all right. As a friend, I mean. And I am willing to forgive and forget the way she treated me. What the hell? Annie will work it out. Then we'll all get drunk together and watch the sun come up. Fix breakfast . . .

Well, Ray, we missed you twice again, going and coming. Then everybody quit trying. I know from Geraldine (believing about half of it, of course) what happened with you all. Thoroughly beaten down, frustrated, you were ripe for a long serious talk. Tears and a plea for forgiveness from her. An appeal to your emotional maturity and natural generosity. Promises for the future.

About that unfortunate incident in the office. Knowing you had an eight o'clock class, I came early. Not to ambush you, as it may have seemed. Nor to go through your desk. I figured that, since we share the same office, I'd better get there first, take what I needed, and cut out. I won't brazenly sit there, I told myself, with my very presence an insult to Ray, until we have straightened it all out. I'll just get what I need from the office, enough for a couple of days. By the Wednesday Department Luncheon everything will be okay, I'm sure.

It was my thought that prior to the Luncheon I would give you the benefit of a wide berth. At the Luncheon I would be as friendly as can be and you would have to respond in kind. Because our Chairman likes that. A friendly Department is a good, productive Department, he says. I intended to make sure he was standing right there when I greeted you effusively and then asked you how the Debate trip went. Not out of irony or a vulgar desire to rub it in. Shock, yes. To shock you into wakeful attention and the possibility of a meaningful dialogue. You would understand my effort to communicate. Being a genuinely sensitive and intelligent guy, you would be amused too. What dramatic irony! You have to stand there and kill me with comradely kindness. One pout, one snarl or sneer, one snotty remark, and you would be on the Chairman's shitlist. Unfriendly guys have no future at John Wesley. And least in the English Department. And you were still trying to hustle yourself a promotion.

Lest I sound cynical and cruel, let me remind you of the truth that if you play a role well enough, becomingly, as it were, it becomes you.

Trouble was, I overslept. And then I forgot that my watch was running slow. Even so, I probably would have had plenty of time to collect my things and get out before you got there. You never in your life arrived one second early for your eight o'clock class. Except on that particular morning . . .

I got to the office, quickly packed my briefcase, and was ready to leave. Felt suddenly a little sad, like I sensed an unhappy ending. Reached for a cigarette. Had forgotten. Remembered you kept a pack somewhere in your desk. Went and sat in your chair to rummage and find . . . one cigarette, that's all. Among some papers a glossy shine, the edges of some photographs caught my eye. Took a look. Some pleasant Polaroid shots of Geraldine. Flipped through the pictures. Whoa, there. Flash of flesh! Geraldine in buff, inimitable birthday suit, taking various and sundry poses. Pretty good horn shots. A natural model. Couldn't help looking, Ray. Once I found them, I mean. Admittedly, it was wrong to poke around in your desk drawers like that. But I found them only by accident.

I thought maybe I would take one, just for a souvenir, so to speak. Which one? Preoccupied, I spread the pictures across top of desk to pick and choose. Put one in my pocket. Figured the next time I was with Geraldine I'd show it to her. Tell her you sold it to me for two dollars. Geraldine sometimes a very gullible person. I was sitting there laughing out loud imagining the possibilities of that scene when you walked in on me.

I was not laughing at you or Geraldine.

Intended to put pictures back where I found them and leave.

Unfortunately, with pictures in hand like a hand of cards, I never had a chance. You came in and made your own erroneous inferences.

You threw your attaché case at me.

Started around the desk after me. I went under the desk, diving and crawling, and made it to the hall. Hall full of students going to class. Bells ringing to add to confusion. I staggered into wall across the way, caught myself, and turned around. You gave me mouthful of knuckles and my head banged hard against wall. Saw pinwheels and stars of light. Trying to duck and to keep from falling. Second blow grazing my ear and side of head.

Bent over, I started to come up with a punch. Then realized I was still holding on to the photographs. Checked my swing. From my position—please try and see it from my point of view—I was helpless. Head ringing, mouth and lips bleeding. All I could see was your two legs firmly planted, solid and set to hit me again. What could I do?

I swear to God, Ray, I never meant to kick you in your bad leg. Second, and by the same highest authority, with my head and eyes down I never even saw that the students had grabbed you and were holding you. Not until you yelled from the pain and fell to the floor. By then it was too late for anything.

I hurled the pictures away and ran off to the parking lot.

Ray, I doubt that you ever fully understood about your unpleasant interview with President Butterman. Objectively speaking, I don't look too good on that one. And I'll be the first one to admit it.

The thing is, the mitigating circumstance, I was desperate. I checked with old Butterman's secretary, Grace. Remember Grace? Not bad; not good-looking; high-spirited and eager to compensate for her lack of beauty by energy, activity, and a sense of adventure. She always responded with enthusiasm and took my intentions for exactly what they were—polite and strictly political. Within those rational limits we got to be good friends.

Grace told me that I didn't have a prayer. She said Butterball was planning to drop me anyway because I still didn't have my Ph.D. She also told me that Butterass hadn't decided what he was going to do about you. You had about an even chance to be allowed to stay on. There were some advantages for him if he did that. For one thing, he would have you permanently over a barrel if not in it. He would have another grateful slave on the faculty.

I want you to know that it was more to wipe that possum grin off his ugly face than to hurt you personally that I did what I did.

Grace told me your appointment was set for Friday afternoon. That gave me some time. I typed the letter over at her place, and then she drove me down to the P.O. so I could mail it off Special Delivery. I have found that many people are inclined to attach an undue importance, certainly a significance which is not intrinsic, to the fact that a letter arrives by Special Delivery.

I'd rather not quote it or fake it, if you don't mind. A confession doesn't have to be completely embarrassing to be efficacious, does it? Indirect discourse will have to suffice.

I said to Butterworth that much as an apology seemed to be called for in view of my unseemly behavior, much as good manners and, yea, even honest self-interest demanded of me at least a measure of regret, a show of repentance and contrition, yet I had no intention of so honoring him. As far as I was concerned he could stick it up his ass now and forever after. That the only time I ever wanted to see his name again was when I would read his obituary. Which, statistically speaking and barring unforeseen accidents and the whims of Fortune, I would almost certainly live to read and enjoy. However, I continued, I would like to do him one last favor before I faded from the scene at John Wesley. I would like for him to know something he really ought to know, lest he should mistakenly misinterpret the Geraldine Wadley Caper and surmise that it must be a one-shot misfired adultery, chiefly distinguished by its comic elements, and very unlikely to recur. Lest he, like stupid, well-meaning Raymond Wadley himself, might reach the conclusion that a single and wholly exceptional infidelity, nipped in the bud, so to speak, might, in the manner of some broken bones, not only heal, but also weld the original union more firmly than before. Geraldine, I hastened to assure him, was no character out of conventional women's magazine fiction. More likely out of Olympia Press.

I then made a list of fourteen members of the faculty who I knew for a certainty had, at one time or another during the current academic year, had one or more rolls in the hay with the aforesaid lovely Geraldine, adding that the list was woefully incomplete, since I did not choose to include members of the Athletic Department, the coaching staff; nor did I wish even to venture even a guess as to whether the entire football team or only the starting lineup had so indulged. Furthermore, I added, in the case of undergraduates, it was practically a professional venture on Geraldine's part. I wished only to call attention to the amateur amatory activities of this charming faculty wife. However, should he wish to check through his sources and spies, his undergraduate stoolies, he might well inquire whether or not a number of compromising photos, not at all unlike the enclosed, of the aforesaid Geraldine Wadley were not at this very moment in well-thumbed circulation in dormitories and frat houses.

I added that I was doing him a hell of a big favor because with a piece of nymphomaniacal dynamite like that in his already partially corrupted University community, a scandal of really major proportions was, by all odds, likely. And the only reason I was doing this was that when it did hit the fan and nothing at John Wesley was left spic and span, he would have no bitch or whine or hand-wringing coming, and I should be entitled to laugh my ass off at his acute discomfort. . . .

By Friday when you appeared, innocent enough, in your best dark suit, with all the dignity an aggrieved cuckold can muster, you had already had the ax, just like me, only you didn't know it. Not knowing any of these things, you must have wondered at the ease and audacity with which he simply fired you. You had probably prepared yourself against the eventuality of being told that you would not be promoted or, even, if worse came to worst, being told that at the conclusion of the current academic year your services would no longer be needed. But—virtually unheard of!—to be fired on the spot. And not gently, but curtly and gruffly. And for what? For "moral turpitude." That old bugaboo, define it as you will, like "incompetence." Defined in this case, neatly and irrevocably, as attacking with fisticuffs a fellow member of the faculty—*in the presence of students!* Never mind why. There is no sufficient cause or justification. For, even should violence have been a legitimate response to whatever wrong Mr. Towne may have done you, it should never, ever have taken place on University property and in the presence of students. Therefore he had no alternative, as chief administrator of this institution, save that of asking you to leave quietly and without untoward theatrics or rancor; for surely you must acknowledge the justice of his decision? Adding that it might well serve your self-interest to accept this verdict gracefully in view of the fact that every time you applied for a job in the academic world in the future, or for that matter in any other field of endeavor, the matter would sooner or later come up and he, Butterman, would be asked confidentially for an explanation of the details and for an evaluation of the man, you, Raymond Wadley. He, Butterman, would then be personally grateful if, upon leaving this office and this campus, you, Wadley, would demonstrate those qualities of patience and fortitude he knew you to possess at your best moments. Your resigned acceptance and self-control would be matched, he promised you, by a willingness on his part to forgive, forget, and to do everything in his not altogether inconsiderable power to assure you a decent second chance in the academic world. In fact, as a token of his faith in your ability to rise above this one surprising lapse, he was willing even now to get on the phone to a friend of his, the Chancellor of a small but honorable agricultural and mechanical institution in South Dakota, and arrange for a job for you there, perhaps at a slight, temporary reduction of salary, but money isn't everything and we all have to tighten our belts and put our shoulders to the wheel from time to time, nobody being perfect. . . .

According to Grace you shook hands with him, gratefully, Ray, tears in your eyes. And he walked you out of the office, the reception room, and the building, briskly to be sure, but with his arm around your shoulder like a real pal.

By Friday night, thanks to her many friends and my many enemies (plus, I guess, my own track record, which helped to impose a certain pattern on the circumstantial evidence), Annie had pretty well figured out everything that happened. At least she knew all she wanted to know.

"You are no damn good, rotten to the core," she told me. "It is bad enough, by all known standards, to fuck your friends' wives. But you don't stop even there. You have to find a way to fuck your friends too."

I had time to get in only one good solid slap across her face when the phone started ringing. She ran to answer it. I lit a cigarette and stood there trying to think of the proper rare quixotic gesture which would work as an effective apology when Annie came back, rubbing the side of her face and looking furious.

"That was Geraldine."

"Geraldine who?"

"Women can be a problem," she said. "They tend to get involved in spite of themselves."

"Oh goddamn . . . !"

"Are you going to beat her up too?"

Bad scene, Ray. Boring and bad. Best I could hope for from then on was a reconciliation. Fall-back position was "a few days for both of us to think it over and sort things out." Which I got. We agreed to separate for a while, beginning the next morning. I could take the car and go somewhere. She was quite comfortable at home, thank you.

Saturday morning I drove out to the Finlandia Sauna. Ready to sweat until I became a pure spirit and could vanish or fly away. There was one of the college wagons parked out there, but it meant nothing to me. I figured a couple of coaches had come to bake out the Friday-night booze. I undressed, noticing some clothes on a hanger but not paying any attention to them either. Grabbed a towel from the stack and slipped into that dry, hot, wonderful, wood-smelling, low-ceilinged little room. Parked my butt gingerly on a hot bench, sweating already, before I looked up and saw you. I must have jumped and started to get out of the room by instant reflex.

"Aw, sit down, Jack," you said. "Can you think of anything sillier than a couple of old crocks like us fighting it out, bare-ass, in a sauna bath?"

"It's my nerves, Ray," I told you. "I guess I just can't take it like I used to. It's been a rough week. Let's see . . . I lost my job and my best friend and I'm about to lose my wife and kids. Old age, Ray. A few years ago I could have taken it with a shrug. Now it kind of smarts."

Well, it was, for an hour or so, like old times. We sweated a lot. We had a few inconsequential laughs. We even stopped at a place down the road on the way back to town and drank a couple of beers together. Nothing like a freezing cold can of beer after you've had a sauna bath.

It was then, with the two of us sitting in the Wesley wagon, drinking beer, that you told me how you and Geraldine had agreed it was better to break up for keeps. You were very calm and sensible about it. She would go off and visit her Aunt Clara this weekend, leaving you time to pack up your things and anything else you felt you wanted. All she wanted was the little red Triumph. Which is why, of course, you were driving the Wesley wagon.

We finished our beers. Shook hands and said good-bye. You drove off to pack up. And I drove to Boston to be Geraldine's Aunt Clara for the rest of the weekend.

We had a wild weekend. Never left the hotel room. Couldn't break it off until Tuesday. (Or maybe, I think now, she may have planned it that way, to give you a whole extra day in the empty, lonely house in case you changed your mind.) We got back to your house after dark. She went in first to look around. Came to the doorway and motioned me to come on inside.

"He left everything!" she said. "All he took with him was his own clothes."

"Oh yeah?"

"I was afraid he would take the TV or the stereo or something, just for spite. But he didn't. It proves I'm right."

"About what?"

"About people," she said. "Trust them and give them freedom and responsibility and they do the right thing almost every time."

"It just proves Ray is a good guy."

"He's a sweetie pie," she said. "Just a sweetie pie."

I grabbed her up in my arms and carried her, laughing and kicking, into the bedroom. Dropped her on top of the bed. Started pulling and peeling her clothes off.

"As I was saying here the last time when we were rudely interrupted . . ."

That seemed to amuse her. Still, Geraldine made me turn the photograph of you, which was on the bureau, to face the wall. That girl was not without a certain sensitivity.

Since folly is, in fact, the subject of this little true confession, I would be lying, Ray, if I didn't say to you that you were a damn fool to do what you did. That fact in no way mitigates my own folly or lessens my need for confession. But goddamn it, Ray, I have been terribly hurt by what you chose to do. Ever since. Did you stop to consider the possible effect on Geraldine and me? Or on other people? If you didn't, you damn well should have. And if you did, then anything you may have hoped to achieve has been deeply undermined by the punitive and vindictive nature of your action.

I refuse to let guilt cripple me. Sure, I have gone right ahead making a wake of mischief behind me, getting into trouble and out of it, goofing off and fouling up. Just like I did before then. And like I guess I am bound to keep on doing for as long as I live. For better or worse. I am the same person. But nothing has ever been quite the same since then.

It must have been around two in the morning when I woke up and wanted a smoke. Out of matches. Geraldine got up, slipped on a robe, and went into the kitchen to fix us something to drink. We looked everywhere for matches. No luck.

"Try the basement," she said. "We used to keep some down there in case that damned old hot-water heater conked out."

I tried the light, but the bulb was out. Stumbled down dark stairs and felt my way toward the hot-water heater. Stubbed my toes on something hard. Felt it in the dark. Felt and hefted it. And then the other one right beside it. Both of them heavy.

"Geraldine," I called. "He left his suitcases in the basement."

I groped in the dark, trying to find the heater and the matches.

"Jack?"

I looked back and saw her framed in the doorway, backlit by light from the hallway.

"Did you say he left his suitcases down there?"

"I believe so. Wait till I light a match."

"I wonder why he did a thing like that?"

"Wait until I can see something . . ."

Ray, I already knew as clearly as if I had seen it in noon sunlight. But I was praying my mind's eye had deceived me this time. I found the matches. They were damp. The first couple wouldn't strike.

"I'll go find a flashlight," she said.

"Just a minute."

The third match caught and flared. I held it up. There were the two suitcases all right. And there, too, over in the corner just before the match went out, there you were. Sprawled and lying in the corner like a broken doll.

"Is he still alive?"

"I don't think so," I said. "Go get that light and I'll take a good look."

While she hunted for the flashlight I came back up and swallowed the drink she had fixed. She gave the light to me and I was sent down again. Ray, you and I both have seen our share of blood and gore in the wars. So I wasn't worried about having to look at a stiff. After a time you learn that the only blood and gore you are entitled to feel anything about is your own. I put the light right on you, Ray.

"He's been dead quite a while," I said.

You had done a job of it, taking half of your face and head. You had, evidently, sat down in a little deck chair, which lay nearby, taken that pistol of yours, and put it in your mouth. And then at some point, early or late, you pulled the trigger. Very brave, in a way. Because there is always the chance that you'll live. I couldn't do it that way, myself, Ray, not with a pistol. For fear I might flinch or twitch and botch it. I stood there looking at you, admiring your courage. On the floor, bloodstained (oh there was plenty of that), there was a framed portrait photograph of her. You must have been holding it in your free hand when you pulled the trigger.

"Is there a note? Do you see a note anywhere?"

Geraldine was right beside me, her face pale and drawn in hard, tight lines of shock. She looked old, Ray, hard and old. I could see what she was going to look like in twenty years. Or less.

"I don't see anything. Maybe he left one some place else in the house."

"Maybe . . ." Then she said, "I wonder if his life insurance has a suicide clause."

She turned back to the stairs and started up slowly.

"That was the only good . . . the only really good picture I ever had taken in my whole life," she said. "And he ruined it."

"I doubt if he wanted to."

"Want! Want!" she shouted at me. "He never knew what he wanted!"

By then she was sobbing and I was sick. Vomiting all over the basement. Puking my guts out. I couldn't cry. But my stomach, the seat of truth, reacted for me. Not out of squeamishness and not even from shame. Not then, not yet. But from sorrow. And not just sorrow for you, but for the three of us. For all of us. For Annie and the children. For all the children you would never have. For scratchy towels and big soft fluffy ones. For television and stitchery. . .

I kept on vomiting until I had the dry heaves. Until there was nothing left to come up. Then I was over it. I went and sat in the kitchen and discussed calling the police. She wanted me to leave first, but I explained that within five minutes they would know I had been there anyway and then there would be some bad trouble.

"He's been dead since sometime Saturday, Sunday at the latest," I said. "That's my guess. We can prove we were in Boston together, and it's clearly a suicide. If we tell the truth, we'll be all right."

She didn't like it, but she agreed. And so the cops came and went, and then the undertaker came and went. By which time it was already full daylight. She fixed breakfast. Oddly, we were both hungry.

"I'm leaving," she said. "I'll get the movers to come later and pack everything up."

"What about the funeral?"

"I told the man I want him cremated."

"I've got to finish out the rest of the semester."

"I know," she said. "It won't look right if you don't. I'll be in touch as soon as I'm settled somewhere."

I just nodded.

"You got a garden hose that will reach down there?"

She pointed to the front yard. I went outside, hooked two sections of hose together, screwed on the nozzle, and then brought it down into the basement. Then went back up and turned the water on. Then back down again.

That's the last thing I ever did for you, Ray. Hose the remaining stains of you, and my vomit, too, off the wall and the floor and down the floor drain. It was clean and drying fast when I left.

There was no note. At least nobody ever found one.

That might have been better, after all. A crazy note. Or a raging note. Or a self-pitying one. Even some heartbreaking and silly message. But you left it all to the imagination. You left each of us, separate and equal, to live with the blank cruelty of it always. Which may have been right and even just, but which was also unforgivable.

Well, I am ready to forgive you for that, Ray.

If St. Augustine is right (and it almost always turns out that he is), the dead have neither interest in nor concern for the living. The dead do not care any more. Finally they are careless. Which means I don't have to ask your forgiveness, too.

But, alive, I am able to forgive you. Not out of my own guilt. If I were ever to entertain guilt seriously, I would join you among the indifferent dead. Not from any guilt, but because forgiveness is the one free act of human love that is still possible for me. Not that people can ever really completely forgive each other. But in the ritual of wishing to and trying to forgive one another, in ceasing to judge one another and leaving Judgment to its proper Author, then for a brief moment we can find and feel the secret energy of divinity in us.

Forgiveness is a simple and glorious act of human freedom. Suicide and lunacy are not. Sartre and Camus were full of shit.

You think I'm too serious all of a sudden? Well, you're right, old buddy. Right about that, anyway.

GEORGE GARRETT DISCUSSES

"A Record as Long as Your Arm," plot, and the angel he must wrestle

PM: When you start to write, do you like to know where you're going, or do you prefer to be surprised?

GG: I like surprise both for me and for the reader. I want (to use Keats's term) to surprise by a fine excess.

For the purpose of surprising myself, it is my habit, for the most part, to write without a clear and present notion of the ending until I am suddenly there. Then, and only then, I will go back and try to make the parts assemble to ask for and create that ending. I like to think that even after a story has been "fixed," my own original sense of discovery will somehow be communicated and create some suspense in the story. Honestly, I didn't know Ray was dead until Towne found him there in the basement. I was probably more surprised than Towne.

PM: How did you decide when to reveal that?

GG: I wanted, if possible, to hold off on that news until near the end. Ideally, it should then "change" the whole story for a reader.

PM: "A Record . . ." begins very much in the middle. How did you decide on your starting point?

GG: The starting point seemed natural to me and, maybe more, to Towne—a "grabber." Guy caught with pants down. An away-we-go opening.

PM: That opening scene also happens to have more dramatic intensity than any other in the story (until we discover the body). In the ebb after that initial crisis, the many plot complications incrementally build again in intensity.

GG: Once I had decided it would end with Ray dead I knew I would have to end it with a strong scene. It would have to be intense. So all I knew and all I needed to know was that it must steadily and gradually turn up the heat.

PM: You seem to have taken to heart Chekhov's advice (that a weapon mentioned in Act I should fire in Act III) by mentioning Ray's gun repeatedly and in some depth early in the story—without it seeming in the least like a setup. What's the trick to pulling that off?

GG: I think the trick, if it works, is the addition of lots of little turns and details as diversions from the algebraic working out of the plot. Take the sauna scene, for instance. The scene itself is in part a kind of diversion. Just so, a detail like the broken hot-water heater and search for matches. Perfectly logical, but at the same time a kind of distraction or diversion. I mean, Towne could just as well have had some matches or a cigarette lighter, but I wanted to build some suspense. Can he strike and light damp matches?

PM: That steambath/bar scene near the end provides a classic calm-before-the-storm moment of relief.

GG: I needed a calm scene and one in which we could believe that Ray and Towne had actually been friends.

It is a scene lifted from "real life." A couple of my colleagues once had a fistfight in a sauna. Nobody knew exactly why, but everybody had a story to go with it. Most presumed they were fighting over some woman. For years afterward I wanted to do a story or maybe a little one-act play about two naked guys duking it out in a sauna. One discovers that the other one has been screwing his wife or girlfriend. I "lifted" it for "Record" and then turned it inside out. I guess you might say, if you wanted to, that the "real" fistfight was the source of the whole story.

One thing more for the record (as long as what?): The story, "Record," is composed of the first and the last scenes of my huge and unfinished novel, *Life with Kim Novak Is Hell.* The novel is in the form of a very long letter from Towne to Ray, maybe written or maybe merely imagined.

PM: Towne also shows up in some of your other published works. When did you first come up with this guy?

GG: I'm not sure exactly. Thanks to a young scholar-critic named Casey Claybough, who is working on a book about my fiction, I now know Towne first appears, or is mentioned by name anyway, as a fishing-tackle salesman who ran off with somebody's wife in the short story "A Game of Catch," which first appeared in the *Transatlantic Review* in 1960. Since then Towne has appeared in any number of shapes and forms, versions and variations. Call him a protean type. He is even mentioned in my Elizabethan trilogy as an actor in *Entered from the Sun*. Turns out there really was an actor named John Towne in the late sixteenth century. I found his name on several cast lists and took it for a sign.

From the beginning, there were always two kinds of Towne characters, not a "good" one or a "bad" one, but one who is more or less realistic, subject to cause and effect and the ravages of time. This one, the one in "Record," is sane enough not to think of himself as a character in a story being composed by somebody else. The other one, like his shadow or twin, believes that he is no more or no less than a character in a work of fiction.

One thing more. The name itself was borrowed, stolen from one of my favorite uncles, a professional dancer who danced as Chester Towne.

PM: Towne seems like a kind of Mr. Hyde to your Dr. Jekyll: you both have degrees from Princeton, both confess a deep and knowledgeable respect for St. Augustine and a belief in the divine nature of forgiveness, and both display a penchant for writing acerbic letters to celebrities. So setting aside your many and presumably larger differences, what accounts for those similarities and your compulsion to explore them?

GG: I believe my connection with the Towne character begins from the fact that I had a brother, not a twin, who was born sometime before I was and who died in infancy. For a long time, until I learned that fact, I felt a deep sense of absence in my life as well as a strange rivalry, as if my brother were truly a twin and we were somehow a variation on the Jacob and Esau story. Jacob, the trickster, has long fascinated me, and I have written about him in poems. But in a sense, by concentrating on Jacob, I have moved away from the story of rivalry and focused more on another aspect—Jacob, and how he wrestled with an angel in the dark at a river's edge and thereby earned a new name and identity. In a sense he became for me a figure for the artist who must descend into the darkest part of the self and there kill a monster or wrestle an imaginary angel to be reborn and gain a true identity. In most myths of this action there is a guide—Virgil for Dante. But if you replace Virgil with John Towne, you end up with comedy, and not a divine one. I reckon then that Towne becomes the monster I must kill and the angel (some angel!) I must wrestle. Sometimes he wins and sometimes I do.

PM: In your 1986 meta-fictional novel *Poison Pen* we are told that after Towne's affair with Geraldine, both couples got divorced. That's quite an alternative scenario to Ray killing himself. Which idea came first? Which do you prefer? And how would you like a reader to think about their mutual existence?

GG: I really and truly don't know how to answer this one. It wasn't an accident, happy or otherwise, but I do think it was typical of Towne to give us two or more versions of the same event, always depending on context. Those readers who happen to notice may have a little fun, may even (as I often allow myself to hope) add their own narrative to my version. I believe that half or more of the value of a work of fiction is the engagement of the reader. Preference? I prefer suicide in the short story, divorce in the novel.

PM: "Plot" sometimes gets a bad rap in quality fiction. What's its proper role?

GG: Some stories, particularly but not only genre stories, have built in plenty of suspense and action, and the job of the writer in that case (and yes, I have done some of this in film and TV scripts, for example) is to be as deftly transparent as possible, to be clear and keep things rolling and try your level best not to get in the way of the material of the story. Let the inherent suspense of the plot and story carry you like a breaking wave. Most "literary" stories lack that built-in suspense and drive. They are constructed from exploration and revelation (as in a striptease) of character, on the investigation of traditional or original themes and on the power and glory of language itself. "Record" is, I hope, a hybrid, a shotgun-wedding-of-a-plot story and literary story.

PM: Much of "Record" plays like farce. Could plot ever assume such a dominant role in a literary story that is more conventionally dramatic?

GG: I like the balance of farce and pathos, but the same story could have been told (with different results) leaning more one way or the other. Sure, plot could assume such a dominant role if, for example, we had opened the story with the discovery of Ray's body, and then the story became a how-did-all-this-come-to-happen tale. Same events but completely different tone. Think about it.

PM: The affair and suicide, absolutely. The misidentified cars crisscrossing one another, for example, a little harder to imagine maybe.

One of the story's strengths and pleasures, in its farce mode, is the way it deliberately calls attention to some of the more contorted bits of choreography. Other than humor, what were you trying to achieve with that self-referential device?

GG: It always interests me in any story to try to discover the relationship of the teller to the tale. I think of this as the man behind the curtain, the Wizard of Oz. Do we get to see him in action or not? The eccentricity of "Record" is that here are two tellers, myself and Towne, each sharing some disguised common characteristics, each one eager to shuck personal responsibility by means of "contorted choreography," both trying, then, in various ways to emphasize the artificiality of the story so as to escape judgment. That probably doesn't make much sense and sounds a lot more serious that it is or ought to be. Most of this I didn't think about at the time of writing. I started things moving and then had to run to catch up with myself.

PM: You include background info about the characters *very* economically; pretty much only as it pertains to each emerging plot development. Is that your standard approach in short story writing?

GG: I knew one thing for sure. "Record" had to get going quickly and then keep moving if it were going to work at all. There could be, and are, different timing and pacing within the story, but it must not look back on itself too much. Another story might need much more background information and detail. Not this one. Is this a habit of mine? I hope not. I aim to do each story as something different from all the others, so that each time I step up to the plate I will face a new and different challenge.

PM: In general, the kind of economy of exposition you employ in "Record" does seem to have become a general feature of contemporary short story writing. Any thoughts about the merits or limits of that?

GG: The strictly economical story is certainly a trend in contemporary American fiction. It was bound to happen as we kept trying to get more and more life into the tight little space of the short story form. That interests me a lot, but right now I am more interested in something else—the small story, writ large, adding to it precisely the things that are usually expendable in the name of economy. I don't see anybody else doing this, though the novella seems to be a form that interests a lot of good people.

PM: What if anything about "Record" might you have done differently were you to write it today?

GG: If I wrote "Record" today, chances are, besides some reflexive cutting and polishing, I would add some more details of the specific time, the good and bad news of the world. Not for any good reason, really, but just because the clash of private and public life is what interests me a lot these days.

PM: Your attraction to "Christian" themes has been noted, and this story is certainly a good example. Are you religious person?

GG: I was raised in the church (Episcopal) and in fact did the whole thing—acolyte, crucifer, lay reader, chalice bearer. Have even preached a few sermons, but it's been a good while since I went to church (my wife goes regularly). I like to think of myself sometimes as a twelfth-century Christian, an Augustinian. I also like to imagine myself as a member-in-good-standing of the tribe of Chaucer. But my religious beliefs are constantly challenged and changing.

PM: Towne's compulsion to confess seems to contrast with Geraldine's less-examined response to guilt. Is Towne redeemable as a sinner? Does "A Record . . . " make that argument?

GG: Here is (maybe) where my religious beliefs do come to bear somewhat. Towne is certainly redeemable. He can't forgive himself, of course, not really. None of us can. But God, by definition, can forgive anybody for anything. That's not the argument of "Record," however.

PM: What do sermon writing and story writing have in common?

GG: The best sermons I have ever heard or read are built around some kind of narrative line and are usually based on the text of some parable. The tradition of the parable—Judaic, Christian, Augustinian—is at the heart of all Western literature. My stories are not sermons. I am not preaching or teaching, but I am certainly trying to tell a meaningful story.

PM: Who influenced you the most as a writer?

GG: If we listed writers, I could fill up your book with the names. I read a lot, all the time, indiscriminately, and everything influences me one way or the other. But let's limit it to people, to my family: my grandfather, Colonel Toomer, who was a great storyteller; some writers in the family on both sides, for example Harry Stillwell Edwards of Macon, Georgia, on my mother's side of the family, or Oliver H. P. Garrett, an Academy Award-winning screenwriter, on my father's side. These two men were glamorous and made the writer's line of work look like a lot of fun. Above all, my father, who started me "writing" before I could read or write, by patiently encouraging me to dictate stories and poems to him. And then, when I could read, he gave me the huge benefit of a houseful of good books. I owe so much to him and to many others. The best I can do in response is to pass it on to others. As John Berryman wrote (in "Homage to Mistress Bradstreet"): "We are on each other's hands who care."

Author of thirty-two books and editor or co-editor of nineteen others, **GEORGE GARRETT** recently retired from the University of Virginia after a forty-year teaching career. Among his honors and awards are the Rome Prize of the American Academy of Arts and Letters, fellowships from the Guggenheim, Ford, and Rockefeller foundations and the National Endowment for the Arts, the T. S. Eliot Award of the Ingersoll Foundation, the Aiken Taylor Award for Modern American Poetry, the PEN/Malamud Award for Excellence in Short Fiction, and the Cleanth Brooks Medal for Lifetime Achievement. He and his wife live in Charlottesville, Virginia.

[illegible]

[illegible]

POINT OF VIEW/VOICE

CHINA

Charles Johnson

CONDOLENCES TO EVERY ONE OF US

Allan Gurganus

CHINA

Charles Johnson

Evelyn's problems with her husband, Rudolph, began one evening in early March—a dreary winter evening in Seattle—when he complained after a heavy meal of pig's feet and mashed potatoes of shortness of breath, an allergy to something she put in his food perhaps, or brought on by the first signs of wild flowers around them. She suggested they get out of the house for the evening, go to a movie. He was fifty-four, a postman for thirty-three years now, with high blood pressure, emphysema, flat feet, and, as Evelyn told her friend Shelberdine Lewis, the lingering fear that he had cancer. Getting old, he was also getting hard to live with. He told her never to salt his dinners, to keep their Lincoln Continental at a crawl, and never run her fingers along his inner thigh when they sat in Reverend William Merrill's church, because anything, even sex, or laughing too loud—Rudolph was serious—might bring on heart failure.

So she chose for their Saturday night outing a peaceful movie, a mildly funny comedy a *Seattle Times* reviewer said was fit only for titters and nasal snorts, a low-key satire that made Rudolph's eyelids droop as he shoveled down unbuttered popcorn in the darkened, half-empty theater. Sticky fluids cemented Evelyn's feet to the floor. A man in the last row laughed at all the wrong places. She kept the popcorn on her lap, though she hated the unsalted stuff and wouldn't touch it, sighing as Rudolph pawed across her to shove his fingers inside the cup.

She followed the film as best she could, but occasionally her eyes frosted over, flashed white. She went blind like this now and then. The fibers of her eyes were failing; her retinas were tearing like soft tissue. At these times the world was a canvas with whiteout spilling from the far left corner toward the center; it was the sudden shock of an empty frame in a series of slides. Someday, she knew, the snow on her eyes would stay. Winter eternally: her eyes split like her walking stick. She groped along the fractured surface, waiting for her sight to thaw, listening to the film she couldn't see. Her only comfort was knowing that, despite her infirmity, her Rudolph was in even worse health.

He slid back and forth from sleep during the film (she elbowed him occasionally, or pinched his leg), then came full awake, sitting up suddenly when the movie ended and a "Coming Attractions" trailer began. It was some sort of gladiator movie, Evelyn thought, blinking, and it was pretty trashy stuff at that. The plot's revenge theme was a poor excuse for Chinese actors or Japanese (she couldn't tell those people apart) to flail the air with their hands and feet, take on fifty costumed extras at once, and leap twenty feet through the air in perfect defiance of gravity. Rudolph's mouth hung open.

"Can people really do that?" He did not take his eyes off the screen, but talked at her from the right side of his mouth. "Leap that high?"

"It's a *movie*," sighed Evelyn. "A *bad* movie."

He nodded, then asked again, "But can they?"

"Oh, Rudolph, for God's sake!" She stood up to leave, her seat slapping back loudly. "They're on *trampolines!* You can see them in the corner—there!—if you open your eyes!"

He did see them, once Evelyn twisted his head to the lower left corner of the screen, and it seemed to her that her husband looked disappointed—looked, in fact, the way he did the afternoon Dr. Guylee told Rudolph he'd developed an extrasystolic reaction, a faint, moaning sound from his heart whenever it relaxed. He said no more and, after the trailer finished, stood—there was chewing gum stuck to his trouser seat—dragged on his heavy coat with her help, and followed Evelyn up the long, carpeted aisle, through the exit of the Coronet Theater, and to their car. He said nothing as she chattered on the way home, reminding him that he could not stay up all night puttering in his basement shop because the next evening they were to attend the church's revival meeting.

Rudolph, however, did not attend the revival. He complained after lunch of a light, dancing pain in his chest, which he had conveniently whenever Mount Zion Baptist Church held revivals, and she went alone, sitting with her friend Shelberdine, a beautician. She was forty-one; Evelyn, fifty-two. That evening, Evelyn wore spotless white gloves, tan therapeutic stockings for the swelling in her ankles, and a white dress that brought out nicely the brown color of her skin, the most beautiful cedar brown, Rudolph said when they were courting thirty-five years ago in South Carolina. But then Evelyn had worn a matching checkered skirt and coat to meeting. With her jet black hair pinned behind her neck by a simple wooden comb, she looked as if she might have been Andrew Wyeth's starkly beautiful model for *Day of the Fair.* Rudolph, she remembered, wore black business suits, black ties, black wing tips, but he also wore white gloves because he was a senior usher—this was how she first noticed him. He was one of four young men dressed like deacons (or blackbirds), their left hands tucked into the hollow of their backs, their right carrying silver plates for the offering as they marched in almost military fashion down each aisle: Christian soldiers, she'd thought, the cream of black manhood, and to get his attention she placed not her white envelope or coins in Rudolph's plate but instead a note that said: "You have a beautiful smile." It was, for all her innocence, a daring thing to do, according to Evelyn's mother—flirting with a randy young man like Rudolph Lee Jackson, but he did have nice, tigerish teeth. A killer smile, people called it, like all the boys in the Jackson family: a killer smile and good hair that needed no more than one stroke of his palm to bring out Quo Vadis rows pomaded sweetly with the scent of Murray's.

And of course, Rudolph was no dummy. Not a total dummy, at least. He pretended nothing extraordinary had happened as the congregation left the little whitewashed church. He stood, the youngest son, between his father and mother, and let old Deacon Adcock remark, "Oh, how strong he's looking now," which was a lie. Rudolph was the weakest of the Jackson boys, the pale, bookish, spiritual child born when his parents were well past forty. His brothers played football, they went into the navy; Rudolph lived in Scripture, was labeled 4-F, and hoped to attend Moody Bible Institute in Chicago, if he could ever find the money. Evelyn could tell Rudolph knew exactly where she was in the crowd, that he could feel her as she and her sister, Debbie, waited for their father to bring his DeSoto—the family prize—closer to the front steps. When the crowd thinned, he shambled over in his slow ministerial walk, introduced himself, and unfolded her note.

"You write this?" he asked. "It's not right to play with the Lord's money, you know."

"I like to play," she said.

"You do, huh?" He never looked directly at people. Women, she guessed, terrified him. Or, to be exact, the powerful emotions they caused in him terrified Rudolph. He was a pud puller, if she ever saw one. He kept his eyes on a spot left of her face. "You're Joe Montgomery's daughter, aren't you?"

"Maybe," teased Evelyn.

He trousered the note and stood marking the ground with his toe. "And just what you expect to get, Miss Playful, by fooling with people during collection time?"

She waited, let him look away, and when the back-and-forth swing of his gaze crossed her again, said in her most melic, soft-breathing voice: *"You."*

Up front, portly Reverend Merrill concluded his sermon. Evelyn tipped her head slightly, smiling into memory; her hand reached left to pat Rudolph's leg gently; then she remembered it was Shelberdine beside her, and lifted her hand to the seat in front of her. She said a prayer for Rudolph's health, but mainly it was for herself, a hedge against her fear that their childless years had slipped by like wind, that she might return home one day and find him—as she had found her father—on the floor, bellied up, one arm twisted behind him where he fell, alone, his fingers locked against his chest. Rudolph had begun to run down, Evelyn decided, the minute he was turned down by Moody Bible Institute. They moved to Seattle in 1956—his brother Eli was stationed nearby and said Boeing was hiring black men. But they didn't hire Rudolph. He had kidney trouble on and off before he landed the job at the Post Office. Whenever he bent forward, he felt dizzy. Liver, heart, and lungs—they'd worn down gradually as his belly grew, but none of this was as bad as what he called "the Problem." His pecker shrank to no bigger than a pencil eraser each time he saw her undress. Or when Evelyn, as was her habit when talking, touched his arm. Was she the cause of this? Well, she knew she wasn't much to look at anymore. She'd seen the bottom of a few too many candy wrappers. Evelyn was nothing to make a man pant and jump her bones, pulling her fully clothed onto the davenport, as Rudolph had done years before, but wasn't sex something else you surrendered with age? It never seemed all that good to her anyway. And besides, he'd wanted oral sex, which Evelyn—if she knew nothing else—thought was a nasty, unsanitary thing to do with your mouth. She glanced up from under her spring hat past the pulpit, past the choir of black and brown faces to the agonized beauty of a bearded white carpenter impaled on a rood, and in this timeless image she felt comforted that suffering was inescapable, the loss of vitality inevitable, even a good thing maybe, and that she had to steel herself—yes—for someday opening her bedroom door and finding her Rudolph face down in his breakfast oatmeal. He would die before her, she knew that in her bones.

And so, after service, Sanka, and a slice of meat pie with Shelberdine downstairs in the brightly lit church basement, Evelyn returned home to tell her husband how lovely the Griffin girls had sung that day, that their neighbor Rod Kenner had been saved, and to listen, if necessary, to Rudolph's fear that the lump on his shoulder was an early-warning sign of something evil. As it turned out, Evelyn found that except for their cat, Mr. Miller, the little A-frame house was empty. She looked in his bedroom. No Rudolph. The unnaturally still house made Evelyn uneasy, and she took the excruciatingly painful twenty stairs into the basement to peer into a workroom littered with power tools, planks of wood, and the blueprints her husband used to make bookshelves and cabinets. No Rudolph. Frightened, Evelyn called the eight hospitals in Seattle, but no one had a Rudolph Lee Jackson on his books. After her last call the starburst clock in the living room read twelve-thirty. Putting down the wall phone, she felt a familiar pain in her abdomen. Another attack of Hershey squirts, probably from the meat pie. She hurried into the bathroom, lifted her skirt, and lowered her underwear around her ankles, but kept the door wide open, something impossible to do if Rudolph was home. Actually, it felt good not to have him underfoot, a little like he was dead already. But the last thing Evelyn wanted was that or, as she lay down against her lumpy backrest, to fall asleep, though she did, nodding off and dreaming until something shifted down her weight on the side of her bed away from the wall.

"Evelyn," said Rudolph, "look at this." She blinked back sleep and squinted at the cover of a magazine called *Inside Kung-Fu,* which Rudolph waved under her nose. On the cover a man stood bowlegged, one hand cocked under his armpit, the other corkscrewing straight at Evelyn's nose.

"Rudolph!" She batted the magazine aside, then swung her eyes toward the cluttered nightstand, focusing on the electric clock beside her water glass from McDonald's, Preparation H suppositories, and Harlequin romances. "It's morning!" Now she was mad. At least, working at it. "Where have you been?"

Her husband inhaled, a wheezing, whistlelike breath. He rolled the magazine into a cylinder and, as he spoke, struck his left palm with it. "That movie we saw advertised? You remember—it was called *The Five Fingers of Death.* I just saw that and one called *Deep Thrust.*"

"Wonderful." Evelyn screwed up her lips. "I'm calling hospitals and you're at a Hong Kong double feature."

"Listen," said Rudolph. "You don't understand." He seemed at that moment as if he did not understand either. "It was a Seattle movie premiere. The Northwest is crawling with fighters. It has something to do with all the Asians out here. Before they showed the movie, four students from a kwoon in Chinatown went onstage—"

"A what?" asked Evelyn.

"A kwoon—it's a place to study fighting, a meditation hall." He looked at her but was really watching, Evelyn realized, something exciting she had missed. "They did a demonstration to drum up their membership. They broke boards and bricks, Evelyn. They went through what's called kata and kumite and . . . " He stopped again to breathe. "I've never seen anything so beautiful. The reason I'm late is because I wanted to talk with them after the movie."

Evelyn, suspicious, took a Valium and waited.

"I signed up for lessons," he said.

She gave a glacial look at Rudolph, then at his magazine, and said in the voice she used five years ago when he wanted to take a vacation to Upper Volta or, before that, invest in a British car she knew they couldn't afford:

"You're fifty-*four* years old, Rudolph."

"I know that."

"You're no Muhammad Ali."

"I know that," he said.

"You're no Bruce Lee. Do you want to be Bruce Lee? Do you know where he is now, Rudolph? He'd dead—dead here in a Seattle cemetery and buried up on Capital Hill."

His shoulders slumped a little. Silently, Rudolph began undressing, his beefy backside turned toward her, slipping his pajama bottoms on before taking off his shirt so his scrawny lower body would not be fully exposed. He picked up his magazine, said, "I'm sorry if I worried you," and huffed upstairs to his bedroom. Evelyn clicked off the mushroom-shaped lamp on her nightstand. She lay on her side, listening to his slow footsteps strike the stairs, then heard his mattress creak above her—his bedroom was directly above hers—but she did not hear him click off his own light. From time to time she heard his shifting weight squeak the mattress springs. He was reading that foolish magazine, she guessed; then she grew tired and gave this impossible man up to God. With a copy of *The Thorn Birds* open on her lap, Evelyn fell heavily to sleep again.

At breakfast the next morning any mention of the lessons gave Rudolph lockjaw. He kissed her forehead, as always, before going to work, and simply said he might be home late. Climbing the stairs to his bedroom was painful for Evelyn, but she hauled herself up, pausing at each step to huff, then sat on his bed and looked over his copy of *Inside Kung-Fu.* There were articles on empty-hand combat, soft-focus photos of ferocious-looking men in funny suits, parables about legendary Zen masters, an interview with someone named Bernie Bernheim, who began to study karate at age fifty-seven and became a black belt at age sixty-one, and page after page of advertisements for exotic Asian weapons: nunchaku, shuriken, sai swords, tonfa, bo staffs, training bags of all sorts, a wooden dummy shaped like a man and called a Mook Jong, and weights. Rudolph had circled them all. He had torn the order form from the last page of the magazine. The total cost of the things he'd circled—Evelyn added them furiously, rounding off the figures—was $800.

Two minutes later she was on the telephone to Shelberdine.

"Let him tire of it," said her friend. "Didn't you tell me Rudolph had Lower Lombard Strain?"

Evelyn's nose clogged with tears.

"Why is he doing this? Is it me, do you think?"

"It's the Problem," said Shelberdine. "He wants his manhood back. Before he died, Arthur did the same. Someone at the plant told him he could get it back if he did twenty-yard sprints. He went into convulsions while running around the lake."

Evelyn felt something turn in her chest. "You don't think he'll hurt himself, do you?"

"Of course not."

"Do you think he'll hurt *me?*"

Her friend reassured Evelyn that Mid-Life Crisis brought out these shenanigans in men. Evelyn replied that she thought Mid-Life Crisis started around age forty, to which Shelberdine said, "Honey, I don't mean no harm, but Rudolph always was a little on the slow side," and Evelyn agreed. She would wait until he worked this thing out of his system, until Nature defeated him and he surrendered, as any right-thinking person would, to the breakdown of the body, the brutal fact of decay, which could only be blunted, it seemed to her, by decaying *with* someone, the comfort every Negro couple felt when, aging, they knew enough to let things wind down.

Her patience was rewarded in the beginning. Rudolph crawled home from his first lesson, hunched over, hardly able to stand, afraid he had permanently ruptured something. He collapsed face down on the living room sofa, his feet on the floor. She helped him change into his pajamas and fingered Ben-Gay into his back muscles. Evelyn had never seen her husband so close to tears.

"I can't *do* push-ups," he moaned. "Or sit-ups. I'm so stiff—I don't know my body." He lifted his head, looking up pitifully, his eyes pleading. "Call Dr. Guylee. Make an appointment for Thursday, okay?"

"Yes, dear." Evelyn hid her smile with one hand. "You shouldn't push yourself so hard."

At that, he sat up, bare-chested, his stomach bubbling over his pajama bottoms. "That's what it means. *Gung-fu* means 'hard work' in Chinese. Evelyn"—he lowered his voice—"I don't think I've ever really done hard work in my life. Not like this, something that asks me to give *every*thing, body and soul, spirit and flesh. I've always felt . . . " He looked down, his dark hands dangling between his thighs. "I've never been able to give *every*thing to *any*thing. The world never let me. It won't let me put all of myself into play. Do you know what I'm saying? Every job I've had, everything I've ever done, it only demanded part of me. It was like there was so much *more* of me that went unused after the job was over. I get that feeling in church sometimes." He lay back down, talking now into the sofa cushion. "Sometimes I get that feeling with you."

Her hand stopped on his shoulder. She wasn't sure she'd heard him right, his voice was so muffled. "That I've never used all of you?"

Rudolph nodded, rubbing his right knuckle where, at the kwoon, he'd lost a stretch of skin on a speedbag. "There's still part of me left over. You never tried to touch all of me, to take everything. Maybe you can't. Maybe no one can. But sometimes I get the feeling that the unused part—the unlived life—*spoils,* that you get cancer because it sits like fruit on the ground and rots." Rudolph shook his head; he'd said too much and knew it, perhaps had not even put it the way he felt inside. Stiffly, he got to his feet. "Don't ask me to stop training." His eyebrows spread inward. "If I stop, I'll die."

Evelyn twisted the cap back onto the Ben-Gay. She held out her hand, which Rudolph took. Veins on the back of his hand burgeoned abnormally like dough. Once when she was shopping at the Public Market she'd seen monstrous plastic gloves shaped like hands in a magic store window. His hand looked like that. It belonged on Lon Chaney. Her voice shook a little, panicky, "I'll call Dr. Guylee in the morning."

Evelyn knew—or thought she knew—his trouble. He'd never come to terms with the disagreeableness of things. Rudolph had always been too serious for some people, even in South Carolina. It was the thing, strange to say, that drew her to him, this crimped-browed tendency in Rudolph to listen with every atom of his life when their minister in Hodges, quoting Marcus Aurelius to give his sermon flash, said, "Live with the gods," or later in Seattle, the habit of working himself up over Reverend Merrill's reading from Ecclesiastes 9:10: "Whatsoever thy hand findeth to do, do it with all thy might." Now, he didn't *really* mean that, Evelyn knew. Nothing in the world could be taken that seriously; that's *why* this was the world. And, as all Mount Zion knew, Reverend Merrill had a weakness for high-yellow choir-girls and gin, and was forever complaining that his salary was too small for his family. People made compromises, nodded at spiritual commonplaces—the high seriousness of biblical verses that demanded nearly superhuman duty and self-denial—and laughed off their lapses into sloth, envy, and the other deadly sins. It was what made living so enjoyably *human:* this built-in inability of man to square his performance with perfection. People were naturally soft on themselves. But not her Rudolph.

Of course, he seldom complained. It was not in his nature to complain when, looking for "gods," he found only ruin and wreckage. What did he expect? Evelyn wondered. Man was evil—she'd told him that a thousand times—or, if not evil, hopelessly flawed. Everything failed; it was some sort of law. But at least there was laughter, and lovers clinging to one another against the cliff; there were novels—wonderful tales of how things should be—and perfection promised in the afterworld. He'd sit and listen, her Rudolph, when she put things this way, nodding because he knew that in his persistent hunger for perfection in the here and now he was, at best, in the minority. He kept his dissatisfaction to himself, but occasionally Evelyn would glimpse in his eyes that look, that distant, pained expression that asked: *Is this all?* She saw it after her first miscarriage, then her second; saw it when he stopped searching the want ads and settled on the Post Office as the fulfillment of his potential in the marketplace. It was always there, that look, after he turned forty, and no new, lavishly praised novel from the Book-of-the-Month Club, no feature-length movie, prayer meeting, or meal she fixed for him wiped it from Rudolph's eyes. He was, at least, this sort of man before he saw that martial-arts B movie. It was a dark vision, Evelyn decided, a dangerous vision, and in it she whiffed something that might destroy her. What that was, she couldn't say, but she knew her Rudolph better than he knew himself. He would see the error—the waste of time—in his new hobby, and she was sure he would mend his ways.

In the weeks, then months that followed Evelyn waited, watching her husband for a flag of surrender. There was no such sign. He became worse than before. He cooked his own meals, called her heavy soul food dishes "too acidic," lived on raw vegetables, seaweed, nuts, and fruit to make his body "more alkaline," and fasted on Sundays. He ordered books on something called Shaolin fighting and meditation from a store in California, and when his equipment arrived UPS from Dolan's Sports in New Jersey, he ordered more—in consternation, Evelyn read the list—leg stretchers, makiwara boards, air shields, hand grips, bokken, focus mitts, a full-length mirror (for heaven's sake) so he could correct his form, and protective equipment. For proper use of his headgear and gloves, however, he said he needed a sparring partner—an opponent—he said, to help him instinctively understand "combat strategy," how to "flow" and "close the Gap" between himself and an adversary, how to create by his movements a negative space in which the other would be neutralized.

"Well," crabbed Evelyn, "if you need a punching bag, don't look at *me.*"

He sat across the kitchen from her, doing dynamic-tension exercises as she read a new magazine called *Self.* "Did I ever tell you what a black belt means?" he asked.

"You told me."

"Sifu Chan doesn't use belts for ranking. They were introduced seventy years ago because Westerners were impatient, you know, needed signposts and all that."

"You told me," said Evelyn.

"Originally, all you got was a white belt. It symbolized innocence. Virginity." His face was immensely serious, like a preacher's. "As you worked, it got darker, dirtier, and turned brown. Then black. You were a master then. With even more work, the belt became frayed, the threads came loose, you see, and the belt showed white again."

"Rudolph, I've heard this before!" Evelyn picked up her magazine and took it into her bedroom. From there, with her legs drawn up under the blankets, she shouted: "I *won't* be your punching bag!"

So he brought friends from his kwoon, friends she wanted nothing to do with. There was something unsettling about them. Some were street fighters. Young. They wore tank-top shirts and motorcycle jackets. After drinking racks of Rainier beer on the front porch, they tossed their crumpled empties next door into Rod Kenner's yard. Together, two of Rudolph's new friends—Truck and Tuco—weighed a quarter of a ton. Evelyn kept a rolling pin under her pillow when they came, but she knew they could eat that along with her. But some of his new friends were students at the University of Washington. Truck, a Vietnamese only two years in America, planned to apply to the Police Academy once his training ended; and Tuco, who was Puerto Rican, had been fighting since he could make a fist; but a delicate young man named Andrea, a blue sash, was an actor in the drama department at the university. His kwoon training, he said, was less for self-defense than helping him understand his movements onstage—how, for example, to convincingly explode across a room in anger. Her husband liked them, Evelyn realized in horror. And they liked him. They were separated by money, background, and religion, but something she could not identify made them seem, those nights on the porch after his class, like a single body. They called Rudolph "Older Brother" or, less politely, "Pop."

His sifu, a short, smooth-figured boy named Douglas Chan, who Evelyn figured couldn't be over eighteen, sat like the Dalai Lama in their tiny kitchen as if he owned it, sipping her tea, which Rudolph laced with Korean ginseng. Her husband lit Chan's cigarettes as if he were President Carter come to visit the common man. He recommended that Rudolph study T'ai Chi, "soft" fighting systems, ki, and something called Tao. He told him to study, as well, Newton's three laws of physics and apply them to his own body during kumite. What she remembered most about Chan were his wrist braces, ornamental weapons that had three straps and, along the black leather, highly polished studs like those worn by Steve Reeves in a movie she'd seen about Hercules. In a voice she though girlish, he spoke of eye gouges and groin-tearing techniques, exercises called the Delayed Touch of Death and Dim Mak, with the casualness she and Shelberdine talked about bargains at Thriftway. And then they suited up, the boyish Sifu, who looked like Maharaj-ji's rougher brother, and her clumsy husband; they went out back, pushed aside the aluminum lawn furniture, and pummeled each other for half an hour. More precisely, her Rudolph was on the receiving end of hook kicks, spinning back fists faster than thought, and foot sweeps that left his body purpled for weeks. A sensible man would have known enough to drive to Swedish Hospital pronto. Rudolph, never known as a profound thinker, pushed on after Sifu Chan left, practicing his flying kicks by leaping to ground level from a four-foot hole he'd dug by their cyclone fence.

Evelyn, nibbling a Van de Kamp's pastry from Safeway—she was always nibbling, these days—watched from the kitchen window until twilight, then brought out the Ben-Gay, a cold beer, and rubbing alcohol on a tray. She figured he needed it. Instead, Rudolph, stretching under the far-reaching cedar in the backyard, politely refused, pushed the tray aside, and rubbed himself with Dit-Da-Jow, "iron-hitting wine," which smelled like the open door of an opium factory on a hot summer day. Yet this ancient potion not only instantly healed his wounds (said Rudolph) but prevented arthritis as well. She was tempted to see if it healed brain damage by pouring it into Rudolph's ears, but apparently he was doing something right. Dr. Guylee's examination had been glowing; he said Rudolph's muscle tone, whatever that was, was better. His cardiovascular system was healthier. His erections were outstanding—or upstanding—though lately he seemed to have no interest in sex. Evelyn, even she, saw in the crepuscular light changes in Rudolph's upper body as he stretched: Muscles like globes of light rippled along his shoulders; larval currents moved on his belly. The language of his new, developing body eluded her. He was not always like this. After a cold shower and sleep his muscles shrank back a little. It was only after his workouts, his weight lifting, that his body expanded like baking bread, filling out in a way that obliterated the soft Rudolph-body she knew. This new flesh had the contours of the silhouetted figures on medical charts: the body as it must be in the mind of God. Glistening with perspiration, his muscles took on the properties of the free weights he pumped relentlessly. They were profoundly tragic, too, because their beauty was earthbound. It would vanish with the world. You are ugly, his new muscles said to Evelyn: old and ugly. His self-punishment made her feel sick. She was afraid of his hard, cold weights. She hated them. Yet she wanted them, too. They had a certain monastic beauty. She thought: *He's doing this to hurt me.* She wondered: What was it like to be powerful? Was clever cynicism—even comedy—the by-product of bulging bellies, weak nerves, bad posture? Her only defense against the dumbbells that stood between them—she meant both his weights and his friends—was, as always, her acid southern tongue:

"They're all fairies, right?"

Rudolph looked dreamily her way. These post-workout periods made him feel, he said, as if there were no interval between himself and what he saw. His face was vacant, his eyes—like smoke. In this afterglow (he said) he saw without judging. Without judgment, there were no distinctions. Without distinctions, there was no desire. Without desire . . .

He smiled sideways at her. "Who?"

"The people in your kwoon." Evelyn crossed her arms. "I read somewhere that most body builders are homosexual."

He refused to answer her.

"If they're not gay, then maybe I should take lessons. It's been good for you, right?" Her voice grew sharp. "I mean, isn't that what you're saying? That you and your friends are better'n everybody else?"

Rudolph's head dropped; he drew a long breath. Lately, his responses to her took the form of quietly clearing his lungs.

"You do what you have to, Evelyn. You don't have to do what anybody else does." He stood up, touched his toes, then brought his forehead straight down against his unbent knees, which was physically impossible, Evelyn would have said—and faintly obscene.

It was a nightmare to watch him each evening after dinner. He walked around the house in his Everlast leg weights, tried push-ups on his finger-tips and wrists, and, as she sat trying to watch "The Jeffersons," stood in a ready stance before the flickering screen, throwing punches each time the scene, or shot, changed to improve his timing. It took the fun out of watching TV, him doing that—she preferred him falling asleep in his chair beside her, as he used to. But what truly frightened Evelyn was his "doing nothing." Sitting in meditation, planted cross-legged in a full lotus on their front porch, with Mr. Miller blissfully curled on his lap, a Bodhisattva in the middle of houseplants she set out for the sun. Looking at him, you'd have thought he was dead. The whole thing smelled like self-hypnosis. He breathed too slowly, in Evelyn's view—only three breaths per minute, he claimed. He wore his gi, splotchy with dried blood and sweat, his calloused hands on his knees, the forefingers on each tipped against his thumbs, his eyes screwed shut.

During his eighth month at the kwoon, she stood watching him as he sat, wondering over the vivid changes in his body, the grim firmness where before there was jolly fat, the disquieting steadiness of his posture, where before Rudolph could not sit still in church for five minutes without fidgeting. Now he sat in zazen for forty-five minutes a day, fifteen when he awoke, fifteen (he said) at work in the mailroom during his lunch break, fifteen before going to bed. He called this withdrawal (how she hated his fancy language) similar to the necessary silences in music, "a stillness that prepared him for busyness and sound." He'd never breathed before, he told her. Not once. Not clear to the floor of himself. Never breathed and emptied himself as he did now, picturing himself sitting in the bottom of Lake Washington: himself, Rudolph Lee Jackson, at the center of the universe; for if the universe was infinite, any point where he stood would be at its center—it would shift and move with him. (That saying,

Evelyn knew, was minted in Douglas Chan's mind. No Negro preacher worth the name would speak that way.) He told her that in zazen, at the bottom of the lake, he worked to discipline his mind and maintain one point of concentration; each thought, each feeling that overcame him he saw as a fragile bubble, which he could inspect passionlessly from all sides; then he let it float gently to the surface, and soon—as he slipped deeper and deeper into the vortices of himself, into the Void—even the image of himself on the lake floor vanished.

Evelyn stifled a scream.

Was she one of Rudolph's bubbles, something to detach himself from? On the porch, Evelyn watched him narrowly, sitting in a rain-whitened chair, her chin on her left fist. She snapped the fingers on her right hand under his nose. Nothing. She knocked her knuckles lightly on his forehead. Nothing. (Faker, she thought.) For another five minutes he sat and breathed, sat and breathed, then opened his eyes slowly as if he'd slept as long as Rip Van Winkle. "It's dark," he said, stunned. When he began, it was twilight. Evelyn realized something new: He was not living time as she was, not even that anymore. Things, she saw, were slower for him; to him she must seem like a woman stuck in fast-forward. She asked:

"What do you see when you go in there?"

Rudolph rubbed his eyes. "Nothing."

"Then *why* do you do it? The world's out here!"

He seemed unable to say, as if the question was senseless. His eyes angled up, like a child's, toward her face. "Nothing is peaceful sometimes. The emptiness is full. I'm not afraid of it now."

"You empty yourself?" she asked. "Of me, too?"

"Yes."

Evelyn's hand shot up to cover her face. She let fly with a whimper. Rudolph rose instantly—he sent Mr. Miller flying—then fell back hard on his buttocks; the lotus cut off blood to his lower body—which provided more to his brain, he claimed—and it always took him a few seconds before he could stand again. He reached up, pulled her hand down, and stroked it.

"What've I done?"

"That's it," sobbed Evelyn. "I don't know what you're doing." She lifted the end of her bathrobe, blew her nose, then looked at him through streaming, unseeing eyes. "And you don't either. I wish you'd never seen that movie. I'm sick of all your weights and workouts—sick of them, do you hear? Rudolph, I want you back the way you were: *sick."* No sooner than she said this Evelyn was sorry. But she'd done no harm. Rudolph, she saw, didn't want anything; everything, Evelyn included, delighted him, but as far as Rudolph was concerned, it was all shadows in a phantom history. He was humbler now, more patient, but he'd lost touch with everything she knew was normal in people: weakness, fear, guilt, self-doubt, the very things that gave the world thickness and made people do things. She *did* want him to desire her. No, she didn't. Not if it meant oral sex. Evelyn didn't know, really, what she wanted anymore. She felt, suddenly, as if she might dissolve before his eyes. "Rudolph, if you're 'empty,' like you say, you don't know who—or what—is talking to you. If you said you were praying, I'd understand. It would be God talking to you. But this way..." She pounded her fist four, five times on her thigh. "It could be *evil* spirits, you know! There are *evil* spirits, Rudolph. It could be the Devil."

Rudolph thought for a second. His chest lowered after another long breath. "Evelyn, this is going to sound funny, but I don't believe in the Devil."

Evelyn swallowed. It had come to that.

"Or God—unless we are gods."

She could tell he was at pains to pick his words carefully, afraid he might offend. Since joining the kwoon and studying ways to kill, he seemed particularly careful to avoid her own most effective weapon: the wry, cutting remark, the put-down, the direct, ego-deflating slash. Oh, he was becoming a real saint. At times, it made her want to hit him.

"Whatever is just *is,"* he said. "That's all I know. Instead of worrying about whether it's good or bad, God or the Devil, I just want to be quiet, work on myself, and interfere with things as little as possible. Evelyn," he asked suddenly, "how can there be *two* things?" His brow wrinkled; he chewed his lip. "You think what I'm saying is evil, don't you?"

"I think it's strange! Rudolph, you didn't grow up in China," she said. "They can't breathe in China! I saw that today on the news. They burn soft coal, which gets into the air and turns into acid rain. They wear face masks over there, like the ones we bought when Mount St. Helens blew up. They all ride bicycles, for Christ's sake! They want what we have." Evelyn heard Rod Kenner step onto his screened porch, perhaps to listen from his rocker. She dropped her voice a little. "You grew up in Hodges, South Carolina, same as me, in a right and proper colored church. If you'd *been* to China, maybe I'd understand."

"I can only be what I've been?" This he asked softly, but his voice trembled. "Only what I was in Hodges?"

"You can't be Chinese."

"I don't want to be Chinese!" The thought made Rudolph smile and shake his head. Because she did not understand, and because he was tired of talking, Rudolph stepped back a few feet from her, stretching again, always stretching. "I only want to be what I *can* be, which isn't the greatest fighter in the world, only the fighter *I* can be. Lord knows, I'll probably get creamed in the tournament this Saturday." He added, before she could reply, "Doug asked me if I'd like to compete this weekend in full-contact matches with some people from the kwoon. I have to." He opened the screen door. "I will."

"You'll be killed—you know that, Rudolph." She dug her fingernails into her bathrobe, and dug this into him: "You know, you never were very strong. Six months ago you couldn't open a pickle jar for me."

He did not seem to hear her. "I bought a ticket for you." He held the screen door open, waiting for her to come inside. "I'll fight better if you're there."

She spent the better part of that week at Shelberdine's mornings and Reverend Merrill's church evenings, rinsing her mouth with prayer, sitting most often alone in the front row so she would not have to hear Rudolph talking to himself from the musty basement as he pounded out bench presses, skipped rope for thirty minutes in the backyard, or shadowboxed in preparation for a fight made inevitable by his new muscles. She had married a fool, that was clear, and if he expected her to sit on a bench at the Kingdome while some equally stupid brute spilled the rest of his brains—probably not enough left now to fill a teaspoon—then he was wrong. How could he see the world as "perfect"?—That was his claim. There was poverty, unemployment, twenty-one children dying every minute, every day, every year from hunger and malnutrition, over twenty murdered in Atlanta; there were sixty thousand nuclear weapons in the world, which was dreadful, what with Seattle so close to Boeing; there were far-right Republicans in the White House: *good* reasons, Evelyn thought, to be "negative and life-denying," as Rudolph would put it. It was almost sin to see harmony in an earthly hell, and in a fit of spleen she prayed God would dislocate his shoulder, do some minor damage to humble him, bring him home, and remind him that the body was vanity, a violation of every verse in the Bible. But Evelyn could not sustain her thoughts as long as he could. Not for more than a few seconds. Her mind never settled, never rested, and finally on Saturday morning, when she awoke on Shelberdine's sofa, it would not stay away from the image of her Rudolph dead before hundreds of indifferent spectators, paramedics pounding on his chest, bursting his rib cage in an effort to keep him alive.

From Shelberdine's house she called a taxi and, in the steady rain that northwesterners love, arrived at the Kingdome by noon. It's over already, Evelyn thought, walking the circular stairs to her seat, clamping shut her wet umbrella. She heard cheers, booing, an Asian voice with an accent over a microphone. The tournament began at ten, which was enough time for her white belt husband to be in the emergency ward at Harborview Hospital by now, but she had to see. At first, as she stepped down to her seat through the crowd, she could only hear—her mind grappled for the word, then remembered—kiais, or "spirit shouts," from the great floor of the stadium, many shouts, for contests were progressing in three rings simultaneously. It felt like a circus. It smelled like a locker room. Here two children stood toe to toe until one landed a front kick that sent the other child flying fifteen feet. There two lean-muscled female black belts were interlocked in a delicate ballet, like dance or a chess game of continual motion. They had a kind of sense, these women—she noticed it immediately—a feel for space and their place in it. (Evelyn hated them immediately.) And in the farthest circle she saw, or rather felt, Rudolph, the oldest thing on the deck, who, sparring in the adult division, was squared off with another white belt, not a boy who might hurt him—the other man was middle-aged, graying, maybe only a few years younger than Rudolph—but they were sparring just the same.

Yet it was not truly him that Evelyn, sitting down, saw. Acoustics in the Kingdome whirlpooled the noise of the crowd, a rivering of voices that affected her, suddenly, like the pitch and roll of voices during service. It affected the way she watched Rudolph. She wondered: Who are these people? She caught her breath when, miscalculating his distance from his opponent, her husband stepped sideways into a roundhouse kick with lots of snap—she heard the cloth of his opponent's gi crack like a gunshot when he threw the technique. She leaned forward, gripping the huge purse on her lap when Rudolph recovered and retreated from the killing to the neutral zone, and then, in a wide stance, rethought strategy. This was not the man she'd slept with for twenty years. Not her hypochondriac Rudolph who had to rest and run cold water on his wrists after walking from the front stairs to the fence to pick up the *Seattle Times*. She did not know him, perhaps she had never known him, and now she never would, for the man on the floor, the man splashed with sweat, rising on the ball of his rear foot for a flying kick—was he so foolish he still thought he could fly?—would outlive her; he'd stand healthy and strong and think of her in a bubble, one hand on her headstone, and it was all right, she thought, weeping uncontrollably, it was all right that Rudolph would return home after visiting her wet grave, clean out her bedroom, the pillboxes and paperback books, and throw open her windows to let her sour, rotting smell escape, then move a younger woman's things onto the floor space darkened by her color television, her porcelain chamber pot, her antique sewing machine. And then Evelyn was on her feet, unsure why, but the crowd had stood suddenly to clap, and Evelyn clapped, too, though for an instant she pounded her gloved hands together instinctively until her vision cleared, the momentary flash of retinal blindness giving way to a frame of her husband, the postman, twenty feet off the ground in a perfect flying kick that floored his opponent and made a Japanese judge who looked like Oddjob shout "ippon"—one point—and the fighting in the farthest ring, in herself, perhaps in all the world, was over.

CHARLES JOHNSON DISCUSSES

"China," point of view and voice, and Alpha Narratives

CJ: This early story (1980) was initially inspired by a rather heated discussion about Buddhism that I had with my friend and former teacher, John Gardner, in person and through letters. The discussion grew out of his reading of my second novel, *Oxherding Tale,* after he saw the final manuscript. Gardner was many things—a medievalist, a critic, a polymathic creator, a man truly immersed in the Western tradition, but something he knew little about was Eastern philosophy and religions, and *Oxherding Tale* is, at heart, a dramatic exploration of non-Western philosophical visions. In a word, Gardner once told me he felt Buddhism was "wrong" because it lacked what he saw at the center of Christianity—love as embodied in the figure of Jesus. His views were, of course, incorrect. *Metta*—loving-kindness—is central to the Buddhadharma, which is a path of supreme compassion for all sentient beings. We argued back and forth about Buddhism in a few letters, then I decided to simply dramatize my position by writing the story "China," knowing that Gardner much preferred to read fiction than arguments. He enjoyed the story, was convinced by it, added a sentence of his own (for voice consistency), then published it in his literary journal, *MSS.*

PM: What questions do you usually ask yourself before deciding the point of view from which to tell a given story?

CJ: Well, as I've told my writing students for the last twenty-eight years, the viewpoint selected should be the one that enables the writer (and reader) to access best—and most fully—the various levels of meaning in a story. To give you an example, in 1971 when I was still an undergraduate I wrote an early draft of *Middle Passage* from the viewpoint of a white ship's captain. That approached failed, at least for me at the time, because the European (or American) captain was far too removed from the culture of the slaves in the hold of his ship. He didn't know them. He couldn't get close to their culture, their individual lives, their dreams. For him, they could never be more than commodities to be sold for profit. In the version of *Middle Passage* that I worked out between 1983 and 1989, the viewpoint is that of a black American freeman, the protagonist Rutherford Calhoun, who can understand *both* the world of the crew of the *Republic* and that of the Allmuseri, the Africans brought onto that ship. He is literally caught between those two worlds, that of the Africans and American mariners, finds himself reflected in both, and is therefore our best guide through the story.

PM: Rust Hills, in *Writing in General and the Short Story in Particular,* argues that point of view should belong to the character whose change is most central to the story. Do you agree, and if so, what about Evelyn's change was more compelling to you than her husband's very striking changes?

CJ: I think Rust Hills's argument is correct. But in "China," we should note that the lives of these two characters—Evelyn and Rudolph—are so intertwined, as husband and wife, that a change in one of them registers a reaction or change in the other. When the story opens they are in stasis. Rudolph is slowly dying—physically, mentally, and most important of all, spiritually. Evelyn accepts this dissolution as the natural order of things. But then, her husband begins training in the martial arts, strengthening his body, then his spirit as he eases into the practice of meditation. Her entire sense of the world and how it works is deeply shaken by this. She resists this change until the very end of the story when, at the tournament, she "lets go" in Buddhist fashion her attachment to certain ideas about how life must be *and* her smug attachment to the belief that she would outlive him.

In effect, the moment of liberation for Evelyn is more wrenching, more emotionally costly, than it is for Rudolph, and precisely because she has clung so tightly to her provincial notions and prejudices. At the story's end, she experiences what I like to call "epistemological humility," the intuition—like a smack from a Zen roshi's bamboo staff—that the universe is far greater than she can conceive, more wondrous, and beyond conceptualization. (Bear in mind that astrophysicists tell us that twenty-three percent of the universe consists of dark matter, another seventy-three percent is made of dark energy, neither of which we know *any*thing about; only four percent of the cosmos can be measured or experienced, which means that we, all of us, find ourselves dwelling in the greatest of mysteries our entire lives.)

PM: One benefit of telling "China" from Evelyn's point of view is that it enlarges the story's stakes beyond Rudolph's transformation to encompass the threat to their marriage. To see the story from Rudolph's eyes is to change the central issue of the story.

CJ: Yes, it would have. Technically speaking, when one has a mysterious or fascinating or unusual character in a story or a novel (Sherlock Holmes, for example), it's often a good idea for the reader to see that character through the eyes of someone else (Watson). In my novels and some short stories, I like to have what someone once called a "magnet character," the sort of actor who the moment he (or she) appears on stage draws all the energy and excitement to himself (or herself). We diminish, I think, the larger-than-life quality of those characters if they tell their own tales.

PM: How consciously do you consider the reader's ability to identify with the point-of-view character?

CJ: I'm very conscious of this. Always when I select a viewpoint I strive to create a character readers can empathize with to some degree.

PM: Why did you choose third-person limited instead of first-person for "China"?

CJ: The story always determines the appropriate viewpoint. Yet I should add, I guess, that first-person and limited third-person are very close—in terms of psychic distance—in the aesthetic effects they achieve. In both we are very close to one character—perched on his (or her) shoulder in third-person, and listening to them speak directly to us in first-person. (Many contemporary readers, I know, prefer the "authority" that comes from first-person testimony, trust it more than they do the "God-like" viewpoint of full omniscience in third-person, but for me one of the charms of say, *Tom Jones*, is that Fielding's narrator becomes as much a character in the tale as his main actors, and with its own personality.) But there are differences worth pointing out, too. In first-person, every sentence (or line) narrates *and* reveals character through diction, observations, etc. With limited third-person, I have a narrator who is telling the story but is not *in* that story as an actor. Such a narrator can use the protagonist's word-choices, he (or she) as narrator can have the "flavor" of the protagonist's worldview but also when necessary step back from that character.

PM: There still remains the "limitation" of not being able to enter another character's mind, and yet there are ways to get around even this, like supposition. For instance on page 126 Evelyn "could tell Rudolph knew . . . " What other devices do you recommend for bypassing the constraints of limited point of view?

CJ: This is potentially a large, interesting, and rich philosophical question—*what* can we know and *how* do we know it? I would suggest readers take a look at Chapter Eleven in my novel *Oxherding Tale.* That chapter is entitled, "The Manumission of First-Person Viewpoint." It is, as the title suggests, a rumination on the epistemology of viewpoint in fiction. If we talk about the "limitation" of a particular viewpoint, not in typical creative workshop terms but in the context of intellectual history, we find we are talking about the limits and possibilities of a perceiving self and of consciousness. So it's necessary to ask, "What is the self that perceives? What is consciousness?" (And chewy, illuminating answers are provided, I think, by David Hume in *A Treatise of Human Nature*, by Kant in *The Critique of Pure Reason*, by phenomenology and Buddhism.)

What, you ask, is the best strategy for overcoming the "constraints of limited viewpoint"? I would say the answer is *imagination.* And thinking, when we write, critically about the creative writing workshop ideas we inherit, asking what precisely do they mean and are they accurate. So much depends on *how* we define a "character," a "self." What if your character is a synaesthetic, one of the tiny percentage of the population who can "see" colors when music is playing? (Such folks and their abilities have been verified empirically). Or what if your character is Shakyamuni Buddha? To a very large degree, our approach to the limits of viewpoint (consciousness) is determined by *who* we're writing about, and what science and philosophy can tell us about the nature of the mind. For me, all definitions of this kind—of mind, viewpoint and consciousness—are provisional, open-ended, and subject to change based upon new evidence and information.

PM: How would you describe the difference between a character's voice and a story's voice? In cases of limited point of view, the distinction is sometimes difficult to grasp.

CJ: Strictly speaking, a character's voice is (for me) how that character speaks: for example, Rutherford Calhoun in *Middle Passage* has a speech laced with the language of the sea and nineteenth-century ships; Andrew Hawkins in *Oxherding Tale* narrates often with the diction of the eighteenth-century novel (Fielding, Stern, etc.); and my fictitious Martin Luther King in *Dreamer* speaks with a language drenched by two thousand years of Christian theology. (Voice and vision, in other words, are united in a character.) If the story is rendered in third-person limited, the voice of the "outside" narrator can—even when it occasionally appropriates the main character's language—step back, as I said earlier, and observe the character *ironically.* That is, the narrator sees things the protagonist doesn't see about himself (or herself).

PM: Some of the clearest examples of that in "China," I think, are to be found in its humor, which, in a gentle way, sometimes comes at Evelyn's expense. Do you have a favorite example?

CJ: The story is so riddled with ironic lines that it's hard for me to select a favorite. However, if I *must* choose, I'd pick Evelyn's desperate utterance—a slip, really, when she says, "Rudolph, I want you back the way you were: *sick*." When she tearfully blurts this out, *every*thing is on the table between these two, i.e., her fears and anger and confusion, their antithetical cultural visions of life and its possibilities.

PM: You convey a strong sense of Evelyn's voice (that "flavor" you referred to) by employing a few of her colloquialisms—"Hershey squirts," for example—and only a few. Other writers, especially beginning writers, might have piled them on. Were you conscious of your own restraint and if so, do you recall when and how you developed such an aesthetic?

CJ: Sometimes in an early draft of a story I may pile on vivid voice moments like the one you flagged, "Hershey squirts." In the first draft I pile them on because I want the story to be complete—it is, in other words, still *evolving* before my eyes; I'm in a state of suspense as I write the first draft (as I hope the reader will be with the final draft), and I don't know until I reach the end everything the story will need to be a complete and generous aesthetic experience. Then, by draft three (or later drafts), as I read through the lines, I mercilessly take out anything that is superfluous, that overstates things, and especially anything that ruins the rhythm, cadence, and flow of a line or paragraph. My editing rule is: any sentence or phrase that *can* come out *should* come out (unless the writer absolutely loves it). Every word, sentence, and paragraph must be able to justify itself being on the page—it must be *doing* something: advancing the plot, deepening character, creating musicality, providing rich imagery, adding humor for entertainment value, etc. Such restraint, as you called it, is crucial in any artistic composition. Often we have to edit out lines and phrases and words we love because they don't add to the work's coherence, consistency and completeness—we must, as the saying goes, "kill our babies."

PM: Do you urge your students to write through characters of a different gender, class, race, etc., than themselves? What principles, if any, do you suggest they follow in such an undertaking?

CJ: I urge them to do this all the time. Doing so is an antidote to students writing the same story over and over about, say, their first sexual experiences—or writing about characters who, if one scratches them deeply enough, are just versions of the writer himself (or herself). I constantly urge my students to imagine *other* lives, *other* visions of the world—not just white, Eurocentric, and Western ones. To be successful at switching race, gender, and class for their characters, a couple of things are required. First, they must have a tremendous degree of empathy for their characters; they must *care* about them. And, secondly, they (as writers) must be able to "let go" their beliefs and perspectival orientations in order to grasp what the world looks like "over there" behind the eyes of the gender Other, the racial Other, or the cultural Other.

You know, as an African American author, I have to do this *all* the time. In one story I may be writing from the viewpoint of a white CEO in Seattle ("Executive Decision"), in another from Martha Washington's viewpoint ("Martha's Dilemma"), and in a third from the viewpoint of Frederick Douglass ("A Lion at Pendleton"). As writers, we *must* be like actors who are able to disappear into numerous roles, for as a famous actress once said, "I've never been more myself than when I'm playing someone else."

PM: How do you feel about the use of multiple points of view in a short story?

CJ: I usually discourage students (and myself) from using multiple viewpoints in a short story. In a novel, that strategy works just fine. But a short story of, oh, between twelve and twenty-five pages, needs to quickly establish our point of reference—whose eyes we're seeing this world through—for the reader's comfort. Once or twice, I've had through necessity to shift third-person from one character to a second in order to fully explore a story's meaning, or to use multiple first-person viewpoints. But generally I shy away from multiple viewpoints in short fiction unless a story absolutely requires that.

Remember, the principle here is this: there is no timeless or rigid "Platonic form" for the short story or novel. Each new, original story or novel teaches us anew what a story or novel can *be.* The aesthetic and formal strategies are always dictated and determined *from within* the individual work by its content, not imposed from outside.

PM: Evelyn's epiphany coming as it does during a moment of "retinal blindness" is a wonderful culmination of that motif. What moved you to afflict her with degenerating retinas in the first place?

CJ: Early in the story her retinal blindness was simply a detail I found interesting to add when she and Rudolph are watching a movie (I have a colleague with that problem and she was on my mind, partly, as I reached for details to characterize Evelyn). At the time I included that detail in Act One of the story I had no idea that as a metaphor it would have greater significance when I reached the final scene in Act Three.

This is how the creative process works—it's a process of *discovery.* Technically, a story can be divided into three parts: beginning, middle, and end. In the story's beginning we have to trust ourselves, as writers. We have to add details that define and despoil the universe of "possibility," which is where we are at a story's opening. (In other words, we can give *any* details we want to a character or her world, but once we make a decision, we've eliminated other possibilities). I tell my students that in the first part of the story—the realm of Possibility—the writer needs a good idea (i.e., an interesting conflict or, as John Barth once put it, a rich "ground situation"). The second part of the story puts us in the realm of Probability, where the character and her universe have already been defined and what now occurs is based *causally* on what came in the beginning. We also need a *second* good idea in the story's middle to deepen and complicate the original conflict. Finally, at the story's end (Act Three), we find ourselves in the realm of Necessity, because everything that happens is predetermined by all the decisions that the writer made in the beginning and middle—at this stage, the story is almost writing itself because causally, only a certain outcome is now possible.

The visual analog for this would be a funnel, big at the opening and quite small at the end. Aristotle in *The Poetics* calls this process "energeia," the actualization of the potential inherent in character and event. At the end of the story we also need a *final good idea* to bring the story to closure, so *three* strong ideas are required for a story to realize itself, at least in terms of my aesthetic.

So all of that above is to say this: at the beginning of a story a writer doesn't know—and doesn't *have* to know—the meaning of every detail he includes. You trust your instincts, your subconscious, when creating. When I reached the end of "China," I remembered that Evelyn had retinal blindness, which erupts when she watches her husband at the tournament, and which by the tale's end I discovered worked well as a metaphor for her cultural and philosophical blindness.

PM: At several times the characters physically take control of each other's eyes: Evelyn wants Rudolph to notice the trampoline in the movie and turns his head toward it; he wants her to be impressed with the magazine cover and shoves it in her face. The battle over point of view actually becomes a component of the conflict.

CJ: In one way or another, all my fiction is about the conflict of interpretations. My novels and stories tend to be Hegelian, that is, my characters have visions of the world that are antinomies—viewpoints that each contain their own partial truth—and in the novels and stories I set those conflicting views at war with each other, letting the characters battle it out until a resolution (or Hegelian synthesis) is dramatically realized.

PM: I've always found Evelyn's question on page 137 one of the story's most provocative: "Was clever cynicism—even comedy—the by-product of . . . [weakness]?" What's your own take on that? What *is* the proper place of comedy in literature and life?

CJ: Well, I think in contemporary America people use clever cynicism as a defense mechanism to protect themselves from ideas and experiences they fear or fail to understand. For me, that's a shallow response to phenomenon—a way of closing oneself off from the unfamiliar, new, and unknown, the exact opposite (for a Buddhist) of egoless listening, which is one of the attributes of love.

PM: How has your own background as a Buddhist and a martial-arts instructor influenced your approach to writing?

CJ: All during my adult life, I've been a Buddhist or someone devoted to the Dharma, though I seldom discussed this with non-Buddhists. I first practiced Vipassana meditation when I was fourteen years old, began the study of martial arts five years later at a Chicago kwoon (practice hall) when I was nineteen, and I've practiced meditation regularly since 1980.

The Chinese martial arts provide a rigorous discipline for the body as well as the mind, and segue into Buddhist study and practice, which is all about disciplining the mind. I specifically discuss the relationship between Buddhist practice and creative work in an essay in my book *Turning the Wheel* entitled, "The Elusive Art of Mindfulness."

PM: Didn't you once mention that as a college student, you cranked out a new practice novel every semester, in addition to your coursework?

CJ: Well, I trained myself when I began writing novels in 1970 at age twenty-two to produce ten pages a day. (I had the same discipline earlier as a professional cartoonist in my late teens and early twenties—I'd do five finished drawings a day.) Each of those apprentice novels went through three drafts in a ten-week academic quarter. When I focus on something, as a Buddhist and meditator, I focus on it wholly and completely to the exclusion of *every*thing else—this is what Buddhists call "mindfulness" or sometimes in Sanskrit we use the word *ekagratha,* "one-pointedness of mind." When I write something, especially a novel, I do it as if it might be the very *last* thing I ever do, my last will and testament in language, so to speak. It must have my best ideas, best feelings, and best skill. And the doing of it allows me to momentarily extinguish the illusion of the "ego." All that I'm focused on is the imaginative object unfolding before my eyes. It's the same focus and intensity that one finds, for example, in the Japanese tea ceremony, the Zen approach to archery, or creating rock gardens.

PM: How long did you spend working on "China," and through how many drafts?

CJ: Given the way I work, concentrating one hundred percent on a creation day and night until it's done, I've never taken more than four or five days to write a short story. (On the other hand, I typically spend five to seven years on novels because I send them through many drafts and around three thousand pages of revisions.)

PM: What single point about fiction writing above all others do you try to convey to aspiring writers now?

CJ: There's one point I emphasize over and over: We have many people today who write fiction or want to, but too few gifted *storytellers.* There's absolutely no reason, I believe, to sit down to write unless one has a truly compelling story to tell. We are blessed if we receive from whatever powers that be *one* rousing good story that will outlive us and delight and enlighten future generations (like Ralph Ellison's *Invisible Man*); if a writer receives *two* such Alpha Narratives (as I call them) to tell, then he (or she) is a major talent in his (or her) time; if he (or she) receives *three* or more, then that writer (like Mark Twain or Shakespeare) is an author whose contributions enrich literary culture, worldwide, for as long as our species exists. We learn technique simply to enable us—as midwives—to deliver that story, that baby undamaged as a gift for our readers. For me, this is the only goal appropriate for apprentice and journeymen writers.

PM: Your creative approach and methods sound very intense. How do your students respond when you describe it all to them?

CJ: The best students understand that art is a *total* affair for the artist. That creating art is hard work (the literal meaning of "kung fu"), with ninety percent of the process involving rewriting over and over. The intensity doesn't frighten them. Rather, it inspires them because they realize that no creative project is impossible if they're willing to go over their pages until every word and phrase and paragraph approaches perfection.

❦

DR. CHARLES JOHNSON, a 1998 MacArthur Fellow, received the National Book Award for his novel *Middle Passage* in 1990, and is a 2002 recipient of the Academy Award for Literature from the American Academy of Arts and Letters. In 2003, he was elected to membership in the American Academy of Arts and Sciences. He has published three other novels, including *Dreamer* (1998), *Oxherding Tale* (1982), and *Faith and the Good Thing* (1974), as well as two story collections, *The Sorcerer's Apprentice* (1986) and *Soulcatcher* (2001). Among his many other books, his newest is *Turning the Wheel: Essays on Buddhism and Writing* (2003). He is the S. Wilson and Grace M. Pollock Endowed Professor of English at the University of Washington in Seattle. You can visit his author's website at www.oxherdingtale.com, and additional information on his work can be found at http://www.siu.edu/~johnson.

CONDOLENCES TO EVERY ONE OF US

Allan Gurganus

Dear Mrs. Whiston,

I was in Africa on Father Flannagan's Tour of the World with your parents when they were killed. I want to tell you how it happened. My son-in-law is a doctor (eye, ear, nose, and throat) at Our Lady of Perpetual Help outside Toledo, and he says I should write down all I know, the sooner the better, to get it out of my system. I am a woman of sixty-seven years. I have a whole box of stationery here. If this doesn't turn out so hot, I'm sorry. My mind is better than ever but sometimes my writing hand gets cramped. I'll take breaks when I need to. I've got all morning.

I blame the tour organizers. They should be informed about the chances of revolution happening while one of their buses is visiting some place. When I first looked at Father Flannagan's literature, I got bad feelings about Tongaville. I'd never even heard of it, but on these package deals you just go where the bus goes. You take the bad cities with the good.

Your parents were the most popular couple on our tour. They always had a kind word for everyone. They'd made several other world trips, so your mother knew to be ready for the worst. She shared her Kaopectate with me when I most needed it outside Alexandria. I'm sending along a picture I took with my new camera at the Sphinx. It's not as sharp as I expected but here it is. Your mother is the one on the saddle and your father's holding his baseball-type cap out like he's feeding her camel. He really stood about ten feet in front of it because we were told they bite. The woman off to the right is Miss Ada McMillan, a retired librarian just full of energy and from Winnetka, Ill. She is laughing here because your father was such a card, always in high spirits, always cheering us up, keeping the ball rolling in ways our tour guide should have. I hope knowing more about your parents' death will be better for you than remaining in the dark. I think I'd want the whole truth. What I've read in American papers and magazines about the revolution is just plain wrong, and I believe that using the photograph of your poor parents lying in the street was totally indecent and unforgivable. I pray you have been spared seeing it. That started as a Polaroid snapshot taken by my neighbor and ex-friend Cora White. She was along on the African tour. I hear she sold the picture to a wire service for 175 dollars. I will never speak to her again, I can promise you that, Mrs. Whiston.

I'm rambling already, so I will begin to sketch out what I remember. If you choose to stop reading here, I can understand that. But I'm going on anyway. If I don't get this Africa business laid out in the open, I know my dreams and housework will stay like they are now, a big mess.

My memory is one thing I've always been proud of. I can rattle off restaurant menus from lunches I ate with my late husband in 1926. Till now, the only good this ability has done me is not needing to keep grocery lists and never forgetting any family member's birthday.

The bus had to wait for sheep to cross the road just outside the capital city. I was putting on my lipstick when we heard the explosion. Tongaville is made of mud walls like what's known as stucco in America. The town was far off, all one color on a flat desert so it looked like a toy fort. One round tower blew into a thousand pieces. The shock waves were so strong that sheep fell against the front of our bus. They got terrified and were climbing up on each other. They don't look like our American sheep but are black and have very skinny legs. Their coats are thick as powder puffs, only greasy. Seeing how scared they were scared me.

Some of us tried talking sense to our tour guide. He wasn't any Father Flannagan. We'd all expected a priest, even though the brochure didn't come right out and promise one. This guide was not even Catholic, but some Arab with a mustache. He spoke English so badly you had to keep asking him to repeat and sometimes even to spell things out. We told him it would be a mistake, driving into a town where this type of thing was happening. But he said our hotel rooms were already paid for—otherwise, we'd just have to sleep on the bus and miss the Game Preserve the next morning. We were so tired. Half of us were sick. Somebody asked for a show of hands. Majority ruled that we go in and take our chances. But my instinct told me, definitely no.

Mrs. Whiston, we'd been in Egypt earlier. It is dry and outstandingly beautiful but as far as a place to live and work, it lags way behind Ohio. But, maybe that's just me. Thanks to Egypt, I had the worst case of diarrhea I have ever heard of or read about. You cannot believe how low a case of diarrhea can bring a person's spirits and better judgment. Because of it, I voted Yes, enter Tongaville. In my condition, a bus parked on the desert, where there's not one blade of grass much less a bush for fifty miles, was just no place to spend the night. So, like a pack of fools, we drove into Tongaville, right into the middle of it.

The bus was air-conditioned, and we couldn't exactly hear what all of them were shouting at us. Then Miss McMillan, who's in your parents' snapshot and at seventy-nine is still sharp as a tack, she said, "CIA, they're yelling CIA," and she was right. First it sounded like some native word but that was because they were saying it wrong. Miss McMillan was on target as usual. The only ones who'd voted to skip Tongaville were her and the three Canadian teachers who often acted afraid of us Americans, especially the Texans, and who wore light sweaters, even in Egypt. "Father Flannagan's World Tours" was spelled out in English all over the bus. Some of our people said it had probably tipped off the natives about our being Americans. But after three weeks with this group, I knew we weren't that hard to spot. I never thought I'd be ashamed of my home country, but certain know-it-all attitudes and rudeness toward Africans had embarrassed me more than once. This might have been my first world trip, but wherever I am I can usually tell right from wrong. The Texans especially were pushy beyond belief.

Hotel workers came out and joined hands and made two lines for protection, a kind of alley from the door of our bus to the lobby of the Hotel Alpha, which was no great shakes but, by this time, looked pretty good to me. Your father, I remember, was the last to get off because he kept photographing rebels through the big tinted black window. They had already started rocking the bus and he was still inside it running up and down the aisle taking pictures of their angry faces near the glass. Your mother just plain told him to come out of there this minute and he finally did. I made it upstairs to my room and looked out the balcony window. The crowd had climbed up on our bus and pried open the door. They swarmed all over it, about a hundred half-dressed people, so skinny it hurt you to look at them. The bus's sunroof was glass and I could see them in there scrambling over every seat. The street in front of our hotel was just crawling with people. One group waved brooms. A few boys had found golf clubs somewhere and were throwing these up then catching them like majorettes would. A naked man and woman danced around, holding a vacuum cleaner over their heads. He lifted the body of it and she'd slung the hose over her shoulder and kept shaking the wand part at people. Even from the second floor, I could tell it was an Electrolux. The crowd didn't seem to know what a vacuum cleaner was. They kept staring up at the thing. Seeing this scared me more than anything so far. Then our bus drove off. Most of the Africans ran after it, all cheering. I stood there at the window thinking, Well, there our only hope goes. This is probably it, what could be worse for us? That's when I noticed our tour guide. He went sneaking across the street, looking left and right, guilt written all over him, and carrying a red Samsonite makeup case exactly like Mimi Martinson's, a rich divorcee's from St. Pete. That little Arab turned the corner. I knew then we were on our own, with this mess out of control.

I decided to build a barricade in front of my door but realized that the rest room was out in the hall. We had to share.

Father Flannagan's leaflet said in big printing, "Rooms with private baths at the best of the earth's four-star hotels." I went to find the bathroom but somebody was in there and four more of our people were waiting in line.

Old Mr. McGuane, one of the Texans, stood around, real casual, holding a pistol. He was telling the others how he'd brought it along just in case, and somebody asked him how he'd gotten it through customs and the hijack inspections and he said he didn't know, it had been right there in his bag all along, but he could tell them one thing, he was mighty glad to have it with him now. Other people asked, just in case, what his room number was. I had to use the bathroom so much but I knew it was going to take forever. Seeing people from our tour had depressed me even more. So I walked back, locked my door, and just sat down on the bed and went ahead and had a good cry. I thought of Teddy and Lorraine, my son-in-law and daughter, who'd given me this trip to get my mind off my husband's death. I couldn't help believing that I'd never see Toledo again. I kept remembering a new Early American spice rack I'd hung in my kitchen just before leaving. It's funny, the kind of thing that gives you comfort when you're scared.

I told myself that if I just lived through this, if I got to go one more time to the Towne and Country restaurant near my home, and order their fantastic blue-cheese dressing, and then drive over to the Old Mill Little Theater and see another production of *Jacques Brel Is Alive and Well,* I'd give five thousand dollars to the Little Sisters of Mercy Orphanage. I vowed this and said a quick prayer to seal it. I found some hotel stationery and sat down and wrote out my will. I already had a legal one back in our safe deposit box, but it soothed my mind so much to write: I leave all my earthly goods to Teddy and Lorraine. I leave all my earthly goods to Teddy and Lorraine. Sitting there, I fell asleep.

I know I'm rambling worse than ever. But in emergencies like this, little things bunch up and get to seem important as the big facts. So I'm putting most everything in.

I woke up and at first didn't know where I was, then I remembered, Africa, and I thought, Oh Lord. Even in Ohio, sometimes the feeling comes over me and I wonder, What exactly am I doing here? In Tongaville, it was that same question but about five hundred times as strong. I crawled to the end of my bed and looked out the balcony window and that's when I saw your mother and father wandering around down on the street. Frankly, Mrs. Whiston, I thought they were pretty foolish to be out there. When our bus was hijacked, its spare fell off, and now the street was totally empty except for your parents and the tire and a beggar who was propped up in a doorway down the block. I think he was only there because the mob had carried off his crutches as two more things to wave around.

Your dad was taking a picture of the tire and your poor mother was looking at the light meter. You probably know how your father asked her to help by testing the brightness of the light. He pretended to include her in his hobby, but, in my opinion, he never really listened to Lily. Many times I'd hear her say, "Fred, it's way too bright out here. Without some filters, every shot is going to be way overexposed. This is Africa, Fred." He'd nod and go on clicking away. She acted like she didn't notice this, but after forty years of a thing, you notice. It made me remember my own marriage to one basically good man. I wondered, Is it wise or crazy to put up with so much for so long. Your dad was mostly kind to her and he didn't mean any harm, but this once I wish he'd told her not to bother, to just go on upstairs and take a nap or something. Instead, there Lily was, two stories down, the poor thing holding out a light meter of no earthly good to anybody, squinting at it and wearing her pretty yellow pantsuit. I should have called to them. If it had been just her I definitely would have, but when a woman's husband is along, you often act different.

Then they both looked down the street. By leaning out the window, I could see a whole parade, this whole mass of people carrying signs painted on sheets stretched between green bamboo poles. The writing was a foreign language, foreign to me, at least. Groups came down the street and sidewalks, pushing, waving scrap lumber and garden tools. They all moved together. They looked organized and almost noble, like they knew just what they wanted and deserved, and, right now, were headed there to get it. I expected your parents to run straight back into our hotel. They had time. But instead, your father changed cameras. He wore about three looped around his neck and he crouched down like a professional and started taking pictures. The Africans were shouting something hard to understand except I think the CIA part was still in there. The chants got louder and echoed between buildings. Your dad stayed put. Lily looked confused but tried to make herself useful anyway and held out that light meter toward the crowd, like she was offering it to them. Lily kept glancing at the hotel doorway. Somebody must have been signaling for her to come inside. But she didn't budge, she stuck out there in the open with your dad. He hunched down facing them. I just stood upstairs and watched. I kept believing he knew things I didn't.

His camera had a long black lens and this was pressed up against his face, and I don't know if people thought it was a gun or what, but along with their chant, I heard this one pop, no louder than a firecracker, and your poor father fell right back. It was as fast and simple as that. It seemed like he did a backflip he'd been planning all along, or got more interested in the sky between buildings than the crowd, because he was lying there staring right up at the sun. He tried to toss the camera to your mother, like the camera mattered most. She caught it and looked down at the thing for a minute. Then she seemed to wake up and she took two shaky steps toward him. But that moment the people shoved past our hotel. There were hundreds of them and they were running fast. Some were banging on pots and garbage-can lids. They carried things along over their heads. A phone pole on its side, people hanging onto the loose wires like these were leashes. Along came what looked like a huge snake held up by dozens of black hands, but it was just the vacuum hose. I could see flashes of her yellow suit down there.

The last of the parade went rushing by, women, children, and some bony dogs hurrying to catch up. Your mother was face down on the street way beyond your dad. People had taken her blouse off. All the cameras were gone, but one that had been trampled. They'd carried off the tire and your poor mother's yellow blouse.

I just fixed myself a cup of coffee, Mrs. Whiston, and ran cold water over my writing hand. I'm in such a state trying to get this down. I plan to start forgetting just as soon as this letter is done. But I think it's important to face the hard facts at the time, and not let yourself off easy.

My Willard died at the cement works where he'd been their employee for thirty-five years. I drove out a week or so after the funeral and talked to the boys he'd worked with on his last morning alive. They told me little things they remembered from that day. One man, a colored fellow named Roy, he'd been with Diamond Cement as long as my husband. He said Willard told a joke just before lunch hour, which is when he passed away. His heart went. The joke was about the three priests trying to catch a train to Pittsburgh. Willard must of told that one about five thousand times. He'd got it down to an art, this priest joke and some other favorites. I asked Roy, Which joke? Like I'd never heard it. He probably guessed that in the twenty years Willard had been telling that corny thing, I'd have to know it by now. But he started up anyway, understanding that I needed it. Roy went through the whole thing, waiting in the right places, adding all Willard's extra touches. When he finished, I laughed out loud like it was new to me, and not just for show but from the heart. Hearing it helped me so much. I'm not sure why I started telling this. I think it's to show why I'm not holding one thing back, not sparing you anything, no matter how bad it sounds.

I tore the sheets off my bed and unlocked the door. People had stacked their luggage as a barricade across the stair landing. I shoved through this, and some fell down the stairwell but I didn't care. I ran into the lobby. A black bellhop tried to stop me but I got past him through the revolving door. Out in the sun and heat, seeing them stunned me all over again. I bent down beside your father and felt him. One camera had been stepped on, lens glass was shining all around his shoulder. Then I ran down the street to your mother and put my hand on the side of her face. Both your folks were dead. Her back looked so bare and white, and the bra strap seemed to be cutting her. I spread the sheet over Lily and then I lifted it up and undid the clip of her strap. The beggar had leaned out of his doorway to stare at me. For some reason, this made me feel guilty, like I could have saved them or was stealing their watches. I stood up dizzy but made it back and called the bellboy to come out here and help me carry your folks inside. I kept waving but he'd just press up against the glass and shake his head no. Then he crooked his finger for me to come back in. I saw something move upstairs and I looked up there, and it astonished me. There were three guests in every balcony window, our whole busload all lined up in rows and staring down at me with your poor parents.

Cora White peeped over the grillework on the third floor. When she saw me looking up, her head jerked back. But one of her arms stayed there holding the Polaroid, then her other hand came out and poked the button. Many people were taking pictures. I put a hand over my eyes for shade and called, "Come help us, come help us. The Madisons are dead," and I pointed to your folks. But nobody budged. It was a scary and terrible sight, Mrs. Whiston. Most windows were closed, so I called louder. Some of the women would look at each other and back at me, but not one soul up there moved. So then, when I saw what was going on, I started screaming names. I'm not a young woman, Mrs. Whiston, but with all my might I hollered upstairs, especially to my friends who, like me, had signed up for this at Holy Assumption. "Deborah Schmidt, Cora White, LaVerne and May Stimson, I see you, and I know you, so you all come right down here and help us." But as I called their names, they'd ease back into the rooms or let the drapes fall over their faces. I was out in the sun, feeling totally lost. I was starting to shake. People weren't even looking at me or your folks any more but along the street in the other direction, and when I saw a crowd headed here even bigger than before, I stooped down and ran right back inside. The bellboy jammed a baggage cart half into the revolving door, then the two of us ducked under the front desk and we stayed there.

I'd turned into just as big a coward as the rest, so who am I to point the finger? All the same, I won't forget how it is to be the person who needs help, and to look up and see your group, your people, lined up like in a department-store window, and every one refusing you. Your dearest friends on earth doing that.

I never figured out how the Marines from the U.S. Embassy knew where we were, but all of a sudden they showed up in a truck, carrying rifles. I was so concerned for my own safety I hardly gave your parents' bodies another thought, Mrs. Whiston. The Marines looked very young, like they couldn't be old enough to drive, and here they were rescuing us. I asked if the Embassy had maybe picked up your parents, because by this time, they were both gone, nothing left but broken glass on the pavement. The Marine said, "No, Ma'am." I wish you could have heard him say that. He was tall and had a sweet pink healthy face. Like all of them, he seemed to talk in a Southern accent, and when this boy told me, "No, Ma'am," it was so full of politeness, so old-fashioned and American in the good way that after what our busload had just done, I broke right down in the lobby. Nobody on our tour would come near me now they'd gathered downstairs, all shy to see me still alive. The Marine looked embarrassed. I thought if he would just put his arm around me for a minute, I'd be all right. And I'm sure he was going to, but when he saw that no one else was rushing over to help, not even one of our women, he said, "Excuse me," and hurried off. He was just shy, a man's body and this little boy's face.

Up drove the Embassy's four black cars to rush us to the airport. American soldiers and government secretaries were driving anything they could lay hands on. They said to leave all the luggage we couldn't carry in our laps. Mimi Martinson asked everyone but me if they'd seen her precious makeup bag, so why should I have told her where it went? More officials arrived, two sports cars and a Buick that looked bigger than ones at home but was a lot like Teddy and Lorraine's, only yellow. For one second, I really thought it was them come for me. That's how crazy I'd turned. By this time, I didn't know Africa from around the block.

A Volkswagen camper with Delaware plates pulled up in front. I rode in that. It belonged to the Ambassador's daughter. We unloaded food from the little refrigerator to take on the plane with us. The freezer was full of Stouffer's Lobster Newburg dinners, and more of these were waiting at the airport in ice chests from the Embassy Commissary.

We'd started for the plane when we heard the biggest explosion yet. An oil refinery, this row of tanks went off like bombs and in one minute the entire sky got black. We had to keep low in the camper, but at an intersection near the refinery I heard something and looked out and saw two sheep running through the empty streets. I think oil had spilled on them and their coats were on fire, Mrs. Whiston. They both ran down the center of the road right along the dotted line. Smoke came blowing off their backs and real flames and they were making noises so human, so terrible I cannot describe it. When I was a child, I was sick a lot and had nightmares full of horrible sights, and this was like some dream from then but worse.

The Embassy man tried to tell me that these sheep were headed toward some river and would be all right. But, if there was a river through the desert, how could it stay a desert and dry? We flew to Athens then to Brussels then home to Kennedy. We were treated like royalty, except by the reporters, who were rude. The Ambassador and his wife acted just like everybody else and weren't a bit stuck up. He said he'd known there was some trouble brewing, but as for a revolution, he guessed he'd been caught napping.

Now, I am home. I'm safe and sound at my own kitchen table. When I walked in here for the first time last week, my new maple spice rack looked like an altar to me. I'm tired and never plan to leave the security of Toledo again.

Mrs. Whiston, it's hard for me to believe that our earth has gotten this bad this quick. I'm not saying your dad was right in doing what he did, rushing outside without understanding how dangerous things are now. He just forgot his place and took way too much for granted. He thought all people on earth were as good-natured as himself, and with as much free time, and would pose for him. But he overlooked hunger. That is bound to make terrible changes in people's dispositions. White or black, people are more miserable and less willing to be scenery than the *National Geographic* would like us to think. Every fact I once held dear has swung around and turned into something else.

As one example, Teddy says there probably *is* no Father Flannagan. It's just a name somebody thought up to suck people in. Anyway, I contributed a gift in honor of your folks and my late husband to the Little Sisters of Mercy Orphanage. I found I had less of a nest egg thanks to the bite the money crunch has made in our economy, so I only gave half of what I promised, but the Sisters seemed happy and Teddy told me I was crazy to do it.

I feel that knowing what I know now, I should start life over. If you asked what Africa taught me, I couldn't spell it out with words but in my heart, I think, something serious has switched. Chances are, my life is too far along for any last-minute change in plans. However, I've been thinking. Maybe we should give up what we own to feed the hungry? But at my age, an old white woman and spoiled like this, I wonder how much I could really do without. It shocks me to understand how greedy I am. Really, I've learned so little.

As a result of being long-winded like this, I am very tired. So listen, across the miles, Mrs. Whiston, I just offer you a hug. I do hate to hit the end of this letter. I would like to buck you up in your time of sorrow but my place, I think, is still here in Toledo in the old neighborhood. This afternoon I'm tending my grandchildren who are way ahead of others their age. They're final stars in whatever crown I'm going to get on earth.

Oh well, so long. We all do what we can, don't we? We just hope that in the end it's worth the hard daily efforts and has been mostly for the best. We are really the lucky ones. The rest think they are outside looking in at happiness. If they only knew. When the highs and lows are so far apart, it's hard to stay in the middle and think of yourself as a good person. But I'm trying.

Teddy and Lorraine said to send their regards. I pass on my deep sympathy to you and, as far as that goes, to every one of us. I'll just sign this as coming from

Yours truly,

Mrs. Willard Gracie (Maria)

P. S. If you write back, wonderful. I don't get much mail.

ALLAN GURGANUS DISCUSSES

"Condolences to Every One of Us," point of view and voice, and the comedy of disaster

AG: The tale's inspiration leapt from one of those news photos we see daily. Civilians, caught in a political crossfire while wearing their best Sunday-shopping clothes, had been killed on the street. Someone had thrown a tarp or sheet over them but, from underneath, one pair of white high heels emerged. A ladies' handbag was still looped within an elbow's crook, protected even in death. This picture tore my heart out. I started thinking how the news of such a death might be "broken to" the dead person's beloved next of kin. What was kindest? To say it quick, or to back into the brunt of it?

To whom could one turn for an explanation of this single casualty? The most logical witness might seem some expert on international terrorism. But for me, as a Democrat and an artist, one ordinary woman's attempt to comprehend these ghastly crimes outstripped in validity any professional pundit's opinion. Mrs. Maria Gracie, with her high-school education and big heart, has a name that refers to "Maria, full of Grace." Like the mother of Christ, she is a small-town girl called up in a plot-conflagration not of her making, one veering mostly beyond her comprehension. Even so, she tries making sense of it. That seems to Maria as much a duty as a right.

With only one box of drug-store stationery as her medium and forum, with a sixty-seven-year-old's hand-cramps slowing her, she does get down the facts. She starts at the top of the event and sees it through. Later she tries, ineptly, to find a "moral" in it and cannot. The humbleness of her clean-up gear stands at odds with the calamitous world-forces that killed her friends while revealing the cowardice and self-interest of fellow touring Americans. Mrs. Gracie's attempt to answer impossible questions about privilege and hunger, entitlement and rage, makes her worth hearing.

PM: She would seem a precursor to your most famous narrator, Lucy Marsden, the title character in *Oldest Living Confederate Widow Tells All*, published more than a decade later. What drew you, even as a young man, toward the point of view of elderly, provincial widows?

AG: I'm sure that Mrs. Gracie served as an early working model for Lucy Marsden. They have much in common: A direct address (although Lucy, half-blind, recites her saga into a student's tape recorder), an assured point of view, a gift for gab, an appetite for metaphor, and a delightful quiet kind of small-town mirth. But, of course, this short story might be like a paint chart sample that predicts the larger spectral demands of a novel. The structural difference between a very short story and a very long novel is like that of tweezing a ship's model into a bottle as opposed to welding then caulking an actual ocean liner. I encourage my students to write stories before they try novels. Fact is, stories are much, much harder, but I don't tell that to the young. With a novel, huge shifts are necessary. You must choose one voice that can prove both singular and choral. It has to be credible for ten autobiographical pages (like "Condolences") but then must subdivide into other souls, ascending to warp-speed overdrive. The novel's voice must also prove various and complex and supple enough to literally imitate eighty other characters for nearly eight hundred pages. A story must crowd all that into ten pages and a narrower register with maximum impact.

Even so, my two widow-women are both witnesses seldom consulted by others but perhaps the more reliable for that. They have been waiting for an occasion that might get them noticed, heard at last. They both have strong senses of right and wrong. Their gift for comedy constitutes, in miniature, their single best equipment for surviving. Lucy speaks at age ninety-nine and I would also predict a similar long life for Mrs. Gracie.

When she catches one of her "former-friends" photographing the dead bodies to sell to the wire services, Maria reassures her letter's recipient, "I will never speak to her again." This simple statement must be accepted as a promise to be trusted. There are, in a world of quicksand ethics and disappearing political integrity, private moral absolutes. The people that evince and practice these remain, in my mind and in my fiction, heroic figures. I contrast the automatic integrity of such women with how far from private ethics our public life has fallen.

I am drawn, I think, to widows because they at last find themselves free to act—after half centuries of lurking and cooking as secondary figures. Husbands gone, they are now freed to act as they wish, without consultation, without always cutting themselves down to size to be "the little woman."

PM: There is something about Mrs. Gracie's humble yet direct voice that is instantly endearing. How would you describe the process behind creating and refining that voice?

AG: We tend to think of articulate people as educated people. That's not necessarily true. Often, on the page, the reverse proves so. Someone who's earned a Ph.D. brings a specialized footnoting overload of information to any situation. Is that eloquence? What makes for direct, emotive storytelling? One rustic joke describes the city feller who, when asked for the time, tells how his watch is made. Mrs. Gracie can tell time. She knows its value.

My own aesthetic system sometimes involves treating complex issues as simply as possible. Maria Gracie is not simple. But her mode of expression has a kind of high-school-theme literalness. She has decided to undertake the difficult task of writing a letter to the daughter of parents who were recently murdered in a horrid public way in distant Africa. This surviving child has just been subjected to the further trauma of seeing her dead folks' images in newspapers and *Time* and *Newsweek*. So there has been nothing private or dignifying in their ritual slaughters. It is part of Mrs. Gracie's genius of decency to imagine that she, in her straight-out address and radical humanity (these are my terms, not hers) might provide consolation, some justifying background, to a grieving young woman whom Mrs. Gracie has never met. Her letter is a forthright attempt to salvage something by telling it plain, fast.

Your term "humble" is a beautiful word for this task she assumes without hope of reward. My story's opening places her in her kitchen and clears her morning of appointments. It is important in a written first-person account that we know where the jotting is taking place and under what conditions.

The Widow Gracie's own modesty is established; her early jokes about Kaopectate and how the Canadian librarians wear light sweaters even in Egypt, these hint that she is not a priss or a bore. She proves herself to be precisely the sort of relaxed contained person one could travel with. A kitchen clock is set in motion at the top of the story. It helps make her wind-up, her expecting her grandchildren's visit, all the more eloquent when it arrives by the last P. S. I use the kids' getting out of school as a sort of implied finale. I think the letter was begun just after ten a.m. and finished just before three p.m. A serious undertaking, this could cramp even a non-arthritic hand.

So apart from its material, the letter comes to have stature because we have witnessed its being made, the emotional struggle of that. I actually picture her handwriting deteriorating as the pages pile up on her kitchen table's oilcloth covering.

PM: Mrs. Gracie's self-deprecation helps keep her from seeming moralistic, even when pointing out the failings of her fellow travelers.

AG: Mrs. Gracie cannot resist accusing her former-friends of hiding from harm, even as they click away in a blaze of flashbulbs from their balconies. In a way, every time we accuse others of acting badly, we imply our own decency should be the planetary model. Sometimes that is the sole reason for reportage—a long roll-call of others' failures. But in this case, supported by the very proof of the long letter itself, Maria's own decency is vouchsafed, assured.

One of my favorite details in the story is how our virtuous widow, confronting the half-dressed body of her friend, reaches under the sheet and releases a bra-strap that seems to be cutting into the dead woman's pale back. Something about her performing this release under the cloth's cover seemed right to me. I showed the story in its early stages to an older painter friend named Maud Morgan. She died quite recently at around age one hundred. She had been one of Hemingway's lovers in Paris and was a lovely person, a real woman of the world. Maud cited that detail and said, "You must've felt good when you came up with that." As a very young artist myself, I considered her psychic for knowing what I ranked among the story's most intimate and telling moments. By that, of course, I mean the event or gesture most indirect, unusual, and improbable but finally true (and therefore, with all those contradictions at work, the detail most human). Often the detail that seems most real is the one most utterly invented.

PM: You've written several stories in the form of letters. And at least two address surviving relatives with news of their lost loved ones. The survivor, in this case, Mrs. Whiston, becomes a sort of stand-in for the reader. What emotional effect do you hope to achieve by this technical choice, and what are some of its other advantages or possible limitations?

AG: Which of us ever gets enough letters? These days especially. Therefore the sight of one, for us alone, always appeals. "Dear . . . " is surely any narrative's most en-dearing opening! I overtip if waitresses call me "dearie." It's a favor I can offer my readers.

One advantage of using the epistolary form is: without our quite knowing it, letters have their own built-in conventions, a set of predictable chord-changes. "How are you? We are fine here mostly. I am sitting here, at this particular time of day between doing thus and so, and this is what I see out my window. The big sad odd news here is . . . "

You can build a story on those several comforting stair-steps. You can also subvert their proffered expectations.

Mrs. Gracie addresses a stranger, assuming she knows nothing, providing everything that person might need to know. She asserts that the news broadcasters got it all wrong. She begins by stating her early doubts concerning the theological pedigree of the tour-organizers; then she takes us by degree into a city that is literally blowing up even as the group's ungainly bus enters it. "I was in Africa on Father Flannagan's Tour of the World with your parents when they were killed. I want to tell you how it happened."

The murder of one parent might prove sufficiently involving for a single letter but how both being slain must provoke and implicate everyone with parents, meaning everybody. The joke about Father Flannagan's spurious organization is at once offset and rushed past by that verb "killed." And the opening's subsequent verbs "want" and "tell" are as earnest and essentializing as any I know. They also perfectly embody the character of this particular letter-writer, her seeming simplicity. We will read on . . . she has made us an offer we cannot refuse.

PM: Though filled with death, grief, and suffering, there's a humorous undertone to much of the story, partly due to Mrs. Gracie's being such a stranger to Tongaville, partly due to her extreme modesty. Describe how you are using her point of view—and in particular her eye for detail—to create this nervous humor.

AG: You'd be right in thinking that a story about two people clubbed to death on the street might not qualify as a laugh riot. But my vision is, thank God, a comic one. I go back to the root for the word "comedy," "komos"—meaning: a dance or pageant ritual. Something about the mob streaming past the Hotel Alpha, something about the stolen bus, something about the Stouffer's frozen dinners coming to the rescue, certainly something about photographing an angry anti-capitalist crowd as if it were an exotic species behind bars at some U.S. zoo, all of it is incipiently hilarious. I even enjoyed making up the town called "Tongaville." There exists some pivot flash-point where Tragedy gets the giggles. And that is where I wish to live. The tragedies just keep on coming, so we might as well get whatever pleasure we can from confronting then re-inventing them.

There is nothing more cliché than Midwestern Americans who rush to Egypt in hopes of being photographed atop ill-tempered camels. I push that by having this photographic-minded couple stage-manage their particular sight-gag shot. There is something crudely funny in this and in so many of the supporting details. Since the Americans are traveling light, whatever props they bring to bear on the action must be portable: the old Texan's smuggled pistol, the rich widow's red Samonsite makeup case full of implied jewelry.

The vacuum cleaner is seen in stages. First it is welcomed as a familiar object, an Electrolux after all, just like the one safe in Mrs. Gracie's hall closet. But then she sees how it is being held aloft as a trophy, notable here for its very strangeness. When, later, the vacuum's hose appears, her own addled imagination turns it into a huge African jungle snake, though this is a desert reality. She herself has already been alienated out of trusting the homeliest of her own home implements. The notation here, and in most all my work, is—however emotionally vexed—essentially comic. By which I mean: it is too serious to be left as merely soggily serious. The tale attempts to "make light" of what's impossible, otherwise, to endure.

PM: But how do you, as the author, manage to present this humor without seeming to make fun of Mrs. Gracie or appearing insensitive to the story's tragic events?

AG: I'll give you an example of something I cut. It proved wrong, even condescending. I came to see it would be satirical at the expense of the story's characters. Again, Maud Morgan, now departed, suggested it was the tale's single wrong word. Maria Gracie used to admire the soon-to-be-killed woman's "pretty yellow polyester pantsuit." The mention of this miracle-plastic-fabric of the period would have been true to the time, true to the class-taste of the ill-fated Mrs. Madison. (Educated people who favor cotton and linen and other natural fabrics always sneered at the leathery non-breathing ugly polyester of the period.) Mrs. Gracie would not have admired anyone's suit simply because it was polyester. Other bus tourists would have worn the same material. Instead she's pleased by the pantsuit's cut and color. By deleting that semi-snide reference, by not nudging my reader's ribs, I sidestepped the one word that might have dated my story by mentioning a dead fad. I also honored the characters from within the story. That is essential, keeping the comedy kind. Of course, to be "kind" means to be "like." "Kin" and "kind" share an ancestor. Chekhov's credo ran, "No one must ever be humiliated."

PM: Naming her church Holy Assumption is a small satirical gem. Did that name present itself in the story's composition, or had you been saving it?

AG: Part of the miracle of fiction is its simplest transaction and ever-unfolding daisy-chain: If *this* is true then *that* might be, and if *that* is then what rests beside *it*? "Holy Assumption" is a popular name for working-class Catholic churches; it also puns on certain American assumptions about power, privilege, and God's being on our side. The short story form, like the poem it so closely resembles, can condense so much into two words.

Such linguistic options only happen on the fly while the writer is in full-out motion. No such detail arrives as conscious separate check-list decisions. They are transitive and spill out of one's utter commitment to the character who's speaking.

PM: Her idea toward the end—"Maybe we should give up what we own to feed the hungry?"—is so naked, bold, and direct, and gains even greater poignancy for being so. Was it always posed as a question? (Actually it's a statement passing as a question.)

AG: Punctuation can have a similar wallop. By putting the question mark after "hungry," I throw the question back at the reader. The Widow has already decided against but is asking the reader to be a referee and to go on record about personal sacrifice, how far said reader would go in giving away earthly goods.

PM: To my ear, there definitely exists a strong, very particular thing as the Gurganus voice. It's noticeable even in this early, first-person story—for example, in that question mark after her statement about feeding the world's hungry. When did you first become aware of your "voice" as a writer? And what do you remember doing to cultivate it and to distinguish it from those predecessors you've most admired?

AG: We're all the sum total of our genetic salad, of everything we've ever read, and sung, and humped. That comes out as a force when we tell (or invent) a story we care about. The knowingness arrives later, secondarily; it's the hotel doctor summoned upstairs only after the shots have been fired.

I talked long before I walked. I was made to memorize stupid little comments (authored by my mother). These were meant to astonish those who stopped to peer into my baby-stroller. The infant lisped, "I read dictionaries and encyclopedias all about rhinoceros and hippopotamuses." I am told I said this as a parrot might, only half understanding why it got an awed amused response. I mention this trick as part of my own linguistic shame and pride. I cite it because it shows how my mother gloried in my being a prodigy, at least smart for a baby on one block in Rocky Mount, North Carolina! But when I tell a story the first time, I try to do it without marveling at the cuteness of my diction, at how many forty-dollar vocabulary words I can mortice into its meander.

My work focuses on middle-middle class or working-class people because—cursed with the curlicue vortex of a Baroque imagination—I always need an element of corset-simplification. Mrs. Gracie gave me that. The action is simple and bold. Her transitions from self-consciousness at her kitchen table in Ohio to recalling the terror in Africa are very stark and poster-like in their suddenness. The letter only seems the work of an untutored writer. I boiled down a twenty-four-page story to its simplest, surest outlines:

> "I'm not sure why... I'm not holding one thing back, not sparing you anything, no matter how bad it sounds.
>
> "I tore the sheets off my bed and unlocked the door. People had stacked their luggage as a barricade across

the stair landing. I shoved through this, and some fell down the stairwell but I didn't care."

She has become a tyro in her efforts to help her friends in trouble. The immediate subject-verb sense of motion helps. She moves like the goddess Diana breaking through all obstacles, strengthened by emotion's pure empowerment.

The language creates emotion while seeming to follow emotion, now clarifying, now muddying the narrative line. Craft happens both from the inside out when the writing is molten hot. And it also comes later, with the cooling of emotion recollected in tranquility; then one can work on it from without with dental tools, with a patience impossible during the heat of composition.

PM: Many aspiring writers fantasize about having a mentor, in the way John Cheever was an early mentor of yours when you were a student at the Iowa Writers' Workshop. Could you talk a little about the pluses and minuses of mentorship and demystify that subject a little?

AG: Cheever said either one of two things about any new story I risked showing him: *Yes* or *No*. When he liked something, I felt giddy and fulfilled and godly. When he said *No*, I had no idea what was wrong with it; therefore I thought something hideous must be wrong with me. He was not a conventional how-to teacher.

I later saw he was asking me to write stories the way he did, after his sixty years' daily practice. He would type one straight out and when all ten pages were there, he'd read it cold and either tear the thing up and start over, or mail it right to *The New Yorker*, where it would appear the next week. John was a sprinter, not a dental technician. Either you clear the hurdles or you can't. He belonged to the generation of the Action Painters. The artist stood before a canvas. He committed something to it. If it didn't work, he'd reach for white gesso, let that dry, and would start the damn thing all over again.

I took what I could from this mentor lesson. But I tend to think that any story one loves enough to write must have a little something right with it. That might just be one living, twitchy sentence. Sometimes only the idea survives its own execution. But since I had an insane determination, and since I so respected Cheever's best clarion heartfelt work, he did help me. He became a strong advocate of those stories of mine he believed in absolutely. The others? They're in a file around here somewhere. He was right; they were born deformed but I still buried them with all the Christian rites and honors.

John was one kind of mentor. Also at Iowa, I worked with Stanley Elkin, a comic writer of the wildest sort of wizardry. He had no bedside manner in class. The third week in class, he told one boy who'd just read his story aloud, "You are the queen of laziness," and we all knew it was true and so did the accused writer. He didn't kill himself. He was, I think, too lazy. But Stanley was the most astute critic of new fiction I've ever met. The reverse of John's laurel wreath either awarded or withheld, Stanley's advice was reassuringly specific. "Cut the last three pages then add a third person synopsis written flat, the tone of prose off a cornflakes box. Then you'll have something fresh. But only then . . ." I would resist his Rx for my story till, as if unaided and for my own reasons, I struck on that very same solution, six tedious months later. Stanley was always right. (Oh, if only the dear man had lived forever and were still here to read over my shoulder. But, no, that's not right either.)

You have teachers in the way you have starter marriages in order to survive those, stronger. You must ruthlessly naturalize and imbibe each separate influence. From Cheever's work I absorbed how a story can emerge from what appears the most drear and conventional neighborhood—each one with its heroes, faded athletes, its shameless ladies' men, its well-diggers of genius. From Elkin I learned the value of the jazz riff that builds to a crescendo nearly unbearable till it passes aloft and almost out of human hearing.

But each mentor offers some single strong lesson. And a new writer is wise to be proudly marked by all of them. Then, once you've inhaled their best advice, you ignore it. And only when the lessons are utterly inherent, only when you think you made yourself up out of a cloud, a dictionary-encyclopedia, and a shoestring, only then are you ready—opinionated into shouting a gruff *Yes* or a *No*—to mentor someone else talented, all too serious, but oh so young.

ALLAN GURGANUS has published novels, essays, and short stories. His longer works include *Oldest Living Confederate Widow Tells All* (1989), *White People* (1991), and *The Practical Heart* (2001). A member of the American Academy of Arts and Sciences, he is winner of the Sue Kaufman Prize from the American Academy, and of the *Los Angeles Times* Book Prize for the best work of American fiction. Having taught at Duke, Stanford, Sarah Lawrence, and the Iowa Writers' Workshop, he now lives in a village of five thousand souls in his native North Carolina.

SETTING

SUR

Ursula K. Le Guin

THE THIRD AND FINAL CONTINENT

Jhumpa Lahiri

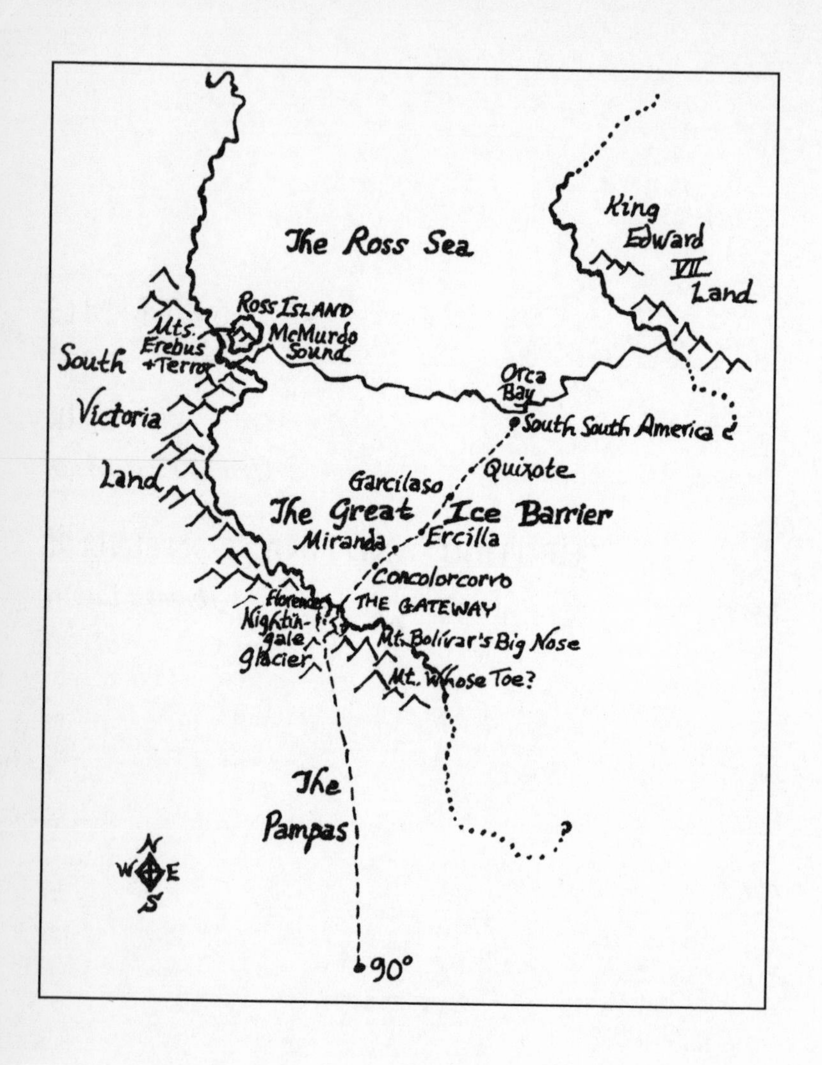

The Ross Sea
King Edward VII Land
Ross Island
Mts. Erebus + Terror
McMurdo Sound
South Victoria Land
Orca Bay
South South America
Quixote
Garcilaso
The Great Ice Barrier
Miranda
Ercilla
Concolorcorvo
Florence Nightin-gale Glacier
THE GATEWAY
Mt. Bolívar's Big Nose
Mt. Whose Toe?
The Pampas
?
N
W
E
S
90°

SUR

Ursula K. Le Guin

A Summary Report of the Yelcho Expedition to the Antarctic, 1909–10

Although I have no intention of publishing this report, I think it would be nice if a grandchild of mine, or somebody's grandchild, happened to find it some day; so I shall keep it in the leather trunk in the attic, along with Rosita's christening gown and Juanito's silver rattle and my wedding shoes and fineskos.

The first requisite for mounting an expedition—money—is normally the hardest to come by. I grieve that even in a report destined for a trunk in the attic of a house in a very quiet suburb of Lima I dare not write the name of the generous benefactor, the great soul without whose unstinting liberality the Yelcho Expedition would never have been more than the idlest excursion into daydream. That our equipment was the best and most modern—that our provisions were plentiful and fine—that a ship of the Chilean government, with her brave officers and gallant crew, was twice sent halfway round the world for our convenience: all this is due to that benefactor whose name, alas! I must not say, but whose happiest debtor I shall be till death.

When I was little more than a child, my imagination was caught by a newspaper account of the voyage of the *Belgica,* which, sailing south from Tierra del Fuego, was beset by ice in the Bellingshausen Sea and drifted a whole year with the floe, the men aboard her suffering a great deal from want of food and from the terror of the unending winter darkness. I read and reread that account, and later followed with excitement the reports of the rescue of Dr. Nordenskjöld from the South Shetland Islands by the dashing Captain Irizar of the *Uruguay,* and the adventures of the *Scotia* in the Weddell Sea. But all these exploits were to me but forerunners of the British National Antarctic Expedition of 1901–04, in the *Discovery,* and the wonderful account of that expedition by Captain Scott. This book, which I ordered from London and reread a thousand times, filled me with longing to see with my own eyes that strange continent, last Thule of the South, which lies on our maps and globes like a white cloud, a void, fringed here and there with scraps of coastline, dubious capes, supposititious islands, headlands that may or may not be there: Antarctica. And the desire was as pure as the polar snows: to go, to see—no more, no less. I deeply respect the scientific accomplishments of Captain Scott's expedition, and have read with passionate interest the findings of physicists, meteorologists, biologists, etc.; but having had no training in any science, nor any opportunity for such training, my ignorance obliged me to forgo any thought of adding to the body of scientific knowledge concerning Antarctica, and the same is true for all members of my expedition. It seems a pity; but there was nothing we could do about it. Our goal was limited to observation and exploration. We hoped to go a little farther, perhaps, and see a little more; if not, simply to go and to see. A simple ambition, I think, and essentially a modest one.

Yet it would have remained less than an ambition, no more than a longing, but for the support and encouragement of my dear cousin and friend Juana ——. (I use no surnames, lest this report fall into strangers' hands at last, and embarrassment or unpleasant notoriety thus be brought upon unsuspecting husbands, sons, etc.) I had lent Juana my copy of *The Voyage of the "Discovery,"* and it was she who, as we strolled beneath our parasols across the Plaza de Armas after Mass one Sunday in 1908, said, "Well, if Captain Scott can do it, why can't we?"

It was Juana who proposed that we write Carlota —— in Valparaíso. Through Carlota we met our benefactor, and so obtained our money, our ship, and even the plausible pretext of going on retreat in a Bolivian convent, which some of us were forced to employ (while the rest of us said we were going to Paris for the winter season). And it was my Juana who in the darkest moments remained resolute, unshaken in her determination to achieve our goal.

And there were dark moments, especially in the spring of 1909—times when I did not see how the Expedition would ever become more than a quarter ton of pemmican gone to waste and a lifelong regret. It was so very hard to gather our expeditionary force together! So few of those we asked even knew what we were talking about—so many thought we were mad, or wicked, or both! And of those few who shared our folly, still fewer were able, when it came to the point, to leave their daily duties and commit themselves to a voyage of at least six months, attended with not inconsiderable uncertainty and danger. An ailing parent; an anxious husband beset by business cares; a child at home with only ignorant or incompetent servants to look after it: these are not responsibilities lightly to be set aside. And those who wished to evade such claims were not the companions we wanted in hard work, risk, and privation.

But since success crowned our efforts, why dwell on the setbacks and delays, or the wretched contrivances and downright lies that we all had to employ? I look back with regret only to those friends who wished to come with us but could not, by any contrivance, get free—those we had to leave behind to a life without danger, without uncertainty, without hope.

On the seventeenth of August, 1909, in Punta Arenas, Chile, all the members of the Expedition met for the first time: Juana and I, the two Peruvians; from Argentina, Zoe, Berta, and Teresa; and our Chileans, Carlota and her friends Eva, Pepita, and Dolores. At the last moment I had received word that María's husband, in Quito, was ill and she must stay to nurse him, so we were nine, not ten. Indeed, we had resigned ourselves to being but eight when, just as night fell, the indomitable Zoe arrived in a tiny pirogue manned by Indians, her yacht having sprung a leak just as it entered the Straits of Magellan.

That night before we sailed we began to get to know one another, and we agreed, as we enjoyed our abominable supper in the abominable seaport inn of Punta Arenas, that if a situation arose of such urgent danger that one voice must be obeyed without present question, the unenviable honor of speaking with that voice should fall first upon myself; if I were incapacitated, upon Carlota; if she, then upon Berta. We three were then toasted as "Supreme Inca," "La Araucana," and "The Third Mate," amid a lot of laughter and cheering. As it came out, to my very great pleasure and relief, my qualities as a "leader" were never tested; the nine of us worked things out amongst us from beginning to end without any orders being given by anybody, and only two or three times with recourse to a vote by voice or show of hands. To be sure, we argued a good deal. But then, we had time to argue. And one way or another the arguments always ended up in a decision, upon which action could be taken. Usually at least one person grumbled about the decision, sometimes bitterly. But what is life without grumbling and the occasional opportunity to say "I told you so"? How could one bear housework, or looking after babies, let alone the rigors of sledge-hauling in Antarctica, without grumbling? Officers—as we came to understand aboard the *Yelcho*—are forbidden to grumble; but we nine were, and are, by birth and upbringing, unequivocally and irrevocably, all crew.

Though our shortest course to the southern continent, and that originally urged upon us by the captain of our good ship, was to the South Shetlands and the Bellingshausen Sea, or else by the South Orkneys into the Weddell Sea, we planned to sail west to the Ross Sea, which Captain Scott had explored and described, and from which the brave Ernest Shackleton had returned only the previous autumn. More was known about this region than any other portion of the coast of Antarctica, and though that more was not much, yet it served as some insurance of the safety of the ship, which we felt we had no right to imperil. Captain Pardo had fully agreed with us after studying the charts and our planned itinerary; and so it was westward that we took our course out of the Straits next morning.

Our journey half round the globe was attended by fortune. The little *Yelcho* steamed cheerily along through gale and gleam, climbing up and down those seas of the Southern Ocean that run unbroken round the world. Juana, who had fought bulls and the far more dangerous cows on her family's *estancia,* called the ship *la vaca valiente*, because she always returned to the charge. Once we got over being seasick, we all enjoyed the sea voyage, though oppressed at times by the kindly but officious protectiveness of the captain and his officers, who felt that we were only "safe" when huddled up in the three tiny cabins that they had chivalrously vacated for our use.

We saw our first iceberg much farther south than we had looked for it, and saluted it with Veuve Clicquot at dinner. The next day we entered the ice pack, the belt of floes and bergs broken loose from the land ice and winter-frozen seas of Antarctica, which drifts northward in the spring. Fortune still smiled on us: our little steamer, incapable, with her unreinforced metal hull, of forcing a way into the ice, picked her way from lane to lane without hesitation, and on the third day we were through the pack, in which ships have sometimes struggled for weeks and been obliged to turn back at last. Ahead of us now lay the dark-grey waters of the Ross Sea, and beyond that, on the horizon, the remote glimmer, the cloud-reflected whiteness of the Great Ice Barrier.

Entering the Ross Sea a little east of Longitude West 160°, we came in sight of the Barrier at the place where Captain Scott's party, finding a bight in the vast wall of ice, had gone ashore and sent up their hydrogen-gas balloon for reconnaissance and photography. The towering face of the Barrier, its sheer cliffs and azure and violet waterworn caves, all were as described, but the location had changed; instead of a narrow bight, there was a considerable bay, full of the beautiful and terrific orca whales playing and spouting in the sunshine of that brilliant southern spring.

Evidently masses of ice many acres in extent had broken away from the Barrier (which—at least for most of its vast extent—does not rest on land but floats on water) since the *Discovery*'s passage in 1902. This put our plan to set up camp on the Barrier itself in a new light; and while we were discussing alternatives, we asked Captain Pardo to take the ship west along the Barrier face toward Ross Island and McMurdo Sound. As the sea was clear of ice and quite calm, he was happy to do so and, when we sighted the smoke plume of Mt. Erebus, to share in our celebration—another half case of Veuve Clicquot.

The *Yelcho* anchored in Arrival Bay, and we went ashore in the ship's boat. I cannot describe my emotions when I set foot on the earth, the barren, cold gravel at the foot of the long volcanic slope. I felt elation, impatience, gratitude, awe, familiarity. I felt that I was home at last. Eight Adélie penguins immediately came to greet us with many exclamations of interest not unmixed with disapproval. "Where on earth have you been? What took you so long? The Hut is around this way. Please come this way. Mind the rocks!" They insisted on our going to visit Hut Point, where the large structure built by Captain Scott's party stood, looking just as in the photographs and drawings that illustrate his book. The area about it, however, was disgusting—a kind of graveyard of seal skins, seal bones, penguin bones, and rubbish, presided over by the mad, screaming skua gulls. Our escorts waddled past the slaughterhouse in all tranquility, and one showed me personally to the door, though it would not go in.

The interior of the hut was less offensive but very dreary. Boxes of supplies had been stacked up into a kind of room within the room; it did not look as I had imagined it when the *Discovery* party put on their melodramas and minstrel shows in the long winter night. (Much later, we learned that Sir Ernest had rearranged it a good deal when he was there just a year before us.) It was dirty, and had about it a mean disorder. A pound tin of tea was standing open. Empty meat tins lay about; biscuits were spilled on the floor; a lot of dog turds were underfoot—frozen, of course, but not a great deal improved by that. No doubt the last occupants had had to leave in a hurry, perhaps even in a blizzard. All the same, they could have closed the tea tin. But housekeeping, the art of the infinite, is no game for amateurs.

Teresa proposed that we use the hut as our camp. Zoe counterproposed that we set fire to it. We finally shut the door and left it as we had found it. The penguins appeared to approve, and cheered us all the way to the boat.

McMurdo Sound was free of ice, and Captain Pardo now proposed to take us off Ross Island and across to Victoria Land, where we might camp at the foot of the Western Mountains, on dry and solid earth. But those mountains, with their storm-darkened peaks and hanging cirques and glaciers, looked as awful as Captain Scott had found them on his western journey, and none of us felt much inclined to seek shelter among them.

Aboard the ship that night we decided to go back and set up our base as we had originally planned, on the Barrier itself. For all available reports indicated that the clear way south was across the level Barrier surface until one could ascend one of the confluent glaciers to the high plateau that appears to form the whole interior of the continent. Captain Pardo argued strongly against this plan, asking what would become of us if the Barrier "calved"—if our particular acre of ice broke away and started to drift northward. "Well," said Zoe, "then you won't have to come so far to meet us." But he was so persuasive on this theme that he persuaded himself into leaving one of the *Yelcho*'s boats with us when we camped, as a means of escape. We found it useful for fishing, later on.

My first steps on Antarctic soil, my only visit to Ross Island, had not been pleasure unalloyed. I thought of the words of the English poet,

> Though every prospect pleases,
> And only Man is vile.

But then, the backside of heroism is often rather sad; women and servants know that. They know also that the heroism may be no less real for that. But achievement is smaller than men think. What is large is the sky, the earth, the sea, the soul. I looked back as the ship sailed east again that evening. We were well into September now, with eight hours or more of daylight. The spring sunset lingered on the twelve-thousand-foot peak of Erebus and shone rosy-gold on her long plume of steam. The steam from our own small funnel faded blue on the twilit water as we crept along under the towering pale wall of ice.

On our return to "Orca Bay"—Sir Ernest, we learned years later, had named it the Bay of Whales—we found a sheltered nook where the Barrier edge was low enough to provide fairly easy access from the ship. The *Yelcho* put out her ice anchor, and the next long, hard days were spent in unloading our supplies and setting up our camp on the ice, a half kilometre in from the edge: a task in which the *Yelcho*'s crew lent us invaluable aid and interminable advice. We took all the aid gratefully, and most of the advice with salt.

The weather so far had been extraordinarily mild for spring in this latitude; the temperature had not yet gone below –20°F, and there was only one blizzard while we were setting up camp. But Captain Scott had spoken feelingly of the bitter south winds on the Barrier, and we had planned accordingly. Exposed as our camp was to every wind, we built no rigid structures above ground. We set up tents to shelter in while we dug out a series of cubicles in the ice itself, lined them with hay insulation and pine boarding, and roofed them with canvas over bamboo poles, covered with snow for weight and insulation. The big central room was instantly named Buenos Aires by our Argentineans, to whom the center, wherever one is, is always Buenos Aires. The heating and cooking stove was in Buenos Aires. The storage tunnels and the privy (called Punta Arenas) got some back heat from the stove. The sleeping cubicles opened off Buenos Aires, and were very small, mere tubes into which one crawled feet first; they were lined deeply with hay and soon warmed by one's body warmth. The sailors called them coffins and worm-holes, and looked with horror on our burrows in the ice. But our little warren or prairie-dog village served us well, permitting us as much warmth and privacy as one could reasonably expect under such circumstances. If the *Yelcho* was unable to get through the ice in February and we had to spend the winter in Antarctica, we certainly could do so, though on very limited rations. For this coming summer, our base—Sudamérica del Sur, South South America, but we generally called it the Base—was intended merely as a place to sleep, to store our provisions, and to give shelter from blizzards.

To Berta and Eva, however, it was more than that. They were its chief architect-designers, its most ingenious builder-excavators, and its most diligent and contented occupants, forever inventing an improvement in ventilation, or learning how to make skylights, or revealing to us a new addition to our suite of rooms, dug in the living ice. It was thanks to them that our stores were stowed so handily, that our stove drew and heated so efficiently, and that Buenos Aires, where nine people cooked, ate, worked, conversed, argued, grumbled, painted, played the guitar and banjo, and kept the Expedition's library of books and maps, was a marvel of comfort and convenience. We lived there in real amity; and if you simply had to be alone for a while, you crawled into your sleeping hole head first.

Berta went a little farther. When she had done all she could to make South South America livable, she dug out one more cell just under the ice surface, leaving a nearly transparent sheet of ice like a greenhouse roof; and there, alone, she worked at sculptures. They were beautiful forms, some like a blending of the reclining human figure with the subtle curves and volumes of the Weddell seal, others like the fantastic shapes of ice cornices and ice caves. Perhaps they are there still, under the snow, in the bubble in the Great Barrier. There where she made them, they might last as long as stone. But she could not bring them north. That is the penalty for carving in water.

Captain Pardo was reluctant to leave us, but his orders did not permit him to hang about the Ross Sea indefinitely, and so at last, with many earnest injunctions to us to stay put—make no journeys—take no risks—beware of frostbite—don't use edge tools—look out for cracks in the ice—and a heartfelt promise to return to Orca Bay on February 20th, or as near that date as wind and ice would permit, the good man bade us farewell, and his crew shouted us a great goodbye cheer as they weighed anchor. That evening, in the long orange twilight of October, we saw the topmast of the *Yelcho* go down the north horizon, over the edge of the world, leaving us to ice, and silence, and the Pole.

That night we began to plan the Southern Journey.

The ensuing month passed in short practice trips and depot-laying. The life we had led at home, though in its own way strenuous, had not fitted any of us for the kind of strain met with in sledge-hauling at ten or twenty degrees below freezing. We all needed as much working out as possible before we dared undertake a long haul.

My longest exploratory trip, made with Dolores and Carlota, was southwest toward Mt. Markham, and it was a nightmare—blizzards and pressure ice all the way out, crevasses and no view of the mountains when we got there, and white weather and sastrugi all the way back. The trip was useful, however, in that we could begin to estimate our capacities; and also in that we had started out with a very heavy load of provisions, which we depoted at a hundred and a hundred and thirty miles south-southwest of Base. Thereafter other parties pushed on farther, till we had a line of snow cairns and depots right down to Latitude 80° 43', where Juana and Zoe, on an exploring trip, had found a kind of stone gateway opening on a great glacier leading south. We established these depots to avoid, if possible, the hunger that had bedevilled Captain Scott's Southern Party, and the consequent misery and weakness. And we also established to our own satisfaction—intense satisfaction—that we were sledge-haulers at least as good as Captain Scott's husky dogs. Of course we could not have expected to pull as much or as fast as his men. That we did so was because we were favored by much better weather than Captain Scott's party ever met on the Barrier; and also the quantity and quality of our food made a very considerable difference. I am sure that the fifteen percent of dried fruits in our pemmican helped prevent scurvy; and the potatoes, frozen and dried according to an ancient Andean Indian method, were very nourishing yet very light and compact—perfect sledding rations. In any case, it was with considerable confidence in our capacities that we made ready at last for the Southern Journey.

The Southern Party consisted of two sledge teams: Juana, Dolores, and myself; Carlota, Pepita, and Zoe. The support team of Berta, Eva, and Teresa set out before us with a heavy load of supplies, going right up onto the glacier to prospect routes and leave depots of supplies for our return journey. We followed five days behind them, and met them returning between Depot Ercilla and Depot Miranda. That "night"—of course, there was no real darkness—we were all nine together in the heart of the level plain of ice. It was November 15th, Dolores's birthday. We celebrated by putting eight ounces of pisco in the hot chocolate, and became very merry. We sang. It is strange now to remember how thin our voices sounded in that great silence. It was overcast, white weather, without shadows and without visible horizon or any feature to break the level; there was nothing to see at all. We had come to that white place on the map, that void, and there we flew and sang like sparrows.

After sleep and a good breakfast the Base Party continued north, and the Southern Party sledged on. The sky cleared presently. High up, thin clouds passed over very rapidly from southwest to northeast, but down on the Barrier it was calm and just cold enough, five or ten degrees below freezing, to give a firm surface for hauling.

On the level ice we never pulled less than eleven miles (seventeen kilometres) a day, and generally fifteen or sixteen miles (twenty-five kilometres). (Our instruments, being British-made, were calibrated in feet, miles, degrees Fahrenheit, etc., but we often converted miles to kilometres, because the larger numbers sounded more encouraging.) At the time we left South America, we knew only that Mr. Ernest Shackleton had mounted another expedition to the Antarctic in 1907, had tried to attain the Pole but failed, and had returned to England in June of the current year, 1909. No coherent report of his explorations had yet reached South America when we left; we did not know what route he had gone, or how far he had got. But we were not altogether taken by surprise when, far across the featureless white plain, tiny beneath the mountain peaks and the strange silent flight of the rainbow-fringed cloud wisps, we saw a fluttering dot of black. We turned west from our course to visit it: a snow heap nearly buried by the winter's storms—a flag on a bamboo pole, a mere shred of threadbare cloth, an empty oil-can—and a few footprints standing some inches above the ice. In some conditions of weather the snow compressed under one's weight remains when the surrounding soft snow melts or is scoured away by the wind; and so these reversed footprints had been left standing all these months, like rows of cobbler's lasts—a queer sight.

We met no other such traces on our way. In general I believe our course was somewhat east of Mr. Shackleton's. Juana, our surveyor, had trained herself well and was faithful and methodical in her sightings and readings, but our equipment was minimal—a theodolite on tripod legs, a sextant with artificial horizon, two compasses, and chronometers. We had only the wheel meter on the sledge to give distance actually traveled.

In any case, it was the day after passing Mr. Shackleton's waymark that I first saw clearly the great glacier among the mountains to the southwest, which was to give us a pathway from the sea level of the Barrier up to the altiplano, ten thousand feet above. The approach was magnificent: a gateway formed by immense vertical domes and pillars of rock. Zoe and Juana had called the vast ice river that flowed through that gateway the Florence Nightingale Glacier, wishing to honor the British, who had been the inspiration and guide of our Expedition; that very brave and very peculiar lady seemed to represent so much that is best, and strangest, in the island race. On maps, of course, this glacier bears the name Mr. Shackleton gave it: the Beardmore.

The ascent of the Nightingale was not easy. The way was open at first, and well marked by our support party, but after some days we came among terrible crevasses, a maze of hidden cracks, from a foot to thirty feet wide and from thirty to a thousand feet deep. Step by step we went, and step by step, and the way always upward now. We were fifteen days on the glacier. At first the weather was hot—up to 20°F—and the hot nights without darkness were wretchedly uncomfortable in our small tents. And all of us suffered more or less from snowblindness just at the time when we wanted clear eyesight to pick our way among the ridges and crevasses of the tortured ice, and to see the wonders about and before us. For at every day's advance more great, nameless peaks came into view in the west and southwest, summit beyond summit, range beyond range, stark rock and snow in the unending noon.

We gave names to these peaks, not very seriously, since we did not expect our discoveries to come to the attention of geographers. Zoe had a gift for naming, and it is thanks to her that certain sketch maps in various suburban South American attics bear such curious features as "Bolívar's Big Nose," "I Am General Rosas," "The Cloudmaker," "Whose Toe?," and "Throne of Our Lady of the Southern Cross." And when at last we got up onto the altiplano, the great interior plateau, it was Zoe who called it the pampa, and maintained that we walked there among vast herds of invisible cattle, transparent cattle pastured on the spindrift snow, their gauchos the restless, merciless winds. We were by then all a little crazy with exhaustion and the great altitude—twelve thousand feet—and the cold and the wind blowing and the luminous circles and crosses surrounding the suns, for often there were three or four suns in the sky, up there.

That is not a place where people have any business to be. We should have turned back; but since we had worked so hard to get there, it seemed that we should go on, at least for a while.

A blizzard came, with very low temperatures, so we had to stay in the tents, in our sleeping bags, for thirty hours—a rest we all needed, though it was warmth we needed most, and there was no warmth on that terrible plain anywhere at all but in our veins. We huddled close together all that time. The ice we lay on is two miles thick.

It cleared suddenly and became, for the plateau, good weather: twelve below zero and the wind not very strong. We three crawled out of our tent and met the others crawling out of theirs. Carlota told us then that her group wished to turn back. Pepita had been feeling very ill; even after the rest during the blizzard, her temperature would not rise above 94°. Carlota was having trouble breathing. Zoe was perfectly fit, but much preferred staying with her friends and lending them a hand in difficulties to pushing on toward the Pole. So we put the four ounces of pisco that we had been keeping for Christmas into the breakfast cocoa, and dug out our tents, and loaded our sledges, and parted there in the white daylight on the bitter plain.

Our sledge was fairly light by now. We pulled on to the south. Juana calculated our position daily. On the twenty-second of December, 1909, we reached the South Pole. The weather was, as always, very cruel. Nothing of any kind marked the dreary whiteness. We discussed leaving some kind of mark or monument, a snow cairn, a tent pole and flag; but there seemed no particular reason to do so. Anything we could do, anything we were, was insignificant, in that awful place. We put up the tent for shelter for an hour and made a cup of tea, and then struck "90° Camp."

Dolores, standing patient as ever in her sledging harness, looked at the snow; it was so hard frozen that it showed no trace of our footprints coming, and she said, "Which way?"

"North," said Juana.

It was a joke, because at that particular place there is no other direction. But we did not laugh. Our lips were cracked with frostbite and hurt too much to let us laugh. So we started back, and the wind at our backs pushed us along, and dulled the knife edges of the waves of frozen snow.

All that week the blizzard wind pursued us like a pack of mad dogs. I cannot describe it. I wished we had not gone to the Pole. I think I wish it even now. But I was glad even then that we had left no sign there, for some man longing to be first might come some day, and find it, and know then what a fool he had been, and break his heart.

We talked, when we could talk, of catching up to Carlota's party, since they might be going slower than we. In fact they used their tent as a sail to catch the following wind and had got far ahead of us. But in many places they had built snow cairns or left some sign for us; once, Zoe had written on the lee side of a ten-foot sastruga, just as children write on the sand of the beach at Miraflores, "This Way Out!" The wind blowing over the frozen ridge had left the words perfectly distinct.

In the very hour that we began to descend the glacier, the weather turned warmer, and the mad dogs were left to howl forever tethered to the Pole. The distance that had taken us fifteen days going up we covered in only eight days going down. But the good weather that had aided us descending the Nightingale became a curse down on the Barrier ice, where we had looked forward to a kind of royal progress from depot to depot, eating our fill and taking our time for the last three hundred-odd miles. In a tight place on the glacier I lost my goggles—I was swinging from my harness at the time in a crevasse—and then Juana broke hers when we had to do some rock-climbing coming down to the Gateway. After two days in bright sunlight with only one pair of snow goggles to pass amongst us, we were all suffering badly from snowblindness. It became acutely painful to keep lookout for landmarks or depot flags, to take sightings, even to study the compass, which had to be laid down on the snow to steady the needle. At Concolorcorvo Depot, where there was a particularly good supply of food and fuel, we gave up, crawled into our sleeping bags with bandaged eyes, and slowly boiled alive like lobsters in the tent exposed to the relentless sun. The voices of Berta and Zoe were the sweetest sound I ever heard. A little concerned about us, they had skied south to meet us. They led us home to Base.

We recovered quite swiftly, but the altiplano left its mark. When she was very little, Rosita asked if a dog "had bitted Mama's toes." I told her yes—a great, white, mad dog named Blizzard! My Rosita and my Juanito heard many stories when they were little, about that fearful dog and how it howled, and the transparent cattle of the invisible gauchos, and a river of ice eight thousand feet high called Nightingale, and how Cousin Juana drank a cup of tea standing on the bottom of the world under seven suns, and other fairy tales.

We were in for one severe shock when we reached Base at last. Teresa was pregnant. I must admit that my first response to the poor girl's big belly and sheepish look was anger—rage—fury. That one of us should have concealed anything, and such a thing, from the others! But Teresa had done nothing of the sort. Only those who had concealed from her what she most needed to know were to blame. Brought up by servants, with four years' schooling in a convent, and married at sixteen, the poor girl was still so ignorant at twenty years of age that she had thought it was "the cold weather" that made her miss her periods. Even this was not entirely stupid, for all of us on the Southern Journey had seen our periods change or stop altogether as we experienced increasing cold, hunger, and fatigue. Teresa's appetite had begun to draw general attention; and then she had begun, as she said pathetically, "to get fat." The others were worried at the thought of all the sledge-hauling she had done, but she flourished, and the only problem was her positively insatiable appetite. As well as could be determined from her shy references to her last night on the hacienda with her husband, the baby was due at just about the same time as the *Yelcho,* February 20th. But we had not been back from the Southern Journey two weeks when, on February 14th, she went into labor.

Several of us had borne children and had helped with deliveries, and anyhow most of what needs to be done is fairly self-evident; but a first labor can be long and trying, and we were all anxious, while Teresa was frightened out of her wits. She kept calling for her José till she was as hoarse as a skua. Zoe lost all patience at last and said, "By God, Teresa, if you say 'José!' once more, I hope you have a penguin!" But what she had, after twenty long hours, was a pretty little red-faced girl.

Many were the suggestions for that child's name from her eight proud midwife aunts: Polita, Penguina, McMurdo, Victoria . . . But Teresa announced, after she had had a good sleep and a large serving of pemmican, "I shall name her Rosa—Rosa del Sur," Rose of the South. That night we drank the last two bottles of Veuve Clicquot (having finished the pisco at 88° 60' South) in toasts to our little Rose.

On the nineteenth of February, a day early, my Juana came down into Buenos Aires in a hurry. "The ship," she said, "the ship has come," and she burst into tears—she who had never wept in all our weeks of pain and weariness on the long haul.

Of the return voyage there is nothing to tell. We came back safe.

In 1912 all the world learned that the brave Norwegian Amundsen had reached the South Pole; and then, much later, we heard the accounts of how Captain Scott and his men had come there after him but did not come home again.

Just this year, Juana and I wrote to the captain of the *Yelcho,* for the newspapers have been full of the story of his gallant dash to rescue Sir Ernest Shackleton's men from Elephant Island, and we wished to congratulate him, and once more to thank him. Never one word has he breathed of our secret. He is a man of honor, Luis Pardo.

* * *

I add this last note in 1929. Over the years we have lost touch with one another. It is very difficult for women to meet, when they live as far apart as we do. Since Juana died, I have seen none of my old sledgemates, though sometimes we write. Our little Rosa del Sur died of the scarlet fever when she was five years old. Teresa had many other children. Carlota took the veil in Santiago ten years ago. We are old women now, with old husbands, and grown children, and grandchildren who might some day like to read about the Expedition. Even if they are rather ashamed of having such a crazy grandmother, they may enjoy sharing in the secret. But they must not let Mr. Amundsen know! He would be terribly embarrassed and disappointed. There is no need for him or anyone else outside the family to know. We left no footprints, even.

URSULA K. LE GUIN DISCUSSES

"Sur," setting, and a place of remote and terrible beauty

PM: At what point as a writer were you drawn to focus on alien worlds?
UKL: The first story I can recall writing was a fantasy involving evil elves who teased a writer, and by twelve or so I had written one concerning time travel and the origin of life on Earth, so it appears that I was pretty well alienated from the start. I began to find my fictional voice at twenty or so, when I discovered the country of Orsinia, which is alien only in being imaginary and, come to think of it, un-American. I really am not sure when I first wrote a story set on a world other than Earth.
PM: What draws you to the idea of invented or barely trodden territory? Is it freeing?
UKL: Apparently I often have to go around a corner in the fourth or fifth dimension in order to view what is under my nose. "Distancing" is not the right word, but I don't know what is. I need indirection. "Write it slant," said Emily {Dickinson}.

But yes, it is freeing, too: despite the labor of inventing and furnishing a world, the imagined setting allows purification, a concentration on what the story is about. Maybe it is for a writer something like painting scenes from the Bible or classical mythology was for painters up to the twentieth century: by shedding the trappings and fashions and inevitable references of the modern, and painting real people in imagined settings, they could achieve a large clarity of actions and emotions, a broad but intense relevance.
PM: Do you typically start with a setting and mine it for its human implications, or start with a character-driven premise, then cast around for a setting in which to showcase it?

UKL: No two stories start the same way, but my experience is mostly that the people and the settings come at the same time, are indissoluble. The setting does sometimes come first, but only marginally; if it doesn't promptly sprout the people who live in it, it's not much use to me as a storyteller.

PM: How did you conceive of a feminist social satire (and would you even call it that) set in Antarctica?

UKL: As a child I read a book about Admiral Byrd's terrier, Igloo, and was fascinated with the landscape of ice. I began to read the accounts and memoirs of the early Antarctic explorers when I was in my twenties. It was hard to get hold of most of them then, but I read all I could get, Scott, Shackleton, Cherry-Garrard, the lot. Over the years I did a great deal of armchair travel by man-hauled sled (and so knew how to describe the journey across the glacier in my novel *The Left Hand of Darkness*). The idea for sending a party of women to the South Pole a little in advance of Scott drifted into my head on an airplane. As soon as I got off the plane and could write, the unnamed narrator of "Sur" began to tell me the story, very directly, plainly, and without pausing for questions. I wrote down what she told me and sent it to *The New Yorker*. They accepted it. She is not the kind of woman you argue with. A reticent person, but firm.

PM: What specific idea, image, or voice fragment occurred to you on that fateful plane ride? Or perhaps the right question is: How did the narrator introduce herself to you?

UKL: I think I just began thinking about what if some women had actually been there before all the famous men but didn't say anything about it . . . and then who were the women . . . and then I saw that they were South American women, and so on from there, so that when I began actually to write the story, my narrator was ready for me, or I for her.

PM: How do you attempt to create the right conditions for inspiration?

UKL: Well, I mostly describe the pre-writing state as "listening," and that's what I do, I listen—for the voice or voices or whatever. It's not a matter of willing something to happen, calling forth, creating conditions, etc. I get nowhere doing that. ("He can summon spirits from the vasty deep."—"Aye, but will they come . . . ?")

Negative capability, yin, wu wei, that's what I depend on. Listening is an intense state. We undervalue reception, receptivity.

PM: The title, being the Spanish word for south, also sounds like the male honorific *sir*, yes? At what point did you come up with it? What other titles did you consider?

UKL: Oh, it is a homage to Jorge Luis Borges, for his story "El Sur" and for being Borges. (I am afraid it sounds more like a drainpipe than an honorific—it rhymes better with *your* or *dour*.) It was always the story's title. The narrator provided it, along with the map, and as I say, argument was out of the question.

PM: The scientific subtitle creates that strong sense of verisimilitude, but is also very generous: it orients us immediately. What inspired it? Had you written any drafts without that device?

UKL: I am ashamed to say that the story didn't have many drafts. Probably I (or the narrator) added the subtitle when I was typing from the first draft making the clean copy to submit. The subtitle is in imitation, of course, of the kind of books I read about South Polar exploration.

PM: You also help the reader keep pace—on a journey that could easily have become surreal and confusing—by beginning many paragraphs with a simple orienting phrase like, "Entering the Ross Sea." Were you conscious of leaving those breadcrumbs?

UKL: This is embarrassing. I have to keep saying that I was taking dictation from a nonexistent person. It sounds like an excuse for narrative irresponsibility.

Anyhow, knowing where one is is tremendously important to an explorer. I did get out my books and maps, and checked the party's positions and sites and camps, distances traveled and travel chronology, etc., with care.

I drew the narrator's sketch-map pretty promptly, as I needed it to refer to. Names of mountains, etc., were added as we traveled.

PM: Upon setting foot on Antarctica, why does the narrator say, "I felt that I was home at last"?

UKL: I know of two reasons among, probably, several more. One is that she, and I, had always dreamed of Antarctica as a place of remote and terrible beauty; when you find yourself in the place you've read and thought about and imagined for years, and find it as remote, terrible, and beautiful as your dreams of it, you may well feel that you have come home.

The other reason I can explain best perhaps by citing the story "The Women Men Don't See," by James Tiptree, Jr.—in which a middle-aged, ordinary American woman and her daughter are marooned with some men in the marshes of the Yucatan. A space ship lands, and presently the women go off on the space ship with the aliens. The men are aghast, but we see that the women feel more at home with the aliens than they do with the men.

The women in my story feel at home in Antarctica because there is nobody telling them that it doesn't belong to them, that men own everything, do everything, are everything. . . .

But this explanation is both crude and approximate. By suggesting it indirectly, the story says it better than any interpretation can do.

PM: Part of the story's indirection lies in the discrepancy between the narrator's voice and the author's. For example, we readers represent just the sort of "strangers" the narrator wishes to keep the document from. How did you conceive of and then maintain that delicate tension between her stated modest agenda and your larger implicit one?

UKL: By not thinking about mine at all. Really, absolutely not. I don't even want to think about it now. When I have a collaborator of the quality of that nameless narrator, I should, I think, be grateful, and shut up.

PM: Allow me to badger you about it just a bit more. So much of the story's artfulness seems to derive from the gap between her professed reticence and the objective "realities" of the document. When she says she doesn't want to break the heart of any male explorer who might follow, I *believe* her. Shouldn't I?

UKL: Of course you should. She wrote the story because it is (you will agree, I hope) a story worth telling; and, as she says, she thinks it might be nice if her grandchild, or somebody's grandchild, found it and read it some day, so she put it in a trunk in the attic, along with the map. She doesn't like to think of nobody ever knowing anything about what she and the others did—utter oblivion. But the idea of publishing—"going public"—is I think genuinely abhorrent to her; as it would have been to most women of her country, class, and kind. Her reticence is real.

If there is any bad faith, it's mine. I invaded her attic.

PM: It's that "bad faith," as you call it, that I find so artful. Another of the story's beautiful strengths is the unusual way it enlarges the ideas of discovery and legacy. And even though in some ways the story is very pointed and critical, its overarching temperament is one of great generosity.

UKL: The older I get, the more I love and admire generosity, magnanimity, and when in moral doubt I try to use it as my guide—to choose the more generous act or word.

PM: The raised footprints on page 196 seem a key image for the story. Where did you learn about the phenomenon and how did you decide what it was going to mean?

UKL: I think it's in one of Shackleton's books. An unforgettable image, which presented itself at the right time. And which I would interpret only once the story is written, if I can interpret it at all, which I don't think I can.

PM: You seem to return to the image very pointedly in the story's last line, when we're reminded this expedition left no footprints, and I infer the reason to be that as women they weighed less and so did not compress the snow tightly enough to leave that strangely raised variety. Am I inventing this?

UKL: It's possible, but I doubt the weight difference would be significant. More likely it was just different weather/snow conditions. Shackleton (or whoever it was) made it clear, or so I recall, that it was not a common phenomenon, not something they saw every time they crossed previous tracks, but was odd, worthy of notice.

PM: The image of reversed footprints also seems to convey the idea that things are not always what people expect.

UKL: That's possible too.

Really, I'm sorry—but as a rule I cannot interpret what images in my work "mean," and I receive strong warnings from within to avoid it. Criticism, analysis, interpretation are all invaluable skills, but they are not the author's job, and often not the author's skills.

I don't mean to come on all woo-woo about this, you know. I do not hear voices, I am not a puppet "controlled" by my characters, and I do not abandon reason when I write.

Put it this way: the story is the text; analysis and interpretation are translations of the text into a different language. I don't always care to translate my own work, and sometimes actively resist being asked to do so, because I know I will both falsify and lessen it.

PM: Your descriptions of the terrain are always serving other functions, like delineating character or articulating theme, or both, in the case of Captain Scott's camp on pages 190–91. How do you achieve that depth of complexity?

UKL: "Fortune favors the prepared mind." I had been reading about that camp for years, how it looked to different expeditions that used it, and how they used it, etc. (It is still there, you know.) There was my data at hand when I wanted it.

As to the larger question, I suppose everything in a short story has to serve several purposes; but one does not plan all those functions consciously and deliberately. If the story is going right, one doesn't grope about for complexity of relevance. It supplies itself as if inevitably, like harmony in music.

PM: You give your narrator's diction a slight formality to help suggest the historical time frame and the fact that she's probably not writing in English, which you also emphasize with few italicized Spanish words. How do you tell when you're doing enough of this and not too much? (A former teacher of mine regrets deeply his decision to spell phonetically all the southern dialect in his first novel.)

UKL: Just pleasing my own ear. I like dialect writing, so long as it "says" itself to the ear through the eye, like the Scots dialogue in Walter Scott, or Burns's or Clare's poetry. I also like it when characters of a historical period talk like people of that period. But I'm allergic to excess of foreign words (seems show-offish) or use of non-English locutions (seems silly).

PM: You're actually fluent in Spanish and have translated a book of poetry; have you ever composed in it yourself? Does having more than one language enhance your facility with English?

UKL: I studied French and Italian language and literature in college and grad school, because I didn't want to be told what to read in English, and because I always loved learning both my own language and other people's languages. I think the more language(s) I know the more surely language is my instrument. I can read several now, but can write only in my own.

PM: Early in "Sur," you reveal the expedition was a "success," thereby dispelling the most obvious element of suspense. Why?

UKL: I don't really know, but it might be because I myself enjoy suspense only very moderately, and often find it to be quite destructive to a story. It is a mechanical device to force and drag the reader forward. As a reader I would rather be lured forward by the interest of what is being told. As a writer I prefer to lure rather than drag.

PM: Your dispensing with it early also seems to free the story to address more important questions, like *how* the women interacted with each other and the wild.

UKL: Exactly!

PM: On a related note, it's worth mentioning how little fanfare attends their arrival at the Pole. Which seems to emphasize that the climax of this particular story is not conquest. If I had to guess, I'd say it's the birth of Teresa's child, Rosa del Sur. Or does this story even have a climax, as its commonly conceived?

UKL: I love that word, *climax*. A whole Theory of Narrative lies within it. Pump, pump pump bam bam faster! faster! faster-fasterfaster! carchase-weeeeoooooo-OOOOO POW!

Am I being awfully rude?

Anyhow, conquest is definitely not the point of the story. Anti-conquest, maybe? Thus involving a degree of Anticlimax (a word that could be read in more than one way) . . . ?

I don't think Rosa's birth is any sort of, er, climax. Why would it be? Is reproductive function inevitably the climactic event of a woman's life, even nine women who also happened to go to the South Pole, eight of whom did not have a baby?

It just happened.

Birth is a thing that tends to happen when women are around.

There were not a lot of childbirths on most Polar expeditions, when one comes to think of it. It wasn't an option for most of them. Poor fellows.

PM: Why did you have the child die five years later?

UKL: Because life is like that. You survive birth in a hole in the ice of Antarctica, and then die at five of chickenpox. It is not fair.

PM: Is there anything about the story you'd change if you were writing it today?

UKL: Yes, I would not be so rude about Punta Arenas. I have visited it twice since I wrote the story, and found it not the harsh and sordid town my narrator describes, but an appealing little city on a grand harbor. And inland of it is all Patagonia. But as I said, I do not argue with that narrator.

PM: I imagine this is a story that has touched readers deeply. What response have you gotten to it?

UKL: Very positive, and it still gets reprinted fairly often. Some people I think are merely amused by the impertinence of the idea; others are indeed moved by it. I was very moved myself, when a soldier who had been with the American South Pole team sent me her Antarctic Service badge. And again, when one of the women who recently crossed Antarctica afoot told me before she set off that she was carrying the story along with her. When every ounce you carry counts . . . that is an unsurpassable honor.

❧

URSULA K. LE GUIN writes in various modes including realistic fiction, science fiction, fantasy, books for children and young adults, essays, and poems. She has published nineteen novels, eleven volumes of short fiction, twelve books for children, three collections of nonfiction, six volumes of poetry, and four of translation. Her most recent books are a collection of talks and essays, *The Wave in the Mind* (2004), and a novel, *Gifts* (2004).

THE THIRD AND FINAL CONTINENT

Jhumpa Lahiri

I left India in 1964 with a certificate in commerce and the equivalent, in those days, of ten dollars to my name. For three weeks I sailed on the SS *Roma,* an Italian cargo vessel, in a cabin next to the ship's engine, across the Arabian Sea, the Red Sea, the Mediterranean, and finally to England. I lived in north London, in Finsbury Park, in a house occupied entirely by penniless Bengali bachelors like myself, at least a dozen and sometimes more, all struggling to educate and establish ourselves abroad.

I attended lectures at LSE and worked at the university library to get by. We lived three or four to a room, shared a single, icy toilet, and took turns cooking pots of egg curry, which we ate with our hands on a table covered with newspapers. Apart from our jobs we had few responsibilities. On weekends we lounged barefoot in drawstring pajamas, drinking tea and smoking Rothmans, or set out to watch cricket at Lord's. Some weekends the house was crammed with still more Bengalis, to whom we had introduced ourselves at the greengrocer, or on the Tube, and we made yet more egg curry, and played Mukesh on a Grundig reel-to-reel, and soaked our dirty dishes in the bathtub. Every now and then someone in the house moved out, to live with a woman whom his family back in Calcutta had determined he was to wed. In 1969, when I was thirty-six years old, my own marriage was arranged. Around the same time I was offered a full-time job in America, in the processing department of a library at MIT. The salary was generous enough to support a wife, and I was honored to be hired by a world-famous university, and so I obtained a sixth-preference green card, and prepared to travel farther still.

By now I had enough money to go by plane. I flew first to Calcutta, to attend my wedding, and a week later I flew to Boston, to begin my new job. During the flight I read *The Student Guide to North America,* a paperback volume that I'd bought before leaving London, for seven shillings six pence on Tottenham Court Road, for although I was no longer a student I was on a budget all the same. I learned that Americans drove on the right side of the road, not the left, and that they called a lift an elevator and an engaged phone busy. "The pace of life in North America is different from Britain as you will soon discover," the guidebook informed me. "Everybody feels he must get to the top. Don't expect an English cup of tea." As the plane began its descent over Boston Harbor, the pilot announced the weather and time, and that President Nixon had declared a national holiday: two American men had landed on the moon. Several passengers cheered. "God bless America!" one of them hollered. Across the aisle, I saw a woman praying.

I spent my first night at the YMCA in Central Square, Cambridge, an inexpensive accommodation recommended by my guidebook. It was walking distance from MIT, and steps from the post office and a supermarket called Purity Supreme. The room contained a cot, a desk, and a small wooden cross on one wall. A sign on the door said cooking was strictly forbidden. A bare window overlooked Massachusetts Avenue, a major thoroughfare with traffic in both directions. Car horns, shrill and prolonged, blared one after another. Flashing sirens heralded endless emergencies, and a fleet of buses rumbled past, their doors opening and closing with a powerful hiss, throughout the night. The noise was constantly distracting, at times suffocating. I felt it deep in my ribs, just as I had felt the furious drone of the engine on the SS *Roma.* But there was no ship's deck to escape to, no glittering ocean to thrill my soul, no breeze to cool my face, no one to talk to. I was too tired to pace the gloomy corridors of the YMCA in my drawstring pajamas. Instead I sat at the desk and stared out the window, at the city hall of Cambridge and a row of small shops. In the morning I reported to my job at the Dewey Library, a beige fortlike building by Memorial Drive. I also opened a bank account, rented a post office box, and bought a plastic bowl and a spoon at Woolworth's, a store whose name I recognized from London. I went to Purity Supreme, wandering up and down the aisles, converting ounces to grams and comparing prices to things in England. In the end I bought a small carton of milk and a box of cornflakes. This was my first meal in America. I ate it at my desk. I preferred it to hamburgers or hot dogs, the only alternative I could afford in the coffee shops on Massachusetts Avenue, and, besides, at the time I had yet to consume any beef. Even the simple chore of buying milk was new to me; in London we'd had bottles delivered each morning to our door.

In a week I had adjusted, more or less. I ate cornflakes and milk, morning and night, and bought some bananas for variety, slicing them into the bowl with the edge of my spoon. In addition I bought tea bags and a flask, which the salesman in Woolworth's referred to as a thermos (a flask, he informed me, was used to store whiskey, another thing I had never consumed). For the price of one cup of tea at a coffee shop, I filled the flask with boiling water on my way to work each morning, and brewed the four cups I drank in the course of a day. I bought a larger carton of milk, and learned to leave it on the shaded part of the windowsill, as I had seen another resident at the YMCA do. To pass the time in the evenings I read the *Boston Globe* downstairs, in a spacious room with stained-glass windows. I read every article and advertisement, so that I would grow familiar with things, and when my eyes grew tired I slept. Only I did not sleep well. Each night I had to keep the window wide open; it was the only source of air in the stifling room, and the noise was intolerable. I would lie on the cot with my fingers pressed into my ears, but when I drifted off to sleep my hands fell away, and the noise of the traffic would wake me up again. Pigeon feathers drifted onto the windowsill, and one evening, when I poured milk over my cornflakes, I saw that it had soured. Nevertheless I resolved to stay at the YMCA for six weeks, until my wife's passport and green card were ready. Once she arrived I would have to rent a proper apartment, and from time to time I studied the classified section of the newspaper, or stopped in at the housing office at MIT during my lunch break, to see what was available in my price range. It was in this manner that I discovered a room for immediate occupancy, in a house on a quiet street, the listing said, for eight dollars per week. I copied the phone number into my guidebook and dialed from a pay telephone, sorting through the coins with which I was still unfamiliar, smaller and lighter than shillings, heavier and brighter than *paisas.*

"Who is speaking?" a woman demanded. Her voice was bold and clamorous.

"Yes, good afternoon, madame. I am calling about the room for rent."

"Harvard or Tech?"

"I beg your pardon?"

"Are you from Harvard or Tech?"

Gathering that Tech referred to the Massachusetts Institute of Technology, I replied, "I work at Dewey Library," adding tentatively, "at Tech."

"I only rent rooms to boys from Harvard or Tech!"

"Yes, madame."

I was given an address and an appointment for seven o'clock that evening. Thirty minutes before the hour I set out, my guidebook in my pocket, my breath fresh with Listerine. I turned down a street shaded with trees, perpendicular to Massachusetts Avenue. Stray blades of grass poked between the cracks of the footpath. In spite of the heat I wore a coat and a tie, regarding the event as I would any other interview; I had never lived in the home of a person who was not Indian. The house, surrounded by a chain-link fence, was off-white with dark brown trim. Unlike the stucco row house I'd lived in in London, this house, fully detached, was covered with wooden shingles, with a tangle of forsythia bushes plastered against the front and sides. When I pressed the calling bell, the woman with whom I had spoken on the phone hollered from what seemed to be just the other side of the door, "One minute, please!"

Several minutes later the door was opened by a tiny, extremely old woman. A mass of snowy hair was arranged like a small sack on top of her head. As I stepped into the house she sat down on a wooden bench positioned at the bottom of a narrow carpeted staircase. Once she was settled on the bench, in a small pool of light, she peered up at me with undivided attention. She wore a long black skirt that spread like a stiff tent to the floor, and a starched white shirt edged with ruffles at the throat and cuffs. Her hands, folded together in her lap, had long pallid fingers, with swollen knuckles and tough yellow nails. Age had battered her features so that she almost resembled a man, with sharp, shrunken eyes and prominent creases on either side of her nose. Her lips, chapped and faded, had nearly disappeared, and her eyebrows were missing altogether. Nevertheless she looked fierce.

"Lock up!" she commanded. She shouted even though I stood only a few feet away. "Fasten the chain and firmly press that button on the knob! This is the first thing you shall do when you enter, is that clear?"

I locked the door as directed and examined the house. Next to the bench on which the woman sat was a small round table, its legs fully concealed, much like the woman's, by a skirt of lace. The table held a lamp, a transistor radio, a leather change purse with a silver clasp, and a telephone. A thick wooden cane coated with a layer of dust was propped against one side. There was a parlor to my right, lined with bookcases and filled with shabby claw-footed furniture. In the corner of the parlor I saw a grand piano with its top down, piled with papers. The piano's bench was missing; it seemed to be the one on which the woman was sitting. Somewhere in the house a clock chimed seven times.

"You're punctual!" the woman proclaimed. "I expect you shall be so with the rent!"

"I have a letter, madame." In my jacket pocket was a letter confirming my employment from MIT, which I had brought along to prove that I was indeed from Tech.

She stared at the letter, then handed it back to me carefully, gripping it with her fingers as if it were a dinner plate heaped with food instead of a sheet of paper. She did not wear glasses, and I wondered if she'd read a word of it. "The last boy was always late! Still owes me eight dollars! Harvard boys aren't what they used to be! Only Harvard and Tech in this house! How's Tech, boy?"

"It is very well."

"You checked the lock?"

"Yes, madame."

She slapped the space beside her on the bench with one hand, and told me to sit down. For a moment she was silent. Then she intoned, as if she alone possessed this knowledge:

"There is an American flag on the moon!"

"Yes, madame." Until then I had not thought very much about the moon shot. It was in the newspaper, of course, article upon article. The astronauts had landed on the shores of the Sea of Tranquility, I had read, traveling farther than anyone in the history of civilization. For a few hours they explored the moon's surface. They gathered rocks in their pockets, described their surroundings (a magnificent desolation, according to one astronaut), spoke by phone to the president, and planted a flag in lunar soil. The voyage was hailed as man's most awesome achievement. I had seen full-page photographs in the *Globe,* of the astronauts in their inflated costumes, and read about what certain people in Boston had been doing at the exact moment the astronauts landed, on a Sunday afternoon. A man said that he was operating a swan boat with a radio pressed to his ear; a woman had been baking rolls for her grandchildren.

The woman bellowed, "A flag on the moon, boy! I heard it on the radio! Isn't that splendid?"

"Yes, madame."

But she was not satisfied with my reply. Instead she commanded, "Say 'splendid'!"

I was both baffled and somewhat insulted by the request. It reminded me of the way I was taught multiplication tables as a child, repeating after the master, sitting cross-legged, without shoes or pencils, on the floor of my one-room Tollygunge school. It also reminded me of my wedding, when I had repeated endless Sanskrit verses after the priest, verses I barely understood, which joined me to my wife. I said nothing.

"Say 'splendid'!" the woman bellowed once again.

"Splendid," I murmured. I had to repeat the word a second time at the top of my lungs, so she could hear. I am soft-spoken by nature and was especially reluctant to raise my voice to an elderly woman whom I had met only moments ago, but she did not appear to be offended. If anything the reply pleased her because her next command was:

"Go see the room!"

I rose from the bench and mounted the narrow carpeted staircase. There were five doors, two on either side of an equally narrow hallway, and one at the opposite end. Only one door was partly open. The room contained a twin bed under a sloping ceiling, a brown oval rug, a basin with an exposed pipe, and a chest of drawers. One door, painted white, led to a closet, another to a toilet and a tub. The walls were covered with gray and ivory striped paper. The window was open; net curtains stirred in the breeze. I lifted them away and inspected the view: a small back yard, with a few fruit trees and an empty clothesline. I was satisfied. From the bottom of the stairs I heard the woman demand, "What is your decision?"

When I returned to the foyer and told her, she picked up the leather change purse on the table, opened the clasp, fished about with her fingers, and produced a key on a thin wire hoop. She informed me that there was a kitchen at the back of the house, accessible through the parlor. I was welcome to use the stove as long as I left it as I found it. Sheets and towels were provided, but keeping them clean was my own responsibility. The rent was due Friday mornings on the ledge above the piano keys. "And no lady visitors!"

"I am a married man, madame." It was the first time I had announced this fact to anyone.

But she had not heard. "No lady visitors!" she insisted. She introduced herself as Mrs. Croft.

My wife's name was Mala. The marriage had been arranged by my older brother and his wife. I regarded the proposition with neither objection nor enthusiasm. It was a duty expected of me, as it was expected of every man. She was the daughter of a schoolteacher in Beleghata. I was told that she could cook, knit, embroider, sketch landscapes, and recite poems by Tagore, but these talents could not make up for the fact that she did not possess a fair complexion, and so a string of men had rejected her to her face. She was twenty-seven, an age when her parents had begun to fear that she would never marry, and so they were willing to ship their only child halfway across the world in order to save her from spinsterhood.

For five nights we shared a bed. Each of those nights, after applying cold cream and braiding her hair, which she tied up at the end with a black cotton string, she turned from me and wept; she missed her parents. Although I would be leaving the country in a few days, custom dictated that she was now a part of my household, and for the next six weeks she was to live with my brother and his wife, cooking, cleaning, serving tea and sweets to guests. I did nothing to console her. I lay on my own side of the bed, reading my guidebook by flashlight and anticipating my journey. At times I thought of the tiny room on the other side of the wall which had belonged to my mother. Now the room was practically empty; the wooden pallet on which she'd once slept was piled with trunks and old bedding. Nearly six years ago, before leaving for London, I had watched her die on that bed, had found her playing with her excrement in her final days. Before we cremated her I had cleaned each of her fingernails with a hairpin, and then, because my brother could not bear it, I had assumed the role of eldest son, and had touched the flame to her temple, to release her tormented soul to heaven.

The next morning I moved into the room in Mrs. Croft's house. When I unlocked the door I saw that she was sitting on the piano bench, on the same side as the previous evening. She wore the same black skirt, the same starched white blouse, and had her hands folded together the same way in her lap. She looked so much the same that I wondered if she'd spent the whole night on the bench. I put my suitcase upstairs, filled my flask with boiling water in the kitchen, and headed off to work. That evening when I came home from the university, she was still there.

"Sit down, boy!" She slapped the space beside her.

I perched beside her on the bench. I had a bag of groceries with me—more milk, more cornflakes, and more bananas, for my inspection of the kitchen earlier in the day had revealed no spare pots, pans, or cooking utensils. There were only two saucepans in the refrigerator, both containing some orange broth, and a copper kettle on the stove.

"Good evening, madame."

She asked me if I had checked the lock. I told her I had.

For a moment she was silent. Then suddenly she declared, with the equal measures of disbelief and delight as the night before, "There's an American flag on the moon, boy!"

"Yes, madame."

"A flag on the moon! Isn't that splendid?"

I nodded, dreading what I knew was coming. "Yes, madame."

"Say 'splendid'!"

This time I paused, looking to either side in case anyone were there to overhear me, though I knew perfectly well that the house was empty. I felt like an idiot. But it was a small enough thing to ask. "Splendid!" I cried out.

Within days it became our routine. In the mornings when I left for the library Mrs. Croft was either hidden away in her bedroom, on the other side of the staircase, or she was sitting on the bench, oblivious to my presence, listening to the news or classical music on the radio. But each evening when I returned the same thing happened: she slapped the bench, ordered me to sit down, declared that there was a flag on the moon, and declared that it was splendid. I said it was splendid, too, and then we sat in silence. As awkward as it was, and as endless as it felt to me then, the nightly encounter lasted only about ten minutes; inevitably she would drift off to sleep, her head falling abruptly toward her chest, leaving me free to retire to my room. By then, of course, there was no flag standing on the moon. The astronauts, I had read in the paper, had seen it fall before they flew back to Earth. But I did not have the heart to tell her.

Friday morning, when my first week's rent was due, I went to the piano in the parlor to place my money on the ledge. The piano keys were dull and discolored. When I pressed one, it made no sound at all. I had put eight one-dollar bills in an envelope and written Mrs. Croft's name on the front of it. I was not in the habit of leaving money unmarked and unattended. From where I stood I could see the profile of her tent-shaped skirt. She was sitting on the bench, listening to the radio. It seemed unnecessary to make her get up and walk all the way to the piano. I never saw her walking about, and assumed, from the cane always propped against the round table at her side, that she did so with difficulty. When I approached the bench she peered up at me and demanded:

"What is your business?"

"The rent, madame."

"On the ledge above the piano keys!"

"I have it here." I extended the envelope toward her, but her fingers, folded together in her lap, did not budge. I bowed slightly and lowered the envelope, but her fingers, folded together in her lap, did not budge. I bowed slightly and lowered the envelope, so that it hovered just above her hands. After a moment she accepted, and nodded her head.

That night when I came home, she did not slap the bench, but out of habit I sat beside her as usual. She asked me if I had checked the lock, but she mentioned nothing about the flag on the moon. Instead she said:

"It was very kind of you!"

"I beg your pardon, madame?"

"Very kind of you!"

She was still holding the envelope in her hands.

On Sunday there was a knock on my door. An elderly woman introduced herself: she was Mrs. Croft's daughter, Helen. She walked into the room and looked at each of the walls as if for signs of change, glancing at the shirts that hung in the closet, the neckties draped over the doorknob, the box of cornflakes on the chest of drawers, the dirty bowl and spoon in the basin. She was short and thick-waisted, with cropped silver hair and bright pink lipstick. She wore a sleeveless summer dress, a row of white plastic beads, and spectacles on a chain that hung like a swing against her chest. The backs of her legs were mapped with dark blue veins, and her upper arms sagged like the flesh of a roasted eggplant. She told me she lived in Arlington, a town farther up Massachusetts Avenue. "I come once a week to bring Mother groceries. Has she sent you packing yet?"

"It is very well, madame."

"Some of the boys run screaming. But I think she likes you. You're the first boarder she's ever referred to as a gentleman."

"Not at all, madame."

She looked at me, noticing my bare feet (I still felt strange wearing shoes indoors, and always removed them before entering my room). "Are you new to Boston?"

"New to America, madame."

"From?" she raised her eyebrows.

"I am from Calcutta, India."

"Is that right? We had a Brazilian fellow, about a year ago. You'll find Cambridge a very international city."

I nodded, and began to wonder how long our conversation would last. But at that moment we heard Mrs. Croft's electrifying voice rising up the stairs. When we stepped into the hallway we heard her hollering:

"You are to come downstairs immediately!"

"What is it?" Helen hollered back.

"Immediately!"

I put my shoes on at once. Helen sighed.

We walked down the staircase. It was too narrow for us to descend side by side, so I followed Helen, who seemed to be in no hurry, and complained at one point that she had a bad knee. "Have you been walking without your cane?" Helen called out. "You know you're not supposed to walk without that cane." She paused, resting her hand on the banister, and looked back at me. "She slips sometimes."

For the first time Mrs. Croft seemed vulnerable. I pictured her on the floor in front of the bench, flat on her back, staring at the ceiling, her feet pointing in opposite directions. But when we reached the bottom of the staircase she was sitting there as usual, her hands folded together in her lap. Two grocery bags were at her feet. When we stood before her she did not slap the bench, or ask us to sit down. She glared.

"What is it, Mother?"

"It's improper!"

"What's improper?"

"It is improper for a lady and gentleman who are not married to one another to hold a private conversation without a chaperone!"

Helen said she was sixty-eight years old, old enough to be my mother, but Mrs. Croft insisted that Helen and I speak to each other downstairs, in the parlor. She added that it was also improper for a lady of Helen's station to reveal her age, and to wear a dress so high above the ankle.

"For your information, Mother, it's nineteen sixty-nine. What would you do if you actually left the house one day and saw a girl in a miniskirt?"

Mrs. Croft sniffed. "I'd have her arrested."

Helen shook her head and picked up one of the grocery bags. I picked up the other one, and followed her through the parlor and into the kitchen. The bags were filled with cans of soup, which Helen opened up one by one with a few cranks of a can opener. She tossed the old soup in the saucepans into the sink, rinsed the pans under the tap, filled them with soup from the newly opened cans, and put them back in the refrigerator. "A few years ago she could still open the cans herself," Helen said. "She hates that I do it for her now. But the piano killed her hands." She put on her spectacles, glanced up at the cupboards, and spotted my tea bags. "Shall we have a cup?"

I filled the kettle on the stove. "I beg your pardon, madame. The piano?"

"She used to give lessons. For forty years. It was how she raised us after my father died." Helen put her hands on her hips, staring at the open refrigerator. She reached into the back, pulled out a wrapped stick of butter, frowned, and tossed it into the garbage. "That ought to do it," she said, and put the unopened cans of soup in the cupboard. I sat at the table and watched as Helen washed the dirty dishes, tied up the garbage bag, watered a spider plant over the sink, and poured boiling water into two cups. She handed one to me without milk, the string of the tea bag trailing over the side, and sat down at the table.

"Excuse me, madame, but is it enough?"

Helen took a sip of her tea. Her lipstick left a smiling pink stain on the inside rim of the cup. "Is what enough?"

"The soup in the pans. Is it enough food for Mrs. Croft?"

"She won't eat anything else. She stopped eating solids after she turned one hundred. That was, let's see, three years ago."

I was mortified. I had assumed Mrs. Croft was in her eighties, perhaps as old as ninety. I had never known a person who had lived for over a century. That this person was a widow who lived alone mortified me further still. It was widowhood that had driven my own mother insane. My father, who worked as a clerk at the General Post Office of Calcutta, died of encephalitis when I was sixteen. My mother refused to adjust to life without him; instead she sank deeper into a world of darkness from which neither I, nor my brother, nor concerned relatives, nor psychiatric clinics on Rash Behari Avenue could save her. What pained me most was to see her so unguarded, to hear her burp after meals or expel gas in front of company without the slightest embarrassment. After my father's death my brother abandoned his schooling and began to work in the jute mill he would eventually manage, in order to keep the household running. And so it was my job to sit by my mother's feet and study for my exams as she counted and recounted the bracelets on her arm as if they were the beads of an abacus. We tried to keep an eye on her. Once she had wandered half naked to the tram depot before we were able to bring her inside again.

"I am happy to warm Mrs. Croft's soup in the evenings," I suggested, removing the tea bag from my cup and squeezing out the liquor. "It is no trouble."

Helen looked at her watch, stood up, and poured the rest of her tea into the sink. "I wouldn't if I were you. That's the sort of thing that would kill her altogether."

That evening, when Helen had gone back to Arlington and Mrs. Croft and I were alone again, I began to worry. Now that I knew how very old she was, I worried that something would happen to her in the middle of the night, or when I was out during the day. As vigorous as her voice was, and imperious as she seemed, I knew that even a scratch or a cough could kill a person that old; each day she lived, I knew, was something of a miracle. Although Helen had seemed friendly enough, a small part of me worried that she might accuse me of negligence if anything were to happen. Helen didn't seem worried. She came and went, bringing soup for Mrs. Croft, one Sunday after the next.

In this manner the six weeks of that summer passed. I came home each evening, after my hours at the library, and spent a few minutes on the piano bench with Mrs. Croft. I gave her a bit of my company, and assured her that I had checked the lock, and told her that the flag on the moon was splendid. Some evenings I sat beside her long after she had drifted off to sleep, still in awe of how many years she had spent on this earth. At times I tried to picture the world she had been born into, in 1866—a world, I imagined, filled with women in long black skirts, and chaste conversations in the parlor. Now, when I looked at her hands with their swollen knuckles folded together in her lap, I imagined them smooth and slim, striking the piano keys. At times I came downstairs before going to sleep, to make sure she was sitting upright on the bench, or was safe in her bedroom. On Fridays I made sure to put the rent in her hands. There was nothing I could do for her beyond these simple gestures. I was not her son, and apart from those eight dollars, I owed her nothing.

At the end of August, Mala's passport and green card were ready. I received a telegram with her flight information; my brother's house in Calcutta had no telephone. Around that time I also received a letter from her, written only a few days after we had parted. There was no salutation; addressing me by name would have assumed an intimacy we had not yet discovered. It contained only a few lines. "I write in English in preparation for the journey. Here I am very much lonely. Is it very cold there. Is there snow. Yours, Mala."

I was not touched by her words. We had spent only a handful of days in each other's company. And yet we were bound together; for six weeks she had worn an iron bangle on her wrist, and applied vermillion powder to the part in her hair, to signify to the world that she was a bride. In those six weeks I regarded her arrival as I would the arrival of a coming month, or season—something inevitable, but meaningless at the time. So little did I know her that, while details of her face sometimes rose to my memory, I could not conjure up the whole of it.

A few days after receiving the letter, as I was walking to work in the morning, I saw an Indian woman on the other side of Massachusetts Avenue, wearing a sari with its free end nearly dragging on the footpath, and pushing a child in a stroller. An American woman with a small black dog on a leash was walking to one side of her. Suddenly the dog began barking. From the other side of the street I watched as the Indian woman, startled, stopped in her path, at which point the dog leapt up and seized the end of the sari between its teeth. The American woman scolded the dog, appeared to apologize, and walked quickly away, leaving the Indian woman to fix her sari in the middle of the footpath, and quiet her crying child. She did not see me standing there, and eventually she continued on her way. Such a mishap, I realized that morning, would soon be my concern. It was my duty to take care of Mala, to welcome her and protect her. I would have to buy her her first pair of snow boots, her first winter coat. I would have to tell her which streets to avoid, which way the traffic came, tell her to wear her sari so that the free end did not drag on the footpath. A five-mile separation from her parents, I recalled with some irritation, had caused her to weep.

Unlike Mala, I was used to it all by then: used to cornflakes and milk, used to Helen's visits, used to sitting on the bench with Mrs. Croft. The only thing I was not used to was Mala. Nevertheless I did what I had to do. I went to the housing office at MIT and found a furnished apartment a few blocks away, with a double bed and a private kitchen and bath, for forty dollars a week. One last Friday I handed Mrs. Croft eight one-dollar bills in an envelope, brought my suitcase downstairs, and informed her that I was moving. She put my key into her change purse. The last thing she asked me to do was hand her the cane propped against the table, so that she could walk to the door and lock it behind me. "Good-bye, then," she said, and retreated back into the house. I did not expect any display of emotion, but I was disappointed all the same. I was only a boarder, a man who paid her a bit of money and passed in and out of her home for six weeks. Compared to a century, it was no time at all.

At the airport I recognized Mala immediately. The free end of her sari did not drag on the floor, but was draped in a sign of bridal modesty over her head, just as it had draped my mother until the day my father died. Her thin brown arms were stacked with gold bracelets, a small red circle was painted on her forehead, and the edges of her feet were tinted with a decorative red dye. I did not embrace her, or kiss her, or take her hand. Instead

I asked her, speaking Bengali for the first time in America, if she was hungry.

She hesitated, then nodded yes.

I told her I had prepared some egg curry at home. "What did they give you to eat on the plane?"

"I didn't eat."

"All the way from Calcutta?"

"The menu said oxtail soup."

"But surely there were other items."

"The thought of eating an ox's tail made me lose my appetite."

When we arrived home, Mala opened up one of her suitcases, and presented me with two pullover sweaters, both made with bright blue wool, which she had knitted in the course of our separation, one with a V neck, the other covered with cables. I tried them on; both were tight under the arms. She had also brought me two new pairs of drawstring pajamas, a letter from my brother, and a packet of loose Darjeeling tea. I had no present for her apart from the egg curry. We sat at a bare table, each of us staring at our plates. We ate with our hands, another thing I had not yet done in America.

"The house is nice," she said. "Also the egg curry." With her left hand she held the end of her sari to her chest, so it would not slip off her head.

"I don't know many recipes."

She nodded, peeling the skin off each of her potatoes before eating them. At one point the sari slipped to her shoulders. She readjusted it at once.

"There is no need to cover your head," I said. "I don't mind. It doesn't matter here."

She kept it covered anyway.

I waited to get used to her, to her presence at my side, at my table and in my bed, but a week later we were still strangers. I still was not used to coming home to an apartment that smelled of steamed rice, and finding that the basin in the bathroom was always wiped clean, our two toothbrushes lying side by side, a

cake of Pears soap from India resting in the soap dish. I was not used to the fragrance of the coconut oil she rubbed every other night into her scalp, or the delicate sound her bracelets made as she moved about the apartment. In the mornings she was always awake before I was. The first morning when I came into the kitchen she had heated up the leftovers and set a plate with a spoonful of salt on its edge on the table, assuming I would eat rice for breakfast, as most Bengali husbands did. I told her cereal would do, and the next morning when I came into the kitchen she had already poured the cornflakes into my bowl. One morning she walked with me down Massachusetts Avenue to MIT, where I gave her a short tour of the campus. On the way we stopped at a hardware store and I made a copy of the key, so that she could let herself into the apartment. The next morning before I left for work she asked me for a few dollars. I parted with them reluctantly, but I knew that this, too, was now normal. When I came home from work there was a potato peeler in the kitchen drawer, and a tablecloth on the table, and chicken curry made with fresh garlic and ginger on the stove. We did not have a television in those days. After dinner I read the newspaper, while Mala sat at the kitchen table, working on a cardigan for herself with more of the bright blue wool, or writing letters home.

At the end of our first week, on Friday, I suggested going out. Mala set down her knitting and disappeared into the bathroom. When she emerged I regretted the suggestion; she had put on a clean silk sari and extra bracelets, and coiled her hair with a flattering side part on top of her head. She was prepared as if for a party, or at the very least for the cinema, but I had no such destination in mind. The evening air was balmy. We walked several blocks down Massachusetts Avenue, looking into the windows of restaurants and shops. Then, without thinking, I led her down the quiet street where for so many nights I had walked alone.

"This is where I lived before you came," I said, stopping at Mrs. Croft's chain-link fence.

"In such a big house?"

"I had a small room upstairs. At the back."

"Who else lives there?"

"A very old woman."

"With her family?"

"Alone."

"But who takes care of her?"

I opened the gate. "For the most part she takes care of herself."

I wondered if Mrs. Croft would remember me; I wondered if she had a new boarder to sit with her on the bench each evening. When I pressed the bell I expected the same long wait as that day of our first meeting, when I did not have a key. But this time the door was opened almost immediately, by Helen. Mrs. Croft was not sitting on the bench. The bench was gone.

"Hello there," Helen said, smiling with her bright pink lips at Mala. "Mother's in the parlor. Will you be visiting awhile?"

"As you wish, madame."

"Then I think I'll run to the store, if you don't mind. She had a little accident. We can't leave her alone these days, not even for a minute."

I locked the door after Helen and walked into the parlor. Mrs. Croft was lying flat on her back, her head on a peach-colored cushion, a thin white quilt spread over her body. Her hands were folded together on top of her chest. When she saw me she pointed at the sofa, and told me to sit down. I took my place as directed, but Mala wandered over to the piano and sat on the bench, which was now positioned where it belonged.

"I broke my hip!" Mrs. Croft announced, as if no time had passed.

"Oh dear, madame."

"I fell off the bench!"

"I am so sorry, madame."

"It was the middle of the night! Do you know what I did, boy?"

I shook my head.

"I called the police!"

She stared up at the ceiling and grinned sedately, exposing a crowded row of long gray teeth. Not one was missing. "What do you say to that, boy?"

As stunned as I was, I knew what I had to say. With no hesitation at all, I cried out, "Splendid!"

Mala laughed then. Her voice was full of kindness, her eyes bright with amusement. I had never heard her laugh before, and it was loud enough so Mrs. Croft had heard, too. She turned to Mala and glared.

"Who is she, boy?"

"She is my wife, madame."

Mrs. Croft pressed her head at an angle against the cushion to get a better look. "Can you play the piano?"

"No, madame," Mala replied.

"Then stand up!"

Mala rose to her feet, adjusting the end of her sari over her head and holding it to her chest, and, for the first time since her arrival, I felt sympathy. I remembered my first days in London, learning how to take the Tube to Russell Square, riding an escalator for the first time, being unable to understand that when the man cried "piper" it meant "paper," being unable to decipher, for a whole year, that the conductor said "mind the gap" as the train pulled away from each station. Like me, Mala had traveled far from home, not knowing where she was going, or what she would find, for no reason other than to be my wife. As strange as it seemed, I knew in my heart that one day her death would affect me, and stranger still, that mine would affect her. I wanted somehow to explain this to Mrs. Croft, who was still scrutinizing Mala from top to toe with what seemed to be placid disdain. I wondered if Mrs. Croft had ever seen a woman in a sari, with a dot painted on her forehead and bracelets stacked on her wrists. I wondered what she would object to. I wondered if she could see the red dye still vivid on Mala's feet, all but obscured by the bottom edge of her sari. At last Mrs. Croft declared, with the equal measures of disbelief and delight I knew well:

"She is a perfect lady!"

Now it was I who laughed. I did so quietly, and Mrs. Croft did not hear me. But Mala had heard, and, for the first time, we looked at each other and smiled.

I like to think of that moment in Mrs. Croft's parlor as the moment when the distance between Mala and me began to lessen. Although we were not yet fully in love, I like to think of the months that followed as a honeymoon of sorts. Together we explored the city and met Bengalis, some of whom are still friends today. We discovered that a man named Bill sold fresh fish on Prospect Street, and that a shop in Harvard Square called Cardullo's sold bay leaves and cloves. In the evenings we walked to the Charles River to watch sailboats drift across the water, or had ice cream cones in Harvard Yard. We bought an Instamatic camera with which to document our life together, and I took pictures of her posing in front of the Prudential building, so that she could send them to her parents. At night we kissed, shy at first but quickly bold, and discovered pleasure and solace in each other's arms. I told her about my voyage on the SS *Roma,* and about Finsbury Park and the YMCA, and my evenings on the bench with Mrs. Croft. When I told her stories about my mother, she wept. It was Mala who consoled me when, reading the *Globe* one evening, I came across Mrs. Croft's obituary. I had not thought of her in several months—by then those six weeks of the summer were already a remote interlude in my past—but when I learned of her death I was stricken, so much so that when Mala looked up from her knitting she found me staring at the wall, the newspaper neglected in my lap, unable to speak. Mrs. Croft's was the first death I mourned in America, for hers was the first life I had admired; she had left this world at last, ancient and alone, never to return.

As for me, I have not strayed much farther. Mala and I live in a town about twenty miles from Boston, on a tree-lined street much like Mrs. Croft's, in a house we own, with a garden that saves us from buying tomatoes in summer, and room for guests. We are American citizens now, so that we can collect social security when it is time. Though we visit Calcutta every few years, and bring back more drawstring pajamas and Darjeeling tea, we have decided to grow old here. I work in a small college library. We have a son who attends Harvard University. Mala no longer drapes the end of her sari over her head, or weeps at night for her parents, but occasionally she weeps for our son. So we drive to Cambridge to visit him, or bring him home for a weekend, so that he can eat rice with us with his hands, and speak in Bengali, things we sometimes worry he will no longer do after we die.

Whenever we make that drive, I always make it a point to take Massachusetts Avenue, in spite of the traffic. I barely recognize the buildings now, but each time I am there I return instantly to those six weeks as if they were only the other day, and I slow down and point to Mrs. Croft's street, saying to my son, here was my first home in America, where I lived with a woman who was 103. "Remember?" Mala says, and smiles, amazed, as I am, that there was ever a time that we were strangers. My son always expresses his astonishment, not at Mrs. Croft's age, but at how little I paid in rent, a fact nearly as inconceivable to him as a flag on the moon was to a woman born in 1866. In my son's eyes I see the ambition that had first hurled me across the world. In a few years he will graduate and pave his way, alone and unprotected. But I remind myself that he has a father who is still living, a mother who is happy and strong. Whenever he is discouraged, I tell him that if I can survive on three continents, then there is no obstacle he cannot conquer. While the astronauts, heroes forever, spent mere hours on the moon, I have remained in this new world for nearly thirty years. I know that my achievement is quite ordinary. I am not the only man to seek his fortune far from home, and certainly I am not the first. Still, there are times I am bewildered by each mile I have traveled, each meal I have eaten, each person I have known, each room in which I have slept. As ordinary as it all appears, there are times when it is beyond my imagination.

JHUMPA LAHIRI DISCUSSES

"The Third and Final Continent," setting, cornflakes, and the "perfect lady"

PM: Your fiction often explores the tension between the place where it's unfolding and some *other* place—the place left behind, say, or a place the character tries to imagine.

JL: There were two physical landscapes in my upbringing. I lived exclusively in the United States, but because my parents remain so closely tied to India and their family, I could never think of myself as being part of just one place.

And I think that still continues to interest me as a writer. Even the more subtle shift of someone growing up in a small town and moving to a city, or growing up in a certain way and then finding him or herself in a new environment, yields a lot for me dramatically.

PM: In "The Third and Final Continent" you have your narrator buy his guide to North America in London and not in India. On the plane to Boston, he reads: "Don't expect an English cup of tea," a nice irony given that his own cultural adjustments will undoubtedly be larger. Do you recall anything about making that choice?

JL: I actually found this book in a closet in our house somewhere. It was my father's book and he had obviously bought it in London. He wouldn't have needed it in India. When he lived in India, he was only going to England, and it was from England that he came here. I based my character on that same path that my father took.

I've never written anything as close to real life as that story. It wasn't my life I was writing about, but still, I was basing quite a bit of it on events that happened.

PM: Did you interview your father for background information when you were writing it, or by that point had you internalized the family stories?

JL: I had always heard this story, this anecdote about my father coming over in 1969 and renting a house in Cambridge that belonged to the one-hundred-three-year-old woman, and how she would want to speak to him every evening about the men who had just been to the moon—all of that my father would relate from time to time. I think it struck me when I was growing up because my father is not a big storyteller.

When I was up at the Fine Arts Work Center in Provincetown, on a writing fellowship for seven months, I invited my father to come and spend a week there. He did, and one evening I invited a few fellow writers over for dinner. One of them happened to ask my father: why did you come to America, talk about that. And so he eventually wound up telling this story again, and for some reason, I saw it not just as a part of my father's past but as a possible story that I could write.

PM: The simultaneity with the moon landing gives the material an amazing shapeliness.

JL: I never thought about it as a parallel or significant in any way. Even when I started writing, it was so much a part of my family lore that it's one of those things you feel so close to, you can't see it. It was only after I had spent quite a bit of time wrestling with the making of the story that it occurred to me that it was such a fascinating confluence of events—one very personal and one so very, very public that changed the world and how human beings think of themselves in relation to the rest of the universe. It was very gratifying to discover. But it was only in the course of the writing. I worked on this story I would say for six or seven months in total.

PM: His plane touches down in Boston as news of the moon landing is announced. I assume there's a certain amount of poetic license you're taking there; it's just too wonderful to have actually been the case.

JL: I think I got that detail from reading accounts of the moon landing and how it was announced on airplanes and things like that. But I think that my father had already been here for a while, and then the moon landing happened. He had maybe been here for a month, but I don't know. At this point it's all sort of mixed up, and it's very hard for me to tease out what was real and what wasn't.

PM: How did you immerse your imagination in the world of the late sixties? Did you look up archived editions of the Boston newspapers?

JL: I did. I got some issues of the *Globe*—the day of the moon landing, and a few follow-up articles on it. And I read one or two books about that particular mission.

PM: You provide a few crisp details about the row house in London, and nothing gets across the chaotic, transitory living space of bachelors quite like dirty dishes soaking in a bathtub.

JL: That was a detail from my parents' early married life in London. The chronology of the story is off. My parents were already married, and I was already born, when this story took place. The timing is delayed. I did that because first of all I wasn't interested in writing any sort of family history. I wanted it to be fiction. And also I felt that the arrival of this man's wife would contribute to his situation. My mother told me, on various occasions, about one of the places they lived in in London, where they didn't have access to a sink and they had to do their dishes in the bathroom. They lived in various shared lodgings and shared a kitchen. And it was either that there was no sink or the sink was far too small. My parents, even back then, entertained a lot of people on a regular basis. So I think there was need for ample sink space.

PM: Your narrator's next stop is the YMCA, and you evoke its unpleasantness with just a couple of very choice sensory details, most importantly the street sounds. Do you recall how you arrived at that? Trying to sleep with your fingers in your ears—that's an elegantly simple yet unendurable situation.

JL: I imagined it would be loud because I know where it is in Cambridge, on Massachusetts Avenue, which is a very busy central avenue. I had never been inside the YMCA until very recently;

I actually did a reading there, which bizarrely brought this whole experience full circle. My father never stayed in the YMCA, but he would go there to read the newspapers and pass the time in the evenings. I asked a friend who had lived in Cambridge for many years about the YMCA. I think he had been there and knew people who stayed there, so he gave me some details.

Regarding the matter of the fingers in the ears, when I first started writing that story, I was up in Provincetown, which is probably the most quiet place on earth. I was there in the wintertime and would hear the sea and the wind and that was about it. But after my fellowship ended, I moved to Manhattan and I was working on this story, in an apartment on Fourteenth Street on the East Side. It was an incredibly noisy apartment facing the street. So I just worked that detail in—what it's like to live in a really noisy place.

PM: Sometimes the mere fact that the narrator is observing a certain detail implies its novelty to him—the wood-shingled house and chain-link fence of Mrs. Croft's house, for instance.

JL: There are certainly no wood-shingled houses in Calcutta to speak of. Nor are there very many in north London. I imagined that the narrator would observe the exterior of the house carefully before entering. I wanted it to be a specific image of Cambridge and its architecture.

PM: As a traveler, he's particularly aware of things that a resident might not be.

JL: I think that's true for anyone who feels new to a place. Your powers of observation are sharpened, heightened. And especially so in a situation where you're contemplating taking up residence there. Basic questions would go through one's mind: Is it safe? Is it solid? So the details, I imagine, would be important.

PM: These powers of observation coincide nicely with your task as a writer: to see things through fresh eyes. Maybe every writer should try a travel story as an exercise.

JL: That's how I see everything in the world. It's hard for me *not* to notice those things.

PM: What do you attribute that to?
JL: I think I'm just hard-wired that way. It's how I relate to the physical world. I am a very visual person and I just tend to notice things. But I don't think I'm unique. I think most writers and painters would say the same thing.
PM: Are you a big walker? Josip Novakovich supposes in the *Fiction Writer's Workshop* that writers had a much more intimate relationship with their cities before driving became so predominant.
JL: I've never owned a car in my life. My parents had a car when I was growing up, obviously, so I rode in cars. But when I went to college in New York City I didn't have a car. I moved to Boston after college—I lived there for eight years—and never had a car. I had a car for those seven months when I was living on Cape Cod, but I rarely used it, except when I had to leave the Cape for some reason. And now I'm back in New York and we still don't have a car, so I do walk a lot, just out of necessity, I suppose.
PM: Do you keep any kind of notebook with details observed either in your daily life or your travels?
JL: I keep a journal. I record this and that, but don't really think of it as material for writing. It's just more of a writing exercise, a sort of daily warm-up for me.
PM: In this story and others, you really tap into food being a huge source of comfort and discomfort.
JL: Yes, absolutely.
PM: When Mala pre-pours the narrator's cornflakes for him, that's a rich gesture: It's touching and gently funny too, and revealing of her character. She doesn't question his choice, she continues to dutifully prepare his breakfast, even a breakfast whose very essence is convenience and lack of preparation.
JL: She's a new wife, and she wants to please and be helpful and do the wifely thing. That would mean doing things so that her husband wouldn't have to. I imagine her as a very traditionally raised woman with a strong sense of duty toward her husband. So that would include what she does with the cornflakes.
PM: Mrs. Croft must have grown up in a world without corn-

flakes herself, and would probably find it a less than proper breakfast. What does Mrs. Croft's kitchen—its contents and the soup regimen—convey about *her* character and situation?
JL: She's sort of eating to survive, in the same way that the narrator is—eating to live, and not the other way around. She's too old and too frail to do anything more elaborate. She can't even open up the cans. I think that for the narrator it would be a very startling thing to find a woman of her age living alone. It is simply unheard of in India, and I think in many other parts of the world as well, but certainly in India. The thought of an elderly person on his or her own would be quite disturbing and upsetting, but also kind of fascinating for the narrator to see. And she does manage, even though she's limited in what she can do.
PM: It's interesting that you mentioned the narrator's in a sort of similar position. He's not yet a householder, and she isn't much of one any longer. And they're both at this crossroads where they're passing one another, and that's something they have in common, two people who at first blush might seem more different than similar.
JL: Right.
PM: There's that nice detail about the table legs in Mrs. Croft's living room, being concealed, as are Mrs. Croft's—the story specifically compares the two on page 216—implying a modesty that is old-fashioned in 1960s Cambridge, but ironically more fitting I'd guess with 1960s Calcutta.
JL: Probably. The Victorian influence in Calcutta is quite strong, and the cultural changes that were in the air during the sixties in the United States had not hit Calcutta.
PM: Miniskirts among them, which seems to scandalize Mrs. Croft. Certainly regarding the propriety between the sexes, Mrs. Croft seems as though she'd be much more at home in Calcutta.
JL: Yes. *(Laughs.)* Probably.
PM: I wanted to talk about the piano bench. When we meet up with Mrs. Croft, it's at the bottom of the stairs, so right after she lets him in, she sits back down, and that's where she's to be found, most of the time.

JL: Right, that's her spot. That was a detail I took from my father's account. The real Mrs. Croft was a piano teacher, and the bench was central to the way he told the story: that she would be sitting there on the bench and would ask him to sit down beside her.

PM: There's a poignance to its being away from the piano—it's clear she no longer plays it.

JL: She's sort of disconnected from her former life. At the end of the story, the bench is back at the piano, because then Mala sits on it.

PM: She does, which also feels like a significant choice.

JL: It seems like that was the place the narrator associates himself and Mrs. Croft being together and now it's he and Mala who are a couple, a true couple. So I suppose that's why her sitting there would be significant.

PM: I also read into it some kind of connection between Mala and Mrs. Croft, because it's shortly afterward that Mrs. Croft deems her "a perfect lady." It makes a kind of quirky sense, given Mrs. Croft's Victorian propriety, that she'd be especially appreciative of Mala's virtues.

JL: Yes, that's another detail that's taken from the real life account. Apparently the real Mrs. Croft pronounced my mother a perfect lady.

PM: It's amazing that such a key element actually occurred. You know how you can read certain works of fiction and they feel constrained by a kind of over-autobiographical feeling and the sense that they're not fully imagined? But that's certainly not the case with this story.

JL: I think the difference is that I am at such a remove. It's one thing to write autobiographically about things that you've experienced. That's when the lack of imagination comes into play because you rely on what you know—but I knew nothing of this story apart from a two- or three-minute anecdote with scattered details about a piano bench, and cornflakes, and the "perfect lady." The rest of it was a completely alien world to me. I was two years old in 1969. I have no memory of the moon landing,

I have no idea what it's like to immigrate, I have no idea what it's like to be a man. I have no idea what it was like for my father. I've never experienced anything remotely similar. The closest I've ever come is going to a foreign country for a week or two and struggling along in a foreign language, with a foreign currency. So even though all of these details were given to me in terms of family history, I had to work extra hard to make them ring true, and to make them seem credible. I was writing about both a time and an experience that I had no consciousness of.

PM: And you've done more than just make them credible. When Mrs. Croft pronounces Mala a perfect lady, it feels like so much has led to that moment. Their couple-ness is being formally recognized in America, and in his mind.

JL: Yes. Because I managed to manipulate the details and the chronology of events, I think that the pronouncement is more significant in the world of the story than perhaps it was in real life. In real life, my parents may have just chuckled over that. I was also in that living room at the time. My parents took me on the visit to the real Mrs. Croft. I was two; god knows what I was doing. It was very funny and interesting to write a scene in which I knew I had been present but I erased myself completely.

PM: I wanted to talk about that small scene on pages 226–27 where the narrator is witnessing the woman in the sari with the baby stroller and there's another woman with a pet dog. There's a sort of mini-drama that's being played out before the narrator, and a small culture clash. I'm guessing that pet dogs are not nearly so popular in 1960s Calcutta?

JL: Not as much, no. I vaguely remember, when I lived in Boston, observing an Indian woman once walking down Mass Avenue; I think I was walking behind her. But you know it could have been a weird image in a dream that lingered. I don't know about the bit with the dog, either. I think I just invented it, but I can't be sure.

PM: The pet seems to convey a sense of American privilege and triviality, as well as a slight menace.

JL: I think of it as the narrator does: The woman is somehow vulnerable, because of her clothing and appearance, which are superficial traits standing for something deeper. Seeing it happen to an Indian woman who isn't his wife allows that realization to penetrate a bit more.

PM: How have some of your readers in India responded to your work?

JL: Oh, very different opinions. *(Laughs.)* Hatred and admiration and everything in between—it's sort of like here.

PM: Hatred? Why?

JL: I don't know. Why not? I mean it's just a matter of personal opinion. There are people who can't stand my writing and don't think I deserve to be published, and then there are other people who are very kind and say nice things. I think for some reason, because my book got more attention than certainly most people, including myself, thought it would, people react very strongly to it, both good and bad.

PM: What has your father had to say about "The Third and Final Continent"?

JL: As I mentioned earlier, my father is generally a man of few words. When he read the story, his reply was, "My whole life is there."

Born in London and raised in Rhode Island, **JHUMPA LAHIRI** is a graduate of Barnard College, where she received a B.A. in English literature, and of Boston University, where she received an M.A. in English, an M.A. in Creative Writing, an M.A. in Comparative Studies in Literature and the Arts, and a Ph.D. in Renaissance Studies. Her short story collection, *Interpreter of Maladies*, won the 2000 Pulitzer Prize for fiction, the PEN/Hemingway Award, *The New Yorker* Debut of the Year, and an American Academy of Arts and Letters Addison Metcalf Award. "The Third and Final Continent," which first appeared in *The New Yorker,* was part of that magazine's winning fiction entry in the 2000 National Magazine Awards, and was reprinted in *The Best American Short Stories 2000*. Lahiri is also the author of a novel, *The Namesake* (2003). She lives in New York with her husband, son, and daughter.

STRUCTURE

DREAM CHILDREN

Gail Godwin

The worst thing. Such a terrible thing to happen to a young woman. It's a wonder she didn't go mad.

As she went about her errands, a cheerful, neat young woman, a wife, wearing pants with permanent creases and safari jackets and high-necked sweaters that folded chastely just below the line of the small gold hoops she wore in her ears, she imagined people saying this, or thinking it to themselves. But nobody knew. Nobody knew anything, other than that she and her husband had moved here a year ago, as so many couples were moving farther away from the city, the husband commuting, or staying in town during the week—as hers did. There was nobody here, in this quaint, unspoiled village, nestled in the foothills of the mountains, who could have looked at her and guessed that anything out of the ordinary, predictable, auspicious spectrum of things that happen to bright, attractive young women had happened to her. She always returned her books to the local library on time; she bought liquor at the local liquor store only on Friday, before she went to meet her husband's bus from the city. He was something in television, a producer? So many ambitious young couples moving to this Dutch farming village, founded in 1690, to restore ruined fieldstone houses and plant herb gardens and keep their own horses and discover the relief of finding oneself insignificant in Nature for the first time!

A terrible thing. So freakish. If you read it in a story or saw it on TV, you'd say no, this sort of thing could never happen in an American hospital.

DePuy, who owned the old Patroon farm adjacent to her land,

frequently glimpsed her racing her horse in the early morning, when the mists still lay on the fields, sometimes just before the sun came up and there was a frost on everything. "One woodchuck hole and she and that stallion will both have to be put out of their misery," he told his wife. "She's too reckless. I'll bet you her old man doesn't know she goes streaking to hell across the fields like that." Mrs. DePuy nodded, silent, and went about her business. She, too, watched that other woman ride, a woman not so much younger than herself, but with an aura of romance—of tragedy, perhaps. The way she looked: like those heroines in English novels who ride off their bad tempers and unrequited love affairs, clenching their thighs against the flanks of spirited horses with murderous red eyes. Mrs. DePuy, who had ridden since the age of three, recognized something beyond recklessness in that elegant young woman, in her crisp checked shirts and her dove-gray jodhpurs. *She has nothing to fear anymore,* thought the farmer's wife, with sure feminine instinct; she both envied and pitied her. "What she needs is children," remarked DePuy.

"A Dry Sack, a Remy Martin, and . . . let's see, a half-gallon of the Chablis, and I think I'd better take a Scotch . . . and the Mouton-Cadet . . . and maybe a dry vermouth." Mrs. Frye, another farmer's wife, who runs the liquor store, asks if her husband is bringing company for the weekend. "He sure is; we couldn't drink all that by ourselves," and the young woman laughs, her lovely teeth exposed, her small gold earrings quivering in the light. "You know, I saw his name—on the television the other night," says Mrs. Frye. "It was at the beginning of that new comedy show, the one with the woman who used to be on another show with her husband and little girl, only they divorced, you know the one?" "Of course I do. It's one of my husband's shows. I'll tell him you watched it." Mrs. Frye puts the bottles in an empty box, carefully inserting wedges of cardboard between them. Through the window of her store she sees her customer's pert bottle-green car, some sort of little foreign car with the engine running, filled with groceries and weekend parcels, and that big silver-blue dog sitting up in the front seat just like a human being. "I think that kind of thing is so sad," says Mrs. Frye; "families breaking up, poor little children having to divide their loyalties." "I couldn't agree more," replies the young woman, nodding gravely. Such a personable, polite girl! "Are you sure you can carry that, dear? I can get Earl from the back. . . . " But the girl has it hoisted on her shoulder in a flash, is airily maneuvering between unopened cartons stacked in the aisle, in her pretty boots. Her perfume lingers in Mrs. Frye's store for a half-hour after she has driven away.

After dinner, her husband and his friends drank brandy. She lay in front of the fire, stroking the dog, and listening to Victoria Darrow, the news commentator, in person. A few minutes ago, they had all watched Victoria on TV. "That's right; thirty-nine!" Victoria now whispered to her. "What? That's kind of you. I'm photogenic, thank God, or I'd have been put out to pasture long before. . . . I look five, maybe seven years younger on the screen . . . but the point I'm getting at is, I went to this doctor and he said, 'If you want to do this thing, you'd better go home today and get started.' He told me—did you know this? Did you know that a woman is born with all the eggs she'll ever have, and when she gets to my age, the ones that are left have been rattling around so long they're a little shopworn; then every time you fly you get an extra dose of radioactivity, so those poor eggs. He told me when a woman over forty comes into his office pregnant, his heart sinks; that's why he quit practicing obstetrics, he said; he could still remember the screams of a woman whose baby he delivered . . . she was having natural childbirth and she kept saying, 'Why won't you let me see it, I insist on seeing it,' and so he had to, and he says he can still hear her screaming."

"Oh, what was—what was wrong with it?"

But she never got the answer. Her husband, white around the lips, was standing over Victoria ominously, offering the Remy Martin bottle. "Vicky, let me pour you some more," he said. And to his wife, "I think Blue Boy needs to go out."

"Yes, yes, of course. Please excuse me, Victoria. I'll just be . . . "

Her husband followed her to the kitchen, his hand on the back of her neck. "Are you okay? That stupid yammering bitch. She and her twenty-six-year-old lover! I wish I'd never brought them, but she's been hinting around the studio for weeks."

"But I like them, I like having them. I'm fine. Please go back. I'll take the dog out and come back. Please . . . "

"All right. If you're sure you're okay." He backed away, hands dangling at his sides. A handsome man, wearing a pink shirt with Guatemalan embroidery. Thick black hair and a face rather boyish, but cunning. Last weekend she had sat beside him, alone in this house, just the two of them, and watched him on television: a documentary, in several parts, in which TV "examines itself." There was his double, sitting in an armchair in his executive office, coolly replying to the questions of Victoria Darrow. *"Do you personally watch all the programs you produce, Mr. McNair?"* She watched the man on the screen, how he moved his lips when he spoke, but kept the rest of his face, his body perfectly still. Funny, she had never noticed this before. He managed to say that he did and did not watch all the programs he produced.

Now, in the kitchen, she looked at him backing away, a little like a renegade in one of his own shows—a desperate man, perhaps, who has just killed somebody and is backing away, hands dangling loosely at his sides, Mr. McNair, her husband. That man on the screen. Once a lover above her in bed. That friend who held her hand in the hospital. One hand in hers, the other holding the stopwatch. For a brief instant, all the images coalesce and she feels something again. But once outside, under the galaxies of autumn-sharp stars, the intelligent dog at her heels like some smart gray ghost, she is glad to be free of all that. She walks quickly over the damp grass to the barn, to look in on her horse. She understands something: her husband, Victoria Darrow lead double lives that seem perfectly normal to them. But if she told her husband that she, too, is in two lives, he would become alarmed; he would sell this house and make her move back to the city where he could keep an eye on her welfare.

* * *

She is discovering people like herself, down through the centuries, all over the world. She scours books with titles like *The Timeless Moment, The Sleeping Prophet, Between Two Worlds, Silent Union: A Record of Unwilled Communication;* collecting evidence, weaving a sort of underworld net of colleagues around her.

A rainy fall day. Too wet to ride. The silver dog asleep beside her in her special alcove, a padded window seat filled with pillows and books. She is looking down on the fields of dried lithrium, and the fir trees beyond, and the mountains gauzy with fog and rain, thinking, in a kind of terror and ecstasy, about all these connections. A book lies face down on her lap. She has just read the following:

> Theodore Dreiser and his friend John Cowper Powys had been dining at Dreiser's place on West Fifty Seventh Street. As Powys made ready to leave and catch his train to the little town up the Hudson, where he was then living, he told Dreiser, "I'll appear before you here, later in the evening."
>
> Dreiser laughed. "Are you going to turn yourself into a ghost, or have you a spare key?" he asked. Powys said he would return "in some form," he didn't know exactly what kind.
>
> After his friend left, Dreiser sat up and read for two hours. Then he looked up and saw Powys standing in the doorway to the living room. It was Powys' features, his tall stature, even the loose tweed garments which he wore. Dreiser rose at once and strode towards the figure, saying, "Well, John, you kept your word. Come on in and tell me how you did it." But the figure vanished when Dreiser came within three feet of it.
>
> Dreiser then went to the telephone and called Powys' house in the country. Powys answered. Dreiser told him what happened and Powys said, "I told you

I'd be there and you oughtn't to be surprised." But he refused to discuss how he had done it, if, indeed, he knew how.

"But don't you get frightened, up here all by yourself, alone with all these creaky sounds?" asked Victoria the next morning.

"No, I guess I'm used to them," she replied, breaking eggs into a bowl. "I know what each one means. The wood expanding and contracting . . . the wind getting caught between the shutter and the latch . . . Sometimes small animals get lost in the stone walls and scratch around till they find their way out . . . or die."

"Ugh. But don't you imagine things? I would, in a house like this. How old? That's almost three hundred years of lived lives, people's suffering and shouting and making love and giving birth, under this roof. . . . You'd think there'd be a few ghosts around."

"I don't know," said her hostess blandly. "I haven't heard any. But of course, I have Blue Boy, so I don't get scared." She whisked the eggs, unable to face Victoria. She and her husband had lain awake last night, embarrassed at the sounds coming from the next room. No ghostly moans, those. "Why can't that bitch control herself, or at least lower her voice," he said angrily. He stroked his wife's arm, both of them pretending not to remember. She had bled for an entire year afterward, until the doctor said they would have to remove everything. "I'm empty," she had said when her husband had tried again, after she was healed. "I'm sorry, I just don't feel anything." Now they lay tenderly together on these weekends, like childhood friends, like effigies on a lovers' tomb, their mutual sorrow like a sword between them. She assumed he had another life, or lives, in town. As she had here. Nobody is just one person, she had learned.

"I'm sure I would imagine things," said Victoria. "I would see things and hear things inside my head much worse than an ordinary murderer or rapist."

The wind caught in the shutter latch . . . a small animal dislodging pieces of fieldstone in its terror, sending them tumbling down the inner walls, from attic to cellar . . . a sound like a child rattling a jar full or marbles, or small stones . . .

"I have so little imagination," she said humbly, warming the butter in the omelet pan. She could feel Victoria Darrow's professional curiosity waning from her dull country life, focusing elsewhere.

Cunning!

As a child of nine, she had gone through a phase of walking in her sleep. One summer night, they found her bed empty, and after an hour's hysterical search they had found her in her nightgown, curled up on the flagstones beside the fishpond. She woke, baffled, in her father's tense clutch, the stars all over the sky, her mother repeating over and over again to the night at large, "Oh my God, she could have drowned!" They took her to a child psychiatrist, a pretty Austrian woman who spoke to her with the same vocabulary she used on grownups, putting the child instantly at ease. "It is not at all uncommon what you did. I have known so many children who take little night journeys from their beds, and then they awaken and don't know what all the fuss is about! Usually these journeys are quite harmless, because children are surrounded by a magical reality that keeps them safe. Yes, the race of children possesses magically sagacious powers! But the grownups, they tend to forget how it once was for them. They worry, they are afraid of so many things. You do not want your mother and father, who love you so anxiously, to live in fear of you going to live with the fishes." She had giggled at the thought. The woman's steady gray-green eyes were trained on her carefully, suspending her in a kind of bubble. Then she had rejoined her parents, a dutiful "child" again, holding a hand up to each of them. The night journeys had stopped.

A thunderstorm one night last spring. Blue Boy whining in his insulated house below the garage. She had lain there, strangely elated by the nearness of the thunderclaps that tore at the sky, followed by instantaneous flashes of jagged light. Wondering shouldn't she go down and let the dog in; he hated storms. Then dozing off again . . .

She woke. The storm had stopped. The dark air was quiet. Something had changed, some small thing—what? She had to think hard before she found it: the hall light, which she kept burning during the week-nights when she was there alone, had gone out. She reached over and switched the button on her bed-side lamp. Nothing. A tree must have fallen and hit a wire, causing the power to go off. This often happened here. No problem. The dog had stopped crying. She felt herself sinking into a delicious, deep reverie, the kind that sometimes came just before morning, as if her being broke slowly into tiny pieces and spread itself over the world. It was a feeling she had not known until she had lived by herself in this house: this weightless though conscious state in which she lay, as if in a warm bath, and yet was able to send her thoughts anywhere, as if her mind contained the entire world.

And as she floated in this silent world, transparent and buoyed upon the dream layers of the mind, she heard a small rattling sound, like pebbles being shaken in a jar. The sound came distinctly from the guest room, a room so chosen by her husband and herself because it was the farthest room from their bedroom on this floor. It lay above what had been the old side of the house, built seventy-five years before the new side, which was completed in 1753. There was a bed in it, and a chair, and some plants in the window. Sometimes on weekends when she could not sleep, she went and read there, or meditated, to keep from waking her husband. It was the room where Victoria Darrow and her young lover would not sleep the following fall, because she would say quietly to her husband, "No . . . not that room. I—I've made up the bed in the other room." "What?" he would want to know. "The one next to ours? Right under our noses?"

She did not lie long listening to this sound before she understood it was one she had never heard in the house before. It had a peculiar regularity to its rhythm; there was nothing accidental about it, nothing influenced by the wind, or the nerves of some lost animal. *K-chunk, k-chunk, k-chunk,* it went. At intervals of exactly a half-minute apart. She still remembered how to time such things, such intervals. She was as good as any stopwatch when it came to timing certain intervals.

K-chunk, k-chunk, k-chunk. That determined regularity. Something willed, something poignantly repeated, as though the repetition was a means of consoling someone in the dark. Her skin began to prickle. Often, lying in such states of weightless reverie, she had practiced the trick of sending herself abroad, into rooms of the house, out into the night to check on Blue Boy, over to the barn to look in on her horse, who slept standing up. Once she had heard a rather frightening noise, as if someone in the basement had turned on a faucet, and so she forced herself to "go down," floating down two sets of stairs into the darkness, only to discover what she had known all the time: the hookup system between the hot-water tank and the pump, which sounded like someone turning on the water.

Now she went through the palpable, prickly darkness, without lights, down the chilly hall in her sleeveless gown, into the guest room. Although there was no light, not even a moon shining through the window, she could make out the shape of the bed and then the chair, the spider plants on the window, and a small dark shape in one corner, on the floor, which she and her husband had painted a light yellow.

K-chunk, k-chunk, k-chunk. The shape moved with the noise.

Now she knew what they meant, that "someone's hair stood on end." It was true. As she forced herself across the borders of a place she had never been, she felt, distinctly, every single hair on her head raise itself a millimeter or so from her scalp.

She knelt down and discovered him. He was kneeling, a little cold and scared, shaking a small jar filled with some kind of pebbles. (She later found out, in a subsequent visit, that they were small colored shells, of a triangular shape, called coquinas: she found them in a picture in a child's nature book at the library.) He was wearing pajamas a little too big for him, obviously hand-me-downs, and he was exactly two years older than the only time she had ever held him in her arms.

The two of them knelt in the corner of the room, taking each other in. His large eyes were the same as before: dark and unblinking. He held the small jar close to him, watching her. He was not afraid, but she knew better than to move too close.

She knelt, the tears streaming down her cheeks, but she made no sound, her eyes fastened on that small form. And then the hall light came on silently, as well as the lamp beside her bed, and with wet cheeks and pounding heart she could not be sure whether or not she had actually been out of the room.

But what did it matter, on the level where they had met? He traveled so much farther than she to reach that room. *("Yes, the race of children possesses magically sagacious powers!")*

She and her husband sat together on the flowered chintz sofa, watching the last of the series in which TV purportedly examined itself. She said, "Did you ever think that the whole thing is really a miracle? I mean, here we sit, eighty miles away from your studios, and we turn on a little machine and there is Victoria, speaking to us as clearly as she did last weekend when she was in this very room. Why, it's magic, it's time travel and space travel right in front of our eyes, but because it's been 'discovered,' because the world understands that it's only little dots that transmit Victoria electrically to us, it's *all right.* We can bear it. Don't you sometimes wonder about all the miracles that haven't been officially approved yet? I mean, who knows, maybe in a hundred years everybody will take it for granted that they can send an image of themselves around in space by some perfectly natural means available to us now. I mean, when you think about it, what *is* space? What *is* time? Where do the so-called boundaries of each of us begin and end? Can anyone explain it?"

He was drinking Scotch and thinking how they had decided not to renew Victoria Darrow's contract. Somewhere on the edges of his mind hovered an anxious, growing certainty about his wife. At the local grocery store this morning, when he went to pick up a carton of milk and the paper, he had stopped to chat with DePuy. "I don't mean to interfere, but she doesn't know those fields," said the farmer. "Last year we had to shoot a mare, stumbled into one of those holes. . . . It's madness, the way she rides."

And look at her now, her face so pale and shining, speaking of miracles and space travel, almost on the verge of tears. . . .

And last night, his first night up from the city, he had wandered through the house, trying to drink himself into this slower weekend pace, and he had come across a pile of her books, stacked in the alcove where, it was obvious, she lay for hours, escaping into science fiction, and the occult.

Now his own face appeared on the screen. "I want to be fair," he was telling Victoria Darrow. "I want to be objective. . . . Violence has always been part of the human makeup. I don't like it anymore than you do, but there it is. I think it's more a question of whether we want to face things as they are or escape into fantasies of how we would like them to be."

Beside him, his wife uttered a sudden bell-like laugh.

(". . . It's madness, the way she rides.")

He did want to be fair, objective. She had told him again and again that she liked her life here. And he—well, he had to admit he liked his own present set-up.

"I am a pragmatist," he was telling Virginia Darrow on the screen. He decided to speak to his wife about her riding and leave her alone about the books. She had the right to some escape, if anyone did. But the titles: *Marvelous Manifestations, The Mind Travellers, A Doctor Looks at Spiritualism, The Other Side* . . . Something revolted in him, he couldn't help it; he felt an actual physical revulsion at this kind of thinking. Still it was better than some other escapes. His friend Barnett, the actor, who said at night he went from room to room, after his wife was asleep, collecting empty glasses. ("Once I found one by the Water Pik, a second on the ledge beside the tub, a third on the back of the john, and a fourth on the floor beside the john. . . . ")

He looked sideways at his wife, who was absorbed, it seemed, in watching him on the screen. Her face was tense, alert, animated. She did not look mad. She wore slim gray pants and a loose-knit pullover made of some silvery material, like a knight's chain mail. The lines of her profile were clear and silvery themselves, somehow sexless and pure, like a child's profile. He no longer felt lust when he looked at her, only a sad determination to protect her. He had a mistress in town, whom he loved, but he had explained, right from the beginning, that he considered himself married for the rest of his life. He told this woman the whole story. "And I am implicated in it. I could never leave her." An intelligent, sensitive woman, she had actually wept and said, "Of course not."

He always wore the same pajamas, a shade too big, but always clean. Obviously washed again and again in a machine that went through its cycles frequently. She imagined his "other mother," a harassed woman with several children, short on money, on time, on dreams—all the things she herself had too much of. The family lived, she believed, somewhere in Florida, probably on the west coast. She had worked that out from the little coquina shells: their bright colors, even in moonlight shining through a small window with spider plants in it. His face and arms had been suntanned early in the spring and late into the autumn. They never spoke or touched. She tried and failed to remember where she herself had gone, in those little night journeys to the fishpond. Perhaps he never remembered afterward, when he woke up, clutching his jar, in a roomful of brothers and sisters. Or with a worried mother or father come to collect him, asleep by the sea. Once she had a very clear dream of the whole family, living in a trailer, with palm trees. But that was a dream; she recognized its difference in quality from those truly magic times when, through his own childish powers, he somehow found a will strong enough, or innocent enough, to project himself upon her still-floating consciousness, as clearly and as believably as her own husband's image on the screen.

There had been six of those times in six months. She dared to look forward to more. So unafraid he was. The last time was the day after Victoria Darrow and her young lover and her own good husband returned to the city. She had gone farther with the child than ever before. On a starry-clear, cold September Monday, she had coaxed him down the stairs and out of the house with her. He held to the banisters, a child unused to stairs, and yet she knew there was no danger; he floated in his own dream with her. She took him to see Blue Boy. Who disappointed her by whining and backing away in fear. And then to the barn to see the horse. Who perked up his ears and looked interested. There was no touching, of course, no touching or speaking. Later she wondered if horses, then, were more magical than dogs. If dogs were more "realistic." She was glad the family was poor, the mother harassed. They could not afford any expensive child psychiatrist who would hypnotize him out of his night journeys.

He loved her. She knew that. Even if he never remembered her in his other life.

"At last I was beginning to understand what Teilhard de Chardin meant when he said that man's true home is the mind. I understood that when the mystics tell us that the mind is a place, they *don't mean it as a metaphor.* I found these new powers developed with practice. I had to detach myself from my ordinary physical personality. The intelligent part of me had to remain wide awake, and move down into this world of thoughts, dreams and memories. After several such journeyings, I understood something else: dream and reality aren't competitors, but reciprocal sources of consciousness." This she read in a "respectable book," by a "respectable man," a scientist, alive and living in England, only a few years older than herself. She looked down at the dog, sleeping on the rug. His lean silvery body actually ran as he slept! Suddenly his muzzle lifted, the savage teeth snapped. Where was he "really" now? Did the dream rabbit in his jaws know it was a dream? There was much to think about, between her trips to the nursery.

Would the boy grow, would she see his body slowly emerging from its child's shape, the arms and legs lengthening, the face thinning out into a man's—like a certain advertisement for bread she had seen on TV where a child grows up, in less than a half-minute of sponsor time, right before the viewer's eyes. Would he grow into a man, grow a beard . . . outgrow the nursery region of his mind where they had been able to meet?

And yet, some daylight part of his mind must have retained an image of her from that single daylight time they had looked into each other's eyes.

The worst thing, such an awful thing to happen to a young woman . . . She was having this natural childbirth, you see, her husband in the delivery room with her, and the pains were coming a half-minute apart, and the doctor had just said, "This is going to be a breeze, Mrs. McNair," and they never knew exactly what went wrong, but all of a sudden the pains stopped and they had to go in after the baby without even time to give her a saddle block or any sort of anesthetic. . . . They must have practically had to tear it out of her . . . the husband fainted. The baby was born dead, and they gave her a heavy sedative to put her out all night.

When she woke the next morning, before she had time to remember what had happened, a nurse suddenly entered the room and laid a baby in her arms. "Here's your little boy," she said cheerfully, and the woman thought, with a profound, religious relief, *So that other nightmare was a dream,* and she had the child at her breast feeding him before the nurse realized her mistake and rushed back into the room, but they had to knock the poor woman out with more sedatives before she would let the child go. She was screaming and so was the little baby and they clung to each other till she passed out.

They would have let the nurse go, only it wasn't entirely her fault. The hospital was having a strike at the time; some of the nurses were outside picketing and this nurse had been working straight through for forty-eight hours, and when she was questioned afterward she said she had just mixed up the rooms, and yet, she said, when she had seen the woman and the baby clinging to each other like that, she had undergone a sort of revelation in her almost hallucinatory exhaustion: the nurse said she saw that all children and mothers were interchangeable, that nobody could own anybody or anything, anymore than you could own an idea that happened to be passing through the air and caught on your mind, or anymore than you owned the rosebush that grew in your back yard. There were only mothers and children, she realized; though, afterward, the realization faded.

It was the kind of freakish thing that happens once in a million times, and it's a wonder the poor woman kept her sanity.

In the intervals, longer than those measured by any stopwatch, she waited for him. In what the world accepted as "time," she shopped for groceries, for clothes; she read; she waved from her bottle-green car to Mrs. Frye, trimming the hedge in front of the liquor store, to Mrs. DePuy, hanging out her children's pajamas in the back yard of the old Patroon farm. She rode her horse through the fields of the waning season, letting him have his head; she rode like the wind, a happy, happy woman. She rode faster than fear because she was a woman in a dream, a woman anxiously awaiting her child's sleep. The stallion's hoofs pounded the earth. Oiling his tractor, DePuy resented the foolish woman and almost wished for a woodchuck hole to break that arrogant ride. Wished deep in a violent level of himself he never knew he had. For he was a kind, distracted father and husband, a practical, hard-working man who would never descend deeply into himself. Her body, skimming through time, felt weightless to the horse.

Was she a woman riding a horse and dreaming she was a mother who anxiously awaited her child's sleep; or was she a mother dreaming of herself as a free spirit who could ride her horse like the wind because she had nothing to fear?

I am a happy woman, that's all I know. Who can explain such things?

GAIL GODWIN DISCUSSES

"Dream Children," structure, and her favorite ghost stories

GG: "Dream Children" was conceived and written during 1973. In 1972, the composer Robert Starer and I had met at Yaddo, the artists' retreat in Saratoga Springs, burnt our bridges and left our former lives (which took a year), and moved together into a two-hundred-fifty-year-old stone farmhouse in Ulster County, New York. Neither of us had ever lived in the country before. Its noises, smells, landscapes, and folkways were new to us. Robert went four days a week to the city to teach at Juilliard and Brooklyn College, and I was by myself for four days and three nights in this old house in Stone Ridge, writing full-time for the first time in my life. I had never had so much time alone!

My dreams in this house were unlike any I'd had before. I had versions of a certain repetitive dream in which I *felt* awake and went floating down the stairs and through the old house and out into the fields. I encountered people, they never spoke, and some of them were pretty primitive. They weren't malevolent, just rough-hewn. To them, I must have seemed like some aberration as they went about their business, which was farm labor. You might say I was steeped in an atmosphere of concurrent worlds, separated only by time. I never knew what I was going to encounter. Once, I dreamed I was walking through the rooms of my house and that I kept finding my own unborn children. They were of different ages: one about two, another in his teens. When I woke up, I was shaken; this particular dream was the true procreator of "Dream Children."

Around this time, a friend had a miscarriage in her eighth month. Her husband, who was my literary agent, called to tell me the bizarre aftermath. At the hospital she was sedated, and was later wakened by a nurse who had mistaken the room number and pressed someone else's newborn boy into her arms. But the event of my story, the thing of major importance, was a realization. My woman realized she lived in a dream with her imagined child and was happy in doing so. And I knew it had to be a short story I was writing, rather than a novel, because stories can better crystallize epiphanies.

PM: How did you decide on the unusual structure of "Dream Children"?

GG: My structures for novels or stories aren't decided in advance, they emerge almost viscerally, the way you might go into a bare room and see what furniture is needed and where it should be placed for the kind of life you want to live in that room. So to me there is nothing unusual about the structure of "Dream Children."

I started with a country setting, an old house, some noises at night, a woman who'd been through something heart-breaking but still goes about her stylish errands and rides her horse and uses her time and solitude to probe for the meaning of what happened to her. That is the core of the story for me, that is what incites and excites the writing: I want to discover what she discovers, given the materials she has available. She gets to read books, she gets to draw conclusions from her own experience. (An example of the latter: she and her husband are watching Victoria on TV, and she comments to him: ". . . because it's been 'discovered,' because the world understands that it's only little dots that transmit Victoria electrically to us, it's *all right* . . . {but} don't you sometimes wonder about all the miracles that haven't been officially approved yet?")

The over-voice in italics, which begins the story and comments intermittently throughout, could be—and, it turns out, *is*—Mrs. McNair's. Initially, she refers to herself in third-person, from the point of view of an outsider, should they become acquainted with her sad history. At the end, when she acknowledges she is in the presence of a mystery, she un-distances herself with first-person to conclude that as long as she resides *within this mystery* she can live as a happy woman.

PM: Since story structures "emerge almost viscerally" for you, how do you open yourself up to their possibilities?
GG: Ever since I realized (in the summer of 1972, at Yaddo, while failing to force *The Odd Woman* into a chronological mold of grandmother, mother, and daughter's stories) that I bore and depress myself and kill works in progress if I force myself to follow a scheme, especially a linear point-to-point scheme, I have allowed myself to proceed more . . . what is the adverb I want here? Not intuitively, not instinctually. *Inherently* is closer, because it pertains to the indwelling, intrinsic possibilities of a story. Those are the possibilities I'm after; that's why I keep writing. I stay fascinated as long as I let the *episodes* lead the way, as long as I stay in the story's vitality zone.

My stories and novels are composed primarily of episodes, not narrative progressions. The episodes develop the ongoing movement—the fate—of the story. Fate is not linear; it is a dynamic design and it is unbound by time. As the story proceeds episode by episode, in a certain direction, opportunities arise for further episodes.
PM: Since most of the story's point of view is Mrs. McNair's, do you intend the smattering of other points of view as projections of hers ("as if her mind contained the entire world" page 252), or belonging to an omniscient narrator, or perhaps something else?
GG: Most, but by no means all, of the story's point of view belongs to Mrs. McNair. However, the "smatterings" of other viewpoints belong to other people, they are not projections. That is not to say she couldn't imagine what her husband, Victoria, farmer DePuy would be likely to think or say about her.
PM: You place a section near the beginning and again near the end from the farmer DePuy's point of view. What appealed to you about his removed, observer's perspective and the symmetry of this structure?
GG: I wanted to show that Mrs. McNair has traveled through time and changed, but he has not. He is still anchored in his

here-and-now work-life, with no time or inclination for other dimensions. He doesn't see her as a woman riding between worlds. He resents her oblivious recreational rides over the woodchuck holes.

PM: Mrs. McNair's meeting with the child is the longest section in "Dream Children." Would you describe how you go about making such pacing decisions?

GG: This meeting is the centerpiece of the story. It has to be worked up to, and then down from. Two Australian screenplays and one thirty-minute Canadian TV drama of "Dream Children" have so far wrecked themselves on the shoals of this meeting. It has to be prepared for, otherwise it's just a simplistic haunting. And Mrs. McNair *has* prepared for it. She is ready. We learn that she had a history of childhood night travels. This also sets us up for the child being able to travel to her. And she has been seeking out information about people like herself, her "underworld net of colleagues," who can travel between worlds.

PM: In addition to being the story's centerpiece, is it fair to say that scene demands the largest leap of imagination on the reader's part and therefore requires the deepest level of sensory detail?

GG: Definitely.

PM: You don't dwell on the fact of the baby's death any longer than necessary, and instead the story places its emphasis on the momentary mix-up in the hospital.

GG: The emphasis is on the mix-up rather than the stillbirth of her own baby because that is the order of priorities her memory has given to the experience. She never held her dead baby in her arms, only the living boy. She chooses to cling to that moment of vitality, and it later becomes her comfort and a means of enlarging her experience.

PM: There's also something about the mix-up that is, more so than the death that precedes it, hair-raising. Its strange irony maybe. And also as you just said, the way it will go on to open the door to the narrator's whole exploration.

You drop hints about the mix-up scene, as on page 254 with the line "he was exactly two years older than the only time she had ever held him in her arms," without fully giving it away. When doling out information like that, what is the key to ensuring the reader won't feel manipulated?

GG: How do I ensure that the reader won't feel manipulated? I don't or can't. I don't remember worrying about it, maybe because I was following her inner route as she doled out the memories to herself.

PM: Is the section on Dreiser and Powys quoted from somewhere, or is it something you invented based on your sense of their historical relationship? Describe the appeal for you of employing that small story-within-the-story.

GG: The story about Powys's experiment with his friend Dreiser can be found in biographies. It happened, or they report it happening, during the time Powys was lecturing in America. I first read about it in a book on occult experiences by the English writer, Colin Wilson. Powys, by the way, was a master of the numinous. For a treat, if your attention span is up to an eleven hundred twenty-page novel, read *A Glastonbury Romance.* Here is one minuscule example of how he bridges worlds and expresses the Mrs. McNair mindset:

Mary, out walking at night, is suddenly transfixed beyond her current disappointments by the presence of the moon.

> "What does it make me feel?" she thought. "Is there something about it that every woman who has ever lived in Glastonbury must feel? Something that the Lake Village women felt? Something that immured, medieval nuns were comforted by?"

A Glastonbury Romance is crowded with Mrs. McNair's "underworld network of colleagues," who can get outside of time through being aware of others like themselves all through the ages.

PM: How do you decide when tangential stories are worth the risk of distracting the reader?

GG: If I feel the urge to put in a tangential story, I usually indulge myself. Then later, if I feel that it's an annoying detour or roadblock, having served no purpose but my gratification, I take it out. Last year, I removed a twenty-five-page girls' school flashback from *Queen of the Underworld,* because it made an ungainly hump in the middle of the novel when the reader should be getting excited by what's happening in the present. It hurt me to excise it, but a year later it has found its niche in a ghost novella I'm writing in the evenings, *The Red Nun.*

The Dreiser-Powys exchange gave authority to the kind of exchange Mrs. McNair will soon experience. Both authors were sensible, intelligent men, not gullible, superstitious fools.

PM: Victoria Darrow provides a counterpoint to Mrs. McNair. Could you discuss how the two characters play off one another?

GG: I enjoy creating foil characters because I like reading about them. Becky Sharp and Amelia Sedley in *Vanity Fair*, etc. Victoria Darrow is a foil to Mrs. McNair because she is aggressively curious, always on the prowl for a "sensational" finding, and not subtle. She has no moat of reserve around her. She doesn't hesitate to advertise and dramatize her private life and would feel restrained if she had a secret to keep. She provides a striking contrast to Mrs. McNair, who cunningly passes herself off as normal and rather dull so she can protect the precious secret of her burgeoning inner life.

PM: Also, Victoria is fearful (and has reason to be, it turns out, since she's about to be put out to pasture). Mrs. McNair is evolving beyond those sorts of mundane concerns.

GG: Fearful, yes. You describe the contrast very well.

There is one thing you didn't ask. Why is she just "Mrs. McNair"? I think because she's beyond having a personal name in the realm that matters most to her. With her, the child doesn't have a name. As the exhausted nurse glimpses, there are simply mothers and children. "Mrs. McNair" is her worldly persona, the carapace that comfortably—and cunningly—shields her main life.

PM: Writing students are sometimes cautioned against including dream sequences in fiction, a "rule" you've certainly managed to find exception to over the years! What do *you* advise aspiring writers about it?

GG: You have to be discerning about making up dreams for your characters, but discernment is developed by practice. Meanwhile, here are some guidelines until you learn to trust your discerning powers.

—What is the dream you had in mind for your character? Did you create it for the character, or are you recycling a dream of your own? If it is from your nightlife, you may need to make some alterations to suit the character's needs.

—What is the dream trying to tell the person/character who dreams it?

—Why does it belong in the story? Does it give us insight into the dreamer? Further the action? Warn the dreamer and alert the reader to a change of pace? Prepare us for the next episode?

Then go ahead and create it, put it in, and if it serves any or all of the above purposes, keep it there until you or someone else, like an editor, persuades you to take it out.

I am haunted to this day by a certain dream sequence in my story "A Sorrowful Woman," (in the *Dream Children* collection) that a fiction editor at *Esquire* persuaded me to remove. The woman will be more inscrutable if you leave out the dreams, he said. Now, thirty years later, "A Sorrowful Woman" has become my most anthologized story. And my web site receives a steady traffic in e-mails from baffled students—and teachers—who want to know why this woman killed herself. If the dreams had been left in, you would know why. But everyone agrees, the woman is inscrutable.

Dreams often reveal designs in your life that you aren't aware of. Dreams dredge up buried treasures. Dreams solve daytime problems: Molecular scientist Friedrich Kekulé's {1829–96} famous dream of a whirling snake seizing its own tail led to his solving the mystery of the benzene ring. Dreams lead into novels: "Last night I dreamed of Manderley" is the first line of Daphne du Maurier's *Rebecca;* "Last night I dreamed of Ursula DeVane" is the first line of my own *The Finishing School.*

Someone can have an intercessory dream—a dream that serves others. Shamans have dreams for their respective communities. At the end of my novel *A Southern Family,* Sister Patrick's dream of Theo Quick, on the first anniversary of his death, brings solace and enlightenment to his mother, Lily Quick.

PM: The haunting presence of the deceased has been a long-standing theme in your work. What do you trace it to?

GG: In my fiction, the dead often haunt in constructive or cautionary ways. Their demise is the catalyst for a big life change in someone, or it acts as a prod: "Don't be like me . . . get going or it'll be too late, etc." Or sometimes their removal from the scene alters the dynamics between those left behind.

To what do I trace this long-standing theme? I can't remember a time when I didn't keep active company with the dead, and I don't think this is at all out of the ordinary. A grandparent is continually telling stories of the dead spouse; parents disappear or expire; children die and break our hearts; our friends lose their loved ones; and we console one another and talk about it and wonder where the dead have gone, we re-live their foibles and worst moments, imitate their gestures, emulate their virtues, and sometimes their vices. We make up myths about them and put up pictures of them on the refrigerator. Thus, in their way, they stay around and partake of our ongoing lives.

Also, I grew up in a milieu particularly friendly to marathon storytelling about the departed. Many people I never knew have found permanent places in my psyche: the gardener who dropped dead after drinking a glass of cold water; the grandfather who was a saint and all the stories about his sainthood; the great aunt who went around secretly baptizing the family's babies into the Catholic faith; the little girl who fell out of the window of the school bus, etc.

In addition, I lost a father, a brother, and a close college friend to the suicide demons. Death by suicide poses questions beyond the big question of "Where are they now?" Those left behind have to ask the "whys." And then the "whats." What led to . . . What might have been different . . . What did I leave undone? What would he be like now?

My mother, at seventy-seven, had a heart attack while driving to the airport. I never saw a person die slowly in a bed until a local professor with cancer admitted me to "his final exam." He was the inspiration for *The Good Husband.* I changed him into a woman, Magda Danvers, who would have amused him greatly.

Robert's death was another experience altogether. We were together almost thirty years. We talked frequently of our eventual separation by death, we frankly indulged ourselves, imagining all the angles ahead of time, and then feeling relieved and celebratory when we remembered it hadn't happened yet. I like to think that because he was so aware and prepared for *not* being here someday, so adept at imagining me going on without him, that somehow he prepared an after-death space for himself. "We still have some time together," he remarked the night before he died, and he was right. *Evenings at Five* is a story about present absences and absent presences. In other words, it is a ghost story.

PM: I imagine you're a big fan of ghost stories generally. What do you like best about them?

GG: What kind of person would *not* be a fan of ghost stories? Are there people who prefer *not* to be scared, ever? Are there people who have no desire to experiment with their tolerance level for dread? Are there people who, if they were given the choice, would choose to live in a world with no mystery, no illusions, no dreams and fantasies, no possibilities of visions or miracles, no new laws of nature to upset the status quo—and, above all, no ambiguity? I must have met a few of these people in my life, though offhand I can't recall a single one.

These are my top-four most admired ghost stories:

"The Black Monk," a novella by Anton Chekhov.

"The Great, Good Place," a story by Henry James.

All Hallows' Eve, a novel by Charles Williams.

"Playmates," a story by A. M. Burrage.

Chekhov's treatment of the supernatural in "The Black Monk" plays on my favorite level of dread. The student in "Monk" has been working too hard and is on the verge of a breakdown. The black monk, a "friendly but crafty" mirage transmitted through obscure laws of optics by a legendary monk who lived a thousand years ago, comes in a series of visitations to prepare Kovrin for his death.

"You're just a mirage," says Kovrin (in Ronald Wilks's translation). "Never mind," says the black monk, "the legend, myself, the mirage, are all products of your overheated imagination." To which the student replies, "That means you don't exist." "Think what you like," counters the apparition, "I exist in your imagination, and your imagination is part of nature, so I exist in nature too."

GAIL GODWIN is the author of eleven novels and two collections of stories, including *Dream Children* (1976), *A Mother and Two Daughters* (1982), *A Southern Family* (1987), and *Evenings at Five* (2003). In addition to three National Book Award nominations, she has received a Guggenheim Fellowship, National Endowment grants for both fiction and libretto writing, and the Award in Literature from the American Academy and Institute of Arts and Letters. She lives in Woodstock, New York.

SMORGASBORD

Tobias Wolff

"A prep school in March is like a ship in the doldrums." Our history master said this, as if to himself, while we were waiting for the bell to ring after class. He stood by the window and tapped the glass with his ring in a dreamy, abstracted way meant to make us think he'd forgotten we were there. We were supposed to get the impression that when we weren't around he turned into someone interesting, someone witty and profound, who uttered impromptu bon mots and had a poetic vision of life.

The bell rang.

I went to lunch. The dining hall was almost empty, because it was a free weekend and most of the boys had gone to New York, or home, or to their friends' homes, as soon as their class let out. About the only ones left were foreigners and scholarship students like me and a few other untouchables of various stripes. The school had laid on a nice lunch for us, cheese soufflé, but the portions were small and I went back to my room still hungry. I was always hungry.

Sleety rain fell past my window. The snow on the quad looked grimy; it had melted above the underground heating pipes, exposing long brown lines of mud.

I couldn't get to work. On the next floor down someone kept playing "Mack the Knife." That one song incessantly repeating itself made the dorm seem not just empty but abandoned, as if those who had left were never coming back. I cleaned my room, then tried to read. I looked out the window. I sat down at my desk and studied the new picture my girlfriend had sent me, unable to imagine her from it; I had to close my eyes to do that, and then I could see her, see her solemn eyes and the heavy white breasts she would gravely let me hold sometimes, but not kiss. Not yet, anyway. But I had a promise. That summer, as soon as I got home, we were going to become lovers. "Become lovers." That was what she'd said, very deliberately, listening to the words as she spoke them. All year I had repeated them to myself to take the edge off my loneliness and the fits of lust that made me want to scream and drive my fists through walls. We were going to become lovers that summer, and we were going to be lovers all through college, true to each other even if we ended up thousands of miles apart again, and after college we were going to marry and join the Peace Corps and do something together that would help people. This was our plan. Back in September, the night before I left for school, we wrote it all down along with a lot of other specifics concerning our future: number of children (six), their names, the kinds of dogs we would own, a sketch of our perfect house. We sealed the paper in a bottle and buried it in her backyard. On our golden anniversary we'd dig it up and show it to our children and grandchildren to prove that dreams can come true.

I was writing her a letter when Crosley came to my room. Crosley was a science whiz. He won the science prize every year and spent his summers working as an intern in different laboratories. He was also a fanatical weight lifter. His arms were so knotty that he had to hold them out from his sides as he walked, as if he was carrying buckets. Even his features seemed muscular. His face had a permanent flush. Crosley lived down the hall by himself in one of the only singles in the school. He was said to be a thief; that supposedly was the reason he'd ended up without a roommate. I didn't know if it was true, and I tried to avoid forming an opinion on the matter, but whenever we passed each other I felt embarrassed and looked away.

Crosley leaned in the door and asked me how things were.

I said okay.

He stepped inside and gazed around the room, tilting his head to read my roommate's pennants and the titles of our books. I was uneasy. I said, "So what can I do for you?" not meaning to sound as cold as I did but not exactly regretting it either.

He caught my tone and smiled. It was the kind of smile you put on when you pass a group of people you suspect are talking about you. It was his usual expression.

He said, "You know García, right?"

"García? Sure. I think so."

"You know him," Crosley said. "He runs around with Hidalgo and those guys. He's the tall one."

"Sure," I said. "I know who García is."

"Well, his stepmother is in New York for a fashion show or something, and she's going to drive up and take him out to dinner tonight. She told him to bring along some friends. You want to come?"

"What about Hidalgo and the rest of them?"

"They're at some kind of polo deal in Maryland. Buying horses. Or ponies, I guess it would be."

The notion of someone my age buying ponies to play a game with was so unexpected that I couldn't quite take it in. "Jesus," I said.

Crosley said, "How about it. You want to come?"

I'd never even spoken to García. He was the nephew of a famous dictator, and all his friends were nephews and cousins of other dictators. They lived as they pleased here. Most of them kept cars a few blocks from the campus, though that was completely against the rules. They were cocky and prankish and charming. They moved everywhere in a body, sunglasses pushed up on their heads and jackets slung over their shoulders, twittering all at once like birds, *chinga* this and *chinga* that. The headmaster was completely buffaloed. After Christmas vacation a bunch of them came down with gonorrhea, and all he did was call them in and advise them that they should not be in too great a hurry to lose their innocence. It became a school joke. All you had to do was say the word "innocence" and everyone would crack up.

"I don't know," I said.

"Come on," Crosley said.

"But I don't even know the guy."

"So what? I don't either."

"Then why did he ask you?"

"I was sitting next to him at lunch."

"Terrific," I said. "That explains you. What about me? How come he asked me?"

"He didn't. He told me to bring someone else."

"What, just anybody? Just whoever happened to present himself to your attention?"

Crosley shrugged.

"Sounds great," I said. "Sounds like a recipe for a really memorable evening."

"You got something better to do?" Crosley asked.

"No," I said.

The limousine picked us up under the awning of the headmaster's house. The driver, an old man, got out slowly and then slowly adjusted his cap before opening the door for us. García slid in beside the woman in back. Crosley and I sat across from them on seats that pulled down. I caught her scent immediately. For some years afterward I bought perfume for women, and I was never able to find that one.

García erupted into Spanish as soon as the driver closed the door behind me. He sounded angry, spitting words at the woman and gesticulating violently. She rocked back a little, then let loose a burst of her own. I stared openly at her. Her skin was very white. She wore a black cape over a black dress cut just low enough to show her pale throat, and the bones at the base of her throat. Her mouth was red. There was a spot of rouge high on each cheek, not rubbed in to look like real color but left there carelessly, or carefully, to make you think again how white her skin was. Her teeth were small and sharp-looking, and she bared them in concert with certain gestures and inflections. As she talked her pointed little tongue flicked in and out.

She wasn't a lot older than we were.

She said something definitive and cut her hand through the air. García began to answer her but she said "No!" and chopped the air again. Then she turned and smiled at Crosley and me. It was a completely false smile. She said, "Where would you fellows like to eat?" Her voice sounded lower in English, even a little harsh. She called us "fallows."

"Anywhere is fine with me," I said.

"Anywhere," she repeated. She narrowed her big black eyes and pushed her lips together. I could see that my answer disappointed her. She looked at Crosley.

"There's supposed to be a good French restaurant in Newbury," Crosley said. "Also an Italian place. It depends on what you want."

"No," she said. "It depends on what you want. I am not so hungry."

If García had a preference, he kept it to himself. He sulked in the corner, his round shoulders slumped and his hands between his knees. He seemed to be trying to make a point of some kind.

"There's also a smorgasbord," Crosley said. "If you like smorgasbords."

"Smorgasbord," she said. Obviously the word was new to her. She repeated it to García. He frowned, then answered her in a sullen monotone.

I couldn't believe Crosley had suggested the smorgasbord. It was an egregiously uncouth suggestion. The smorgasbord was where the local fatties went to binge. Football coaches brought whole teams there to bulk up. The food was good enough, and God knows there was plenty of it, all you could eat, actually, but the atmosphere was brutally matter-of-fact. The food was good, though. Big platters of shrimp on crushed ice. Barons of beef. Smoked turkey. No end of food, really.

"You—do you like smorgasbords?" she asked Crosley.

"Yes," he said.

"And you?" she said to me.

I nodded. Then, not to seem wishy-washy, I said, "You bet."

"Smorgasbord," she said. She laughed and clapped her hands. "Smorgasbord!"

Crosley gave directions to the driver, and we drove slowly away from the school. She said something to García. He nodded at both of us and gave our names, then looked away again, out the window, where the snowy fields were turning dark. His face was long, his eyes sorrowful as a hound's. He had barely talked to us while we were waiting for the limousine. I didn't know why he was mad at his stepmother, or why he wouldn't talk to us, or why he'd even asked us along, but by now I didn't really care.

She studied us and repeated our names skeptically. "No," she said. She pointed at Crosley and said, "El Blanco." She pointed to me and said, "El Negro." Then she pointed to herself and said, "I am Linda."

"Leen-da," Crosley said. He really overdid it, but she showed her sharp little teeth and said, *"Exactamente."*

Then she settled back against the seat and pulled her cape close around her shoulders. It soon fell open again. She was restless. She sat forward and leaned back, crossed and recrossed her legs, swung her feet impatiently. She had on black high heels fastened by a thin strap; I could see almost her entire foot. I heard the silky rub of her stockings against each other, and breathed in a fresh breath of her perfume every time she moved. That perfume had a certain effect on me. It didn't reach me as just a smell. It was personal, it seemed to issue from her very privacy. It made the hair bristle on my arms, and sent faint chills across my shoulders and the backs of my knees. Every time she moved I felt a little tug and followed her motion with some slight motion of my own.

When we arrived at the smorgasbord—Swenson's or Hansen's, some such honest Swede of a name—García refused to get out of the limousine. Linda tried to persuade him, but he shrank back into his corner and would not answer or even look at her. She threw up her hands. "Ah!" she said, and turned away. Crosley and I followed her across the parking lot toward the big red barn. Her dress rustled as she walked. Her heels clicked on the cement.

You could say one thing for the smorgasbord; it wasn't pretentious. This was a real barn, not some quaint fantasy of a barn with butter-churn lamps and little brass ornaments nailed to the walls on strips of leather. The kitchen was at one end. The rest of it had been left open and filled with picnic tables. Blazing light bulbs hung from the rafters. In the middle of the barn stood what my English master would have called "the groaning board"—a great table heaped with food, every kind of food you could think of, and more. I'd been there many times and it always gave me a small, pleasant shock to see how much food there was.

Girls wearing dirndls hustled around the barn, cleaning up messes, changing tablecloths, bringing fresh platters of food from the kitchen.

We stood blinking in the sudden light, then followed one of the waitresses across the floor. Linda walked slowly, gazing around like a tourist. Several men looked up from their food as she passed. I was behind her, and I looked forbiddingly back at them so they would think she was my wife.

We were lucky; we got a table to ourselves. Linda shrugged off her cape and waved us toward the food. "Go on," she said. She sat down and opened her purse. When I looked back she was lighting a cigarette.

"You're pretty quiet tonight," Crosley said as we filled our plates. "You pissed off about something?"

"Maybe I'm just quiet, Crosley, you know?"

He speared a slice of meat and said, "When she called you El Negro, that didn't mean she thought you were a Negro. She just said that because your hair is dark. Mine is light, that's how come she called me El Blanco."

"I know that, Crosley. Jesus. You think I couldn't figure that out? Give me some credit, okay?" Then, as we moved around the table, I said, "You speak Spanish?"

"*Un poco.* Actually more like *un poquito.*"

"What's García mad about?"

"Money. Something about money."

"Like what?"

"That's all I could get. But it's definitely about money."

I'd meant to start off slow, but by the time I reached the end of the table my plate was full. Potato salad, ham, jumbo shrimp, toast, barbecued beef, eggs Benny. Crosley's was full too. We walked back toward Linda, who was leaning forward on her elbows and looking around the barn. She took a long drag off her cigarette, lifted her chin, and blew a stream of smoke up toward the rafters. I sat down across from her. "Scoot down," Crosley said, and bumped in beside me.

She watched us eat for a while.

"So," she said, "El Blanco. Are you from New York?"

Crosley looked up in surprise. "No, ma'am," he said. "I'm from Virginia."

Linda stabbed out her cigarette. Her long fingernails were painted the same deep red as the lipstick smears on her cigarette butt. She said, "I just came from New York and I can tell you that is one crazy place. Just incredible. Listen to this. I am in a taxicab, you know, and we are stopping in this traffic jam for a long time and there is a taxicab next to us with this fellow in it who stares at me. Like this, you know." She made her eyes go round. "Of course I ignore him. So guess what, my door opens and he gets into my cab. 'Excuse me,' he says, 'I want to marry you.' 'That's nice,' I say. 'Ask my husband.' 'I don't care about your husband,' he says. 'I don't care about my wife, either.' Of course I had to laugh. 'Okay,' he says. 'You think that's funny? How about this.' Then he says—" Linda looked sharply at each of us. She sniffed and made a face. "He says things you would never believe. Never. He wants to do this and he wants to do that. Well, I act like I am about to scream. I open my mouth like this. 'Hey,' he says, 'okay, okay. Relax.' Then he gets out and goes back to his taxicab. We are still sitting there for a long time again, and you know what he is doing? He is reading the newspaper. With his hat on. Go ahead, eat," she said to us, and nodded toward the food.

A tall blonde girl was carving fresh slices of roast beef onto a platter. She was hale and bosomy—I could see the laces on her bodice straining. Her cheeks glowed. Her bare arms and shoulders were ruddy with exertion. Crosley raised his eyebrows at me. I raised mine back, though my heart wasn't in it. She was a Viking dream, pure gemütlichkeit, but I was drunk on García's stepmother and in that condition you don't want a glass of milk, you want more of what's making you stumble and fall.

Crosley and I filled our plates again and headed back.

"I'm always hungry," he said.

"I know what you mean," I told him.

Linda smoked another cigarette while we ate. She watched the other tables as if she was at a movie. I tried to eat with a little finesse and so did Crosley, dabbing his lips with a napkin between every bulging mouthful, but some of the people around us had completely slipped their moorings. They ducked their heads low to receive their food, and while they chewed it up they looked around suspiciously and circled their plates with their forearms. A big family to our left was the worst. There was something competitive and desperate about them; they seemed to be eating their way toward a condition where they would never have to eat again. You would have thought they were refugees from a great hunger, that outside these walls the land was afflicted with drought and barrenness. I felt a kind of desperation myself; I felt like I was growing emptier with every bite I took.

There was a din in the air, a steady roar like that of a waterfall.

Linda looked around her with a pleased expression. Though she bore no likeness to anyone here, she seemed completely at home. She sent us back for another plate, then dessert and coffee, and while we were finishing up she asked El Blanco if he had a girlfriend.

"No, ma'am," Crosley said. "We broke up," he added, and his red face turned almost purple. It was clear that he was lying.

"You. How about you?"

I nodded.

"Ha!" she said. "El Negro is the one! So. What's her name?"

"Jane."

"Jaaane," Linda drawled. "Okay, let's hear about Jane."

"Jane," I said again.

Linda smiled.

I told her everything. I told her how my girlfriend and I had met and what she looked like and what our plans were—everything. I told her more than everything, because I gave certain coy but definite suggestions about the extremes to which our passion had already driven us. I meant to impress her with my potency, to enflame her, to wipe that smile off her face, but the more I told her the more wolfishly she smiled and the more her eyes laughed at me.

Laughing eyes—now there's a cliché my English master would have eaten me alive for. "How exactly did these eyes laugh?" he would have asked, looking up from my paper while my classmates snorted around me. "Did they titter, or did they merely chortle? Did they give a great guffaw? Did they, perhaps, *scream* with laughter?"

I am here to tell you that eyes can scream with laughter. Linda's did. As I played Big Hombre for her I could see exactly how complete my failure was. I could hear her saying *Okay, El Negro, go on, talk about your little gorlfren, but we know what you want, don't we? You want to suck on my tongue and slobber on my titties and bury your face in me. That's what you want.*

Crosley interrupted me. "Ma'am . . ." he said, and nodded toward the door. García was leaning there with his arms crossed and an expression of fury on his face. When she looked at him he turned and walked out the door.

Her eyes went flat. She sat there for a moment. She began to take a cigarette from her case, then put it back and stood up. "We go," she said.

García was waiting in the car, rigid and silent. He said nothing on the drive back. Linda swung her foot and stared out the window at the passing houses and bright, moonlit fields. Just before we reached the school, García leaned forward and began speaking to her in a low voice. She listened impassively and didn't answer. He was still talking when the limousine stopped in front of the headmaster's house. The driver opened the door. García fixed his eyes on her. Still impassive, she took her pocketbook out of her purse. She opened it and looked inside. She meditated over the contents, then withdrew a bill and offered it to García. It was a hundred-dollar bill. "Boolshit!" he said, and sat back. With no change of expression she turned and held the bill out to me. I didn't know what else to do but take it. She got another one from her pocketbook and presented it to Crosley, who hesitated even less than I did. Then she gave us the same false smile she had greeted us with, and said, "Good night, it was a pleasure to meet you. Good night, good night," she said to García.

The three of us got out of the limousine. I went a few steps and then slowed down, and turned to look back.

"Keep walking!" Crosley hissed.

García yelled something in Spanish as the driver closed the door. I faced around again and walked with Crosley across the quad. As we approached our dorm he quickened his pace. "I don't believe it," he whispered. "A hundred bucks." When we were inside the door he stopped and shouted, "A hundred bucks! A hundred dollars!"

"Pipe down," someone called.

"All right, all right. Fuck you!" he added.

We went up the stairs to our floor, laughing and banging into each other. "Do you believe it?"

I shook my head. We were standing outside my door.

"No, really now, listen." He put his hands on my shoulders and looked into my eyes. He said, "Do you fucking *believe* it?"

I told him I didn't.

"Well, neither do I. I don't fucking believe it."

There didn't seem to be much to say after that. I would have invited Crosley in, but to tell the truth I still thought of him as a thief. We laughed a few more times and said good night.

My room was cold. I took the bill out of my pocket and looked at it. It was new and stiff, the kind of bill you associate with kidnappings. The picture of Franklin was surprisingly life-like. I looked at it for a while. A hundred dollars was a lot of money then. I had never had a hundred dollars before, not in one chunk like this. To be on the safe side I taped it to a page in *Profiles in Courage*—page 100, so I wouldn't forget where it was.

I had trouble getting to sleep. The food I had eaten sat like a stone in me, and I was miserable about the things I'd said. I understood that I had been a liar and a fool. I kept shifting under the covers, then I sat up and turned on my reading lamp. I picked up the new picture my girlfriend had sent me, and closed my eyes, and when I had some peace of mind I renewed my promises to her.

We broke up a month after I got home. Her parents were away one night, and we seized the opportunity to make love in their canopied bed. This was the fifth time we'd made love. She got up immediately afterward and started putting her clothes on. When I asked her what the problem was, she wouldn't answer me. I thought, Oh Christ, what now. "Come on," I said. "What's wrong?"

She was tying her shoes. She looked up and said, "You don't love me."

It surprised me to hear this, not so much that she said it but because it was true. Before this moment I hadn't known it was true, but it was—I didn't love her.

For a long time afterward I told myself that I'd never really loved her, but this wasn't true.

We're supposed to smile at the passions of the young, and at what we recall of our own passions, as if they were no more than a series of sweet frauds we'd fooled ourselves with and then wised up to. Not only the passion of boys and girls for each other but the others, too—passion for justice, for doing right, for turning the world around. All these come in their time under our wintry smiles. Yet there was nothing foolish about what we felt. Nothing merely young. I just wasn't up to it. I let the light go out.

Sometime later I heard a soft knock at my door. I was still wide awake. "Yeah," I said.

Crosley stepped inside. He was wearing a blue dressing gown of some silky material that shimmered in the dim light of the hallway. He said, "Have you got any Tums or anything?"

"No. I wish I did."

"You too, huh?" He closed the door and sat on my roommate's bunk. "Do you feel as bad as I do?"

"How bad do you feel?"

"Like I'm dying. I think there was something wrong with the shrimp."

"Come on, Crosley. You ate everything but the barn."

"So did you."

"That's right. That's why I'm not complaining."

He moaned and rocked back and forth on the bed. I could hear real pain in his voice. I sat up. "You okay, Crosley?"

"I guess," he said.

"You want me to call the nurse?"

"God," he said. "No, that's all right." He kept rocking. Then, in a carefully offhand way, he said, "Look, is it okay if I just stay here for a while?"

I almost said no, then I caught myself. "Sure," I told him. "Make yourself at home."

He must have heard my hesitation. "Forget it," he said bitterly. "Sorry I asked." But he made no move to go.

I felt confused, tender toward Crosley because he was in pain, repelled because of what I'd heard about him. But maybe what I'd heard about him wasn't true. I wanted to be fair, so I said, "Hey Crosley, do you mind if I ask you a question?"

"That depends."

He was watching me, his arms crossed over his stomach. In the moonlight his dressing gown was iridescent as oil.

"Is it true that you got caught stealing?"

"You prick," he said. He looked down at the floor.

I waited.

"You want to hear about it," he said, "just ask someone. Everybody knows all about it, right?"

"I don't."

"That's right, you don't. You don't know shit about it and neither does anyone else." He raised his head. "The really hilarious part is, I didn't actually get caught stealing it, I got caught putting it back. Not to make excuses. I stole it, all right."

"Stole what?"

"The coat," he said. "Robinson's overcoat. Don't tell me you didn't know that."

"Well, I didn't."

"Then you must've been living in a cave or something. You know Robinson, right? Robinson was my roommate. He had this camel's hair overcoat, this really just beautiful overcoat. I kind of got obsessed with it. I thought about it all the time. Whenever he went somewhere without it, I'd put it on and stand in front of the mirror. Then one day I just took the fucker. I stuck it in my locker over at the gym. Robinson was really upset. He'd go to his closet ten, twenty times a day, like he thought the coat had just gone for a walk or something. So anyway, I brought it back. Robinson came into the room right when I was hanging it up." Crosley bent forward suddenly, then leaned back.

"You're lucky they didn't kick you out."

"I wish they had," he said. "The dean wanted to play Jesus. He got all choked up over the fact that I'd brought it back." Crosley rubbed his arms. "Man, did I want that coat. It was ridiculous how much I wanted that coat. You know?" He looked right at me. "Do you know what I'm talking about?"

I nodded.

"Really?"

"Yes."

"Good." Crosley lay back against the pillow, then lifted his feet onto the bed. "Say," he said, "I think I figured out how come García invited me."

"Yeah?"

"He was mad at his stepmother, right? He wanted to punish her."

"So?"

"So I'm the punishment. He probably heard I was the biggest douchebag in school, and figured whoever came with me would have to be a douchebag, too. That's my theory, anyway."

I started laughing. It killed my stomach but I couldn't stop. Crosley said, "Come on, man, don't make me laugh," and he started too, laughing and moaning at the same time.

We lay without talking, then Crosley said, "El Negro."

"Yeah."

"What are you going to do with your C-note?"

"I don't know. What are you going to do?"

"Buy a woman."

"Buy a woman?"

"I haven't got laid in a really long time. In fact," he said, "I've never gotten laid."

"Me either."

I thought about his words. *Buy a woman.* He could actually do it. I could do it myself. I didn't have to wait, didn't have to burn like this for month after month until Jane decided she was ready to give me relief. Three months was a long time to wait. It was an unreasonable time to wait for anything if you had no good reason to wait, if you could just buy what you needed. And to think that you could buy this—buy a mouth for your mouth, and arms and legs to wrap you tight. I had never considered this before. I thought of the money in my book. I could almost feel it there. Pure possibility.

Jane would never know. It wouldn't hurt her at all, and in a certain way it might help, because it was going to be very awkward at first if neither of us had any experience. As a man, I should know what I was doing. It would be a lot better that way.

I told Crosley that I liked his idea. "The time has come to lose our innocence," I said.

"*Exactamente,*" he said.

And so we sat up and took counsel, leaning toward each other from the beds, holding our swollen bellies, whispering back and forth about how this thing might be done, and where, and when.

TOBIAS WOLFF DISCUSSES

"Smorgasbord," structure, and consequences

PM: Most of "Smorgasbord" plays as though it's unfolding when the narrator was in school, but of course it's really being told in retrospect. How would you describe this story's structure?

TW: Stories are about choice and consequence, and that is certainly reflected in the structure of the story: he is still mulling over the loss of his first great love and is beginning, through the telling of the story, to understand how that might have happened by the confusion of love and desire and the corruption of love through the indulgence of desire, objectified. And so the structure of the story reflects the narrator's process of meditation. But I didn't want him to be overly present in the story. I wanted the reader to feel the story not as under the control of the adult narrator but unfolding naturally. And to be in the world of the boys and not the world of the adult. So there's really only a stab here and there to remind the reader that this is actually being told from a distance of years.

PM: The first time we get an inkling of that is in the limo—

TW: "I bought perfume for women . . . "

PM: It's a deceptively simple line and hugely important.

TW: I wanted to register the presence of an older narrator who has been interested in several different women, and has approached them on certain terms. I mean, there's a certain kind of man who buys perfume for women. And that gives a hint—he's already talked about the love of his life and how they were going to get married and have six kids, and golden retrievers and so on. And already now, we've encountered the fact that this did not happen. He's bought perfume for women over the years. So in that one line there's a subtle undoing of his idealistic youthful notion of the future.

PM: It's the sort of line that I imagine many readers might not be fully conscious of on first read.

TW: That's probably true. I hope that readers will reread my stories, but I can't count on it. I just have to write them as best I can. But I take great pleasure in those sorts of moves in other people's stories, where with a single line one feels the ground move a little beneath you. You're looking at the world from a different angle after that line. This is such a moment for me in the story, and I just have to have some faith that a reader will pick it up or at least *feel* it. Sometimes you understand something without actually thinking it through. It works at the level of intuition. And that is really what I hope the effect of that will be: to give the reader an *intuition* of the future that will play into the present reading of the story.

PM: You give the perfume a nice little bump a couple of pages later when you're describing in greater detail its intoxicating effect on the narrator.

TW: She's crossing and uncrossing her legs and he's affected by this, right.

PM: It's interesting that you choose to elaborate on the perfume there rather than near that first mention of it.

TW: It would have been the wrong place to do it. This is the kind of thing that would come over you gradually, because the smell of the perfume has to build in this enclosed space. He has to be there for a while and he has to be paying attention to her. He's going to be *looking* at her first. Then these other, collateral senses begin to operate.

PM: Waiting also lets you create a reference to that first line about the perfume, with its associations about the future, but without leaving the limo, so you can luxuriate more in the unfolding moment.

TW: I also wanted the reader to feel the intense pitch at which the senses of this boy are operating, especially in relation to women and in the service of his appetites. So, yes, I needed to slow time down to capture that.

PM: Let's talk about the longer flash-forward toward the end of the story where you recount the breakup. Can you describe your decision to place it where you did, instead of in more chronological order at the ending?

TW: William Gass has a line in one of his essays describing a certain kind of ending that *snaps home like a cheap lock.* Had I put that revelation at the end, it would have snapped home like a cheap lock.

As it is, you understand when you reach the end—or I hope you do, at least intuitively—how this loss of love could have occurred—and the kind of moral failure that leads him to say, *God, I could buy this.* And then he's thinking, *Well, it'll be better with Jane and me if I do this, I'll have more experience. I'll know what I'm doing*—those ancient male rationalizations for the reduction of love to the purely physical. By the end of the story, he's already set up the conditions by which he will not be able to love her, really, because he's thinking of making love to a body, not to a person. He's not making any great distinction between the prostitute he plans to hire and the girl he claims to love.

And so it shines a light back, shows how it is that she could sense a lack of love in him and that he could hear the truth in her accusation, and how he could become a man who keeps trying with different women to re-create this experience of youth when his senses were at their highest pitch, even overwhelmed. This story is the beginning of understanding for him. So there is a kind of moral progress implied by the story, but in a sequence more intuitive than logical.

PM: Also, it's much more haunting to end with the mood being one of excitement and optimism, given what we know.

TW: Exactly. I like a story to continue in the reader's mind when the reader has finished it, not be closed down, all possibilities and circumstances accounted for. I like the trust that a writer has in me to understand things and to go on after the last word, to feel the characters' lives continuing off the page.

PM: Using that flash-forward also seems to buy you more leeway when the narrator's talking about the waning of passion, and he enlarges the scope to include all sorts of passions. I don't think the story would have given him the platform to do that at the very end.

TW: I agree. I like it that he speaks that way at this point in the story. I would not like it if he were to speak that way at the end of the story—you haven't really heard that voice before, and all of a sudden it gets tacked on at the end. There are writers who do that, and I always find myself bridling a little. It's a question of taste.

PM: And emphasis. There's some sleight of hand at work by tucking it in.

TW: I want the reader to forget this for a while, until the end, when you see what these boys are up to, what they're planning. Then I hope you feel the shadow of that future falling on those last lines. And then: *Boys, what are you doing?* Right? *Where are you going with this? What is going to be the consequence of this?* Well, we know what the consequence is going to be for the narrator. But we don't want it to be told in plain terms at the end of the story.

PM: *Wanting the reader to forget* is an interesting way to put it, because that's also what you seem to be doing right after that first sentence about the perfume. Immediately you cut to a paragraph where García's making a big fuss—it's like you're deliberately creating a diversion.

TW: That's right. I want the narrator there, but I don't want readers to feel as if he's controlling the action too much.

PM: Is one of your reasons for introducing that early line about the perfume to prepare readers, however subliminally, for the extended use of this perspective later on?

TW: Oh, yes. To have the narrator enter with both feet later on, without any hint of him being someone who's telling the story from a distance of years, would be too great a shock. There has to be some preparation for the entrance of that older narrator's voice. And that slight hint of who he is, that you get there—I didn't want it very obtrusive, but I wanted it there, and it makes it possible by sounding that note there to elaborate at greater length when I think it's more opportune. I wouldn't want the reader to *expect* it, but when it does come, I hope the reader feels: *Oh, this narrator has been with me before. I know who this is.*

PM: Was your guiding principle regarding that line to put it as early as you could without drawing attention to it?

TW: Exactly.

PM: The relationship between the time of a story's events and the time of its narration is such a vital choice, but aspiring writers often don't exploit it.

TW: It is one of the great questions in choosing point of view: From what vantage are you going to tell the story? Can you tell it from more than one point of view in time? Can you have multiple levels of time at work? And obviously, the simultaneity of these two different periods in this narrator's life is part of what makes the story. It *does* make the story. I don't think you really have a story without that older narrator. You have an anecdote, but you don't sense the consequences of these events, and the consequences on his character—which is the reason to tell the story at all.

Writers use time in very interesting ways. Look how Tolstoy begins "The Death of Ivan Ilych." He begins it on the day of Ivan Ilych's wake, so of course Ivan isn't even there. His colleagues are talking about him, then that night they go over to his house, and only *after that night* do we begin the story of Ivan Ilych himself. After he's already died. Well, then we read everything that happens to him in the light of the knowledge of his death. And not only the knowledge of his death but the knowledge of how people reacted to his death, which is not a way that any of us would want people to react to our own deaths, though in fact it's probably pretty much how most of us will fare. And so the operation of these two time frames in the story becomes extremely important to understanding the story.

PM: Was it Hemingway who once said something like: "when writing a story about love, never use the word *love*"? I've been trying to find that quote, and I just can't.

TW: I don't know who said that, but it's pretty good advice.

PM: Let's pretend Hemingway said it. It's the sort of thing he might have said. What do you imagine he was warning against?
TW: Vulgarity. Obviousness. And the destruction of an emotion by the limitations of a name. To put the name "love" on a relationship is to immediately empty it of all its nuance, its peculiarity, and also the reader's ability to feel it. Because the reader has an already accumulated number of emotions that attach themselves to that word and they will obscure whatever it is the story has to show about it in this particular case.
PM: "Smorgasbord" suffers from none of those issues; I just found it gutsy and refreshing that in a story very much about the loss of innocence, the characters are actually bandying about the phrase itself.
TW: Well, I don't think it's so much the *loss* of innocence. So many stories are about loss of innocence. I hope this one is different; this is about the *discarding* of innocence. This is the willful attempt to leave innocence behind and enter a fallen world of experience. And I think most of us do that. Obviously some people *lose* their innocence, people who are molested as children have lost their innocence. They've literally had it taken from them, but most of us really decide to just put it by.
PM: Yes, the fact that he's completely implicated is a key distinction. Besides which, I think there are other ways you avoid those pitfalls Hemingway might have had in mind. For instance, you raise the idea very early, as one of the story's givens, in the gonorrhea scene. And also you're having the kids make fun of the idea.
TW: Exactly. Kids naturally would make fun of that if they heard it. But then the double irony is that is exactly what they're going to do.
PM: By the time they repeat the phrase at the end—and here, too, it seems crucial to the story's tone that they're joking about it still—we already know what the narrator has lost, so the joke becomes eerie and sad.
TW: He's saying what he's going to do, and he's going to do it. And it is eerie and sad.

PM: I wanted to talk about that little story-within-the-story Linda's telling, about the taxi ride, that takes us a step or two out of the main narrative.
TW: No, she's recognizing the effects she has on men there, and provoking them as well. She's talking about a man staring at her and claiming he wants to leave his wife for her. There's a playfulness in her way of telling this story and the recognition of her own power to draw men's attention and desire, and that acts very strongly on the narrator, it isn't just a digression in the story.
PM: Not a digression so much as a parallel: this married man's apparent willingness to throw away his previously solemn vows.
TW: He's just saying that, of course. He wants to get together with her. The importance of the story is her willingness to tell it to these hungry boys who are not that much younger than she is.
PM: But even though the guy in the taxi is just saying that, the narrator will eventually more or less do it.
TW: Right. He'll be that kind of guy.
PM: Crosley's entrance seems significant. It comes just as the narrator has expressed his most romantic, idealistic thoughts about Jane.
TW: He barges in twice on the narrator when he's been thinking about Jane.
PM: And there's a structural parallel between those two times: When Crosley first shows up and says that García's buddies are off in Maryland, the narrator is stunned by the notion of buying ponies for a game in very much the way he will be stunned when Crosley later presents the idea of buying sex.
TW: Yes. And he's getting a new appreciation, if that's the right word, for money. When he gets that hundred dollars, he thinks of it as pure possibility. It can encompass buying horses or buying women. This is a new thought for him.
PM: Where did you first learn to imbue even the simple entrances and exits of characters with additional meaning?
TW: Every time I have a character come in I don't necessarily think it's got to mean something. But certainly we choose the moments in our stories very carefully; we don't have the leisure

of the novelist, as short story writers. A novel can tolerate a certain amount of serendipity and digressiveness, and the short story really can't. Things must be purposeful in a short story, but one must not make them feel purposeful.

These guys are alone; everybody seems to have gone off, at least in their dorm, for the weekend, and the narrator is not going to seek Crosley out, because he's got this cloud hanging over him, this rumor. But Crosley's lonely and looking for some company. And so, yeah, he would seek out the narrator. It has to seem inevitable in their social situation. There's some pattern to the events of the story, but not too obtrusive a pattern. You can't be assigning value *x* or *y* to every movement of every character, or it'll feel like algebra. When you're writing, you have to be open to surprises which you as writer may understand only in the gradual accumulation of details in the story.

PM: Generally speaking, do you find yourself observing your characters' actions and then subsequently inferring meaning from them?

TW: There's a reciprocity that develops as you write a story and then rewrite it and rewrite. You're observing it and leading it at the same time.

When you sit down to write the first draft, you obviously have to have *some* notion of what you're doing, but you also have to be absolutely willing to let that notion go by the boards as things develop in the story that are more interesting than the story you had originally conceived.

And that almost always happens to me. I end up writing a different story than the one I started out to write, and if I don't, it's usually not very good. If I just write the story I set out to write, I've learned nothing in the writing, I've felt no excitement of discovery, and the reader will sense that.

Obviously, by the time you get to the last draft of a story you know exactly why everybody's doing what they're doing. That last draft is lapidary work. It's making sure the form and the sentences are exactly the way you want them. You already have your story, so it's finding the best expression for the story—the process that Evan Connell describes as taking commas out and putting them back in.

It's hard to say *drafts* now. Since I've been writing on a computer, I don't have these stacks of manuscript anymore. I used to type a draft. Then I'd type another draft. Then I'd type another draft. That's gone now. The computer's been a gift, as far as I'm concerned, because I rewrite *so* much; I was doing so much manual labor. I often change my characters' names in the course of writing a story, for example, and that was really a pain in the ass, as you can imagine. I've always used my early drafts to experiment with tenses and point of view, and it was just playing havoc.

PM: How long does it usually take you to complete a story?

TW: That depends on the story. As little as a month, as long as five months, which is ridiculous. How I do that without going crazy is a mystery. Or maybe it's the proof that I *am* crazy.

TOBIAS WOLFF lives in Northern California and teaches at Stanford University. The author of three story collections, two memoirs, and the novels *Old School* (2004) and *The Barracks Thief* (1984), he has received the Rea Award for excellence in the short story, the Los Angeles Times Book Prize, and the PEN/Faulkner Award. "Smorgasbord" was included in the 1987 *Best American Short Stories*.

THEME

RICH
Ellen Gilchrist

Tom and Letty Wilson were rich in everything. They were rich in friends because Tom was a vice-president of the Whitney Bank of New Orleans and liked doing business with his friends, and because Letty was vice-president of the Junior League of New Orleans and had her picture in *Town and Country* every year at the Symphony Ball.

The Wilsons were rich in knowing exactly who they were because every year from Epiphany to Fat Tuesday they flew the beautiful green and gold and purple flag outside their house that meant that Letty had been queen of the Mardi Gras the year she was a debutante. Not that Letty was foolish enough to take the flag seriously.

Sometimes she was even embarrassed to call the yardman and ask him to come over and bring his high ladder.

"Preacher, can you come around on Tuesday and put up my flag?" she would ask.

"You know I can," the giant black man would answer. "I been saving time to put up your flag. I won't forget what a beautiful queen you made that year."

"Oh, hush, Preacher. I was a skinny little scared girl. It's a wonder I didn't fall off the balcony I was so scared. I'll see you on Monday." And Letty would think to herself what a big phony Preacher was and wonder when he was going to try to borrow some more money from them.

Tom Wilson considered himself a natural as a banker because he loved to gamble and wheel and deal. From the time he was a boy in a small Baptist town in Tennessee he had loved to play cards and match nickels and lay bets.

In high school he read *The Nashville Banner* avidly and kept an eye out for useful situations such as the lingering and suspenseful illnesses of Pope Pius.

"Let's get up a pool on the day the Pope will die," he would say to the football team, "I'll hold the bank." And because the Pope took a very long time to die with many close calls there were times when Tom was the richest left tackle in Franklin, Tennessee.

Tom had a favorite saying about money. He had read it in the *Reader's Digest* and attributed it to Andrew Carnegie. "Money," Tom would say, "is what you keep score with. Andrew Carnegie."

Another way Tom made money in high school was performing as an amateur magician at local birthday parties and civic events. He could pull a silver dollar or a Lucky Strike cigarette from an astonished six-year-old's ear or from his own left palm extract a seemingly endless stream of multicolored silk chiffon or cause an ordinary piece of clothesline to behave like an Indian cobra.

He got interested in magic during a convalescence from German measles in the sixth grade. He sent off for books of magic tricks and practiced for hours before his bedroom mirror, his quick clever smile flashing and his long fingers curling and uncurling from the sleeves of a black dinner jacket his mother had bought at a church bazaar and remade to fit him.

Tom's personality was too flamboyant for the conservative Whitney Bank, but he was cheerful and cooperative and when he made a mistake he had the ability to turn it into an anecdote.

"Hey, Fred," he would call to one of his bosses. "Come have lunch on me and I'll tell you a good one."

They would walk down St. Charles Avenue to where it crosses Canal and turns into Royal Street as it enters the French Quarter. They would walk into the crowded, humid excitement of the quarter, admiring the girls and watching the Yankee tourists sweat in their absurd spun-glass leisure suits, and turn into the side door of Antoine's or breeze past the maitre d' at Galatoire's or Brennan's.

When a red-faced waiter in funeral black had seated them at a choice table, Tom would loosen his Brooks Brothers' tie, turn his handsome brown eyes on his guest, and begin.

"That bunch of promoters from Dallas talked me into backing an idea to videotape all the historic sights in the quarter and rent the tapes to hotels to show on closed-circuit television. Goddamnit, Fred, I could just see those fucking tourists sitting around their hotel rooms on rainy days ordering from room service and taking in the Cabildo and the Presbytere on T.V." Tom laughed delightedly and waved his glass of vermouth at an elegantly dressed couple walking by the table.

"Well, they're barely breaking even on that one, and now they want to buy up a lot of soft porn movies and sell them to motels in Jefferson Parish. What do you think? Can we stay with them for a few months?"

Then the waiter would bring them cold oysters on the half shell and steaming pompano *en papillote* and a wine steward would serve them a fine Meursault or a Piesporter, and Tom would listen to whatever advice he was given as though it were the most intelligent thing he had ever heard in his life.

Of course he would be thinking, "You stupid, impotent son of a bitch. You scrawny little frog bastard, I'll buy and sell you before it's over. I've got more brains in my balls than the whole snotty bunch of you."

"Tom, you always throw me off my diet," his friend would say, "damned if you don't."

"I told Letty the other day," Tom replied, "that she could just go right ahead and spend her life worrying about being buried in her wedding dress, but I didn't hustle my way to New Orleans all the way from north Tennessee to eat salads and melba toast. Pass me the French bread."

Letty fell in love with Tom the first time she laid eyes on him. He came to Tulane on a football scholarship and charmed his way into a fraternity of wealthy New Orleans boys famed for its drunkenness and its wild practical jokes. It was the same old story. Even the second-, third-, and fourth-generation blue bloods of New Orleans need an infusion of new genes now and then.

The afternoon after Tom was initiated he arrived at the fraternity house with two Negro painters and sat in the low-hanging branches of a live oak tree overlooking Henry Clay Avenue directing them in painting an official-looking yellow-and-white-striped pattern on the street in front of the property. "D-R-U-N-K," he yelled to his painters, holding on to the enormous limb with one hand and pushing his black hair out of his eyes with the other. "Paint it to say D-R-U-N-K Z-O-N-E."

Letty stood near the tree with a group of friends watching him. He was wearing a blue shirt with the sleeves rolled up above his elbows, and a freshman beanie several sizes too small was perched on his head like a tipsy sparrow.

I'm wearing this goddamn beanie forever," Tom yelled. "I'm wearing this beanie until someone brings me a beer," and Letty took the one she was holding and walked over to the tree and handed it to him.

One day a few weeks later, he commandeered a Bunny Bread truck while it was parked outside the fraternity house making a delivery. He picked up two friends and drove the truck madly around the Irish Channel, throwing fresh loaves of white and whole-wheat and rye bread to the astonished housewives.

"Steal from the rich, give to the poor," Tom yelled, and his companions gave up trying to reason with him and helped him yell.

"Free bread, free cake," they yelled, handing out powdered doughnuts and sweet rolls to a gang of kids playing baseball on a weed-covered vacant lot.

They stopped off at Darby's, an Irish bar where Tom made bets on races and football games, and took on some beer and left off some cinnamon rolls.

"Tom, you better go turn that truck in before they catch you," Darby advised, and Tom's friends agreed, so they drove the truck to the second-precinct police headquarters and turned themselves in. Tom used up half a year's allowance paying the damages, but it made his reputation.

In Tom's last year at Tulane a freshman drowned during a hazing accident at the Southern Yacht Club, and the event frightened Tom. He had never liked the boy and had suspected him of being involved with the queers and nigger lovers who hung around the philosophy department and the school newspaper. The boy had gone to prep school in the East and brought weird-looking girls to rush parties. Tom had resisted the temptation to blackball him as he was well connected in uptown society.

After the accident, Tom spent less time at the fraternity house and more time with Letty, whose plain sweet looks and expensive clothes excited him.

I can't go in the house without thinking about it," he said to Letty. "All we were doing was making them swim from pier to pier carrying martinis. I did it fifteen times the year I pledged."

"He should have told someone he couldn't swim very well," Letty answered. "It was an accident. Everyone knows it was an accident. It wasn't your fault." And Letty cuddled up close to him on the couch, breathing as softly as a cat.

Tom had long serious talks with Letty's mild, alcoholic father, who held a seat on the New York Stock Exchange, and in the spring of the year Tom and Letty were married in the Cathedral of Saint Paul with twelve bridesmaids, four flower girls, and seven hundred guests. It was pronounced a marriage made in heaven, and Letty's mother ordered masses said in Rome for their happiness.

They flew to New York on the way to Bermuda and spent their wedding night at the Sherry Netherland Hotel on Fifth Avenue. At least half a dozen of Letty's friends had lost their virginity at the same address, but the trip didn't seem prosaic to Letty.

She stayed in the bathroom a long time gazing at her plain face in the oval mirror and tugging at the white lace nightgown from the Lylian Shop, arranging it now to cover, now to reveal her small breasts. She crossed herself in the mirror, suddenly giggled, then walked out into the blue and gold bedroom as though she had been going to bed with men every night of her life. She had been up until three the night before reading a book on sexual intercourse. She offered her small unpainted mouth to Tom. Her pale hair smelled of Shalimar and carnations and candles. Now she was safe. Now life would begin.

"Oh, I love you, I love, I love, I love you," she whispered over and over. Tom's hands touching her seemed a strange and exciting passage that would carry her simple dreamy existence to a reality she had never encountered. She had never dreamed anyone so interesting would marry her.

Letty's enthusiasm and her frail body excited him, and he made love to her several times before he asked her to remove her gown.

The next day they breakfasted late and walked for a while along the avenue. In the afternoon Tom explained to his wife what her clitoris was and showed her some of the interesting things it was capable of generating, and before the day was out Letty became the first girl in her crowd to break the laws of God and the Napoleonic Code by indulging in oral intercourse.

Fourteen years went by and the Wilsons' luck held. Fourteen years is a long time to stay lucky even for rich people who don't cause trouble for anyone.

Of course, even among the rich there are endless challenges, unyielding limits, rivalry, envy, quirks of fortune. Letty's father grew increasingly incompetent and sold his seat on the exchange, and Letty's irresponsible brothers went to work throwing away the money in Las Vegas and L.A. and Zurich and Johannesburg and Paris and anywhere they could think of to fly to with their interminable strings of mistresses.

Tom envied them their careless, thoughtless lives and he was annoyed that they controlled their own money while Letty's was tied up in some mysterious trust, but he kept his thoughts to himself as he did his obsessive irritation over his growing obesity.

"Looks like you're putting on a little weight there," a friend would observe.

"Good, good," Tom would say, "makes me look like a man. I got a wife to look at if I want to see someone who's skinny."

He stayed busy gambling and hunting and fishing and being the life of the party at the endless round of dinners and cocktail parties and benefits and Mardi Gras functions that consume the lives of the Roman Catholic hierarchy that dominates the life of the city that care forgot.

Letty was preoccupied with the details of their domestic life and her work in the community. She took her committees seriously and actually believed that the work she did made a difference in the lives of other people.

The Wilsons grew rich in houses. They lived in a large Victorian house in the Garden District, and across Lake Pontchartrain they had another Victorian house to stay in on the weekends, with a private beach surrounded by old moss-hung trees. Tom bought a duck camp in Plaquemines Parish and kept an apartment in the French Quarter in case one of his business friends fell in love with his secretary and needed someplace to be alone with her. Tom almost never used the apartment himself. He was rich in being satisfied to sleep with his own wife.

The Wilsons were rich in common sense. When five years of a good Catholic marriage went by and Letty inexplicably never became pregnant, they threw away their thermometers and ovulation charts and litmus paper and went down to the Catholic adoption agency and adopted a baby girl with curly black hair and hazel eyes. Everyone declared she looked exactly like Tom. The Wilsons named the little girl Helen and, as the months went by, everyone swore she even walked and talked like Tom.

At about the same time Helen came to be the Wilsons' little girl, Tom grew interested in raising Labrador retrievers. He had large wire runs with concrete floors built in the side yard for the dogs to stay in when he wasn't training them on the levee or at the park lagoon. He used all the latest methods for training Labs, including an electric cattle prod given to him by Chalin Perez himself and live ducks supplied by a friend on the Audubon Park Zoo Association Committee.

"Watch this, Helen," he would call to the little girl in the stroller, "watch this." And he would throw a duck into the lagoon with its secondary feathers neatly clipped on the left side and its feet tied loosely together, and one of the Labs would swim out into the water and carry it safely back and lay it at his feet.

As so often happens when childless couples are rich in common sense, before long Letty gave birth to a little boy, and then to twin boys, and finally to another little Wilson girl. The Wilsons became so rich in children the neighbors all lost count.

"Tom," Letty said, curling up close to him in the big walnut bed, "Tom, I want to talk to you about something important." The new baby girl was three months old. "Tom, I want to talk to Father Delahoussaye and ask him if we can use some birth control. I think we have all the children we need for now."

Tom put his arms around her and squeezed her until he wrinkled her new green linen B. H. Wragge, and she screamed for mercy.

"Stop it," she said, "be serious. Do you think it's all right to do that?"

Then Tom agreed with her that they had had all the luck with children they needed for the present, and Letty made up her mind to call the cathedral and make an appointment. All her friends were getting dispensations so they would have time to do their work at the Symphony League and the Thrift Shop and the New Orleans Museum Association and the PTAs of the private schools.

All the Wilson children were in good health except Helen. The pediatricians and psychiatrists weren't certain what was wrong with Helen. Helen couldn't concentrate on anything. She didn't like to share and she went through stages of biting other children at the Academy of the Sacred Heart of Jesus.

The doctors decided it was a combination of prenatal brain damage and dyslexia, a complicated learning disability that is a fashionable problem with children in New Orleans.

Letty felt like she spent half her life sitting in offices talking to people about Helen. The office she sat in most often belonged to Dr. Zander. She sat there twisting her rings and avoiding looking at the box of Kleenex on Dr. Zander's desk. It made her feel like she was sleeping in a dirty bed even to think of plucking a Kleenex from Dr. Zander's container and crying in a place where strangers cried. She imagined his chair was filled all day with women weeping over terrible and sordid things like their husbands running off with their secretaries or their children not getting into the right clubs and colleges.

"I don't know what we're going to do with her next," Letty said. "If we let them hold her back a grade it's just going to make her more self-conscious than ever."

"I wish we knew about her genetic background. You people have pull with the sisters. Can't you find out?"

"Tom doesn't want to find out. He says we'll just be opening a can of worms. He gets embarrassed even talking about Helen's problem."

"Well," said Dr. Zander, crossing his short legs and settling his steel-rimmed glasses on his nose like a tiny bicycle stuck on a hill, "let's start her on Dexedrine."

So Letty and Dr. Zander and Dr. Mullins and Dr. Pickett and Dr. Smith decided to try an experiment. They decided to give Helen five milligrams of Dexedrine every day for twenty days each month, taking her off the drug for ten days in between.

"Children with dyslexia react to drugs strangely," Dr. Zander said. "If you give them tranquilizers it peps them up, but if you give them Ritalin or Dexedrine it calms them down and makes them able to think straight."

"You may have to keep her home and have her tutored on the days she is off the drug," he continued, "but the rest of the time she should be easier to live with." And he reached over and patted Letty on the leg and for a moment she thought it might all turn out all right after all.

Helen stood by herself on the playground of the beautiful old pink-brick convent with its drooping wrought-iron balconies covered with ficus. She was watching the girl she liked talking with some other girls who were playing jacks. All the little girls wore blue-and-red-plaid skirts and navy blazers or sweaters. They looked like a disorderly marching band. Helen was waiting for the girl, whose name was Lisa, to decide if she wanted to go home with her after school and spend the afternoon. Lisa's mother was divorced and worked downtown in a department store, so Lisa rode the streetcar back and forth from school and could go anywhere she liked until 5:30 in the afternoon. Sometimes she went home with Helen so she wouldn't have to ride the streetcar. Then Helen would be so excited the hours until school let out would seem to last forever.

Sometimes Lisa liked her and wanted to go home with her and other times she didn't, but she was always nice to Helen and let her stand next to her in lines.

Helen watched Lisa walking toward her. Lisa's skirt was two inches shorter than those of any of the other girls, and she wore high white socks that made her look like a skater. She wore a silver identification bracelet and Revlon nail polish.

"I'll go home with you if you get your mother to take us to get an Icee," Lisa said. "I was going last night but my mother's boyfriend didn't show up until after the place closed so I was going to walk to Manny's after school. Is that O.K.?"

"I think she will," Helen said, her eyes shining. "I'll go call her up and see."

"Naw, let's just go swing. We can ask her when she comes." Then Helen walked with her friend over to the swings and tried to be patient waiting for her turn.

The Dexedrine helped Helen concentrate and it helped her get along better with other people, but it seemed to have an unusual side effect. Helen was chubby and Dr. Zander had led the Wilsons to believe the drug would help her lose weight, but instead she grew even fatter. The Wilsons were afraid to force her to stop eating for fear they would make her nervous, so they tried to reason with her.

"Why can't I have any ice cream?" she would say. "Daddy is fat and he eats all the ice cream he wants." She was leaning up against Letty, stroking her arm and petting the baby with her other hand. They were in an upstairs sitting room with the afternoon sun streaming in through the French windows. Everything in the room was decorated with different shades of blue, and the curtains were white with old-fashioned blue-and-white-checked ruffles.

"You can have ice cream this evening after dinner," Letty said, "I just want you to wait a few hours before you have it. Won't you do that for me?"

"Can I hold the baby for a while?" Helen asked, and Letty allowed her to sit in the rocker and hold the baby and rock it furiously back and forth crooning to it.

"Is Jennifer beautiful, Mother?" Helen asked.

"She's O.K., but she doesn't have curly black hair like you. She just has plain brown hair. Don't you see, Helen, that's why we want you to stop eating between meals, because you're so pretty and we don't want you to get too fat. Why don't you go outside and play with Tim and not try to think about ice cream so much?"

"I don't care," Helen said, "I'm only nine years old and I'm hungry. I want you to tell the maids to give me some ice cream now," and she handed the baby to her mother and ran out of the room.

The Wilsons were rich in maids, and that was a good thing because there were all those children to be taken care of and cooked for and cleaned up after. The maids didn't mind taking care of the Wilson children all day. The Wilsons' house was much more comfortable than the ones they lived in, and no one cared whether they worked very hard or not as long as they showed up on time so Letty could get to her meetings. The maids left their own children with relatives or at home watching television, and when they went home at night they liked them much better than if they had spent the whole day with them.

The Wilson house had a wide white porch across the front and down both sides. It was shaded by enormous oak trees and furnished with swings and wicker rockers. In the afternoons the maids would sit on the porch and other maids from around the neighborhood would come up pushing prams and strollers and the children would all play together on the porch and in the yard. Sometimes the maids fixed lemonade and the children would sell it to passersby from a little stand.

The maids hated Helen. They didn't care whether she had

dyslexia or not. All they knew was that she was a lot of trouble to take care of. One minute she would be as sweet as pie and cuddle up to them and say she loved them and the next minute she wouldn't do anything they told her.

"You're a nigger, nigger, nigger, and my mother said I could cross St. Charles Avenue if I wanted to," Helen would say, and the maids would hold their lips together and look into each other's eyes.

One afternoon the Wilson children and their maids were sitting on the porch after school with some of the neighbors' children and maids. The baby was on the porch in a bassinet on wheels and a new maid was looking out for her. Helen was in the biggest swing and was swinging as high as she could go so that none of the other children could get in the swing with her.

"Helen," the new maid said, "it's Tim's turn in the swing. You been swinging for fifteen minutes while Tim's been waiting. You be a good girl now and let Tim have a turn. You too big to act like that."

"You're just a high yeller nigger," Helen called, "and you can't make me do anything." And she swung up higher and higher.

This maid had never had Helen call her names before and she had a quick temper and didn't put up with children calling her a nigger. She walked over to the swing and grabbed the chain and stopped it from moving.

"You say you're sorry for that, little fat honky white girl," she said, and made as if to grab Helen by the arms, but Helen got away and started running, calling over her shoulder, "Nigger, can't make me do anything."

She was running and looking over her shoulder and she hit the bassinet and it went rolling down the brick stairs so fast none of the maids or children could stop it. It rolled down the stairs and threw the baby onto the sidewalk and the blood from the baby's head began to move all over the concrete like a little ruby lake.

The Wilsons' house was on Philip Street, a street so rich it even had its own drugstore. Not some tacky chain drugstore with everything on special all the time, but a cute drugstore made out of a frame bungalow with gingerbread trim. Everything inside cost twice as much as it did in a regular drugstore, and the grown people could order any kind of drugs they needed and a green Mazda pickup would bring them right over. The children had to get their drugs from a fourteen-year-old pusher in Audubon Park named Leroi, but they could get all the ice cream and candy and chewing gum they wanted from the drugstore and charge it to their parents.

No white adults were at home in the houses where the maids worked so they sent the children running to the drugstore to bring the druggist to help with the baby. They called the hospital and ordered an ambulance and they called several doctors and they called Tom's bank. All the children who were old enough ran to the drugstore except Helen. Helen sat on the porch steps staring down at the baby with the maids hovering over it like swans, and she was crying and screaming and beating her hands against her head. She was in one of the periods when she couldn't have Dexedrine. She screamed and screamed, but none of the maids had time to help her. They were too busy with the baby.

"Shut up, Helen," one of the maids called. "Shut up that goddamn screaming. This baby is about to die."

A police car and the local patrol service drove up. An ambulance arrived and the yard filled with people. The druggist and one of the maids rode off in the ambulance with the baby. The crowd in the yard swarmed and milled and swam before Helen's eyes like a parade.

Finally they stopped looking like people and just looked like spots of color on the yard. Helen ran up the stairs and climbed under her cherry four-poster bed and pulled her pillows and her eiderdown comforter under it with her. There were cereal boxes and an empty ice cream carton and half a tin of English cookies under the headboard. Helen was soaked with sweat and her little Lily playsuit was tight under the arms and cut into her flesh. Helen rolled up in the comforter and began to dream the dream of the heavy clouds. She dreamed she was praying, but the beads of the rosary slipped through her fingers so quickly she couldn't catch them and it was cold in the church and beautiful and fragrant, then dark, then light, and Helen was rolling in the heavy clouds that rolled her like biscuit dough. Just as she was about to suffocate they rolled her face up to the blue air above the clouds. Then Helen was a pink kite floating above the houses at evening. In the yards children were playing and fathers were driving up and baseball games were beginning and the sky turned gray and closed upon the city like a lid.

And now the baby is alone with Helen in her room and the door is locked and Helen ties the baby to the table so it won't fall off.

"Hold still, Baby, this will just be a little shot. This won't hurt much. This won't take a minute." And the baby is still and Helen begins to work on it.

Letty knelt down beside the bed. "Helen, please come out from under there. No one is mad at you. Please come out and help me, Helen. I need you to help me."

Helen held on tighter to the slats of the bed and squeezed her eyes shut and refused to look at Letty.

Letty climbed under the bed to touch the child. Letty was crying and her heart had an anchor in it that kept digging in and sinking deeper and deeper.

Dr. Zander came into the bedroom and knelt beside the bed and began to talk to Helen. Finally he gave up being reasonable and wiggled his small gray-suited body under the bed and Helen was lost in the area of arms that tried to hold her.

Tom was sitting in the bank president's office trying not to let Mr. Saunders know how much he despised him or how much it hurt and mattered to him to be listening to a lecture. Tom thought he was too old to have to listen to lectures. He was tired and he wanted a drink and he wanted to punch the bastard in the face.

"I know, I know," he answered, "I can take care of it. Just give me a month or two. You're right. I'll take care of it."

And he smoothed the pants of his cord suit and waited for the rest of the lecture.

A man came into the room without knocking. Tom's secretary was behind him.

"Tom, I think your baby has had an accident. I don't know any details. Look, I've called for a car. Let me go with you."

Tom ran up the steps of the house and into the hallway full of neighbors and relatives. A girl in a tennis dress touched him on the arm, someone handed him a drink. He ran up the winding stairs to Helen's room. He stood in the doorway. He could see Letty's shoes sticking out from under the bed. He could hear Dr. Zander talking. He couldn't go near them.

"Letty," he called, "Letty, come here, my god, come out from there."

No one came to the funeral but the family. Letty wore a plain dress she would wear any day and the children all wore their school clothes.

The funeral was terrible for the Wilsons, but afterward they went home and all the people from the Garden District and from all over town started coming over to cheer them up. It looked like the biggest cocktail party ever held in New Orleans. It took four rented butlers just to serve the drinks. Everyone wanted to get in on the Wilsons' tragedy.

In the months that followed the funeral Tom began to have sinus headaches for the first time in years. He was drinking a lot and smoking again. He was allergic to whiskey, and when he woke up in the morning his nose and head were so full of phlegm he had to vomit before he could think straight.

He began to have trouble with his vision.

One November day the high yellow windows of the Shell Oil Building all turned their eyes upon him as he stopped at the corner of Poydras and Carondelet to wait for a street-light, and he had to pull the car over to a curb and talk to himself for several minutes before he could drive on.

He got back all the keys to his apartment so he could go there and be alone and think. One afternoon he left work at two o'clock and drove around Jefferson Parish all afternoon drinking Scotch and eating potato chips.

Not as many people at the bank wanted to go out to lunch with him anymore. They were sick and tired of pretending his expensive mistakes were jokes.

One night Tom was gambling at the Pickwick Club with a poker group and a man jokingly accused him of cheating. Tom jumped up from the table, grabbed the man and began hitting him with his fists. He hit the man in the mouth and knocked out his new gold inlays.

"You dirty little goddamn bond peddler, you son of a bitch! I'll kill you for that," Tom yelled, and it took four waiters to hold him while the terrified man made his escape. The next morning Tom resigned from the club.

He started riding the streetcar downtown to work so he wouldn't have to worry about driving his car home if he got drunk. He was worrying about money and he was worrying about his gambling debts, but most of the time he was thinking about Helen. She looked so much like him that he believed people would think she was his illegitimate child. The more he tried to talk himself into believing the baby's death was an accident, the more obstinate his mind became.

The Wilson children were forbidden to take the Labs out of the kennels without permission. One afternoon Tom came home earlier than usual and found Helen sitting in the open door of one of the kennels playing with a half-grown litter of puppies. She was holding one of the puppies and the others were climbing all around her and spilling out onto the grass. She held the puppy by its forelegs, making it dance in the air, then letting it drop. Then she would gather it in her arms and hold it tight and sing to it.

Tom walked over to the kennel and grabbed her by an arm and began to paddle her as hard as he could.

"Goddamn you, what are you trying to do? You know you

aren't supposed to touch those dogs. What in the hell do you think you're doing?"

Helen was too terrified to scream. The Wilsons never spanked their children for anything.

"I didn't do anything to it. I was playing with it," she sobbed.

Letty and the twins came running out of the house and when Tom saw Letty he stopped hitting Helen and walked in through the kitchen door and up the stairs to the bedroom. Letty gave the children to the cook and followed him.

Tom stood by the bedroom window trying to think of something to say to Letty. He kept his back turned to her and he was making a nickel disappear with his left hand. He thought of himself at Tommie Keenen's birthday party wearing his black coat and hat and doing his famous rope trick. Mr. Keenen had given him fifteen dollars. He remembered sticking the money in his billfold.

"My god, Letty, I'm sorry. I don't know what the shit's going on. I thought she was hurting the dog. I know I shouldn't have hit her and there's something I need to tell you about the bank. Kennington is getting sacked. I may be part of the housecleaning."

"Why didn't you tell me before? Can't Daddy do anything?"

"I don't want him to do anything. Even if it happens it doesn't have anything to do with me. It's just bank politics. We'll say I quit. I want to get out of there anyway. That fucking place is driving me crazy."

Tom put the nickel in his pocket and closed the bedroom door. He could hear the maid down the hall comforting Helen. He didn't give a fuck if she cried all night. He walked over to Letty and put his arms around her. He smelled like he'd been drinking for a week. He reached under her dress and pulled down her pantyhose and her underpants and began kissing her face and hair while she stood awkwardly with the pants and hose around her feet like a halter. She was trying to cooperate.

She forgot that Tom smelled like sweat and whiskey. She was thinking about the night they were married. Every time they made love Letty pretended it was that night. She had spent thousands of nights in a bridal suite at the Sherry Netherland Hotel in New York City.

Letty lay on the walnut bed leaning into a pile of satin pillows and twisting a gold bracelet around her wrist. She could hear the children playing outside. She had a headache and her stomach was queasy, but she was afraid to take a Valium or an aspirin. She was waiting for the doctor to call her back and tell her if she was pregnant. She already knew what he was going to say.

Tom came into the room and sat by her on the bed.

"What's wrong?"

"Nothing's wrong. Please don't do that. I'm tired."

"Something's wrong."

"Nothing's wrong. Tom, please leave me alone."

Tom walked out through the French windows and onto a little balcony that overlooked the play yard and the dog runs. Sunshine flooded Philip Street, covering the houses and trees and dogs and children with a million volts a minute. It flowed down to hide in the roots of trees, glistening on the cars, baking the street, and lighting Helen's rumpled hair where she stooped over the puppy. She was singing a little song. She had made up the song she was singing.

"The baby's dead. The baby's dead. The baby's gone to heaven."

"Jesus God," Tom muttered. All up and down Philip Street fathers were returning home from work. A jeep filled with teenagers came tearing past and threw a beer can against the curb.

Six or seven pieces of Tom's mind sailed out across the street and stationed themselves along the power line that zigzagged back and forth along Philip Street between the live oak trees.

The pieces of his mind sat upon the power line like a row of black starlings. They looked him over.

Helen took the dog out of the buggy and dragged it over to the kennel.

"Jesus Christ," Tom said, and the pieces of his mind flew back to him as swiftly as they had flown away and entered his eyes and ears and nostrils and arranged themselves in their proper places like parts of a phrenological head.

Tom looked at his watch. It said 6:15. He stepped back into the bedroom and closed the French windows. A vase of huge roses from the garden hid Letty's reflection in the mirror.

"I'm going to the camp for the night. I need to get away. Besides, the season's almost over."

"All right," Letty answered. "Who are you going with?"

"I think I'll take Helen with me. I haven't paid any attention to her for weeks."

"That's good," Letty said, "I really think I'm getting a cold. I'll have a tray up for supper and try to get some sleep."

Tom moved around the room, opening drawers and closets and throwing some gear into a canvas duffel bag. He changed into his hunting clothes.

He removed the guns he needed from a shelf in the upstairs den and cleaned them neatly and thoroughly and zipped them into their carriers.

"Helen," he called from the downstairs porch. "Bring the dog in the house and come get on some play clothes. I'm going to take you to the duck camp with me. You can take the dog."

"Can we stop and get beignets?" Helen called back, coming running at the invitation.

"Sure we can, honey. Whatever you like. Go get packed. We'll leave as soon as dinner is over."

It was past 9:00 at night. They crossed the Mississippi River from the New Orleans side on the last ferry going to Algier's Point. There was an offshore breeze and a light rain fell on the old brown river. The Mississippi River smelled like the inside of a nigger cabin, powerful and fecund. The smell came in Tom's mouth until he felt he could chew it.

He leaned over the railing and vomited. He felt better and walked back to the red Chevrolet pickup he had given himself for a birthday present. He thought it was chic for a banker to own a pickup.

Helen was playing with the dog, pushing him off the seat

and laughing when he climbed back on her lap. She had a paper bag of doughnuts from the French Market and was eating them and licking the powdered sugar from her fingers and knocking the dog off the seat.

She wasn't the least bit sleepy.

"I'm glad Tim didn't get to go. Tim was bad at school, that's why he had to stay home, isn't it? The sisters called Momma. I don't like Tim. I'm glad I got to go by myself." She stuck her fat arms out the window and rubbed Tom's canvas hunting jacket. "This coat feels hard. It's all dirty. Can we go up in the cabin and talk to the pilot?"

"Sit still, Helen."

"Put the dog in the back, he's bothering me." She bounced up and down on the seat. "We're going to the duck camp. We're going to the duck camp."

The ferry docked. Tom drove the pickup onto the blacktop road past the city dump and on into Plaquemines Parish.

They drove into the brackish marshes that fringe the Gulf of Mexico where it extends in ragged fingers along the coast below and to the east of New Orleans. As they drove closer to the sea the hardwoods turned to palmetto and water oak and willow.

The marshes were silent. Tom could smell the glasswort and black mangrove, the oyster and shrimp boats.

He wondered if it were true that children and dogs could penetrate a man's concealment, could know him utterly.

Helen leaned against his coat and prattled on.

In the Wilson house on Philip Street Tim and the twins were cuddled up by Letty, hearing one last story before they went to bed.

A blue wicker tray held the remains of the children's hot chocolate. The china cups were a confirmation present sent to Letty from Limoges, France.

Now she was finishing reading a wonderful story by Ludwig Bemelmans about a little convent girl in Paris named Madeline who reforms the son of the Spanish ambassador, putting an end to his terrible habit of beheading chickens on a miniature guillotine.

Letty was feeling better. She had decided God was just trying to make up to her for Jennifer.

The camp was a three-room wooden shack built on pilings out over Bayou Lafouche, which runs through the middle of the parish.

The inside of the camp was casually furnished with old leather office furniture, hand-me-down tables and lamps, and a walnut poker table from Neiman-Marcus. Photographs of hunts and parties were tacked around the walls. Over the poker table were pictures of racehorses and their owners and an assortment of ribbons won in races.

Tom laid the guns down on the bar and opened a cabinet over the sink in the part of the room that served as a kitchen. The nigger hadn't come to clean up after the last party and the sink was piled with half-washed dishes. He found a clean glass and a bottle of Tanqueray gin and sat down behind the bar.

Helen was across the room on the floor finishing the beignets and trying to coax the dog to come closer. He was considering it. No one had remembered to feed him.

Tom pulled a new deck of cards out of a drawer, broke the seal, and began to shuffle them.

Helen came and stood by the bar. "Show me a trick, Daddy. Make the queen disappear. Show me how to do it."

"Do you promise not to tell anyone the secret? A magician never tells his secrets."

"I won't tell. Daddy, please show me, show me now."

Tom spread out the cards. He began to explain the trick.

"All right, you go here and here, then here. Then pick up these in just the right order, but look at the people while you do it, not at the cards."

"I'm going to do it for Lisa."

"She's going to beg you to tell the secret. What will you do then?"

"I'll tell her a magician never tells his secrets."

Tom drank the gin and poured some more.

"Now let me do it to you, Daddy."

"Not yet, Helen. Go sit over there with the dog and practice it where I can't see what you're doing. I'll pretend I'm Lisa and don't know what's going on."

Tom picked up the Kliengunther 7 mm. magnum rifle and shot the dog first, splattering its brains all over the door and walls. Without pausing, without giving her time to raise her eyes from the red and gray and black rainbow of the dog, he shot the little girl.

The bullet entered her head from the back. Her thick body rolled across the hardwood floor and lodged against a hat rack from Jody Mellon's old office in the Hibernia Bank Building. One of her arms landed on a pile of old *Penthouse* magazines and her disordered brain flung its roses north and east and south and west and rejoined the order from which it casually arose.

Tom put down the rifle, took a drink of the thick gin, and, carrying the pistol, walked out onto the pier through the kitchen door. Without removing his glasses or his hunting cap he stuck the .38 Smith and Wesson revolver against his palate and splattered his own head all over the new pier and the canvas covering of the Boston Whaler. His body struck the boat going down and landed in eight feet of water beside a broken crab trap left over from the summer.

A pair of deputies from the Plaquemines Parish sheriff's office found the bodies.

Everyone believed it was some terrible inexplicable mistake or accident.

No one believed that much bad luck could happen to a nice lady like Letty Dufrechou Wilson, who never hurt a flea or gave anyone a minute's trouble in her life.

No one believed that much bad luck could get together between the fifteenth week after Pentecost and the third week in Advent.

No one believed a man would kill his own little illegitimate dyslexic daughter just because she was crazy.

And no one, not even the district attorney of New Orleans, wanted to believe a man would shoot a $3,000 Labrador retriever sired by Super Chief out of Prestidigitation.

ELLEN GILCHRIST DISCUSSES
"Rich," theme, imagery, and learning from Huckleberry Finn

EG: This was the first real, finished, serious short story that I ever wrote. It was 1976 probably, or '77. I had a dinner party one night and Jim Whitehead and Bill Harrison, the directors of the [University of Arkansas] writing program at the time, were there. I had been in the writing program for about six months. I was working as a poet. At the dinner party they were asking me about New Orleans, and I remember thinking: How could anyone explain that complicated, multi-layered old city to anyone who hadn't lived there?

I'd not only lived there, I'd been visiting my relatives there—my uncle was the editor of the *Times-Picayune*—since I could remember. It's just part of my life. But how could I explain it to him? Especially uptown New Orleans, the part where I lived. Because during the years when I lived there, when I was married, I lived in a world where everyone was very rich. There was just so much money and so many beautiful European things. So many beautiful fabrics and clothes and things like that. I was *shocked* by the excess, in a way. I mean I *liked* it. I wanted some of all that stuff, too.

The excesses of a wealthy urban culture are all tied up in the story. And people were *mean* to each other in a way that I'd never seen. At cocktail parties, after they'd had a few drinks, people would say things to one another that nobody I knew in Mississippi would ever have been graceless enough to say. And it read to me like *meanness*.

PM: One of the themes "Rich" seems to grapple with is how unnerving the desire to be socially accepted can be. That seems universally true.

EG: I would have found this if I'd been on the Upper East Side of New York City, probably. In any big city I would have found the same thing, it's just that I happened to encounter it in New Orleans. Read that fabulous new translation of *Anna Karenina*—good *God*, it's the same thing I was writing about.
PM: This need to be accepted can turn very self-destructive.
EG: There had been a number of really terrible suicides within the circle of people in which we moved. They weren't our close friends, but they were people we knew and had been to parties with. There were three or four, and I think they were all men who had done things like jump off the Mississippi River Bridge. This unbelievably handsome man, married to a woman who was so beautiful—they were like the beautiful couple—shot himself. And one man had shot his dog before he shot himself. A wealthy man who was married to probably the smartest woman I ever got to talk to in New Orleans. Someone I admired greatly for her brilliance.

And so all of these suicides—I mean how could people who have everything in the world, all the money that they need—I couldn't understand how these people could kill themselves, because at the time I didn't know enough to know about clinical depression. And how clinical depression is exacerbated by drinking—I had kind of figured that out, which is why I let that lead up to it. Different sorts of clinical depression and suicide are caused by drugs and alcohol. That's what happened to Tom.
PM: Maybe those are important clinical reasons, but the most interesting poetic reason the story seems to suggest is that he just gives up believing he can maintain the illusion of belonging to this social world.
EG: Absolutely. Absolutely. It's falling apart for him. He came down there with all his natural skills and beauty and promise and got eaten alive by the culture. If he'd stayed in a small town in Tennessee he'd be all right. I'm sorry to say that, but I probably believe that.
PM: It feels thematically significant that the neighbors see a

physical resemblance between Tom and Helen, because Helen is also an outsider.
EG: Like Tom. The outsider; she's that.
PM: You've got that pitiful moment on page 306 when Helen's eyes are "shining," at the prospect of Lisa wanting to come home after school with her. It's heartbreaking. Helen is not the most likable child in the world, but in that moment it's—
EG: You don't have to be chubby and dyslexic to have that happen to you.
PM: Sure. Anybody can identify with that longing.
EG: And here's Lisa, who has, compared to Helen, nothing in the world. And yet she's got some sort of charismatic power that makes other people let her decide, you know—she's got the stuff.
PM: And Helen wants to be near that.
EG: Helen wants a friend.
PM: On page 303, you have this simple transition: "At about the same time Helen came to be the Wilsons' little girl, Tom grew interested in raising Labrador retrievers." Which I always found wonderfully ironic, since the Wilsons are mystified about Helen's pedigree. Tom seems to be compensating.
EG: I wasn't thinking that when I was writing it. I was just making up a story.
PM: Let's talk about the side story about the drowned fraternity pledge.
EG: That's a true story. All the little side stories like that are true stories. And I had thousands to choose from. I chose the ones that really shocked me.
PM: He's an outsider, as well, trying too hard to belong.
EG: Well, if I was thinking in those terms, and I probably wasn't, I was thinking: What would drive Tom to Letty? Just because she was wealthy, that wouldn't be enough. Because he'd have his pick. It was because she liked him and because she was quiet and because it seemed peaceful. And the good part of Tom, the good things about him are why he turned his back on that world.

PM: That scene where Letty's saying, Let go of it, it wasn't your fault, reflects better on him than it does on her. He's more troubled by the drowning. He suffers more moral confusion over it.
EG: He's smarter than she is. He's just plain old smarter than she is. She's been very, very sheltered and she's simple.
PM: The scene also establishes Tom as—if this story has a main character, it's Tom.
EG: A lot of my work is character-driven, in the deepest, truest sense. But this is really about a time and a place.
PM: The thing that's always struck me about "Rich" is the way it operates as both a short story and a satire. As a satire, society is its main subject, but at the same time you've gone to a lot of trouble to characterize Tom—with his tragic, human flaws—as a protagonist.
EG: Well, I always get involved with my characters. As soon as I name them I believe them. I believe them, just like they're real people. So I can't help making things character-driven because I believe the products of my own imagination.
PM: Religion seems to be one of the social conventions the story seems to be satirizing. For these characters at any rate, religion seems to have less to do with spirituality than it does with social appearance.
EG: I didn't mean that. I've never really been religious. I respect religions much more than I ever did when I was young. The older I get the more I respect the good things about religions and what they bring.
PM: Helen is the only one in the story who more or less prays—when she's hiding under the bed and dreaming the dream of the heavy clouds.
EG: Those are my own childhood memories, when something would go wrong. My dogs were always getting run over. During the Second World War we had to live all over Indiana and Illinois while my father built the airports and my grandfather would send me little fox terriers, because he raised hunting dogs on his plantation. I'd come home from school and my mother'd be standing there: "Another fox terrier got run over."

And I'd crawl under the bed and hold onto the bedsprings for hours. I don't know whether I was just being a drama queen or what. I used to pray when my dogs would die, or when I'd lose something. When I wanted something, I'd pray like crazy, but the rest of the time, I didn't care a thing about God.

PM: I wanted to talk about some of the images in the story—a couple in particular. The baby's blood spreading out like a ruby lake—

EG: I remember writing that. Bill Harrison had told me that every story should have at least one really memorable simile. And I thought, shoot, I've been a poet for years, I can do that.

PM: That metaphor of Helen's brain flinging its roses forth—

EG: Well, I think that's a little over the top. I'd edit that out now.

PM: Both of those images seem especially fresh because you're describing something horrible by comparing it to something that would conventionally be considered beautiful.

EG: I know it. Because I'm not a horror writer.

PM: Is that a conscious choice, to search for imagery in the opposite direction?

EG: It's not a conscious choice. That's not how poets work. Not really how writers work, I don't think. Or didn't for me. I just think something up and write it down. That's really the truth. I don't go looking for something except for titles.

PM: Don't you discard things? Keep thinking until you get to something you like?

EG: Nope. I don't do that either. I throw away big sections of things, and I take extraneous words out. But I don't go think, Oh, well, that's not good, I could—I don't go get one thing and then replace it with another thing. Either the whole thing works or it doesn't. See, I got *into* this story when I was writing it. Like I do with anything I'm writing, the only way I could find out what happened next was to keep on writing it.

Bill Harrison challenged me, because he was helping me and I was talking to him when I was writing, and I don't know how much of it he read or didn't read, but he said, "In the first place, it's got to have a really dramatic ending, and you've set it up that somebody's got to die." So I wrote the last three or four paragraphs, because I was fascinated with that idea.

Oh, *that's* how the labs got in the story, because I was thinking about that man who shot his dog and then shot himself. And I was thinking about how everybody always talked about how much those dogs cost. How much they were sold for and all that, which I thought was just ridiculous. I'd pay four thousand dollars *not* to have a lab locked up in my backyard. It bothered me that in New Orleans all these yards were full of all these penned-up dogs, these great big beautiful working dogs all penned up in yards, and maybe once a week they'd take them out and let them pretend to work. I mean who am I to have all these judgments about what other people are doing, but the Labrador retriever thing in New Orleans just blew me away.

So I wrote the ending, and I wrote the rest of the story to justify the ending that I'd written. Does that make sense? I used to do that a lot.

PM: Do you remember what Bill Harrison was referring to when he said you've set it up that somebody has to die? Maybe he was talking about the fraternity drowning, because that does seem to—

EG: Foreshadow it?

PM: Yes.

EG: I may just think he said something like that. Anyway, he said, you know, I want to see you write a really dynamite ending for this story. He was just trying to show how to write a short story. Trying to show me the process. Or *a* process by which you could write one.

PM: How have readers reacted to this story?

EG: They've liked it, except young women with small children were horrified by it. People who are readers of my stories and love my work were horrified by the fact that I'd let someone kill someone. Because that's really not like me. It was just an exercise to show Bill that I could write something horrible if I wanted to. I don't like having written somebody shooting somebody, especially a child and a dog. It's really not the way I look at the world. That's why I left it out of my *Collected Stories*. I had to leave out something, so I just decided to take out all the stories that had a murder or a suicide. Because I have thirteen grandchildren. I kept thinking, "Oh, I'm their grandmother, I don't want them to read that stuff."

But the good writing in it—you know, that's good writing in it.

Rereading it, the stuff I like are the things that I think are funny. Well, not funny, I guess *irony* would be a better word. "He was rich in being satisfied to sleep with his own wife." "She took her committees seriously and actually believed that the work she did made a difference in the lives of other people." *(Laughs.)* "Letty became the first girl in her crowd to break the laws of God and the Napoleonic code by indulging in oral intercourse."

PM: Would you please read a couple of paragraphs out loud on pages 316 to 317, starting with Tom in the silent marsh while meanwhile Letty's reading a bedtime story about the chicken guillotine from a *Madeline* book?

EG: *(Reading)* ". . . She had decided God was just trying to make up to her for Jennifer."

Isn't the human spirit wonderful? To live in a world where people behead chickens all day long? And don't invite each other to cocktail parties? And then on the other hand, well, easy come, easy go with the babies!

PM: Those two scenes seem wonderfully juxtaposed against each other: Letty surrounded by her confirmation teacups, reading that gruesome story, while Tom is river-boating into the heart of darkness. And the story's moving into this very primal, brutal place, where Tom finally allows himself to wonder that unbearable epiphany: that he can be known utterly.

EG: It's scary country down there. All my cousins, people who hunt down there, like those swamps. There are alligators in those swamps, and people go out in those little flat-bottom boats? What would they want to do that for? To kill some ducks? It takes all day to make duck taste good.

This is the end of the story: I love this. And I remember writing it: *(Reading)* "A pair of deputies from the Plaquemines Parish sheriff's office found the bodies. . . . And no one, not even the district attorney of New Orleans, wanted to believe a man would shoot a three-thousand-dollar Labrador retriever sired by Super Chief out of Prestidigitation." Those are real dogs' names; my cousin had those dogs.

PM: Great name, Prestidigitation—

EG: It means sleight of hand.

PM: Very suitable for Tom, the lifelong illusionist. What I find most striking about the end is the brutal order of it: how it implies people might comprehend the child being killed before they could understand the dog.

EG: Right. Why shoot the dog? I remember when that horrible suicide happened, people would say when they'd hear about it, "He shot the *dog*?"

PM: What does that say about people?

EG: *(Laughs.)* Right.

PM: By the way, when the story says, no one believed that a man would kill his own illegitimate dyslexic daughter, I've always read that as just the—

EG: Everyone had decided that she was really his, but it's not the case. That's the kind of rumors that get started and people believe them because they want to.

PM: I wanted to ask you about the special challenges of writing about race and racism.

EG: It's a challenge for every Southern writer. But I try just to write what I saw the way I saw it, as Faulkner did. The main thing, as Faulkner knew, is that the narrator, voice of the author, must be a voice of respect and reason. But when you're writing dialogue, dialogue has to sound like what it sounded like—

PM: Or a character's thoughts—

EG: Or else we can just give up writing. Writing literature is not public discourse. I don't think it's the same thing as being on a talk show.

PM: I recall hearing somewhere that you consider yourself more a short story writer by temperament than a novelist. Is that true?

EG: Yes, I think so. I like the shorter forms. Having read and written poetry most of my life.

PM: It's been said the short story has more in common with poetry than with the novel.

EG: I believe it's true. You're always trying to pack as much as you can into a small space, because it'll have more power that way. The laws of physics. "Rich" is a poet's short story if there ever was one. It flows from paragraph to paragraph and it's beautiful language, full of surprises, I think, but I wasn't trying to do that, I was just trying to find out how to write a short story. Now obviously four pages of it wasn't going to be enough, and then I wrote an ending. And I was going to see how I was going to find my way toward the ending, and the only model that I had was, I'd just open up *Huckleberry Finn* to any page and find out anything I wanted to know. Any question.

I remember getting up from the dining room table one night and saying, "Freddy," I said, "I don't know how to get them from one room to the next." So I remember I opened up *Huckleberry Finn* to the chapter where Huck is locked up in the cabin and his daddy—his father's left to go get some more whiskey—and he goes through a series of actions to free himself, and then he gets out of the cabin and gets in the boat and leaves. He kills a pig and leaves blood all over the place so people will think he died. Remember that? But it's after Pap leaves and it's everything he does to get out of the cabin. That is just textbook. What could anyone tell you about how to move characters around that would be as meaningful as that? I remember thinking: "Oh! Well, that's all there is to it! These are the steps that it took for him to get out of there: he did this and this and this and this and then he opened the door, and then he left the blood trail, and then he threw the pig away and then he got in the skiff and then he was on the Mississippi River." And because it was such a logical sequence of events, you believed this highly illogical stuff! Have you ever been on the

Mississippi River, even in a big boat? It's completely illogical that anyone could get into a skiff and push out and get into the currents of the Mississippi River. Don't go trying it.
PM: How long have you been teaching now?
EG: This will be my fifth year. I love it. I've learned so much from my students; I like them so much. I've been teaching long enough to see their work come to fruition, and they've had some success. One of my students won the *Playboy* fiction contest last year. One of them sold two stories at once to *The Atlantic*. For three years my students have won the undergraduate fiction award, and this year won the undergraduate fiction award *and* the undergraduate poetry award. I don't know what it is. I'm not probably as good a teacher as some of the other teachers, but I'm able to inspire some of the students, and that thrills me.

ELLEN GILCHRIST is the author of seventeen works of fiction, including *In the Land of Dreamy Dreams* (1981), in which "Rich" first appeared; *Victory Over Japan* (1984), which won the National Book Award; *Collected Stories* (2001); and *Nora Jane: A Life in Stories* (2005). Her nonfiction includes *Falling Through Space: The Journals of Ellen Gilchrist* (1987) and *The Writing Life* (2005). She lives in Fayetteville, Arkansas, and teaches at the University of Arkansas.

NEVER MARRY A MEXICAN

Sandra Cisneros

Never marry a Mexican, my ma said once and always. She said this because of my father. She said this though she was Mexican too. But she was born here in the U.S., and he was born there, and it's *not* the same, you know.

I'll *never* marry. Not any man. I've known men too intimately. I've witnessed their infidelities, and I've helped them to it. Unzipped and unhooked and agreed to clandestine maneuvers. I've been accomplice, committed premeditated crimes. I'm guilty of having caused deliberate pain to other women. I'm vindictive and cruel, and I'm capable of anything.

I admit, there was a time when all I wanted was to belong to a man. To wear that gold band on my left hand and be worn on his arm like an expensive jewel brilliant in the light of day. Not the sneaking around I did in different bars that all looked the same, red carpets with a black grillwork design, flocked wallpaper, wooden wagon-wheel light fixtures with hurricane lampshades a sick amber color like the drinking glasses you get for free at gas stations.

Dark bars, dark restaurants then. And if not—my apartment, with his toothbrush firmly planted in the toothbrush holder like a flag on the North Pole. The bed so big because he never stayed the whole night. Of course not.

Borrowed. That's how I've had my men. Just the cream skimmed off the top. Just the sweetest part of the fruit, without the bitter skin that daily living with a spouse can rend. They've come to me when they wanted the sweet meat then.

So, no. I've never married and never will. Not because I couldn't, but because I'm too romantic for marriage. Marriage has failed me, you could say. Not a man exists who hasn't disappointed me, whom I could trust to love the way I've loved. It's because I believe too much in marriage that I don't. Better to not marry than live a lie.

Mexican men, forget it. For a long time the men clearing off the tables or chopping meat behind the butcher counter or driving the bus I rode to school every day, those weren't men. Not men I considered as potential lovers. Mexican, Puerto Rican, Cuban, Chilean, Colombian, Panamanian, Salvadorean, Bolivian, Honduran, Argentine, Dominican, Venezuelan, Guatemalan, Ecuadorean, Nicaraguan, Peruvian, Costa Rican, Paraguayan, Uruguayan, I don't care. I never saw them. My mother did this to me.

I guess she did it to spare me and Ximena the pain she went through. Having married a Mexican man at seventeen. Having had to put up with all the grief a Mexican family can put on a girl because she was from *el otro lado,* the other side, and my father had married down by marrying her. If he had married a white woman from *el otro lado,* that would've been different. That would've been marrying up, even if the white girl was poor. But what could be more ridiculous than a Mexican girl who couldn't even speak Spanish, who didn't know enough to set a separate plate for each course at dinner, nor how to fold cloth napkins, nor how to set the silverware.

In my ma's house the plates were always stacked in the center of the table, the knives and forks and spoons standing in a jar, help yourself. All the dishes chipped or cracked and nothing matched. And no tablecloth, ever. And newspapers set on the table whenever my grandpa sliced watermelons, and how embarrassed she would be when her boyfriend, my father, would come over and there were newspapers all over the kitchen floor and table. And my grandpa, big hardworking Mexican man, saying Come, come and eat, and slicing a big wedge of those dark green watermelons, a big slice, he wasn't stingy with food. Never, even during the Depression. Come, come and eat, to whoever came knocking on the back door. Hobos sitting at the dinner table and the children staring and staring. Because my grandfather always made sure they never went without. Flour and rice, by the barrel and by the sack. Potatoes. Big bags of pinto beans. And watermelons, bought three or four at a time, rolled under his bed and brought out when you least expected. My grandpa had survived three wars, one Mexican, two American, and he knew what living without meant. He knew.

My father, on the other hand, did not. True, when he first came to this country he had worked shelling clams, washing dishes, planting hedges, sat on the back of the bus in Little Rock and had the bus driver shout, You—sit up here, and my father had shrugged sheepishly and said, No speak English.

But he was no economic refugee, no immigrant fleeing a war. My father ran away from home because he was afraid of facing his father after his first-year grades at the university proved he'd spent more time fooling around than studying. He left behind a house in Mexico City that was neither poor nor rich, but thought itself better than both. A boy who would get off a bus when he saw a girl he knew board if he didn't have the money to pay her fare. That was the world my father left behind.

I imagine my father in his *fanfarrón* clothes, because that's what he was, a *fanfarrón.* That's what my mother thought the moment she turned around to the voice that was asking her to dance. A big show-off, she'd say years later. Nothing but a big show-off. But she never said why she married him. My father in his shark-blue suits with the starched handkerchief in the breast pocket, his felt fedora, his tweed topcoat with the big shoulders, and heavy British wing tips with the pin-hole design on the heel and toe. Clothes that cost a lot. Expensive. That's what my father's things said. *Calidad.* Quality.

My father must've found the U.S. Mexicans very strange, so foreign from what he knew at home in Mexico City where the servant served watermelon on a plate with silverware and a cloth napkin, or mangos with their own special prongs. Not like this, eating with your legs wide open in the yard, or in the kitchen hunkered over newspapers. *Come, come and eat.* No, never like this.

* * *

How I make my living depends. Sometimes I work as a translator. Sometimes I get paid by the word and sometimes by the hour, depending on the job. I do this in the day, and at night I paint. I'd do anything in the day just so I can keep on painting.

I work as a substitute teacher, too, for the San Antonio Independent School District. And that's worse than translating those travel brochures with their tiny print, believe me. I can't stand kids. Not any age. But it pays the rent.

Any way you look at it, what I do to make a living is a form of prostitution. People say, "A painter? How nice," and want to invite me to their parties, have me decorate the lawn like an exotic orchid for hire. But do they buy art?

I'm amphibious. I'm a person who doesn't belong to any class. The rich like to have me around because they envy my creativity; they know they can't buy *that.* The poor don't mind if I live in their neighborhood because they know I'm poor like they are, even if my education and the way I dress keeps us worlds apart. I don't belong to any class. Not to the poor, whose neighborhood I share. Not to the rich, who come to my exhibitions and buy my work. Not to the middle class from which my sister Ximena and I fled.

When I was young, when I first left home and rented that apartment with my sister and her kids right after her husband left, I thought it would be glamorous to be an artist. I wanted to be like Frida or Tina. I was ready to suffer with my camera and my paintbrushes in that awful apartment we rented for $150 each because it had high ceilings and those wonderful glass skylights that convinced us we had to have it. Never mind there was no sink in the bathroom, and a tub that looked like a sarcophagus, and floorboards that didn't meet, and a hallway to scare away the dead. But fourteen-foot ceilings was enough for us to write a check for the deposit right then and there. We thought it all romantic. You know the place, the one on Zarzamora on top of the barber shop with the Casasola prints of the Mexican Revolution. Neon BIRRIA TEPATITLÁN sign round the corner, two goats knocking their heads together, and all those Mexican bakeries, Las Brisas for *huevos rancheros* and *carnitas* and *barbacoa* on Sundays, and fresh fruit milk shakes, and mango *paletas,* and more signs in Spanish than in English. We thought it was great, great. The barrio looked cute in the daytime, like Sesame Street. Kids hopscotching on the sidewalk, blessed little boogers. And hardware stores that still sold ostrich-feather dusters, and whole families marching out of Our Lady of Guadalupe Church on Sundays, girls in their swirly-whirly dresses and patent-leather shoes, boys in their dress Stacys and shiny shirts.

But nights, that was nothing like what we knew up on the north side. Pistols going off like the wild, wild West, and me and Ximena and the kids huddled in one bed with the lights off listening to it all, saying, Go to sleep, babies, it's just firecrackers. But we knew better. Ximena would say, Clemencia, maybe we should go home. And I'd say, Shit! Because she knew as well as I did there was no home to go home to. Not with our mother. Not with that man she married. After Daddy died, it was like we didn't matter. Like Ma was so busy feeling sorry for herself, I don't know. I'm not like Ximena. I still haven't worked it out after all this time, even though our mother's dead now. My half brothers living in that house that should've been ours, me and Ximena's. But that's—how do you say it?—water under the damn? I can't ever get the sayings right even though I was born in this country. We didn't say shit like that in our house.

Once Daddy was gone, it was like my ma didn't exist, like if she died, too. I used to have a little finch, twisted one of its tiny red legs between the bars of the cage once, who knows how. The leg just dried up and fell off. My bird lived a long time without it, just a little red stump of a leg. He was fine, really. My mother's memory is like that, like if something already dead dried up and fell off, and I stopped missing where she used to be. Like if I never had a mother. And I'm not ashamed to say it either. When she married that white man, and he and his boys moved into my father's house, it was as if she stopped being my mother. Like I never even had one.

Ma always sick and too busy worrying about her own life, she would've sold us to the Devil if she could. "Because I married so young, *mi'ja,"* she'd say. "Because your father, he was so much older than me, and I never had a chance to be young. Honey, try to understand . . . " Then I'd stop listening.

That man she met at work, Owen Lambert, the foreman at the photo-finishing plant, who she was seeing even while my father was sick. Even then. That's what I can't forgive.

When my father was coughing up blood and phlegm in the hospital, half his face frozen, and his tongue so fat he couldn't talk, he looked so small with all those tubes and plastic sacks dangling around him. But what I remember most is the smell, like death was already sitting on his chest. And I remember the doctor scraping the phlegm out of my father's mouth with a white washcloth, and my daddy gagging and I wanted to yell, Stop, you stop that, he's my daddy. Goddamn you. Make him live. Daddy, don't. Not yet, not yet, not yet. And how I couldn't hold myself up, I couldn't hold myself up. Like if they'd beaten me, or pulled my insides out through my nostrils, like if they'd stuffed me with cinnamon and cloves, and I just stood there dry-eyed next to Ximena and my mother, Ximena between us because I wouldn't let her stand next to me. Everyone repeating over and over the Ave Marías and Padre Nuestros. The priest sprinkling holy water, *mundo sin fin, amén.*

Drew, remember when you used to call me your Malinalli? It was a joke, a private game between us, because you looked like a Cortez with that beard of yours. My skin dark against yours. Beautiful, you said. You said I was beautiful, and when you said it, Drew, I was.

My Malinalli, Malinche, my courtesan, you said, and yanked my head back by the braid. Calling me that name in between little gulps of breath and the raw kisses you gave, laughing from that black beard of yours.

Before daybreak, you'd be gone, same as always, before I even knew it. And it was as if I'd imagined you, only the teeth marks on my belly and nipples proving me wrong.

Your skin pale, but your hair blacker than a pirate's. Malinalli, you called me, remember? *Mi doradita.* I liked when you spoke to me in my language. I could love myself and think myself worth loving.

Your son. Does he know how much I had to do with his birth? I was the one who convinced you to let him be born. Did you tell him, while his mother lay on her back laboring his birth, I lay in his mother's bed making love to you.

You're nothing without me. I created you from spit and red dust. And I can snuff you between my finger and thumb if I want to. Blow you to kingdom come. You're just a smudge of paint I chose to birth on canvas. And when I made you over, you were no longer a part of her, you were all mine. The landscape of your body taut as a drum. The heart beneath that hide thrumming and thrumming. Not an inch did I give back.

I paint and repaint you the way I see fit, even now. After all these years. Did you know that? Little fool. You think I went hobbling along with my life, whimpering and whining like some twangy country-and-western when you went back to her. But I've been waiting. Making the world look at you from my eyes. And if that's not power, what is?

Nights I light all the candles in the house, the ones to La Virgen de Guadalupe, the ones to El Niño Fidencio, Don Pedrito Jaramillo, Santo Niño de Atocha, Nuestra Señora de San Juan de los Lagos, and especially, Santa Lucía, with her beautiful eyes on a plate.

Your eyes are beautiful, you said. You said they were the darkest eyes you'd ever seen and kissed each one as if they were capable of miracles. And after you left, I wanted to scoop them out with a spoon, place them on a plate under these blue blue skies, food for the blackbirds.

The boy, your son. The one with the face of that redheaded

woman who is your wife. The boy red-freckled like fish food floating on the skin of water. That boy.

I've been waiting patient as a spider all these years, since I was nineteen and he was just an idea hovering in his mother's head, and I'm the one that gave him permission and made it happen, see.

Because your father wanted to leave your mother and live with me. Your mother whining for a child, at least *that.* And he kept saying, Later, we'll see, later. But all along it was me he wanted to be with, it was me, he said.

I want to tell you this evenings when you come to see me. When you're full of talk about what kind of clothes you're going to buy, and what you used to be like when you started high school and what you're like now that you're almost finished. And how everyone knows you as a rocker, and your band, and your new red guitar that you just got because your mother gave you a choice, a guitar or a car, but you don't need a car, do you, because I drive you everywhere. You could be my son if you weren't so light-skinned.

This happened. A long time ago. Before you were born. When you were a moth inside your mother's heart, I was your father's student, yes, just like you're mine now. And your father painted and painted me, because he said, I was his *doradita,* all golden and sun-baked, and that's the kind of woman he likes best, the ones brown as river sand, yes. And he took me under his wing and in his bed, this man, this teacher, your father. I was honored that he'd done me the favor. I was that young.

All I know is I was sleeping with your father the night you were born. In the same bed where you were conceived. I was sleeping with your father and didn't give a damn about that woman, your mother. If she was a brown woman like me, I might've had a harder time living with myself, but since she's not, I don't care. I was there first, always. I've always been there, in the mirror, under his skin, in the blood, before you were born. And he's been here in my heart before I even knew him. Understand? He's always been here. Always. Dissolving like a hibiscus flower, exploding like a rope into dust. I don't care what's right anymore. I don't care about his wife. She's not *my* sister.

And it's not the last time I've slept with a man the night his wife is birthing a baby. Why do I do that, I wonder? Sleep with a man when his wife is giving life, being suckled by a thing with its eyes still shut. Why do that? It's always given me a bit of crazy joy to be able to kill those women like that, without their knowing it. To know I've had their husbands when they were anchored in blue hospital rooms, their guts yanked inside out, the baby sucking their breasts while their husbands sucked mine. All this while their ass stitches were still hurting.

Once, drunk on margaritas, I telephoned your father at four in the morning, woke the bitch up. Hello, she chirped. I want to talk to Drew. Just a moment, she said in her most polite drawing-room English. Just a moment. I laughed about that for weeks. What a stupid ass to pass the phone over to the lug asleep beside her. Excuse me, honey, it's for you. When Drew mumbled hello I was laughing so hard I could hardly talk. Drew? That dumb bitch of a wife of yours, I said, and that's all I could manage. That stupid stupid stupid. No Mexican woman would react like that. Excuse me, honey. It cracked me up.

He's got the same kind of skin, the boy. All the blue veins pale and clear just like his mama. Skin like roses in December. Pretty boy. Little clone. Little cells split into you and you and you. Tell me, baby, which part of you is your mother. I try to imagine her lips, her jaw, her long long legs that wrapped themselves around this father who took me to his bed.

This happened. I'm asleep. Or pretend to be. You're watching me, Drew. I feel your weight when you sit on the corner of the bed, dressed and ready to go, but now you're just watching me sleep. Nothing. Not a word. Not a kiss. Just sitting. You're taking me in, under inspection. What do you think already?

I haven't stopped dreaming you. Did you know that? Do you

think it's strange? I never tell, though. I keep it to myself like I do all the thoughts I think of you.

After all these years.

I don't want you looking at me. I don't want you taking me in while I'm asleep. I'll open my eyes and frighten you away.

There. What did I tell you? *Drew? What is it?* Nothing. I knew you'd say that.

Let's not talk. We're no good at it. With you I'm useless with words. As if somehow I had to learn to speak them all over again, as if the words I needed haven't been invented yet. We're cowards. Come back to bed. At least there I feel I have you for a little. For a moment. For a catch of the breath. You let go. You ache and tug. You rip my skin.

You're almost not a man without your clothes. How do I explain it? You're so much a child in my bed. Nothing but a big boy who needs to be held. I won't let anyone hurt you. My pirate. My slender boy of a man.

After all these years.

I didn't imagine it, did I? A Ganges, an eye of the storm. For a little. When we forgot ourselves, you tugged me, I leapt inside you and split you like an apple. Opened for the other to look and not give back. Something wrenched itself loose. Your body doesn't lie. It's not silent like you.

You're nude as a pearl. You've lost your train of smoke. You're tender as rain. If I'd put you in my mouth you'd dissolve like snow.

You were ashamed to be so naked. Pulled back. But I saw you for what you are, when you opened yourself for me. When you were careless and let yourself through. I caught that catch of the breath. I'm not crazy.

When you slept, you tugged me toward you. You sought me in the dark. I didn't sleep. Every cell, every follicle, every nerve, alert. Watching you sigh and roll and turn and hug me closer to you. I didn't sleep. I was taking *you* in that time.

Your mother? Only once. Years after your father and I stopped seeing each other. At an art exhibition. A show on the photographs of Eugène Atget. Those images, I could look at them for hours. I'd taken a group of students with me.

It was your father I saw first. And in that instant I felt as if everyone in the room, all the sepia-toned photographs, my students, the men in business suits, the high-heeled women, the security guards, everyone, could see me for what I was. I had to scurry out, lead my kids to another gallery, but some things destiny has cut out for you.

He caught up with us in the coat-check area, arm in arm with a redheaded Barbie doll in a fur coat. One of those scary Dallas types, hair yanked into a ponytail, big shiny face like the women behind the cosmetic counters at Neiman's. That's what I remember. She must've been with him all along, only I swear I never saw her until that second.

You could tell from a slight hesitancy, only slight because he's too suave to hesitate, that he was nervous. Then he's walking toward me, and I didn't know what to do, just stood there dazed like those animals crossing the road at night when the headlights stun them.

And I don't know why, but all of a sudden I looked at my shoes and felt ashamed at how old they looked. And he comes up to me, my love, your father, in that way of his with that grin that makes me want to beat him, makes me want to make love to him, and he says in the most sincere voice you ever heard, "Ah, Clemencia! *This* is Megan." No introduction could've been meaner. *This* is Megan. Just like that.

I grinned like an idiot and held out my paw—"Hello, Megan"—and smiled too much the way you do when you can't stand someone. Then I got the hell out of there, chattering like a monkey all the ride back with my kids. When I got home I had to lie down with a cold washcloth on my forehead and the TV on. All I could hear throbbing under the washcloth in that deep part behind my eyes: *This* is Megan.

And that's how I fell asleep, with the TV on and every light in the house burning. When I woke up it was something like three in the morning. I shut the lights and TV and went to get some aspirin, and the cats, who'd been asleep with me on the couch, got up too and followed me into the bathroom as if they knew what's what. And then they followed me into bed, where they aren't allowed, but this time I just let them, fleas and all.

This happened, too. I swear I'm not making this up. It's all true. It was the last time I was going to be with your father. We had agreed. All for the best. Surely I could see that, couldn't I? My own good. A good sport. A young girl like me. Hadn't I understood . . . responsibilities. Besides, he could *never* marry *me.* You didn't think . . . ? *Never marry a Mexican. Never marry a Mexican* . . . No, of course not. I see. I see.

We had the house to ourselves for a few days, who knows how. You and your mother had gone somewhere. Was it Christmas? I don't remember.

I remember the leaded-glass lamp with the milk glass above the dining-room table. I made a mental inventory of everything. The Egyptian lotus design on the hinges of the doors. The narrow, dark hall where your father and I had made love once. The four-clawed tub where he had washed my hair and rinsed it with a tin bowl. This window. That counter. The bedroom with its light in the morning, incredibly soft, like the light from a polished dime.

The house was immaculate, as always, not a stray hair anywhere, not a flake of dandruff or a crumpled towel. Even the roses on the dining-room table held their breath. A kind of airless cleanliness that always made me want to sneeze.

Why was I so curious about this woman he lived with? Every time I went to the bathroom, I found myself opening the medicine cabinet, looking at all the things that were hers. Her Estée Lauder lipsticks. Corals and pinks, of course. Her nail polishes—mauve was as brave as she could wear. Her cotton balls and blond hairpins. A pair of bone-colored sheepskin slippers, as clean as the day she'd bought them. On the door hook—a white robe with a MADE IN ITALY label, and a silky nightshirt with pearl buttons. I touched the fabrics. *Calidad.* Quality.

I don't know how to explain what I did next. While your father was busy in the kitchen, I went over to where I'd left my backpack, and took out a bag of gummy bears I'd bought. And while he was banging pots, I went around the house and left a trail of them in places I was sure *she* would find them. One in her lucite makeup organizer. One stuffed inside each bottle of nail polish. I untwisted the expensive lipsticks to their full length and smushed a bear on the top before recapping them. I even put a gummy bear in her diaphragm case in the very center of that luminescent rubber moon.

Why bother? Drew could take the blame. Or he could say it was the cleaning woman's Mexican voodoo. I knew that, too. It didn't matter. I got a strange satisfaction wandering about the house leaving them in places only she would look.

And just as Drew was shouting, "Dinner!" I saw it on the desk. One of those wooden babushka dolls Drew had brought her from his trip to Russia. I know. He'd bought one just like it for me.

I just did what I did, uncapped the doll inside a doll inside a doll, until I got to the very center, the tiniest baby inside all the others, and this I replaced with a gummy bear. And then I put the dolls back, just like I'd found them, one inside the other, inside the other. Except for the baby, which I put inside my pocket. All through dinner I kept reaching into the pocket of my jean jacket. When I touched it, it made me feel good.

On the way home, on the bridge over the *arroyo* on Guadalupe Street, I stopped the car, switched on the emergency blinkers, got out, and dropped the wooden toy into that muddy creek where winos piss and rats swim. The Barbie doll's toy stewing there in that muck. It gave me a feeling like nothing before and since.

Then I drove home and slept like the dead.

These mornings, I fix coffee for me, milk for the boy. I think of that woman, and I can't see a trace of my lover in this boy, as if she conceived him by immaculate conception.

I sleep with this boy, their son. To make the boy love me the way I love his father. To make him want me, hunger, twist in his sleep, as if he'd swallowed glass. I put him in my mouth. Here, little piece of my *corazón.* Boy with hard thighs and just a bit of down and a small hard downy ass like his father's, and that back like a valentine. Come here, *mi cariñito.* Come to *mamita.* Here's a bit of toast.

I can tell from the way he looks at me, I have him in my power. Come, sparrow. I have the patience of eternity. Come to *mamita.* My stupid little bird. I don't move. I don't startle him. I let him nibble. All, all for you. Rub his belly. Stroke him. Before I snap my teeth.

What is it inside me that makes me so crazy at 2 A.M.? I can't blame it on alcohol in my blood when there isn't any. It's something worse. Something that poisons the blood and tips me when the night swells and I feel as if the whole sky were leaning against my brain.

And if I killed someone on a night like this? And if it was *me* I killed instead, I'd be guilty of getting in the line of crossfire, innocent bystander, isn't it a shame. I'd be walking with my head full of images and my back to the guilty. Suicide? I couldn't say. I didn't see it.

Except it's not me who I want to kill. When the gravity of the planets is just right, it all tilts and upsets the visible balance. And that's when it wants to out from my eyes. That's when I get on the telephone, dangerous as a terrorist. There's nothing to do but let it come.

So. What do you think? Are you convinced now I'm as crazy as a tulip or a taxi? As vagrant as a cloud?

Sometimes the sky is so big and I feel so little at night. That's the problem with being a cloud. The sky is so terribly big. Why is it worse at night, when I have such an urge to communicate and no language with which to form the words? Only colors. Pictures. And you know what I have to say isn't always pleasant.

Oh, love, there. I've gone and done it. What good is it? Good or bad, I've done what I had to do and needed to. And you've answered the phone, and startled me away like a bird. And now you're probably swearing under your breath and going back to sleep, with that wife beside you, warm, radiating her own heat, alive under the flannel and down and smelling a bit like milk and hand cream, and the smell familiar and dear to you, oh.

Human beings pass me on the street, and I want to reach out and strum them as if they were guitars. Sometimes all humanity strikes me as lovely. I just want to reach out and stroke someone, and say There, there, it's all right, honey. There, there, there.

SANDRA CISNEROS DISCUSSES

"Never Marry a Mexican," theme, imagery—and exploring the heart's darkness

SC: Before I began this story I had the premise of seeking revenge on a love by seducing his son. I thought, *Can you imagine if a woman was so angry that she slept with her lover's son and did some harm to the son so her lover could understand what that pain was like?*

I was proposing it out loud one day to somebody, just talking and laughing, because at that time the big nemesis in my life, his child was just getting into his teen years and I was saying, *Wow, he's old enough to be seduced!* I was just joking, and then I thought, *Oh that's a good idea, why don't I write a story like that?* Because a lot of times my stories are things I wouldn't dare do in real life, they're just, what if . . . ?

PM: By nemesis, you mean like a professional nemesis?

SC: Oh no, I never have professional nemeses. My nemeses are always love nemeses. My nemesis is always this love nemesis. I had a great passion in my life: Someone in my twenties who became a catalyst for a lot of my stories and poems. Someone who was in my life for twenty years or something like that. The big love of my life.

PM: So when did you decide it was time to develop this premise of seducing a lover's son?

SC: When I was writing *Woman Hollering Creek* I was compelled to have my antenna open for any subject because I was writing it on a deadline. I was running out of money. I had to get the second part of the advance quickly because I had stopped working so that I could work on this manuscript. It was the first time that I was writing something for a major press, and this was going to be my debut collection. *The House on Mango Street* had already been bought, but I had written that a decade before, so I was working in this period of high panic in this little apartment in San Antonio, and I really tried to use anything and everything that I possibly could to make fiction. I felt like I was back in graduate school trying to meet the deadline writing my thesis.

I didn't think I was opening this can of worms when I began the story, and I really didn't expect that it was going to come out as forceful as it did; I thought it was just going to be some little story, but it just had all this pent-up energy in it.

PM: The story reads as though it has an important sense of mission behind it—there never seems to be any doubt that it has something to say and it's going to say it. I've been wondering if there's any relationship between that and a strong sense of theme.

SC: I don't ever know what the theme of a story is before I begin. I have a kind of emotion maybe, a kind of glimmer toward some direction.

PM: What about now, in hindsight?

SC: I think it's a story about the power of rage, revenge, bitterness, hatred, and how in our pain we often aim it towards ourselves or innocent bystanders. The object of her hate is Drew and the establishment and the powers that hold her with such contempt, but she's such a victim of racism that she hates herself. And she's broken and ill because of it.

I don't think it's a perfect story. I always felt that character was the only character in my collection who was broken. And maybe that's why the story's flawed for me. Because usually women in my work come to some peace at the end. They somehow wind up victorious. There's some sort of happy ending. And this is the one story where the character's tragic. Maybe I didn't develop this story long enough. Maybe it really wanted to be a novel and not a short story. But at the end of the story I felt very frightened of her. And there never was any kind of reward or evolution in her development. She was really just damaged.

PM: She is, but there's something about that last paragraph, where she's letting the reader see a side that she seems to have

kept hidden from *herself* for so long. That small movement feels satisfying to me.
SC: You see, I thought it just made her crazier. When she looks at everybody and has this absolute moment of connection, it made me more terrified of her. That she could do that kind of switch. When I heard an actress perform this part, it gave me the creeps.
PM: It *is* a scary story. How betrayal seems to breed betrayal. And heartbreak breeds heartbreak. And how prejudice turns inward, as you were saying a moment ago, and becomes self-hatred.
SC: And part of the reason why I wrote the story was not only the what-if premise, but because I've met women like Clemencia. I see a lot of women who hate who they are and can be validated only if they are loved by a white man. I wanted to explore that.

The other influence was this woman who had an incredibly tempestuous relationship with her mother and it shocked me, because you don't expect that in our culture. In our culture, there's a reverence of the mother. Especially by men. An absurd reverence for the mother. When you look at Latina writing, it's a reverence for the grandmother. That's why I wanted to do something a little different, and I liked the idea of shocking a Latina reader by breaking that taboo.

I took all three ideas and put them all together in one story and thought, well, what if we write a modern-day Malinche story, what would it look like? The whole Mexican myth of the Malinche fascinates me and I was trying to update it.
PM: Malinche was Cortez's translator—
SC: Yes. She was a very gifted woman, and she was from a noble house. She wasn't a slave, she was a noble woman *sold* into slavery by her own mother, who wanted to make room for her new husband and his children. And so she learned different languages and eventually she was traded by her captors to Cortez, or gifted to him, and wound up serving him and was instrumental in the conquest because of her gift of tongues. And then, of course, he married her off to one of his military men, even though she bore children to him. She was betrayed and betrayed and betrayed.

PM: Clemencia's path toward Drew also seems to have been set in motion by her family. A lot of meaning seems to emerge from the juxtaposition of those two halves of the story. Because her later sense of grievance seems to begin in the hospital scene with her father.
SC: I used the great pain of a recent incident with my father, who had been hospitalized and just started the decline of ill health. It was the last ten years of my father's life, and it was his first hospitalization that caused me to realize how tenuous his life was. I used that fear and that emotion and the powerlessness of that memory, which was very recent as I was writing.
PM: When the narrator's watching her father in the hospital, she says she feels like her insides are being yanked out through her nostrils. And that image of "guts yanked inside out" is repeated a couple of pages later when she's imagining her rivals giving birth. There does seem to be a very rich counterpoint between those two moments. Because when the narrator's witnessing her father's suffering, part of what she's most upset about is that her mother has already started a romance with somebody else. So it's striking that the narrator would then avenge her sense of betrayal on the hospitalized wives of other men.
SC: I don't think I made the connection when I was writing it. I really was just trying to be very honest to the experience of seeing someone else who's ill and that feeling of powerlessness. And then I remembered when we were growing up how fascinated I was with the mummies in the Chicago Field Museum. That was one of my favorite places to go. They used to keep the mummies in the creepy basement and make it feel as if you were entering a tomb. And I remember reading how they prepared the mummies and how they pulled all of the entrails out of the nostrils. And I didn't remember that I remembered that until I wrote that sentence.
PM: That's the sort of image that'll stick in a kid's subconscious!

When you were structuring this story, did you have any concerns about how well readers might synthesize the two halves of the family material and the Drew material?

SC: No, because I'm really in the story; I can't see the structure. And I'm not the type of writer who thinks the story through. I'm very intuitive when I create. And I don't know what I've created even now after all these years.

It's always fascinating to listen to critics analyze it, because when I was writing it, I was being directed by the emotional power. Even that ending, I didn't know I was going to use that ending. I'm always looking around and seeing if I have anything in my dead-end file. I'm looking for buttons. By buttons I mean little finished pieces of writing that have no beginning, middle, or end that I've written in the past that I could possibly use. Something to finish off a garment.

I have a lot of literary buttons in my writing files. And I found that paragraph. It was really part of a letter I wrote when I was living in Berkeley and I was walking through the UC-Berkeley campus when I felt this moment of being connected to everyone. And it was a good piece of writing, so I put it in my Button Box. And when I was finishing the story, I had no idea how it was going to end, and I thought, well, *what if we put this here?* And to me it was *brilliant*. I thought *that's it, that's the ending! (Laughs.)* But I had no idea. I didn't plan that out.

PM: I think it's a brilliant ending, too, partly because I feel a moment of poignance for the narrator, scary as she may be.

SC: The story's very ambiguous and can be read in so many different ways. Maybe that's why people like it. But I'm always shocked that they like it. People always comment on that story, and it sparks a lot of discussion.

PM: What responses have you gotten?

SC: You know what really surprised me? It was white women who liked that story. (Not to say Latinas don't, too—they love it.) But I really thought that it was not a story for them. That they would be offended by it. Because it's a woman who hates white women—but they *like* that story. I don't know why.

PM: What's the most common misreading of the story?

SC: I think the misreading that I generally hear from readers is "I feel that way, too," and they mean about the title or their whole sense of anger toward Mexican men, and they'll say, "Oh that's my favorite story, I feel the same way." And I'll say, "Well, *I* don't feel like the narrator." So that's, I think, a misreading—that they feel I approve of this character.

PM: Clemencia tries to take control of her broken heart in several ways including her art, her portraits of Drew. And even her seduction of the son feels almost like a kind of art project. And it raises an interesting paradox of the artist not just as a creator, but as a destroyer—

SC: Well, that's the whole thing about the artist. I always think that Coatlicue, the creative-destructive goddess, is really the model, you know? She's a pre-Colombian goddess, predecessor of the Virgen de Guadalupe. She's this horrible goddess who was dug up from underground where she'd been—where I guess maybe the Spaniards put her. And when she was excavated, she was so frightening they had to bury her again. She's in the anthropology museum now. She looks like a square pillar, and she has a necklace of hearts.

PM: The narrator views her portraits of Drew as a form of power over him. And so one of the other questions I think the story raises is: Can art vindicate life? Or is the story pointing out the limitations of that notion?

SC: I feel that for me art is certainly a way of re-looking at things. Because I feel as if I'm always repainting the same story over again when I write, but with the years, I come to some place of illumination.

PM: That doesn't seem to be working as well for Clemencia.

SC: Well, maybe she needs to sit another ten years. To me, writing is always like a sitting meditation and sometimes we don't sit with a subject long enough.

PM: If creating her portraits of Drew really empowered her, she wouldn't feel the need to go after the son.

SC: Yes, I guess you're right.

PM: So, looking off the page, what does the future hold for her and the son?

SC: Oh, I think she doesn't have any attachment to the son. It's just a moment of creating pain and being a character that hobbles along the rest of her life, with a great deal of hatred for herself. I see a lot of Clemencias in the world. I see them all the time in people who never have a sense of love for themselves so they can never love other people.

PM: So things are looking pretty bleak for the son, too.

SC: Well, I think the son's a little boy. So I don't think *bleak*. I just think she wants to create a heartache for somebody that is a way of getting back at the father. I don't think his life is bleak.

PM: But since she's likely to go through with her project—breaking the son's heart—part of what I find chilling about that is the implication that his damage will then have its own repercussions.

SC: Yes, that'll be someone who will just be totally aloof and unwilling to be generous and loving and have a normal relationship.

PM: So the cycle of betrayal has the potential to go on infinitely.

SC: Yes. I guess it does. Oh, what a horrible story! I wouldn't be so irresponsible if I was writing that story now.

I think I would write it completely differently now. The last ten years of my life, I've come to some other place, some other *plane*. So the story would be very different now. I don't think that it would just end with a character who was broken or mad. I really feel that there'd be some spiritual enlightenment at least—even if it was very slight. Maybe that's not realistic. But somehow the character would move. I wouldn't just leave her there in that kind of deranged state. I think also, my whole idea of relationships, marriage, and people is very different.

I wrote that when I was in my thirties. I was a young woman, and I had a lot of rage that I had never been allowed to express. Except in poems, which were just little blips. This story came out from a very black part of my heart, you know, a part that I didn't talk about or think about.

I remember when I was writing it that I let myself think or say anything that I liked, that I had absolute freedom to say or think the unthinkable, even though in my everyday life maybe I would always try to be nice, or *quedar bien,* as we say in

Spanish, which means to come off being nice or being polite.

PM: You've mentioned that sometimes when you're working on material that feels dangerous or even ugly you pretend that other people won't read it in your lifetime. Did this story require that sort of extra-private process?

SC: Well, I know that when I wrote this story, lots of painful memories came up. And I felt like Goya when he did that engraving of *The Sleep of Reason*. It really did feel like I was letting loose the bats and monsters and owls and ugly things that were in my psyche with this story. There were a couple of taboo things; as I said, it's not just about one autobiographical incident, it's about all of the nemeses in my life. There was that big love of my life—and I used him for the catalyst because I had such a difficult time communicating with him.

And I remember that it really was a story that took a lot out of me to write. I felt exhausted. I was writing very, very late and falling asleep waking up on top of the pages. I fell asleep with my clothes on when I was writing this story. And I had nightmares.

PM: About the material?

SC: I don't remember. I just felt as if I released, I gave my permission for a lot of dark things to come out that I didn't even know I had in my heart. So, you know, I feel in a way—I'm not Clemencia, but I *am* Clemencia, and I'm all the characters in my books. And I'm not them, at all. But I think we're full of so many hydra that make up who we are.

So there were things that I did in my life—different *parts* of my life—that I didn't feel very proud about, but I got to get them out of my system with this story. It was as if I took all the blackness of all my experiences and put them into this one character. With *no* forgiveness, which is why I named her Clemencia. Imagine that.

I really did steal someone's little wooden doll. And I'm ashamed to say I've never felt happier. And I threw it in the sewer in Chicago. It was a stupid thing to do, but I was so jealous and upset. I remember stuffing it in a manhole, in Pilsen, and shoving it in there where all the rats—and I, I walked away triumphant.

The neighborhood that she describes in the west side of San Antonio is really the south side of Chicago—the buildings and some of the things that she describes are specific buildings I went past when I used to teach in Pilsen, not feeling like I belonged to part of that world. I just plucked them up and moved them.

There is a bridge that divides the west side of San Antonio from downtown, and there is a very murky, awful grungy little arroyo down there. Sometimes it's dry and dusty and sometimes it's just a little trickle.

PM: And this is where Clemencia disposes of her version of the doll, the littlest Russian nesting doll.

SC: Yes. I thought about some really awful place where you would have to throw something. And, of course, I picked a real place, some sort of geographic dividing line between the classes in San Antonio.

PM: The nested doll is such a wonderful symbolic kind of prop.

SC: It is. Of the baby.

PM: The baby in its womb.

SC: Yes. But in real life I took the entire set of nesting dolls and threw them all away. I did all sorts of silly things. Like I broke a framed map of South America with my shoe once. I've always been a very jealous woman. But I didn't kill anybody.

PM: It's good to know where to draw the line.

SC: Yes. *(Laughs.)*

PM: So you've got this set of nesting dolls hovering in the back of your real-life experience, and you're writing this story, and at what point do you decide or intuit the rightness of using them as an image?

SC: You know, I always kind of think of things that I've never told anyone. I'm a very open person—I talk a *lot*. And I tell everything, so I don't have a lot of secrets. But when you write, you try to tap into the things you've never told *anyone.* You have to put your head under the water and go into those deep dark subterranean places. And so I had to rummage about in my memory and think: What have I ever done that I've never told anyone about? And I remembered those dolls.

PM: The dolls work well as an image as they get smaller, but they also work in the other direction as they radiate outward. Also the scattering of the gummy bears—they're being sown in preparation for some future discovery.

SC: I stole that idea from Michael Cunningham. Michael had a story called "Pearls" he showed me. A lover leaves little pearls all over, kind of like a trail of bread, and I guess that memory stayed with me, so I stole the idea. Have to give credit where credit is due.

PM: Let's look at that scene—the long weekend in Drew's house when his wife is away. Clemencia and Drew are having this conversation about their future—

SC: Or lack of—

PM: Exactly. And—what page is that on?

SC: I was looking for that, too.

PM: Page 340. Right after the line break. I read an essay that seemed to believe the sentences "Never marry a Mexican . . . " were actually words that Drew was speaking. Which is not how I read it.

SC: No. I don't read it that way either. I think she's just remembering her mother's words. And suddenly they're in this context. They flip around.

PM: Her mother's indictment has hit home. And all that long-held intolerance against others comes back to indict the narrator in her own mind. It's a devastating moment for her.

SC: I think it was a surprise to me when I wrote that line. I didn't realize the title was going to be the snake that would turn around and bite her. Because Clemencia doesn't see herself as Mexican until that moment. Her mother's words had desexed men, castrated them in a sense. Made them seem like eunuchs, not potential lovers. But it is she who becomes the victim of this racism.

PM: The words turn around and echo in a way that she hadn't anticipated. You also employ another very bold and unusual device that reinforces this motif of echoes: you have the narrator addressing *both* Drew and the son as *you*.

SC: Yes! I got that from Rulfo. Juan Rulfo, the Mexican writer. We think of the page as having limitations, but Juan Rulfo takes those limitations and turns them on their head and makes them an advantage. And what you *can* do on the printed page that you can't do with radio, with audio, or with film is switch the object to whom the narrator is speaking, in that way. And so seamlessly. I was fascinated by that. And I tried when I was writing this book to use everything I'd learned from the masters and do something new technically, craft-wise, with every story I wrote.
PM: The change seems to occur first on page 336. It's almost like a handoff in a relay race.
SC: Yes, that's right.
PM: So how did you decide to do it then and in that way?
SC: I just remember that Rulfo gave me permission. I filed that away in my brain somewhere. I think I was writing the story and it just happened that I remembered I could make a little switch like that. I was just experimenting to see if it could work.
PM: And was that the first spot you experimented with it? Or did you try it in some other spot first?
SC: I don't write a story in a linear fashion. I just write scenes. And every day I write whatever scene I feel most passionate about, and then I stitch them together. So this whole section may not have been written all as one section.

In one day I usually write about a page and quarter. But I remember that this story came out rather quickly, over a series of weeks. And as I said, a lot of it stirred up things I hadn't spoken about for a long time.
PM: Coming back to the question of rage; you've called it a wonderful emotion if you don't aim it at any living thing, especially yourself. Of course, a lot of Clemencia's rage *is* aimed at herself, and while that may be unhealthy in life, it's very interesting in art. So how is rage best used in art? And how does one make that crucial transformation that elevates and universalizes it?
SC: One of the things I learned from all the years of practicing my art is that my best work always comes from some place of

rage. Versus this long period of impotency. I'm really in a very impotent place right now as far as the responsibilities and the questions that get thrown at me all the time as an author regarding the world and politics. And so I'm in that place just before I get angry. *(Laughs.)* And then the rage that comes out moves me out of my silence. For me, that's been the process.

I wonder about my siblings and my mother and other people around me, how everyday people cope with the blows that life gives you. Because I feel that one of the privileges of being an artist is we can take all of those stories, whether they're ours or stories that we've witnessed, and we have not only the privilege but we have the profession of sitting with them over a long period. Almost as if we were assigned to do a sitting meditation with these stories over a decade. Over six months. Over several weeks. Most of society doesn't like to think about these things. The kind of obsessive stories that would damage one's psyche. Most people cope by *not* thinking. And I think that's where it's most damaging, because it grows. They become ghosts inside you. Whereas for the artists, that's their job.

You know, my mother doesn't have time to sit and think about these things all day long, to live her life backwards, but that's my job, and I'll do it for her, and for other people in the community. I think writers are the shamans of the community. I think that everybody sins and you just process it and purify it for them.

SANDRA CISNEROS is the author of two poetry collections, *My Wicked Wicked Ways* (1987) and *Loose Woman* (1994); *Woman Hollering Creek and Other Stories* (1991), which won the PEN Center West Fiction Award, the Quality Paperback Book Club New Voices Award, the Anisfield-Wolf Book Award, and the Lannan Foundation Literary Award; a children's book, *Hairs/Pelitos* (1994); and two novels, *The House on Mango Street* (1991) and *Caramelo* (2002). The recipient of a MacArthur Foundation Fellowship and many other honors, she lives in San Antonio, Texas.

The editor and publisher wish to thank the contributors and their literary agents and publishers, who made this volume possible.

Sandra Cisneros: "Never Marry a Mexican," from *Woman Hollering Creek.* Copyright © 1991 by Sandra Cisneros. Published by Vintage Books, a division of Random House, Inc., New York and originally in hardcover by Random House, Inc. Reprinted by permission of Susan Bergholz Literary Services, New York. All rights reserved.

Kim Edwards: "The Story of My Life," from *The Secrets of a Fire King* by Kim Edwards. Copyright © 1997 by Kim Edwards. Used by permission of W. W. Norton & Company, Inc.

George Garrett: "A Record as Long as Your Arm," from *An Evening Performance* by George Garrett. Copyright © 1978 by George Garrett. Reprinted by permission of the author.

Ellen Gilchrist: "Rich," from *In the Land of Dreamy Dreams* by Ellen Gilchrist. Copyright © 1981 by Ellen Gilchrist. Reprinted by permission of Don Congdon Associates, Inc.

Gail Godwin: "Dream Children," from *Dream Children* by Gail Godwin. Copyright © 1976 by Gail Godwin. Used by permission of Alfred A. Knopf, a division of Random House, Inc.

Allan Gurganus: "Condolences to Every One of Us," from *White People* by Allan Gurganus, copyright © 1991 by Allan Gurganus. Used by permission of Alfred A. Knopf, a division of Random House, Inc.

Charles Johnson: "China," from *The Sorcerer's Apprentice*, copyright ©1983 by Charles Johnson. Reprinted with the permission of Scribner, an imprint of Simon & Schuster Adult Publishing Group.

Walter Kirn: "The Hoaxer," copyright © 1994 by Walter Kirn. First published in *Story*. Reprinted by permission of the author.

Jhumpa Lahiri: "The Third and Final Continent," from *The Interpreter of Maladies* by Jhumpa Lahiri. Copyright © 1999 by Jhumpa Lahiri. Reprinted by permission of Houghton Mifflin Company. All rights reserved.

Ursula K. Le Guin: "Sur," from *Compass Rose* by Ursula K. Le Guin. Copyright © 1982 by Ursula K. Le Guin; first appeared in *The New Yorker;* reprinted by permission of the author and the author's agents, the Virginia Kidd Agency, Inc.

Elizabeth Tallent: "Prowler," from *Honey* by Elizabeth Tallent. Copyright © 1993 by Elizabeth Tallent. Reprinted by permission of the author.

Tobias Wolff: "Smorgasbord," from *The Night in Question* by Tobias Wolff. Copyright © 1996 by Tobias Wolff. Reprinted by permission of International Creative Management.